THE POWWOW HIGHWAY

THE POWWOW HIGHWAY

A NOVEL

DAVID SEALS

UNIVERSITY OF NEW MEXICO PRESS ◡ ALBUQUERQUE

First University of New Mexico Press edition published 2014 by arrangement with the author.
Printed in the United States of America
19 18 17 16 15 14   1 2 3 4 5 6

Library of Congress Cataloging-in-Publication Data
Seals, David.
  The Powwow highway : a novel / David Seals. — University of New Mexico Press edition.
      pages ; cm
  ISBN 978-0-8263-5489-1 (pbk. : alk. paper) — ISBN 978-0-8263-5490-7 (electronic)
  1. Indians of North America—Fiction. I. Title.
  PS3569.E1725P69 2014
  813'.54—dc23
                                    2014001754

COVER ILLUSTRATION: *Aquí Cantamos*, courtesy of Leopoldo Romero
BOOK DESIGN: Catherine Leonardo
Composed in ScalaOT Reg. 11.2/15
Display type is Asphaltum WF and ScalaSansOT

To my family

PREFACE

The Origins of the Sacred Pony

This is the story of a machine and of the people who made a story of its movements and of what happened to the machine and its people. For the Indians who passed along the endless wanderings of the Powwow Highway had felt themselves to be a trickle on an ancient river. They were something of a raiding party in the old dilapidated automobile, not unlike a hunting party of the Old Ones. They came upon the immigrants in a black belching chaos of fear and gasoline and passed along their way like jackrabbits darting past startled drivers on a lonely night. Their eyes flashed like sorcerers' in the headlights and then disappeared behind metal and rubber.

Lame Deer, the agency village of the Northern Cheyenne in Montana, knew the old heap well. But not at first. Rarely had a new vehicle entered upon the traditional lands of the Morning Star People, and this Buick was no exception.

It had been the proud new steed of a vice president of the Billings Bank & Trust for the first two years of its life. It knew the joys of every rambunctious youth, flush with good health, an integral part of the brand-new and very traditional suburb in

Billings. The extravagant cream-colored Buick frolicked alongside the other healthy children of that booming blond-headed city, a proud emblem among emblems of its prosperous neighborhood. If a machine were alive and could be happy—things of which mechanics and inventors were convinced—then this 1964 Buick LeSabre had found its destiny.

Alas, time is no less cruel unto man-made joys than it is unto the creator's own fragile framework. Illusions do not dissipate very quickly, at first. A piece of rubber insulation fell off the driver's door. It was glued back on. The soap ran out of the automatic window washer. It was easily replaced. But then a tire picked up an imperfection out at the rodeo grounds and blew. As the twelve-month guarantee ran out, so did the water pump. The seats began to show wear. The industrious banker cared less to keep the carpets cleaned of Coca-Cola and the dog's muddy footprints. Crayons melted on the dashboard. The front bumper showed suspicious signs of rust.

The old dreams found replacements. The banker was promoted to senior vice president. He had a larger office now, he was picky about his carpeting, his lovely wife had another baby girl. It was time to discover new realms, new possibilities, a new car. Two new cars. The Buick was left on the A-OK lot and its family drove off into new frontiers—a 1966 Buick LeSabre and a Mustang convertible. Mobility had fertilized. Independence had offered its outlet unto whiteman once again, as a young girl might have offered herself to the wind.

Red Siskiewicz, a lonely bachelor from Butte, picked up the '64 buggy on a real deal. New prospects presented themselves to him. Freedom was again a possible route to happiness. Within a week he rolled it down Turner Hill, killing himself and the bleached-blond schoolteacher he had just picked up at the Eldorado Lounge.

The Buick sat for seven months in DeBaca's Wrecking Yard. After a body shop banged it roughly back into shape, it was stripped of every part it possessed, inside and out, by Fidel DeBaca. It sat naked, a lumpy frame, a body only. Fidel sold the parts to his best customers, mechanics from the garages around town.

Wayne and Reed Garrison took it off Fidel's hands one warm day in June, when school was out for the summer. They lifted the '55 Chevy engine from their recently burned-out '47 Ford coupe; put in straight pipes, solid lifters, Naugahyde seats, racing slicks in the rear, mag hubcaps; painted it bright red; and raked the chassis so that it looked to be perpetually rolling downhill. By August they had dubbed it the Cherry Showboat.

By September, the wiring caught fire and Wayne and Reed barely escaped with their lives.

It sat in DeBaca's for three years after that. No one wanted it. The engine and the body were burned shit-brown. A family of skunks made a nest in the backseat. It seemed to be the end of a country-western hard-luck story. It was one down-and-out machine that nobody could love.

Then, one cold and arctic afternoon, a glacial wind blew Manny Bono against the shack of Fidel DeBaca. Manny was on his way to the Purple Orchid, one of many Indian bars huddling among warehouses and wrecking yards and the refuse of every city that no one but Indians and other foolish people who do not understand the twentieth century could want. It was the Indian section of town. Manny ducked into the shack on the sidewalk, even though Fidel was only a goddamn Mexican. Fidel sat by a leaky gas stove, staring unbelievingly at a *Playboy* centerfold.

"Fidel, this wind has frozen my asshole shut. I want to buy one of your fine ponies."

"Shit," Fidel pronounced in his odd Castilian accent, "look around."

Manny did not want to look around. It was too goddamn cold. He looked out the window to see a shit-brown old Buick sticking out among the demolished pickups and Chryslers. It seemed to call to him. It was as if an eagle had shown him the light of this beautiful thing.

"That is a nice one. Does it run?"

"That? Shit."

"It has no engine?"

"It has an engine."

"No tires?"

"Tires."

"I will go start it up."

Miracle of the valley that shivering day as Manny walked bow-legged among the junk, his crew-cut black hair sweating under his brown straw cowboy hat, his pointed boots ignoring the frozen mud holes. He looked at the huge racing slicks in the rear and the bald blackwalls in the front. They had air. He sat on the Naugahyde seats. They were only a little torn. He found the key in the ignition, turned it to on, pumped it twice, and it purred gratefully back to life. He drove past Fidel's shack, very slowly so as not to be seen or heard. Why should he pay a brown whiteman, after all he had done to him? Fidel did not even look out the grimy window, never expecting to see an Indian with a shit-eating grin drive by, or a frantic family of skunks peering out the scent-blackened back window.

And that is how that Buick, like so many American dreams resurrected back unto reality, came to the Cheyenne reservation.

It ran without fault for nine years, until Manny traded it to his cousin Philbert in 1978 for two ounces of marijuana and a worthless horse saddle.

CHAPTER 1

How Protector and Philbert and Buddy
Came to Share Friendship, and
How They Left on Their Sacred Quest

EVERYONE IN LAME DEER knew that old shit-brown Buick. It
had become an integral part of the tribe. Perhaps not as timeless
as the four sacred arrows bequeathed to the Maxkeometaneo by
the ancestral hero Sweet Medicine, it was nevertheless essential
to the daily image of the Cheyenne. That Buick was the talisman
of the whiteman, the medicine to explain modern spirits that
ailed and healed the redman of his technological woes, the sacred
bundle to protect the superstitious Morning Star People from the
whiteman's evils.

Philbert nicknamed the Buick Protector. He then eased his
three hundred pounds behind the steering wheel, grunting carefully. It was a stoic maneuver, for he had not quite recovered from
his celebration with Manny over the new acquisition, and his
head hurt. The steering wheel touched his great fat belly, but only
a little. It made him confident. He reached out for the door, panting to complete the steel-enclosed security. He rested from his
efforts, lighting a roach he found in the ashtray. He let the memory of the epic events of the past three days wash over him in a
cannabis smoke of pleasure.

It was a great thing to have such a war pony. It had been important how he had earned this fine honor. His grandfather had often spoken of raids against the Shoshone for animals of much less quality than Protector. Herds of ponies were a thing of honor to a Cheyenne. It was not a game, this steel-enforced bone he sat upon, this thing that now made him, Philbert Bono—Indian name Whirlwind—a warrior. He put the roach on the cigarette lighter and skillfully snuffed the last medicine of the weed.

He and Manny had gone to pray over this beautiful thing that had happened to them. They drove to the top of a hill overlooking the Custer Battlefield, twenty-five miles from Cheyenne land, on the huge Crow reservation. They sat on the hood of the Protector and terrified the tourists. It was not difficult, for Philbert was a great giant of an Indian, six-foot-four, with long black hair down to his waist tied in a single greasy braid. Two beaded barrettes of green and white added the only color to his uniform, which of course was cowboy jeans, top to bottom. They both had down vests on as well, to keep out the December winds. No, it was not difficult to scare the whiteman in this simple way; indeed, it was fun.

They sat on the hood of the Protector with a case of beer and stared. They finished off one of the ounces of grass with which Philbert had solemnly acquired Protector. One ounce of grass is a lot of dope in twenty-four hours, even for two Indians. So it could be excused if their minds might have wandered.

Manny was watching the heavy traffic pull in and out of the Visitors' Center of the National Monument. He watched the people in the machines who watched him. It seemed odd to him that people did not look at the machines when they were inside them. They always looked to find a face inside, behind glass. It made him, Manny Bono, on the hood of his horse, laugh. He began to convulse with laughter at the movements of the heads inside the machines swiveling to see other heads. He was very stoned, so he

2

saw great meaning in these glimpses, as if they were grainy photographs out of the past, of great artistic sensitivity.

Philbert was having a vision. He saw himself in a sweat hut of the old days, naked and sweating. He was losing a lot of weight, he was preparing for battle, he was listening to the Powers of the Sky and the Earth and everything in between. It was making him very hungry.

"Hey, man, we need munchies."

But Manny only continued his laughing, a high-pitched whoop that the tourists mistook for a war cry, as he drove off in Protector. Some short-haired Crow who worked at the Monument came outside to stare at them as they left, the care of responsibility a hollow frown on their faces. Their ancestors had also stared at Cheyenne upon a hill, with equal anxiety. They went back inside to their janitor jobs.

"Goddamn Cheyenne," they muttered.

Philbert and Manny had many adventures on that whoop, but they would be too many for the telling now and of such profundity as to only make the great red skull of Philbert Bono ache. Enough that it be said Manny found Darla and Letitia Whitehorse in Forsyth and passed out with them in their living room in Busby, on the Res. Philbert had stumbled out to greet the noon sun, shining on his new sign of wealth, and brought himself back to the beginning of this fuzzy recollection. He turned the key to on and the machine gurgled, gasped, and finally spat to life like a horse after a long drink of water. Philbert gingerly put the column lever to D for Drive, avoiding any sudden movements, as the transmission liked to jump back and forth if a careless driver ran the lever over R and P and back to D. It was a delicate instrument, this marvel of the whiteman. Lurching to a painful roll, the man and beast rattled around a broken sewage main in the middle of the unpaved street, trundled carefully past two dogs sleeping in the intersection, and triumphantly eased onto the highway to Lame Deer, sixteen miles away. An arrogant magpie did not move out of the road where it was feasting on a flattened jackrabbit. Protector obligingly skirted the irritable scavenger.

They were on their way, for no particular reason other than they might possibly find a party going on. Lame Deer could be a pretty wild place sometimes.

Just as Philbert was puzzling over his miserable lot, his drive shaft fell out on the road. It was a thunderous metallic crash and the Buick swerved to the side of Highway 212. When he had Protector firmly in hand and had stopped on the shoulder, he looked in the rearview mirror. All he saw was the snowy hillside in front of him, and a concrete REA pumping station. He had forgotten the rearview mirror had been destroyed in a fight with some Sioux from Fort Peck several years ago.

Rolling down the window with difficulty, and then only halfway because it was warped inside the door, he looked out behind him. He saw a long rusty cylinder roll into the weeds on the side of the road. Sure that it must be as necessary to Protector as oats to an animal, Philbert determined he would have to confront the situation. Bracing himself, he opened the door and stood out on his ancestral land. A stiff wintry breeze blew an old Mounds candy wrapper into his face, and then carried it off to new surprises among the piles of modern tumbleweeds lodging along the road. It nestled among a box of Pampers, aluminum foil, and Pepsi pop-tops.

Philbert took a deep breath, stunned at the purity of the air that existed outside his sanctuary. He surveyed the homeland of his people through bloodshot eyes. It made little sense to his brain, but his spirit knew that everything, or anything, of Philbert Bono that was whole was here. He took a leak, just as Bobbie Short went by with his kids in his Ford pickup. They waved out of habit, undisturbed at the activities of the others. It was enough that they were moving.

Philbert remembered the drive shaft. Limping from years of no exercise, he went back to the weeds. He couldn't pick up the strange aperture that had flown from the bowels of his mysterious possession, so he rolled it back to the beast. Sparks flew furiously as the iron rolled across the asphalt, complaining of the cruelty of man to machine. Able to crawl underneath only through the good luck of a slant on the road's shoulder that left Protector on a tilt, Philbert saw one hole in the engine up front, and another hole in the rear. Perhaps he could stick the rusty tube in those holes and be on his way.

With only a few dozen grunts and a preposterous ease that would have amazed a mechanic, that's just what happened. He stuck the six-foot drive shaft back in and proceeded to Lame Deer. It took an Indian to understand truly the mysteries of the world, Philbert thought. This . . . this whiteman, who is he to a people that has known all the tricks of survival in this country for 125,000 years? What is meant to be is meant to be.

Philbert passed his journey with these thoughts, taking Protector to its maximum limit of forty-five miles per hour. An astounding speed, considering it had not had an oil change in twelve years.

The journey proceeded without further incident—if the usual clatters and clangs and scrapes emitting from the agonized bowels of the encrusted machine were taken as ordinary complaints of a whiteman's tool. Philbert thought it was purring more sweetly than ever.

He was, in fact, happier than he had ever been in his life. He was often like that. It was one of those many absolute moments of purity that only occasionally visit other lesser men.

Philbert had had an ordinary life, for an Indian. He had known happiness, as well as tranquillity and fulfillment. There had been moments of sorrow, of anger, of loss, of hopelessness. But they were only moments. Philbert had conquered failure with doggedness. He plowed through poverty with thoughts of wealth. He overcame depression by simply denying its existence. He had his drugs and his food. He had life to overwhelm the aches and pains of intelligence. Good cheer and comradeship overcame the frustrations of knowledge. Philbert was not a seeker, for he had already found what made him the best possible Philbert.

He was a Cheyenne, and all the shit of the world could not erase that.

He was a Cheyenne, even though it meant misery. There was a unity in misery, and therefore he had more than the whiteman ever had in his wealth. That had given Philbert great comfort as early as he could remember. Perhaps even as a baby he knew his dirty blankets and watery milk were a badge of cultural harmony, his one invincible hope. Driving down into the gloomy late afternoon of the center of the Cheyenne race, he felt the joy of belonging to Lame Deer. Here in these muddy streets and tiny house trailers dwelt the joy of his race. A people with a culture, and not just a powerful society of fed and warm immigrant babies. Ugh! He felt pity for whiter, skinnier men.

He was born fat and he stayed fat throughout his thirty-three years. It was a sign of health, a destiny he could not lightly discard. As a boy at the mission school in Lame Deer, he endured the jeers of the other boys and the repulsion of the girls with magnanimity. He was a Cheyenne. He was a great vegetable. The Powers of the Earth had served him unto his people as a platter of nourishment.

He drove past street corners and front yards that recalled incidents of his life. Here, beside a rotting box elder, he had been beaten up for talking to a Crow cheerleader, in town for a basketball game. The four Crow boys exhausted themselves pounding away at his blubber, while the loafers in front of the recreation center hooted their approval of the fat boy through their toothless old mouths. Philbert had relished the fame that beating had brought him. It inspired a minor war between the two tribes, of great satisfaction to everyone.

Another time he had fallen in love. There, beside Angel

Taylor's front yard, the white fence gray from years of never being painted, there he had stood for many hours on many evenings, afraid to knock on her door. He hid behind the pines as many other boys came for her, until a cowboy came from Sheridan in Wyoming and took her away. Angel Taylor. Philbert got a hard-on just thinking about her. He remembered her in waist-length black hair and ankle-length doeskin dresses she wore to pow-wows. She could have won a contest for Miss Indian America, if she had tried. But now she was gone, sunk out of sight into the anonymous quicksand of a whiteman's city.

Past hopes, past excuses, past regrets lay thickly upon his soul, like fat on a side of bacon. Memory was always a thing of the present to an Indian. All he had to do was walk past a piece of dirt and he would be reminded of the sorrows of Little Wolf. The cries of the past could never die in a man who dwelt on the soil where his ancestors were buried. They became the cries of these his children today.

Laughter was there too. So many would like to forget that. But forgetting was impossible in Montana.

Slowly circling the familiar streets, showing off his war pony to the people who pretended indifference, prouder than it was possible for any other man to be proud, Philbert remembered a joke here by a ditch, a drink there by the agency story, a fight—

"Philbert, stop! For chrissake!"

Obediently, he stopped. He recognized the voice of Buddy Red Bird but as yet could not make out his lanky form out there in the approaching dusk. The sun had not set, but the valley where the town lay between steep, pinewooded hills was already in shadow. It was dark, while the sunlit blue sky above spoke of an eternal protection to these cold, weather-beaten people huddling against all odds.

The passenger door of Protector shrieked open, resigned to never knowing grease again upon its parched units. Philbert was startled as the cold air outside came quickly in with Buddy Red

Bird, who quickly closed the door again, amidst screams of outraged metal bending back into unnatural shapes. The doorjamb held, however. Why or how was beyond human explanation.

"What're ya doin' with Manny's junker?" Buddy asked without rancor. "And, Jesus, doesn't the heater work?"

"It's on. Where to?"

"I don't feel anything." Buddy shivered, looking for some sense to the dashboard or the electrical mysteries underneath. All he found for his probing was a box of Kotex Super some friend of Manny's had forgotten in the glove compartment, which had no door, no tools in it, no registration, and of course no gloves. Perhaps, if only in the imagination of hopeful innocents who believe in Candyland and Santa Claus, perhaps there was a faint breeze from some valiant heater lost to the memory of a man. A wisp of heat. It was a hope that Philbert and Buddy could not let die, and so they soon forgot the cold, confident of warmth. It was to be the modus operandi of their impending adventures.

"What're ya doin' with Manny's junker?"

Philbert said, "We made a trade, as of the days when men possessed nothing. The earth alone knows what we may know." Philbert was not astounded at his new elocutionary honesty. Protector wept.

"What the hell . . . ?" Buddy was astounded. "Anyway . . . whatever you said, it's yours, right?"

"Right."

"Good. Then we have to go to New Mexico." Buddy, it was becoming clear, was in an excitable state of mind. These were the words that had been on his mind for a great while. Perhaps even an hour. Time, it must be understood, is not as comprehensible a mystery to the Indian understanding as it is to the whiteman's. Buddy had not made a passionate determination, no matter what the temporal programming.

"New Mexico?" Philbert asked dumbly. He was driving past some schoolgirls and honked casually. They paid no attention

8

since the horn didn't work. Occasionally it might let out a pitiful belch, but this was only upon a random stroke of fortune.

"Yes, Jesus, you know this is a real omen." Buddy talked fast, lighting up a joint. He could talk, smoke, and drink all at once. It was one of the many talents that made him a leader of the tribe. The Tribal Council had long had their eye on him as a future member of their all-powerful body.

"I needed wheels immediately, and at that very moment you splashed by. You really got old Lefty Taylor, Angel's old man, did you know that?"

"No."

"You did."

"What omen?" Philbert liked to arrive at the point. It was an extension of his logical mind.

"Bonnie called about an hour ago. She got busted down in Santa Fe. Pigs pulled her over for no license plates and saw two pounds of Colombian sitting on the seat. Her and some guy named Tony Parelli."

"Who's he?"

"Some Mexican, I guess. She's been dealing pretty heavy. Bought a Volvo, you know, doin' really well."

The smoke from their joint was fogging up the window. Philbert turned on the defroster, but all that came out was a cockroach from the vent on the dashboard. Philbert rubbed the fog off the window with his shirtsleeve. They watched the cockroach wander along the metal of the dashboard. It had been padded, before Manny had torn it all off in an aesthetic rage five years earlier. He said plastic padding made it look cheap.

"She's in jail; we gotta bail her out," Buddy began again, using some of the unused Kotex to clean off his window. "I can use the money the Council gave me yesterday to buy those bulls from the government down at Birney. I'm the goddamn agricultural purchasing agent, you know. Goddamn."

Buddy was a vet and a football star. They trusted him.

9

"They'll be cool about it," Buddy added with his usual confidence.

Philbert kept driving, up and down the dirt trails in the gullies that made up the town. A few houses on either side were puffing out regular streams of smoke from the tin chimneys of the BIA homes. It was cold outside, but Protector was snug and away from all that.

"You got gas money, then?" Philbert asked as he turned a corner sharply, watching the cockroach slide the width of the car on the unpainted metal of the dashboard. It was like a figure skater losing his balance and sliding across the ice on his butt. Outside, a pack of dogs was nearly massacred as Protector jumped an irrigation ditch in Philbert's cockroach distraction. The dogs sprinted away in silent panic. They were also a little hurt that someone would try to run them down.

"Two thousand dollars," Buddy replied, appreciating Philbert's creative driving.

Protector swerved to a stop beside two boys on bicycles, swapping copies of *Penthouse* magazine. They were oblivious to the cold and the excited shouts inside the car.

"The Council gave you two thousand dollars in cash?" Philbert tried to grasp this fact and its awesome implications.

"A check," Buddy explained nonchalantly. Philbert lost his grip on the facts again. What could it mean? He looked for the cockroach. It had disappeared.

"I can cash it, no problem. The trick is to get down to Santa Fe, bail out Bonnie, get her out of the state, and get back here before the Council starts looking for their bulls. We pay for the bulls with another check, and the other one in Santa Fe bounces. We get Bonnie on the Res and they can't touch her."

Buddy took a breath and lit up another joint, satisfied with his plan. The fact that it was riveted with holes did not make it impossible. Facts were inferior truths to these Indians. The bugs would work themselves out.

True, they sort of couldn't touch Bonnie. She was a genuine, registered Cheyenne Indian. State cops had no jurisdiction. It was a fight in the courts because the cops didn't like Indians coming into town and getting drunk and busting up furniture and windows and various other items of private property and then escaping to the reservations and avoiding prosecution. Many a cops-and-Indians chase had developed over just such a states'-rights-versus-federal-jurisdiction dispute: Indians fleeing back to their own sovereign borders with enraged lines of police cruisers on their tails. But Buddy didn't foresee any of that. (That none of it was accurate didn't matter a bit.)

"We gotta bust ass, Philbert," Buddy gently admonished. "We gotta shake our tail feathers down south, and I mean five minutes ago!" Buddy was enjoying the prospect.

His words grated upon Philbert's ears, where his poetic consciousness lay like telephone wires buried between his auditory apparatus and his heart. Nay, his soul. Philbert wanted Buddy's colloquial prospects to be an eloquent voyage, or what would be the point in the going?

"Let's stop by my trailer, where we can pick up sleeping bags and gear. I got a Conoco credit card."

"You said you had two thousand dollars?" Philbert quietly inquired. He was sure his voice sounded like a bird in flight.

"We can't touch that, you dumb fart," Buddy said. He pointed Philbert and Protector down a narrow alley to the ancestral Red Bird circle of trailers, his own a twelve-by-seventy.

"It's Bonnie's bail money. I have some bread left over from this month's welfare check. It'll be enough."

He paused, the drug weariness sweeping upon him in waves of nostalgic tenderness. A family sentiment famous in the emotional Red Birds of Lame Deer brought instant tears into his cynical eyes.

"It's my sister, goddammit! I ain't lettin' no Wasichu bastards lock her up!"

The sheer violence of his sincerity silenced them. Philbert drove along in a respectful stupor, bouncing over boulders and slipping around five-foot potholes into the inner reaches of their little village.

Buddy Red Bird knew full well how to obtain any desired effect. He was a leader; he knew the power of fear, of anger, of arrogance. Self-righteousness was his most effective weapon. It had won him many battles. He need only remind the weaklings of the white and the black and the brown races of their bad record with the red race, and any amount of cowing was possible. Intimidation was desirable with congressmen, businessmen, cocktail women, arts-and-crafts women, and all their precocious children. They were capable of the greatest guilts, and Buddy self-righteously relished their cowardice. There was no emotion he could not feel and would not use with these, the most powerful forces in America.

But there were also the gas attendants and short-order cooks and forest rangers who wouldn't take any of that shit. In their ignorance, their refusal to accept any blame or responsibility, Buddy had found his greatest allies. The dumb shits of the West had more in common with the Indians of the West than any professor of anthropology could begin to understand. It was a perception whose uniqueness Buddy felt would save the West from those contemptible East Coast intellectuals who had come to use the West for their own private fuck, ever since Lewis and Clark opened the dark pages of the West unto the light of European wisdom. The East was the enemy, knowledge was the force of evil, compassion and peace and understanding were the drugs of the indoorsmen. War and laughter and life were the only signs of heaven to Buddy Red Bird.

He had not come to these insights easily. Years of hurt went into them. Years of success.

Buddy played football and still held the state records for rushing and punt return. He got a scholarship to Yale, where he overwhelmed the social sciences department with his honest hatred of everything about them. He got a commission in the Marines, served two years in Vietnam, and won three bronze medals overwhelming the gooks, who reminded him of the Chippewa. Then came Alcatraz, the BIA Occupation in Washington, and Wounded Knee.

Buddy was there, to the ecstatic delight of the East Coast darlings. Indians became the rural branch of radical chic on the East Coast cocktail-party circuit. Buddy failed to mention that he had beat up an FBI agent later and had let a Menominee take the rap. The hell with it; tribes were meant to be enemies.

Buddy had the larger visions. To be Cheyenne was everything.

The great world out there was doomed. Even the Sioux were damned. Civil war after Wounded Knee was tearing them apart. They had always been the obvious target of the secret police. The Cheyenne would lie low until America spent itself and its economic glory into inevitable oblivion. Even the Navaho knew it was coming.

It remained only for the Cheyenne to pull together, and not in some phony reproduction of the past. Even poor old Philbert, whom everyone loathed, harbored some hopes of returning like eagles to caves in Bear Butte, where Sweet Medicine began their race. Ugh!

They pulled across a pile of wet cardboard beside Buddy's trailer. The air seemed ready to rain, although no clouds hovered within sight. Stopping the car, they got out. Philbert exhaled, to let his belly fold over naturally. He would soon get used to the pressure of the steering wheel.

"We'll just be a minute," Buddy said as he hurried up the broken steps to the trailer door. He leapt athletically over and around a slalom course of new and old piles of dog shit. They varied in shades from light tawny to dark mahogany.

"Buddy . . ." An urgency in Philbert's soft voice stopped Buddy. "What?"

"The sun . . ." Philbert breathed quietly. "It's not setting."

"What the hell are you talkin' about?"

"It's . . . exactly where it was when I drove into town, I'm sure of it." Philbert was looking across the hills to a notch where the sun was listing like a yellow bubble on a carpenter's level. He did not move, an extraordinary feat for one of his bulk. Not even a ricochet of fat moved in the usual momentum of his flesh.

"Waiting."

The sound of the trailer door opening and slamming and Buddy's annoyed "Jesus" struck Philbert like a slap in the face. He moved, and his body rippled with a sigh of relief. He went inside the trailer, into utter darkness. Taking a step, something soft underneath cried out in rubbery mockery, "Mama, mama."

"God!" Philbert jumped.

A fragile voice out of the dark said, "It's only Trudy's baby-doll, fat boy."

Philbert closed his eyes, terrified. It was the voice of his mother, long dead. But who was Trudy?"

"I'll be out in a minute, Phil," he heard Buddy shout from somewhere else in the trailer. "Get the beer out of the fridge."

"Mama?" Philbert whispered. "Mama? Do you have a message for me?"

"Yeah." The same croak came out of the shadows. "Turn on a light, I can't see shit."

Philbert, baffled at the strange ways of the cosmos, groped for a light. He found the TV, and turned it on. The blinking blue effervescence added a further eeriness to the stagnant light of the Indian sun.

"For natural hair, use Revlon Ultra-Color. That's Revlon," it droned on.

"You and Harriet gettin' it on, Philbert, boy?" Buddy queried, coming back into the room. He had a great armload of nylon sleeping bags and a Coleman stove and extra electric blankets, doubling his size into a shadowy grotesqueness. The warped storm door slammed as Buddy went outside with his load. Philbert jumped again.

"Harriet?" his over-nutritioned mind asked, staring at the karma of a commercial for Dodge pickups. He watched for meaning as the metal stallion leapt heroically off a hill and down away into the voice-overs and psychedelic graphics of creative advertising. "Happiness is a Dodge Truck," it said in ten colors.

"No, yer mama." The croak laughed. Philbert turned to see the outline of Buddy's ancient Aunt Harriet, sitting off in the gloom on a couch, her bony silhouette before a plastic-covered window. Trudy was one of the stray Black Buffalo kids up the block.

"Boy, you are really spooked, ain't ya?" Harriet laughed again. "Turn the channel."

One obedient flick found "teeth whiter than white"; another flick and they discovered the joys of headache relief.

"Aunt Harriet, how goes it with you?" Philbert found a chair, and sat on a box of crackers. With the artificial light of civilization now illuminating the room, he recognized the usual trash everywhere. Buddy's folks lived in a trailer next door, but Aunt Harriet didn't like them—"Too clean," she often grumbled—so she often came over to Buddy's to sit in the dark and mumble about Uncle Mob, who had run off twenty years ago. She was sixty-one and looked eighty-one.

"What're you two worthless bucks up to?" she asked facetiously. Everyone knew she worshiped Buddy. In fact, there were few people who didn't admire Buddy. Philbert and he had never had much in common, however.

Buddy slammed back in before Philbert could answer. "Bonnie's in jail, Auntie, we're gonna bust her out." He went back down a short passageway to his bedroom.

"Get the beer, Philbert, goddammit!" he ordered out of the dark disorder.

Philbert rose listlessly, crackers stuck to his seat, remembering his dead mama and wishing Harriet had been her. Somehow, as he got four beers from the empty refrigerator in the tiny kitchen behind the TV, his happiness of that afternoon was fading. The unnatural state of some faint responsibility was exerting itself upon him.

"Let's go," Buddy barked, reappearing with another armload of backpacks and clothes. "I got some old Marine fatigues you can rip out and wear. We'll buy toothpaste."

The storm door did not slam this time. Philbert looked and saw a boot had caught in it. It looked like a foot caught in a trap torn from some wild animal.

"Aunt Harriet," Philbert stated, still standing in the kitchen. He leaned over the TV from behind, his hands on the top of the warm machine, his fat fingers hanging over the edge to make a zigzag design on another automobile commercial.

"Aunt Harriet, you're an Elder—"

"You're covering up the picture."

"Sorry." He drew his hands away but kept them on the top of the plastic box for warmth. "You remember your mother talking about the old days? Perhaps your grandmother too?"

"You mean the Depression?"

"Well, no . . ." Philbert hesitated. He didn't even know what to say, let alone how to say it.

"Well, then, what?" she asked impatiently. A pause. "Oh, you want to know about the blanket skins. Well, I get a little sick about bein' asked for some good of Indian wisdom all the time. I ain't got none, so get out of here!" she said loudly, suddenly angry.

He started heavily for the door. Buddy was yelling outside to get going. The TV blared its apocalyptic nonsense. Trash overwhelmed him, inside the trailer and outside on the ground. Despair was ready to show him its true face. Hope cried out for a merciful extermination.

"Hey, fat Philbert," the cynical voice in the room behind him said. He stopped. "I got one quote from Dull Knife he once told my uncle Benny Two Ankles, who told it to my grandmother. He said, 'Keep your pony out of my garden.'"

That was it. Philbert waited for more, for an explanation. Anything. But she was silent, bitterly reaching inside her Montgomery Ward dress to adjust a recalcitrant bra strap. Buddy had begun pounding furiously on the hood of Protector.

With divine realization, Philbert suddenly felt a sense of purpose and strode with renewed greatness out of the trailer to his car. He now had a fresh sense of confusion to keep him going, and it would be cultivated with care. Such experiences of the Old Ones were to be dissected with reverence, and savored over weeks and months like a quart jar of beef jerky. Dull Knife's stringy truth rang within his brain: *Keep your pony out of my garden.* It was a joy to his heart.

Buddy sat at the wheel of Protector, idling the remaining fifty or sixty horses that were usually a symphonic triumph to Philbert. Without him, Whirlwind, at the wheel, though, the rattling music was a chorus of humiliation to Philbert Bono.

"I will make with the driving."

"What?"

"It is my pony," Philbert said, more adamantly than Buddy had ever heard him. "Move!"

Buddy moved over and Philbert leapt behind the wheel. They drove silently out the alleyways of Lame Deer, the glow of twilight descending upon the sleepy camp. Buddy began talking about the route, where to cash the check, all the details of their rescue mission. He drank beer and rolled another joint for them from a plastic bag in the pocket of his red woolen shirt.

Philbert was stoic, both hands on the cracked steering wheel. He regretted leaving Lame Deer. But he drove fast, without looking back, as only a brave man would. It would be for the Powers to decide if he would ever return to the camp. It was a warrior's duty to ride.

It was fifteen miles before the sun would set. Protector brought them to the southeastern edge of their land and the banks of that beautiful river. Buddy watched his tribesman's intensity with sardonic awe. Philbert jumped from the car, as much as Philbert could jump, and the scarlet fury imbuing the earth hit him like the annihilating heat of ten thousand steel smelters. Buddy turned also to the west and took another toke.

Philbert jumped in the river.

"You dumb shit!" Buddy yelled, running to the bank, truly alarmed.

"Hey-hey-hey-hey," Philbert began to chant, standing waist-deep in the freezing water. It was a war chant, a song of life and mystic sorrow. Buddy stared at his tribesman, utterly amazed.

"Hey-heyya-heyya-hey!"

The light wrought its own unknown power. All that can be said is that Buddy Red Bird the Hypocrite and Philbert Bono the Dreamer stood at a small place on the earth and stared at each other. Then they waded wordlessly into the middle of the river and chanted together unto some great understanding that lit up their eyes like sorcerers' in the dark.

CHAPTER 2

How the Princess Came
to Be in Jail, and the
Adventures of Her Friends

NOBILITY LAY HEAVILY upon Bonnie Red Bird. It had been her destiny to be an Indian princess, and she had accepted her destiny. She had the immaculate auburn skin that made the Cheyenne among the most handsome of all the Plains Indians. She had the restrained features that gave the Cheyenne a pure and peaceful look. Her raven-black waist-length hair glistened even in the dark; her figure was full without being immodest; her walk, her posture, her voice—they were all perfectly erect and dignified. She was, in short, beautiful.

Eight packs of cigarettes a day and more men than she could remember did not change this. A healthy quantity of alcohol and drugs only added luster to her cheeks. Two children had made her abdomen flatter, her small breasts fuller. A hard life of living with reality had only strengthened her ideals. She was an indestructible woman.

How she had come to be in the Santa Fe city jail was no mystery to her. It was the racism of the whiteman and of the brownman. She was an Indian; therefore they had been ready to nail her as soon as they saw her ancient face, which drew a veil of fear and ignorance over their insecure and atheistic heritages. The strength of her culture reminded them of the weakness of theirs. It was written, in the sociology books.

Here, then, is the story of Bonnie Red Bird, of her capture by the savages, of how she was raised in the heathen ways, and within which lay some of the truths of many an Indian maiden. It is something that is not in the sociology books.

Maiden she had been until she was fourteen. The Cheyenne, after all, have always been very strict with their women. The Cheyenne woman was the symbol of modesty, the shining example that lit the way for the Sioux and the Arapaho. The Cheyenne woman had a great burden laid upon her from birth, the burden of purity. It was a task unto which many rose valiantly. Many a Cheyenne woman has walked meekly through many an Indian village, and all heads had turned to see her and had felt shame in their breasts for their own lustful and selfish lives. She was the superstructure of their society. They could not approach her devastating goodness.

Bonnie said to hell with all that. She knew that the duties of a modern princess lay in individual fulfillment. She knew she must be liberated if she were to bring her people into the twentieth century. She would be a symbol, yes, but a relevant one.

She saw no contradiction in going to New York City when she was seventeen. It was part of her role in her Montana tribe. She had to find herself in the whiteman's world if she was ever going to keep the redman's world from being lost. It was simple logic. She was a smart girl, she had talents, she would make sense of the two cultures, she would see them come to share the good things they each had to offer.

She attacked the masculine mystique as one very good way to discover this greatest of all possible syntheses. Through men, Bonnie pursued the noble goals of her life's work. She had to experience the personalities of the ruling animal—the white middle-class American male, the most privileged primate on earth.

Bonnie set about her researches with enthusiasm. Being beautiful and rather exotic to New Yorkers, she easily got a job in a glamorous jewelry store on Fifth Avenue. She soon met and allured men of many shapes and pocketbooks. If sex became a part of her experiment, then sex became a tool she could no more do without than a Mercedes-Benz mechanic could do without a ratchet.

It was a tool that she wielded with pleasure. She had always appreciated the boys on the reservations, and the studs in the small-town bars, but these men of New York City were men! They knew a girl's desires, and they gave them to her. Fancy restaurants, Broadway plays, weekend trips to Connecticut, considerate sex, passionate sex, selfish sex—goddammit but it was a good life!

She succumbed completely to America. She made money, accepted gifts, and maintained her pride throughout the foolish declarations of love by half a dozen men.

Then she fell in love with a Communist. He was handsome. A professor of economics at Columbia, his book, *Communism in Corporate America*, made him the hit of the cocktail-party circuit. His salt-and-pepper beard, his understanding of tribal society and its similarity to Communism, the effective bulge in his trousers, all drove her to lay her sweetest enticements upon him at one of the parties. Her voluptuous modesty never failed to drive intelligent men mad.

From then on they were seen everywhere, a sociological triumph of the communal man and the tribal woman. She fell hopelessly in love. He was kind, gentle, and treated her like an equal. She gratified his every pain and pleasure. They had everything to live for, and it seemed that the comforts of American anonymity were slowly but surely seeping into their radical philosophies like antidote into a poison.

Then he was hit by a bus on Lexington Avenue and died immediately. The driver was arguing with a woman passenger about inflation, and didn't see the bearded man lost in his thoughts.

Bonnie dropped out of high society. She told herself it was because the Vietnam War made high society despicable. She marched, she burned her bra, she worked for Eugene McCarthy, and at night she wept in unbearable loneliness.

She could not return home. She could not face her people, her land, her memory of Dull Knife's tragic children. She had responsibilities to fulfill. She must find out what it was that made the whiteman superior.

She began to frequent revolutionary hangouts. America, after all, had always been in a state of change, of search, of growth. These vital dissatisfactions were as much a part of its strength as the stable and patriotic citizenry. It was written in the history books.

She was accepted immediately. She was told Indians were among the certified oppressed people. She took to drinking sherry in coffeehouses with Czechoslovakians, smoking dope in East Village lofts with Cubans, and giggling through less than surreptitious porno flicks in dingy cinemas with Blacks. She was *in*. Indians were admired. She went to plays about Brazilian dictators at off-off-off-Broadway theaters. She started hanging around modern jazz dancers, poets, crippled news vendors. The real people. The people who saw through capitalist propaganda, Communist decadence, greed, and corruption.

She met Kevin McNamara, a fiery Irish devotee of IRA plays, and they got married. He talked about the Irish and the Indians as two great wild peoples of the world. She took acting lessons. Ellen Stewart of Cafe LaMama formed a Native American Theater Company, after Ellen had read *Bury My Heart at Wounded Knee*. Bonnie was asked to be a member of the company. Kevin was the director. Two dozen Indians crawled out of the conglomerate woodwork of New York ethnos, and the chaos was immediate. Crow and Sioux would not work together, Apache just got drunk, Seminole and Seneca wanted to do ritual pageants, and an Eskimo wanted to do Tennessee Williams.

They argued, fought, smoked to peace, walked the streets of Chinatown in shows of beaded and feathered unity, argued, and fought. Ellen pleaded for them to rise above tribal disharmony, to Mohawk shamans in Vermont to come down to New York for powwows, to the Bureau of Indian Affairs for grants.

Kevin began to beat Bonnie. She came to rehearsals with black eyes. She got pregnant and delivered a boy, Sky, effortlessly. Then a girl, Jane. They lived on welfare, she began to paint graphic eagles flying into fluorescent suns, Kevin directed Pawnee and Shawnee in existential plays about the deterioration of the Western myths.

The collapse was inevitable.

Half a dozen of the company went to Atlanta to a Black Ensemble Theater. Others went to Chicago for improv, to Seattle to learn Kwakiutl mask making, and to Los Angeles for the big time in films. Kevin, Bonnie, Sky, and Jane were on their way to L.A. when their car broke down in Oklahoma City.

Even so, it was good to be back in the West. The style simplified. Life became purer, clearer, cleaner. The East was doomed.

A year in Oklahoma City completed Kevin's alcoholism. He beat Bonnie and she would run away. Then she would come back. He totaled their car and wasn't even scratched. He ran tabs up at the local hippie bars day and night. Bonnie worked in a jewelry store selling authentic Indian turquoise to pay the bills. The kids grew, developing uniquely neurotic personalities.

Reality was doomed, however, if it even tried to approach Bonnie Red Bird McNamara. If anything, she grew more beautiful, more innocent, more oblivious physically and spiritually to the rude effects of her own creeping alcoholism. The protestations of her beloved but neglected children only made her more confident of her motherhood. The pathological wildness of her husband only assured her of his great love for his family.

She had grown to become an integral speck of the vast American universe. She had friends, a job, a cute house, a color TV. She had a family, made more believable because of its problems. Above all, it was a white family. She was in. The kids only looked a little Indian.

A friend of hers named Rabbit LeLouche suggested one night in the Orange Lily that there was big money in drugs. They sat on the bar stools of the white hippie bar to which Indians were bona fide brothers, drinking Black Russians, while her husband roared in the back room over his pool game about how theater in America was for shit. Other concerned hippies roared back at him about how There-Was-a-Revolution-Going-on-Outside as they clanged their Budweiser bottles down on the warped pool table.

"Bonnie and Rabbit were buddies." Rabbit was singing drunkenly at the bar. She was a short curly-headed Oklahoman with a twangy rap that left everyone dazzled. Bonnie sat dignified beside her, her seventh Black Russian squarely in front of her. The kids were at a friend's.

"Bonnie, Rabbit, bunny rabbit, get it?" Rabbit laughed. Bonnie smiled politely, trying to be above the humor. But she would repeat something funny with a short giggle, as if she were amazed people could be comic in this miserable world.

"Bunny rabbit!" she repeated, giggling slightly contemptuously.

"Bunny!" Rabbit leaned over, in her most confidential precision. "Bunny!" Bonnie giggled.

"I can make you three grand a week, maybe more," Rabbit said matter-of-factly. She was always very aware of the serious things of the world she had to contend with. "Those suckers in Texaco country and the Tejas hogback El Grande Mexico Coca-Cola are dying—"

"El Grande Coca-Cola!" Bonnie giggled, ordering another round.

"—fer fuckin' distributors. We truck about, sample our own flower tops 'n' coke 'n' such, fuck, suck, and goose the piggy bank like it was chicken today and feathers tomorrow! That's it, you 'n' me. Dump that bum of yers. I guarantee I got friends down in Texas, they'll set us up. We'll be in gravy more permanent than mud on a fence!"

"I got a family, Rabbit," Bonnie pleaded halfheartedly.

"Fuck," Rabbit summarized.

"Yeah," Bonnie had to agree. She was an agreeable person.

"Dump that bum. Three big ones a week, think of it, every week." Rabbit's eyes glowed. "Illegal profiteering has always been the American way. Drug traffic is now number three on the unofficial stock exchange, behind GM and ITT. Bunny rabbit, it's the best way to shellac the corporate process—"

"Shellac the—"

"They expect it, they thrive on it. But this is perfect, baby, because it's a society out there, under there. Underground. Think about it," Rabbit concluded, putting on a floor-length rabbit coat. It was getting chilly, after all. "Bring the kids," she added. "I take Jennifer everywhere."

"Why do you need me?" Bonnie asked.

"You're an Indian, I can trust you."

As Rabbit left to find her five-year-old fatherless child at some babysitter's or other, Bonnie reached the first philosophical crisis of her young adulthood. If you can't join one whiteman, then join another whiteman. They had a vast scheme to their organization. She had tried to join one way, to hitch up her wagon to the corporate star, but that particular ride had been too bumpy.

Well, she could compromise. Compromise, after all, was a mature process everyone considered honorable. It was in the history books.

She fingered the bruise on her cheek the whiteman of the arts, her husband, had given her. She quickly brushed off the painful memory of the whiteman of education she had loved. She never could quite swallow the racism of the whiteman in the business world or the sexism of the whiteman in the society world or the boredom of the whiteman in the working-class world, she suddenly realized. She saw that they all contributed to the culture she sought to understand, but they were beyond including her in the secret of their success. They could never include a redwoman into the ingredients of their secret formula. The melting pot was already overspiced.

So she would fight them, as a traditionally proven way of joining them. Sell illegal drugs to get rich. Kill two birds with one rationalization. Belong to an underground that respected Indians.

There were a few snags to untangle. She informed her husband that night she was leaving, and he threw a butcher knife at her. She managed to hide in the closet with the phone and call the police, while he kicked his foot through the door and the kids screamed in terror in another room. The police arrived with half the neighborhood on their front lawn watching Kevin roll around in the flower bed, then climb up the gutter drains to the roof, and jump off screaming obscenities at all women. He broke his leg, but it still took four cops to handcuff his arms to the Elcar iron fence post. The ambulance arrived for him as six other cops tried variously to coerce and then to pry Bonnie and her two kids, who clung to her like terrified monkeys, out of their locked car, where they had fled from Kevin's lunacy.

In court, Kevin provided half a dozen witnesses to testify about Bonnie's promiscuity. She was judged unfit for custody of the children, and he moved to Santa Fe, with them, and with the blessings of the state of Oklahoma.

Bonnie vowed to get her children back. She left two days later with Rabbit in her Ford station wagon for Austin, Texas, home of funky country-western music and Big Lester, Rabbit's Texas connection.

Big Lester Mardewcki was a boisterous boy from back East. Big brown freckles, a bulbous Eastern European nose, long brown hair and red beard—he was a lover of life, a Leo who had come to know west-central Texas as the center of good-ol'-boy hippie simplicity and big money, Lester was just folks. He had a twenty-acre ranch on a lake outside town, a Mercedes 300SL, two funky pickups, two Great Danes, and a green-eyed lady named Doris. Meat Loaf and Bob Dylan blared from a three thousand–dollar quadraphonic stereo and tape system as they sat on simple handmade leather cushions from Bangkok on the polished oak floor. Moroccan hash was brought out for the guests. Lester and Doris rapped about the oppression of Indians. Vegetarian steak, taters, greens, and a bottle of Baron Rothschild Chateau de Philippe 1961 fed their good, drugged appetites. Psilocybin mushrooms were brought out for dessert. They talked business, as Linda Ronstadt lulled their heightened awareness. Big Les invited them all to his hot tub. Naked dogs and the child floated in the hot water along with the sensitized adults. A water pipe for further explorations was stationed on a permanent island in the center of the redwood tub in the center of the solar greenhouse. Cactus flowers and jade plants added photosynthetic profundity to the human communications, as Doris brought them dainty glasses of amaretto, her freckled breasts not as full as Rabbit's, or as small as Bonnie's "champagne glass–size tits," Doris laughed. They openly enjoyed each other's nakedness, without the pressures of sex. It was freedom. Bonnie couldn't remember being so happy, so certain of her destiny, as she lay back in the hot water, Waterford crystal glass at her elbow in a special notch for refreshments, psilocybin visions filling her overworked brain.

Les and Rabbit talked business. He would have to check with the Scarlattis in San Antonio and Dallas, but it should be no problem for her to get a piece of the West Texas franchise. Southwestern New Mexico might even need drugs. This brought laughter. It was a matter of territory. More laughter as they sang a chorus of "76 Trombones." Returning to a serious note, Lester thought that with Bonnie along they might even crack the Parelli monopoly on the Indian traffic. Bonnie opened her eyes to see Rabbit sidle up against Big Les, and reach over playfully to Doris on the other side to touch a soft nipple. Big Les put one arm obligingly around each of them, and the three talked about how far-out the water was on their skin, the openness of their pores a turn-on to their karma. Bonnie nodded agreeably to herself—her mind was floating, exactly as her body was. It was mystical.

Lester kissed Rabbit. She kissed Doris. They both felt for Lester's penis underwater and the dogs started barking. Bonnie rose and put them outside, then carried Jennifer to bed. Then she sat in the living room in a white terry-cloth robe, smoking Benson & Hedges, listening to Jerry Jeff Walker. She heard splashes in the other room and gasps of pleasure from her three friends. It was beautiful. It was honest.

Yes, the whiteman of the hippie world was where it was at. Not the simplistic flower-child mentality of the sixties and early seventies, but this . . . this advanced pragmatism. Nothing wrong with enjoying the benefits of capitalistic industry, as long as you knew they were bullshit. This realization made Bonnie pure within herself, unlike before.

The next day she and Rabbit and Jennifer drove to San Antonio. Big Lester had given them an address and a recommendation for Vito Scarlatti. The next several months were filled with surreptitious trips by plane, car, and goat wagon into and out of Mexico. Smuggling became a tremendous adventure. It was the stuff of outlaws, Billy the Kid bravado that all Americans openly desired. Bonnie was beside herself. She made love to Mexicans, Texas cowboys, sailors in Mazatlan, surfers in Galveston, and even an Indian in Hermosillo, Sonora, one hot afternoon. She bought a new Volvo with the proceeds of a deal she made in one day at a rented room of an El Paso Holiday Inn. She and Rabbit went hungry for a few dry spells, were frightened many times by *federales* and DEA agents at the border, and got thirsty in the blistering desert; but they never got bored.

They spent all their money on drugs. Good acid, bad acid, mediocre acid, Michoacan marijuana, speed, uppers, downers, and more grass. Synthetics, chemicals, organics—they explored. It was profound. It was subtle, ecstatic, terrifying, mellowing, funny, tiring, ugly, and beautiful.

She had a fight with Rabbit, who wanted to take a vacation, and they split. She infiltrated the Parelli empire by infiltrating Tony Parelli's bulging blue jeans. A two-hour multiple blow job on Interstate 10 won him over to her exotic aboriginal tastes. He was hers and she left the Scarlattis for the Parellis. After all, he was handsome, rich, glib. He was the power.

It was time to go for her kids.

"Tony, honey," she cooed one night in their lavish suite at the Hilton in Albuquerque, "let's go to Santa Fe tomorrow." They were naked, fondling each other with considerate fingers. The room was cozy, their lives were secure, they may even have contemplated love some day.

"Sure," and he stuck his unselfish tongue into her vagina.

Which brings Bonnie back to the city jail. Bitterly she remembered the events of her denouement, guessing at the details. She called to the jailer to purchase another carton of Salems for her, and the Spanish woman grinned an unfriendly, piteous look at yet another worthless Indian. Ink was still on Bonnie's hands, where they had recorded her fingerprints the morning before. She rubbed them on her blue prison dress. She looked out at the leafless cottonwoods of the Pueblo village, which had become a chic metropolis for wealthy immigrants. What had gone wrong?

They had come up from Albuquerque a week ago, full of good cheer and cocaine. She had told Tony of her ex-husband and her children, and he vowed to talk to a judge who was a friend of the family on the New Mexico Supreme Court. Even though he was only twenty-seven, Tony Parelli, of the Kansas City Parellis, was an important man. He wore suits made at Savile Row in London, England.

They came into La Villa Real Santa Fe de San Francisco past five miles of motels, hamburger joints, and used-car lots. It was a vigorous driveway, heartening to the realistic couple, who felt they were pulling into the collective garage of every American city. They belonged to this part of town.

Winding their way into the four-hundred-year-old adobe downtown district was a culture shock. It was foreign, except for the mini traffic jam on the narrow streets. One week before their rendezvous with the realities of the city jail, they parked their car at La Posada Inn, sobered by the quiet beauty of this alien place. It looked poor enough for Bonnie to feel twinges of other Indian feelings.

But it was rich. That was the appeal of quaint chic. The mud buildings and chamisa weeds only looked poor. The glorious crimson sunsets and milk-chocolate adobe coloring only seemed natural. Actually, the price tags were gloriously precious. Tony signed them into a bungalow for seventy-five dollars a day. It reproduced the squat scenery of a prairie dugout down to every detail—except for the modern plumbing, color TV, and electricity. Recognizing the charm of it all, they got into the spirit and bought some authentic Mexican clothes at properly exclusive prices. They paid aristocratic sums for Indian silver, of which the flunky Indians got five percent. They even walked two blocks to dinner. There was no sacrifice too great to make in this rare and folksy atmosphere.

At the Bull Ring, over frozen blackberry margaritas and continental chile rellenos, they laid out their strategy to recapture Bonnie's children. They would hire two desperate caballeros to beat the hell out of Kevin. Then they would say he was an irresponsible father, and Tony's friend the judge would give them to Bonnie. Tony didn't particularly relish having two half-breed brats around, but Bonnie was too good a piece of ass to throw away. Besides, he had orders from KC to crack the Indian market, coming out of Central America. He made a call to Judge Jerry Sisneros, who obeisantly asked them over for drinks after dinner.

FBI Special Agent Doug Lewis noted the telephone number from his table across the room. He had excellent vision. They had been watching Bonnie for months. They had a complete dossier on her. The liaison with a Parelli had cleared up a great deal of suspicion at headquarters. The Wop, of course, was untouchable, but the redskin they wanted. Agent Lewis was assigned to her full-time.

Scurrying through empty windblown streets back to the car was a wintry shock. This was supposed to be the tropics, not seven thousand feet in the mountains! Agent Lewis made a note in his pad of them sticking their hands in each other's pants to keep warm, an awkward movement when scurrying. He followed in his unobtrusive Ford Pinto as the Volvo drove to the unfashionable west side of town where the Spanish lived—and the Anglo hippies who were tired of being fashionable. It looked exactly like the fashionable adobe and dirt roads of the East Side, except that it was the West Side. The Volvo parked for an hour in front of the ordinary stucco adobe house with a real but very unfashionable front lawn.

Inside the house, Bonnie was weeping. She had forgotten how much she missed her children. Judge Sisneros was duly impressed. Tony Parelli hated women who cried. He was getting tired of this flat-breasted whore. Bonnie went to the bathroom to blow her nose. She returned to the strangers and graciously accepted another Scotch and water. She had remembered she was in the presence of power. No people on earth could oppose a Spanish judge in New Mexico, or an Italian wise guy with connections. She relaxed.

"So there'll be no problem, Jerry?" Tony commanded. He had his family's instinct for authority.

"I don't foresee any, Mr. Parelli." Judge Sisneros hated this Anglo *pendejo*. "I believe Santa Fe will be more than hospitable, to both you and the young lady."

"I don't want any trouble," Bonnie felt compelled to say. "I just want my children."

Tony winced. He'd have to leave her at the room from now on if she was going to gum up the negotiations with sentiment.

"I understand." Judge Sisneros had had a nephew seriously injured in a car wreck several years ago, when a drunken Zuni Pueblo plowed into him from the rear. He hated all Indians.

As Bonnie and Tony left, walking around broken toys strewn on the flagstone sidewalk, Judge Jerry Sisneros waved good-bye with hatred in his heart. Those people were ruining his state. The heirs of Los Conquistadores were having their land stolen by Anglo buccaneers and Indian lawyers. He returned to his placid house, where his family crept out to watch TV, now that the old man was through with business. The old man was forty-seven, bitter, and influential. He had a right to be.

He had not seen the second car down the street, a yellow Pinto, pull out after the beige Volvo.

Events lost meaning after that for Bonnie as she stared out her jail cell. She was in a solitary cubicle, so great was her crime. The accumulated sensations of hostility gave her the worst feelings she had ever known. A climax of racial prejudice might have driven her to hate them, if she had not been so sensible.

They had gone to see Kevin and the two kids and the surfer girl who lived with them in an apartment. They were polite. They talked about how theater in Santa Fe was for shit. The kids took their mother to their room to show her their toys, and they all wept silently in each other's arms. They returned to the adults and didn't cry. Tony and Bonnie left after an hour.

Tony paid a man to pay two other men to ambush Kevin as he came out of the hippie theater bar on St. Francis Drive. Agent Lewis saw Tony make the payment, and he saw the terrible beating the two thugs gave Kevin at 1 a.m., after he staggered out of the bar and down an alley to his car. The agent did not try to stop the beating. He did not call an ambulance when the thugs left the poor bleeding fool twisted on the road. He drove away to write his report.

Two Spanish policemen interrogated Kevin from his hospital bed the next day. They were members of Our Lady of Guadalupe Catholic Church, of which Judge Jerry Sisneros and his lovely family were also members. The two policemen soon discovered that Mr. McNamara was a habitual drunkard, that he often got into fights, and that there was evidence he had been associating with known criminal elements in town. And, incredibly enough, he had custody of two children, who lived with him in a questionable neighborhood. These were serious matters, and they would have to make an unfavorable report to the judge. They were very polite about it. Their mothers had taught them the courtesy of Santa Domingo.

Two days later a visibly disturbed Judge Sisneros awarded the custody of the said children in question to their mother. He surprised the courtroom with an emotional appeal for the duties of parents to their children. He was usually so formal and unemotional. His secretary made fresh coffee, she was so touched.

Bonnie was beside herself with joy. She took Sky and Jane to Baskin-Robbins. She took them to the Museum of Navaho Ceremonial Art. She told them they were Indians too.

That night Agent Lewis removed the license plates from their Volvo as it sat parked at La Posada. The children slept in one double bed inside as Bonnie and Tony slept in another. Agent Lewis put a one-pound paper sack of the finest Colombian marijuana under the seat. Sky was awakened as he heard his mother and that man quarreling about something she refused to do for him. He heard a slap and he lay back down.

The next morning Patrolman Sanchez pulled them over on Cerrillos Road. They were on their way to Denny's for breakfast.

Bonnie was driving with the two kids in the front. Tony had excused himself. He said he had other important business in town and would meet them for lunch. He had leased a Cadillac Eldorado to get around.

"May I see your driver's license, ma'am?" Officer Sanchez had asked politely.

"Yes," she replied, blowing Jane's nose. "What's the trouble?" She handed over the Oklahoma license when the policeman did not answer. He took a great deal of time examining the license. Heavy traffic was slowing to a crawl around them on the busy four-lane street. There was no shoulder on which to pull over. Irate drivers gave them dirty looks as they inched past. Officer Sanchez seemed oblivious that a major traffic jam was developing.

"Excuse me a minute, ma'am," he said, returning to his cruiser, parked behind her. The red and blue lights were still flashing from atop the blue car. Only a few people thought it a little strange to see a highway patrol car within the city limits.

They were stopped in front of the Institute of American Indian Arts, a vast government installation erected for Indian artists. Its buildings and facilities were truly impressive. It had very few students. Several lovely Indian girls walked by, behind the eight-foot iron fence separating the school from the road. Bonnie stared blankly at the girls, waiting patiently for the policeman to return. The girls paid her and the traffic snarl no attention.

Bonnie became aware of the beautiful morning air, the blue sky unparalleled anywhere in the United States. The adobe colorings lent a blazing contrast to the subtle beauty. Satisfaction came upon her, with her children sitting quietly beside her, looking with wonder at the traffic and the flashing lights strobing in time to the honking rush-hour melee.

"I'll have to ask you to follow me, ma'am," the officer said, interrupting her reverie.

"I'm sorry?"

"Follow me, please." He returned to his cruiser.

"Why?"

Another cruiser came screaming up from the other direction, completing the chaos of traffic both ways now. The Indian girls inside the fence condescended to cast a hasty glance unto the whiteman noise. Then they hurried on to the school's cafeteria.

Bonnie went to jail. The kids were put in custody of the court and taken off somewhere. Bonnie was booked and fingerprinted. Tony had disappeared. Agent Lewis flew back to his regional office in Kansas City to prepare the case against her. Judge Sisneros would personally see to her case.

She hit the newspapers, big.

She called the Northern Cheyenne Tribal Council in Lame Deer, Montana, for help. It was the first time she had communicated with anyone from her tribe in twelve years. They would not accept the collect call.

She got the number of her big brother from information, and Aunt Harriet took the call.

"Who?" she had croaked.

"Bonnie . . . Bonnie, goddammit!" she had yelled in desperation as a matron oversaw her every moment at the pay phone in the hall.

"Buddy? Yeah, he's here, I'll get him," Aunt Harriet answered, dropping the phone on the floor of the trashed-out trailer.

"That means they accept, Operator," Bonnie had pleaded.

"Yes, ma'am," a polite voice responded.

She could hear voices in the background, and finally a long-familiar but long-forgotten masculine voice picked up the magical transmitter.

"Who?" Buddy asked through a hangover.

"Oh, Buddy, Buddy, it's you, oh God, oh God!" She started sobbing. "Buddy, I'm in jail, the pigs, dope, Mafia, oh Buddy, what'm I gonna do?"

"Who is this?" A long pause. "Bonnie?" he asked, incredulous.

"They've got my children, Buddy."

"Okay, honey, okay, I'll get 'em back. Goddammit, you say the pigs, honey? Have they beat ya?"

"Everyone."

"Okay, okay, I better come get ya. Where are ya?"

"Santa Fe."

"Where's that?"

"I don't know, the jail is all I know."

"Santa Fe? Oh, hey, that's New Mexico. What the hell ya doin' there?"

"I'm in jail, dammit! They planted two pounds of Colombian grass on me. Pulled me over for not havin' plates or somethin' on my Volvo, me 'n' Tony Parelli. No, he's not—"

"I thought you was in New York."

"It's been a nightmare! I don't know how these things happen! You gotta come get me! I got bail at two thousand dollars."

"Bail?"

"Oh, Buddy, you can do it; please, please!"

"The pigs, the goddamn pigs! Fascist Gestapo think they can—"

"Buddy—"

"Fuck fuck fuck!"

"Buddy!"

"Goddammit! Fuck shit piss!"

"That's right."

"Yeah, I'm comin', honey, your people won't let ya down, goddammit, we'll drive all night—"

"Why don't you fly?"

"I'll get the bread, I'll be there, we'll blow those fucks off the map!"

"Okay. And Buddy?"

"Yeah, listen, don't you worry, you're a Cheyenne; those racist pigs ain't gonna screw us. I'll be there, baby sister. You just watch out for those Lesbian creeps and don't blow it, ya gotta be cool. Ya understand? Be cool."

"Yeah. Thanks, Buddy."

"You bet your ass. You're my sister, ain't ya?"

"Yeah."

"Yeah. See ya faster'n a horse can piss."

"Okay."

He hung up and cursed America.

As she hung up, the matron grinned at her and pulled her back down the hall to her cell.

"It ain't two thousand dollars, you stupid squaw," she said. "Your bail has been set at *twenty* thousand."

"What!"

CHAPTER 3

A Lesson in Money
and the
Aesthetics of the Prairie

IT WAS DIFFICULT for Buddy to deal with money. Perhaps it can be said that it was difficult for Indians to deal with money, but that would be a generalization. Any two Indians had never been alike, let alone any two Indian tribes. The Cheyenne and the Sioux were as much alike as any two tribes of the plains warrior societies, and they weren't much alike at all. Well-meaning white-men arrived at many insights about the Indians through the centuries. One particular perception was that Indians could have defeated the European invaders with splendid dispatch if only they had united. Conservative as well as militant organizers today still plead for unity. Vast organizations have been formed to offer a united Indian front to the vast organizations that have been formed to resist a united Indian front. But Indians don't want to be united. They never have. They are among the greatest individuals of the tribal world. That is the nature of the most primitive and the most enduring of all forms of society. Tribalism goes back to the cave, a proven form of social get-togethers. For ten thousand years man hunted in packs, and who were the Indians to rock the ox cart? Berber tribes in the Libyan deserts still don't question the effectiveness of their ways. If a Berber wants to ride out with his tribesmen against a Turk or an Arab, he will. If he doesn't, he won't. It's as simple as charging over a sand dune for glory and plunder, or staying at home and watching television. Some of the pure plains warriors before the whiteman enjoyed the sheer thrill of an attack, that's true. After the whiteman, it was sheer desperation that made them take thrilling chances, not heroism. It still is. But it was always every man for himself, and it still is. If it was convenient to join up with some buddies because you might be outnumbered by those sneaky Crow, then you did what was convenient. But nobody ever, ever told an Indian what to do. And nobody ever will.

So Buddy Red Bird the warrior felt that two thousand–dollar tribal check was burning a hole in the pocket of his anti-collective conscience. He knew there was a beautiful disorganization to every Indian tribe. There were chiefs of spiritual insight, and the sorcerers who could scare the hell out of the careless individualists. They were respected, feared, and hated for their meddling. But they could zap you, so you had to be cool. You couldn't push them too far, because they had the rituals and the curses and the knowledge of thousands of years tucked away in their medicine bundles, and you didn't fuck with the heap big medicine of the cosmos. You just didn't.

But it was tempting. Warriors had always been taught social responsibility, and they had always taken their personal recklessness to the very edge of sanity—for the good of the community, of course. The best warriors had, anyway. They were taught mortality. They practiced immortality. They charged as screaming individualists into battle in as many different ways as there were different warriors. They were showing off to their fellows for honors, and coups. Tactics were silly. They were there to embarrass their enemies and their buddies alike. They defied death, whether it triumphed or not. If a warrior must die, he would at least have stories told about him. His spirit would haunt the campfires of his lesser, more mortal brothers. It was the ultimate mockery of mankind.

That it was the ultimate reason for their defeat at the hands of the palefaces was unavoidable. It was not their fault that they were defeated by the inferior science of tactics and group soldiering.

It had been what made Buddy a fanatic in Vietnam. Life was silly, order was silly, draft dodging was silly. The act of defying death and embarrassing life was everything. The only trouble in 'Nam was that the whiteman, in their nameless groups, could have given a shit to tell the story of their dead around the campfires. The old science of tactics fell apart, because the gooks easily learned about the tactics and transcended them by telling stories around *their* campfires. They had enough humility to die.

The two thousand–dollar check was aflame within his pocket. It was not his conscience or any other Christian hoopla that kept him from broaching the subject to Philbert, who sat at his side in the car, the two of them still wet from the river—it was fear. That goddamn Billy Little Old Man would send a black eagle or something after him. He was the medicine arrow chief and he was just spiteful enough to have some sorcerer's devil peck out Buddy's heart for misusing tribal money. Goddammit, there must be some way to achieve an honorable *act* of embarrassment!

In the old days it had been easy. A man knew he had only to scream and charge at a Crow or a Chippewa, tap the overwhelmed fool lightly on the forehead with a coup stick, and ride away giggling. The Chippewa usually died from the shame, not the wound.

But these days who the hell could tell where honor lay?

It was dark outside, soggy inside. Brotherhood had become a cold and hungry moral dilemma. Philbert had indeed ripped out one of Buddy's Marine fatigues, but his long hair was still wet and he looked more ridiculous than ever in the olive drabs. He was cold and starving. He had not eaten all day, an unprecedented

41

omission. He drove Protector numbly, shivering. His teeth were actually chattering. But it had been good to thank his mother the earth for another day. This his brain told his unimpressed body.

"I've changed my mind," Buddy said. "We'll cash the check at the drive-up window. Cash is better." They were pulling into the dead village of Birney. They were all of two miles off the reservation.

"Can't we eat first?" Philbert chattered. He slowed as they approached the Cheyenne Cafe on the one and only main street of the dejected little town.

"No," said Buddy, "the bank closes at six. It's almost that now."

Philbert drove Protector down the two reluctant blocks of the town, where the Northern Wyoming First National Bank, Birney Branch, sat in the mud. It was a tiny affair, not much bigger than a closet. But a line of pickups and Broncos snaked around behind it, where the drive-up window was lit with two blazing hundred-watt bulbs. They were the only refuge against the darkness that had come up immediately in the foothills.

Protector took its place in line. Buddy shifted on the wet seat. He had put on dry jeans, but he hadn't any shorts, so his cold rump chafed within the raw denim. He pulled the check out of his soggy billfold.

"Goddamn."

It was sopping wet, the ink had run, but a scrupulous observer might make out "Pay to the Order of BIA Cattle Company, $2,000." Buddy endorsed it on the back, adding "For Billy Little Old Man," who had signed it, although of course this had nothing to do with the BIA Cattle Company. An idea sprang into his brain with the mysterious swiftness of all ideas.

"You know, Philbert?" he said nonchalantly. "I remember seein' those BIA bulls a few days ago when I was down here to get some feed fer my old man. They were the scrawniest-lookin' excuses I ever seen."

Philbert was having a vision. A plate of cheeseburgers was set in front of him, along with a cherry pie and a six-pack of Coors. All that he was conscious of were the four pickups in front of him, unmoving, maliciously keeping him from the culinary fantasies of the Cheyenne Cafe. He honked the horn but it didn't work. He flashed his headlights, but only one of them worked, and that one was walleyed and shone off across the sagebrush, lighting up an overflowing trash can behind a house trailer, where a mongrel dog was reveling in discarded enchiladas from a TV dinner.

"Yep," Buddy persevered, "pitiful-lookin' bulls. We better go by the stockyard when we're through here. I don't know if I can accept inferior stock on the hoof."

"Me eat," Philbert grunted. There was treason in his voice. A pickup had pulled out, and Protector gunned a machine-length closer to the cashier behind the illuminated glass.

"Sure," Buddy agreed. "I'll drop ya off at the cafe and go check out those bulls."

Philbert panicked. "No one drives Protector but me." It was a crisis.

"Jesus Christ, Philbert, I gotta see those bulls."

"Me drive." His stomach growled rebelliously. Another pickup left. They came closer to Nirvana.

"Okay," Buddy said.

Philbert was miserable. They sat. It grew darker, even though it was already completely dark. The bank lights and the car lights emphasized their own puniness amidst the great vastness of the night.

Another pickup left. They were on deck. They could see the girl inside the glass, making her dispensations.

Philbert was in agony. It would be an hour before he would eat. The prospect was unbearable. He squirmed. His hands were blue on the steering wheel. His stomach roared, and the people in the pickup in front turned around, puzzled at some strange accusation rumbling at them from the earth. They were

43

the Vanishing Bears from Miles City, and Buddy waved. Philbert only glowered.

The Vanishing Bears got their pneumatic tube of goodies and drove off into the night. Protector straight-piped under the canopy, its raked and rusty torso suddenly ablaze in the attentive glow of the Northern Wyoming First National Bank, Birney Branch.

"Good evening," the polite person inside said through a metallic larynx. The Indian heads inside their machine swiveled to see the young blond head inside her prefabricated box. She was on the driver's side.

"Yeah, I wanna cash this," Buddy yelled, leaning over and above Philbert's bulk to his window. He didn't trust Philbert with this tricky transaction. But both of them were trying to reach the pneumatic tube that lay on the proffered arm-door of a stainless-steel platter. But it was just out of reach.

"I'm tryin' to . . . oh, hell!" Buddy cursed as he gave up and went back to his door. He opened it and went around outside to the box on the roadway. It was cold out there. "I wanna cash this," he said, bending down absurdly to speak into the larynx of the thing. He started to put the check in the tube for underground delivery into the core of the bank when the voice within stopped him.

"I'm sorry, sir, we can't accept transactions from pedestrians."

"I'm not a pedestrian, I'm in that car!" Buddy yelled, feeling guilty about being afoot.

"I'm sorry, sir, you'll have to get back in your car. The fire department forbids pedestrians at the drive-up window."

"Jesus Christ!"

The pickups behind him started honking and flashing their lights. Buddy shot them all the bird. Louie Short Hair leapt out of the truck directly behind them.

"Watch that shit around my family, Buddy!" Louie shouted. He was five-foot-two inches tall, so of course had a reputation as a tough guy. His wife and three kids stared wide-eyed at the two angry men from their crowded cab.

"Watch yer own shit, Louie!" Buddy fired back in a not un-friendly greeting, circling around the front of Protector and back to his passenger door. Philbert sat numbly, staring ahead in weakened confusion.

Louie was on Buddy like buckshot on a goose. Buddy didn't even see it coming, but he knew with the instincts of a combat veteran that Louie's fists were the things raining upon him faster than a blender mincing onions. He threw the pugnacious Indian off him like a grizzly discarding lice, but Louie was back up and on him in an instant. Buddy smacked him a gigantic elbow to the jaw, and Louie flew twenty feet and landed in a muddy snow-bank. A little blood trickled from Buddy's lip, and his ribs didn't feel as good as they had a few moments ago, but he was hitting his stride.

"C'mon, you chickenshit Cheyenne!" he dared to the line of machines idling out in the dark, and truck doors opened and slammed immediately, releasing Skins who were rushing to join in the fun.

"Oh, shit," Philbert cursed, and got out, too, to help his idiotic friend. It was required. The metallic larynx was blatting some-thing unintelligible about the jail.

Partisans for the underdog leapt at Buddy, while ex-vets and Philbert leapt on the partisans. Four boys and a man pulled Buddy to the ground, while three men and a woman pulled them off him. Louie leapt on Philbert, who was pulling the four boys off the woman, and Buddy cross-body blocked Louie. Six kids threw dirty snowballs at all of them, and another half dozen women cheered everyone on. A grandmother was brought out and a folding lawn chair was set up for her at the fringe of the melee. She popped open a Budweiser and watched the fun objec-tively. They were joined by a pack of alert dogs, one of which was promptly sent yelping through the air by one of the men. They kicked, cracked knuckles, and grunged up their clean jeans on the oil stains on the driveway. A siren sent them scurrying, as sure of their escape routes as badgers of their burrows. The old grandma scooted out of sight, along with the rest of their younger combatants. Within twenty seconds they were all back in their machines, as if nothing had happened.

The cops pulled up as Buddy put his wadded check in the pneumatic tube. Philbert was hunkering down in his driver's seat as low as he could go.

"What's going on here?" the white highway patrolman asked through Buddy's window. Buddy rolled the window down in genuine bewilderment. He sat meekly in his seat. Only a little blood showed at his lip.

"Officer? What can I do for you?"

"There's been a call about a brawl," the erect guardian of the peace said. Another guardian in sunglasses joined him.

"I don't know anything—oh, excuse me." Buddy turned back to the bank window, from whence had come a garbled transmission.

"Could I speak to the officers?" it repeated.

"I'm sorry, we're in a terrible hurry," Buddy replied to it. A frantic young man in a stylish suit had joined the girl inside the quarantined box.

"We're not going to have the sort of conduct just—" it began in the young man's resonant tone of ire before Buddy graciously interrupted.

"I'm sorry, but could you complete our transaction? We have some important business to conduct." Then the equalizer: "Or should we just go to another bank?" Buddy oozed unctuousness.

"I don't know if I can even read this check," the robot voice within relented.

"Sir?" the patrolman said at his other side.

"Officer?" Buddy replied.

"Is that blood on your lip?" the officer asked. The other officer leaned closer for a look.

"Ketchup," Buddy replied. "I just had a hamburger."

Philbert salivated.

"You're probably referring to a disturbance caused by the gentlemen in the truck behind us," Buddy continued. "I think it would expedite matters to question him." Buddy had not gone to Yale for nothin'.

"Oh," the guardian replied, looking to Louie and the four wide-eyed faces in the cab beside him, who all sat meekly bewildered. They walked back.

"Sir?" the robot voice queried. "The manager would like to speak with you."

"Certainly."

Philbert cringed.

A stylish older-young whiteman came to the microphone behind the steel and glass. Quite a bit of scurrying was going on inside the closet-size bank. He was examining the smeared and wadded piece of paper Buddy had rudely thrust upon his unsmeared and unwadded enterprise.

"You represent the BIA Cattle Company?" a more resonant robot asked.

"BIA Cattle Company, yes," Buddy answered. "I'm the agricultural purchasing agent. Yes."

"I see."

Philbert turned around to see that the two patrolmen had been referred to the subsequent pickup behind Louie. He saw the guardians give each other the familiar "goddamn Indians" look as they walked in exasperation out into the darkness of the waiting trucks.

"Who is the other gentleman?" the robot voice asked.

"That's Philbert."

"Hi," Philbert said, unable to think of anything else.

"Sir," the robot said, "you have endorsed a check made out to the BIA Cattle Company and signed it for Billy Little Old Man, who signed the check in the first place."

"That's the government for you."

"Yes," the robot replied. Buddy had inspired a smile. Buddy knew the code words.

"We need to buy bulls for the tribe from the government stockyards," Buddy explained. "The tribe is under the governmental protectorate, therefore the government stockyards are really tribal stockyards. Almost."

"Yes."

"They're just down the road. I thought this was done all the time here," Buddy concluded.

The transmission got garbled again; the manager was arguing with the other young man, who turned to the girl staring out the window, who turned back to them with a shrug. The two men stalked off. They gave up. Let the girl pay the Indians. Back down the line, the patrolmen also gave up. It was impossible to deal with these people.

The girl cashed their check in hundreds, and they drove away. It had almost been fun, this metaphor of innocence triumphant.

The two noble savages fingered the twenty hundred-dollar bills in astounded silence. Even Protector rolled solemnly into the road. Philbert had unconsciously taken his foot off the stump of an accelerator pedal as he stared at the green pile of pay money. Like a good calf-roping pony that holds a calf with the saddle horn, Protector turned right onto the paved road. There was nothing better than a well-trained pony. It had been the ultimate aspiration of every cowboy and Indian since Cortés. Protector drove itself out of town, heading southwest.

"Yep," Buddy said, breaking the silence. "We better go check on them bulls."

The government pens were a half mile south on a dirt road. It was a familiar gathering place for Indians, who loved to look at animals. There were often several pickups parked outside the pens and slaughterhouse, their riders parked on the corral fence watching in silence upon the yearling steers, laughing in wonder at the calves, nodding in philosophic contemplation as they were butchered or sold. This was where the whiteman made meat. To the grinning and furious Indians, meat was all life and all death. They sat for many hours and watched whitemen in bloody white aprons herd the food onto mass-production conveyor belts. Perhaps the Indians sat on the fences and tried to put some meaning back into the killing, some sense of power, by their presence. If one or two of them caught fleeting remembrances of ancient buffalo hunts in the bloody stench that arose from within the warehouse beside the pens, if three or four caught a flash of purposeful death in their histories, then only their firm and silent faces expressed it.

Philbert began to slaver uncontrollably as they entered the rackety slaughterhouse. Beeves hung in juicy row upon row. Beeves were being ground into hamburger, hacked into steaks, sawed into roasts. Bellowings from still-living statistics echoed frantically from across the huge stinking warehouse that never shut down. The smell of grain-stuffed excrement permeated from outside in the pens, where the animals were fattened up. Blood stench arose from the conveyor belt, where hundreds of the genetically stupefied beasts were clubbed to death daily and their throats cut. The vomit of fear and the reek of intestines testified to this most essential industry of the West.

Philbert and Buddy walked in past it all to the offices of Sven Sundersen, the man in charge. Even at this late hour they found him at work on his accounts. He need not look up from his ledgers and out his glass walls to the stainless-steel holocaust of mechanized murder of the warehouse to know how many lives had been converted into sustenance for the American family. It was on the printouts before him, in black and white.

But some ominous threat that suddenly darkened his work

light did make him look up. Two wet and battered Indians were staring down upon him and his accounts like avenging angels.

"Oh!" he gasped in surprise. He focused his bifocals upon the unmoving pillars. "Buddy, is that you?"

"Yes."

"I've been expecting you," he said, standing, offering his hand in a friendly, businesslike way. Buddy did not offer his. Sven retrieved his, embarrassed. Buddy felt a minor *act* accomplished.

Goddamn Indians, Sven thought, they'll never learn. Philbert recognized the familiar look above the thoughts.

"I came to see our bulls," Buddy said.

"Oh, yes, surely. You can sign the voucher, and I'll have it—"

"I want to see them first," Buddy said adamantly, his triumph emboldening his audacity. Philbert stood by, lending an air of bulk to Buddy's discourtesy.

"I don't understand," Sven said. He was getting his own dander up now. He could be just as rude as this jerk. "Billy Little Old Man has already seen them."

"I don't care. I'm the agricultural purchasing agent."

"You were supposed to deliver me a check," Sven said, sitting back down. "And pick up three Hereford breeding bulls."

"It doesn't matter if you show them to me or not," Buddy said. "I saw them a few days ago and they ain't worth shit."

"Now, what are you trying to pull here? They are prime beef."

"The hell they are!" Buddy yelled, enjoying his self-righteousness. The point here was racism, regardless of whether Buddy had actually seen the particular bulls in question. "They are scrawny old stock, fit only fer Indians at seven hundred bucks apiece!"

"They were bought *from* Indians, Mandans in North Dakota!" Sven said, making a point.

"That figures!"

"Now listen here, you can't—" Sven tried to say.

"No, I don't," Buddy said, completing the thought. "You been gyppin' us with leftover suet for a hundred years, fella, you and your pals at Safeway and the Chicago packing plants."

"I don't have to listen—"

"You have charged the government outrageous prices to feed the poor starvin' Injuns, then take ninety percent of the meat and flour and beans and leave us the gristle and the bugs and the mildew!"

"This is an Indian-owned stockyard!" Sven said, adding some factual basis to his own creeping hysteria.

"You're not handin' us that murderous bullshit as a front for your own dinner anymore, Mr. Swede!"

"Get out of here!" Sven yelled, his pale face purple with rage. He drew the line of tolerance at racial slurs. Philbert scooted to the door.

"You get us three real bulls by next week," Buddy calmly summarized, "or I'm talkin' to our lawyers."

"I'll just call up Billy Little Old Man," Sven said, reaching for the phone, "and see what he has to say about all this."

Buddy slammed his fist down on the phone, and it leapt over spasmodically to the floor. "And I mean I'm gonna have documentation, fucker."

They stared: the power and the glory. Sven had the power, he had the common sense, he had the companionship of the ruling elite beside him—the white American men. Despite a busy day of dope and jumping in the frozen river, Buddy had the glory. Perhaps he had it because of the dope and the frozen river. Neither of them gave an inch. But Buddy blinked. He had no family, except his folks, who hated his militancy, and his sister, whom he barely remembered. Sven had six children and a pretty wife who loved him. He had an important position in county government, he had his own airplane, and he kept in shape for a man of fifty-three. He believed in his country. Buddy had only Philbert, and the gut ache of his illiterate, drunken, and forlorn tribesmen.

"I'll be back in a week," Buddy said, breaking the duel. "And you'll get your check then, if you've gotten some decent beef."

He turned and exited, Philbert following him. Buddy's eyes were moist, but his erect and defiant stride did not betray them.

Sven grinned in his bookkeeping pinnacle, overlooking his empire. He had won.

Buddy kicked Protector in the fender when they got outside. The kick made no dent on the flaked brown scar that was the Buick's skin. It sat very still, as if very hurt to have been blamed. Philbert winced to see his animal abused, but he understood. Sometimes a man's horse is the only friend he has, and friends are to know a man's sorrow as well as his good cheer.

"So much for that," Buddy said.

They got inside and drove back to the Cheyenne Cafe, for Philbert would not be waylaid from survival for another moment. They amiably greeted Louie Short Hair, who had commandeered two tables for his family. There was only a small purple-green bruise on his jaw. Louie waved back, as did most of the other folks in there who had been in the brawl at the bank. The Vanishing Bears were also there, and Charlotte Two Wolves with her new boyfriend from the Fort Belknap Reservation, and Buffalo Horns, and the Gunpowder boys from Lodge Grass. The place was packed with hungry, laughing Skins.

Philbert made a beeline for the counter, where the service was faster. Betty, a redheaded cowgirl from Idaho, irritably took his order of three cheeseburgers deluxe and a strawberry malt. She was overworked. Buddy absentmindedly ordered a BLT and coffee, and Betty hurried off into the tiny clattering kitchen behind swinging doors.

Buddy felt like thinking aloud. "Philbert, I'm bummed out."

Buffalo Horns came over. He was a pimply squirt who worked for the Highway Department. He had on a yellow

Caterpillar cap over his stylish, ear-length hair. "What're you two worthless fucks up to?" he asked, sitting down, sucking on a toothpick.

"Nothin'," Philbert said, staring at the swinging doors leading to the kitchen, waiting for them to fly open and save his life. "What're you doin, Buff?"

"Just got off work, headin' fer some pussy tonight in Sheridan," Buffalo Horns replied pleasantly, a cowboy twang unconsciously hopscotching out of his mouth. He was a half-breed with a mustache.

"Nothin' ain't exactly what we're doin'," Buddy interjected. "We're takin' off to New Mexico to get my sister, Bonnie."

"Oh, yeah?" Buffalo Horns was interested. "That goodlookin' stuff that went off to New York City?"

"Yeah."

"Jeee-heee-heeee-zussss, she was a hot number," Buffalo Horns larrooped respectfully. Buddy cast him a sudden menacing glance. "I mean, not that she weren't yer sister er anything. I know she was. I mean, I, uh . . . hey, Betty, how 'bout you 'n' me goin' to Sheridan tonight?"

"A pig's ass," Betty said in a clipped tone as she went back to the kitchen. She had brought Philbert and Buddy their drinks. Buffalo Horns stared over the counter at Betty's vanishing rump.

"She's a spunky bitch," he said, "that goddamn Betty." He respected her.

"She's married to the cook," Philbert said between slurps of his malt.

"So?"

"What's all the hoo-rah about Sheridan tonight?" Buddy asked, listlessly stirring sugar into his coffee.

"Why, hell, Christmas is in five days, it's Friday night, all the bars and shops'll be full of fa-la-la and horny little elves," Buffalo Horns explained, laughing at all the fun he was gonna have.

"I guess we'll go on through there tonight," Buddy said. He put his hand in his front pocket and felt the wad of bull money he had crammed in. "It's on our way."

"Well, you better hurry." Buffalo Horns stood up, eyeing two girls who had just come in. "The stores close at nine." He left.

"Fer Christmas shoppin', yeah." Buddy's eyes gleamed, a light bulb clicking to life another idea, more pure than the epistemological daydreams of Plato. Perhaps it was an original idea, or perhaps it was the coagulation of old ideas. It is hard to tell with philosophers.

"Philbert," Buddy said. But Philbert had his cheeseburgers and was not available for comment.

"Mwagh?"

"I'm a little worried about you."

"Blwhatt?"

Hemingwayesque camaraderie spurted out of Buddy. Genuine concern seeped into every syllable he addressed to his gluttonous compeer. Philbert recognized the celestial tones, and his mouth stopped chomping mid-gorge. His great brown eyes turned in radiant wonderment upon his friend.

"I am concerned about your appearance," Buddy said sympathetically. Philbert looked down at the great balloon that was his body, like a circus tent wrapped in the damp fatigues, the seams ripped to their outer limits, his cowboy boots that pinched his corns, his yard-length hair that looked like a pony's tail matted into knots by pony shit.

"Ungah?" Pounds of cheeseburgers began again their semi-automatic evaporation within the cavernous estuaries of Philbert's digestive system.

"If you are going to be a warrior, you must look like a warrior." Verisimilitude lapsed as Buddy made efforts at authenticity. (Grammarians are painstaking people.)

Philbert flipped his hair around behind him. It was getting in the way of his mouth, which had resumed the battle. But his great elk eyes never left the sound of Buddy's remonstrances. (George Armstrong Custer once said that Indians could hear with their eyes.)

"You must dress the part," Buddy concluded solemnly. "It is an essential ritual."

"Nugs me lenevey sham."

"What?"

"Nugs me lenevey sham!" Philbert repeated, annoyed.

"Is that Indian?"

"No," Philbert said, finding a pause between pickles and lettuce. "I got no bread for buckskin."

He took another bite; the matter was closed, as far as his stomach was concerned.

"And your pony?" Buddy said casually, taking a bite of his BLT. It was his trump card, and he played it masterfully. Philbert swung around on the stool, panic bulging from his eyes, french fries crammed in his mouth.

"Mah Plonlie?"

The most solemn accusation against any soldier of the "prevailing way" was about to fall from Buddy's lips. It was a curse too terrible to ignore.

"You have no music."

Gasp!

"Your pony is not prepared for battle."

Cruelty!

"Where is your radio?"

Unmentionable!

"Stereo tape deck? CB? FM! And your speakers? You don't even have any speakers."

Vicious truths! Alas, truth can be vicious, and tears of shame welled into Philbert's eyes. He had not even noticed that the hole in his pony's dashboard where a radio had once been was a vital deficiency of his new wealth, so frail and limited was his wisdom. He gulped the last of his french fries.

"You're right," were all the words he could summon to express the most ethical bankruptcy of his destiny. He could never again face his pony. He would walk for the rest of his days, as penance for his sin. And soon, very soon, he would collapse in exhaustion into some snowbank and die. It would be more than he would deserve.

"It's not hopeless," Buddy's crystalline voice said, his words rising into the gloom of Philbert's incinerated hopes like the phoenix from its ashes. "The stores are open in Sheridan until nine. We can make it. It's only fifty miles."

"Make it?"

"We must not be irresponsible on this great quest of ours," Buddy said, his voice taking on the evangelism of a furniture salesman. "Safety dictates that we get a CB; pride dictates that the songs of our forefathers and our revolutionary brothers of the pop-rock industry echo throughout our eardrums; responsibility itself dictates that we be properly prepared for our quest, morally and spiritually. RadioShack has some great triaxial speakers on sale. I saw it on TV the other day."

"Let's go!" Philbert leapt from his stool, redeemed. He paused only to get a cherry pie, to go.

Protector took 19.8 gallons of regular into its 20-gallon tank at the Conoco station, and they were off, flying down the unnumbered state road that crisscrossed the Tongue River, then intersected with another unnumbered road that showed only as a thin blue line on the map, then past the Tongue River Reservoir and the glories of a Bureau of Land Management recreation area with the earth subdivided into tracts and lots and sold and resold by clever realtors many, many times. But Buddy and Philbert didn't even care that night. They were bound for glory! It was only a matter of time before Waylon Jennings would have their feet stomping to heart-breaking rhythms, before Dolly Parton would send their libidos into the ionosphere of electric-guitar art, before Kiss and Devo and Dr. Hook and the Stones and Alice Cooper and Hoyt Axton and Johnny Paycheck would bring them back down to earth and catapult them into amplified ecstasy!

How many more miles, Daddy? Are we almost there?

These were two Skins who were ready for renewal! It had been a bummer day. It was time to be A Part of It All!

"Maybe I do need some jeans," Philbert said gingerly, breaking into their reveries. Jeans were the buckskin of the day. He gobbled the last of the cherry pie.

"Sure," Buddy said happily. "The money is for Bonnie. We gotta be at our best. It's gonna be heavy down there in New Mexico."

Logic had many forms. Reality was one of them. Truth was another. The lessons of money had not been lost on Buddy, and he knew he was hitting his stride with the logic of reality and truth. Pride was a reality and pride was a truth. He and Philbert had to stand tall if they were gonna free Bonnie from jail. The money was only a superficial manifestation of the deeper demands that they, her knights in shining belt buckles, would be called upon to fulfill. The money was therefore meaningless, in the higher logic of immediate personal needs and their automobile's effectiveness. What good were two thousand dollars if the boys could not carry the day, if the car could not make their getaway? It was beyond rhetoric—it was logic. Buddy was hitting his stride.

"The hell with them flea-bitten bulls," he said.

They crossed into Wyoming. The Tongue River continued to follow the road, anyway.

Furthermore, Buddy reasoned, reality and truth are emotional issues. They rarely follow strict guidelines. Happiness was a truth, but it had no logical parameters. The river was a reality, but it made no analytical sense of its meanderings. Logic was just as illogical as it was logical. This was part of its scientific totality. Buddy felt deductive as hell.

"This way, that money'll do a lot more for the tribe," he said.

They picked up Interstate 90. The flow of the land and mathematics are understood only by mathematicians. They are irrelevant to anyone else. Decimals and ergs and joules were the toys of unlimited possibilities. But how could infinity be logical? Horseshit, Buddy concluded, horseshit could be analyzed but it could never be understood. Not in all its meanings. Logic, therefore, was as much emotion as it was reason. There were only a few pioneers in the science of emotionology in this world, but Buddy Red Bird was one of them.

"Besides, nobody'll know for a week, and we'll be back by then," he said.

He would have to wait for further insights, however, because they were now pulling off into the collective garage of four miles of motels, hamburger joints, and used-car lots that was Sheridan, Wyoming, United States of America.

It was only a coincidence that Christmas now struck them in all its tinsel extravagance in the town named after the man who once had said: "The only good Indian is a dead Indian." Much debate had centered around this succinct quote—some people were sure it was uttered by General Phil Sheridan (the hero of the incineration of the Shenandoah Valley); others confused him with General Sherman (a natural mistake, for he was the hero of the incineration of the state of Georgia); others said it was Mark Twain (who knew a clever sentence when he saw one); or Abraham Lincoln (who only freed blackmen); or George A. Custer (who had it coming). The Indians were sure that Sitting Bull had said it in a moment of exasperation. Any version made sense, as long as it and other pithy remarks could be attributed to some dime-novel hero to include in an anthology of Western myth.

"Deck the halls with boughs of holly! Fa-la-la-la-la . . . la-la-la-la!" It had a good beat. Phil Sheridan himself might have cracked a smile.

Philbert and Protector came to life. They drove past aluminum holly hanging above the streets and bright red stars of Bethlehem in flashing neon loveliness, they circled around the fifty-foot blue spruce decorated with the popping exuberance of a culture come to life, they cruised to "Jingle Bells" and "Frosty the Snowman" (an ancient legend of the Iroquois), until Protector started to tap-dance to all the gaiety. Philbert would have sworn his pony was so glad to see all his motorized brethren in the shop windows and on the honking streets that he did a soft shoe, he did a waltz to the snowmobiles in trailers behind Scouts and Jeep Cherokees, he did a boogaloo to the Comanche motorcycles, a Latin hustle to the toasters in the windows, a two-step gourd dance to the blazing streetlights lighting up the darkness, with vim and vigor and gasoline-powered excitement (operated by the Big Chief Power and Light Company)! Protector was in his element, the prodigal had returned unto his long-lost relatives, he was back in the OK Corral of his childhood! God, it was good to be alive!

Protector knew that America approached a true cultural uniqueness in its celebration of Christmas. Santa Claus in a Cadillac was one of a kind.

The two aboriginal refugees from this utter cultural certainty found a parking place two blocks away from RadioShack. Hideous prospect—they had to walk. They joined the other resigned pilgrims afoot and a little lost in the unfamiliar throng of merciless parking meters. And like everyone else, they bravely forged ahead, hopeful of returning soon to find their companion and nemesis still safe and firmly locked away from horse thieves, patiently waiting for its master.

"'Tis the season to be jolly! Fa-la-la-la-la . . . la-la-la-la!" The good city fathers had installed speakers in the central shopping area to brighten the holiday season with songs of joy. Pocketbooks and billfolds and purses pushed and shoved against each other as the season's goodwill quickened. The pace was exhilarating.

Two pilgrims strode sullenly through the gay crowds. It was

clear they were above it all, apart from it all. They strode as an afterthought to the conscientious generosity of the season's gift-giving fever. Naturally they drew stares.

Secretly desperate to be a part of it all, and yet openly incapable of being anything but above it, they sank with scorn to be below it all. They did not belong, they could not accept it, they could not understand it. So they made fun of it. It was the way of all the disenfranchised folk who were only tributaries to the great mainstream. They were trickles of ice water submerged beneath torrents of good booze.

"Clowns," Buddy muttered, in a show of insouciant cheerfulness. They crowded into RadioShack.

Twenty-five amok eyeballs flickered at them in the wall-to-wall room of technological genius. Televisions of every size and range of colors, hues, tones, and chromatic subtlety were stacked up on each other to the ceiling. Furniture bargains, mouthwash securities, automobile glories, and cartoons synchronized a dissonant visual symphony of exquisite electronic chaos. They flashed stroboscopically beyond human comprehension.

Two pilgrims sidled past a young and stylish salesman hypnotizing a fivesome with a gleaming pile of dials and blue lights. They listened, spellbound.

"You merely program the computer: It controls the auto program locate device. This unique feature skips ahead or back to any song you select (up to nineteen songs) and plays it automatically. A few specs really tell the story: S/N ratio; 64 dB with Dolby; wow and flutter, a minimal 0.06 percent frequency response; 16–30,000 Hz for FeCr. It's your own electronic tape counting, *and* second counting liquid-crystal display and private computer, with the built-in quartz clock as a timing device."

"Yeah, but what is it?" Buddy asked. They all turned in horror at this alien from Mars.

"It's a computer that plays music," the salesman explained, struggling to form the simple sentence.

"I'll take one," a girl of nineteen said. "It's for my boyfriend."

"That'll be three thousand with tax."

She gave him a MasterCard and the aliens stumbled away.

"Can I help you?" a suave, elderly gentleman in a suit asked them. He had swarmed down upon them the instant their barbaric selves had wedged into his store. He had panic under control. He was a Chivas Regal man, and could clearly handle these two beer drinkers.

"Yeah," Buddy said. "We need a stereo tape deck FM radio with CB for our car."

"Right this way." Buddy knew the passwords. "I have a very nice Fujitsu Ten in-dash-GS-7881 AM/FM/MPX auto-reverse cassette with Dolby. It programs fast forward, locking rewind, and FM muting, as well as a built-in noise blanker to eliminate interference."

"Nah," Philbert said thoughtfully. "What else you got?"

Buddy laughed right out loud at the salesman's mouth, which was working to overcome his outrage.

"For our area the R3 Road-Rated Receiver is probably more what you're looking for," the salesman continued blithely. "It pulls in and holds even very weak stations, and with amazing fidelity."

"What's that?" Philbert asked, pointing to a yellow line of numbers flashing in the midst of the R3 display.

"That is the digital station readout that becomes a digital clock when the radio is off." The salesman clearly was beginning to wish he were somewhere else, where he wouldn't have to explain these elementary details. He was an artist, after all.

"We'll take it," Buddy said. "Can we get a CB to go along with it?"

"Certainly. Forty channels?"

"Sure." (Whatever that meant.) "We also need some speakers. I heard about some triaxial—"

"Jensen triaxial three-way with separate woofer, tweeter, and midrange?"

"Sure."

The bill came to $549.64 with tax. Eyebrows hit the ceiling when he paid with cash, a hasty managerial conference was called to order, and they reluctantly consented to accept cash instead of credit. But it was a dangerous precedent. The pilgrims showed Tommy the technician to their car and left him for half an hour to install new life into Protector.

They bought ten cassette tapes, mostly country-western, at $7.95 a piece. Philbert got a Stetson for $35, buckskin pants at $95, boots $85, two shirts, underwear, and socks at Penney's for $41.85. Buddy needed a sheepskin coat at $125, and so did Philbert, but they didn't have any his size, so he settled for a denim parka at $70. They went back to Penney's just as it was closing because Buddy had forgotten to get himself some boxer shorts and wool socks for $24. They were doing their damnedest to join in the holiday spirit. They got back to Protector looking like Indians now. Tommy was finishing the wiring.

"This is some jalopy ya got here." Tommy panted, putting his tools away. He was not at all sure he would have liked to get in it while it was moving, though. "But she's wired for sound, bro."

"Thanks," Buddy said, giving him a five-dollar tip. "Merry Christmas."

"You too," and Tommy hurried out of the cold and back into the store.

Breathlessly they got in Protector. They closed their doors. They looked at each other, spruce and spiffy in their clothes. Philbert adjusted his hat and wished he had a rearview mirror.

"Why don't we put on a tape," Buddy said matter-of-factly.

"I don't know," Philbert said. "What do you want to hear?"

"Got any Waylon Jennings?"

It just so happened they did. Anticipation mounted. Philbert tore the cellophane off the tape. They had agreed in the tape store that the tough but sensitive cowboy singer was both their favorite. Waylon Jennings would initiate the new era of the quest. Philbert touched the tape to its rectangular trapdoor. Lovingly he slid it all the way into its lyrical cave.

Nothing happened.

They waited. These marvels of the whiteman took time to warm up. Juice needed material momentum. It was not automatic, these ebbs and flows of electrical generation. They waited for ten seconds, a minute. Two minutes.

"Maybe it's not turned on."

They turned a knob. Something glowed green. Triumph, as one static crackle erupted and died. Now it had life breathed into it. Now batteries and acid would transform dirt and chemicals into the pulsating pleasure of man's most ancient joy, praise, lament, and the blues.

Nothing happened.

"Maybe we need to turn the car on."

Protector spat to life and a coven of hot spiced wine and Grand Marnier sours outside on the sidewalk jumped at the sudden otherworldly commotion spitting from this once tranquil machine.

Still nothing of a melodic nature happened inside.

They fiddled with every dial, they turned the car off, they turned it back on, they took the tape and turned it over, and still nothing happened. Juice refused to flow, transistor components refused to spark, wires refused to respond to other wires.

"Goddamn this country!"

It was time for Buddy to rave. It was time to feel the frustrations every fragile victim had felt of every callous machine, wagon axle, and stone wheel since the beginning of time. At least since the first man put a tool in his hand and crunched his fingers, man had raved at his society for putting the tool in his hand.

"Fuck shit piss!"

Philbert could have cried, so sensitive was his nature.

"I can't fuckin' believe this!" Buddy raved. "Five hundred and forty-nine fuckin' dollars and it's a piece of shit! A piece of shit!"

And he slammed his fist into the insolent hardware at his side. A plastic dial flew off from the thing. "Look at that! Look at that! Cheap fuckin' shit breaks off at any little touch! Fuck it, I'm goin' back in that store and raising hell! They'll fix it or I'll shove it up their asses and then destroy their store! I'll fuckin' chop it to pieces with an ax!"

He threw the door open and stormed out. "I'll throw their fancy fuckin' worthless junk through the window, them and their fuckin' computers! What a joke!"

And he was gone, stalking up the sidewalks past the thinning crowds, who stared angrily at him as he passed, as he was apparently gushing obscenities.

In his crazed sorrow Philbert picked up the bulky instruction manual that had sat on the seat beside him, where Tommy had thoughtfully placed it. Distractedly he opened it up to the front page.

HOW TO TURN ON YOUR NEW R3 ROAD-RATED RECEIVER: PUNCH THE TUNER DIAL ON THE RIGHT OF THE STATION READOUT.

Punch a dial? Was this a new deviousness of the whiteman? Gingerly, cautiously beyond caution, Philbert pushed in the tuner dial.

"Mah babeee baaaby baaa-haaa-beee don't love me no more!" roared Waylon Jennings from the four corners of the earth. The bass and treble dials were all screwed up from their primitive manipulations, but it was on! It worked. Bangu-bangu headhunters in Western Borneo could not have been more fascinated with a cigarette lighter than that Cheyenne beer drinker in Wyoming was with his new music box.

"She don't love me don't love me don't love me, she don't love me nooooooooooooooo more!"

Over and above and throughout these wailing strains, Philbert heard sirens outside in the streets. Their wailing strains alerted instant reflexes within his Indian nervous system. Mad kamikazes in gray-and-black Chryslers were zeroing in on some hapless battleship in the streets of Sheridan like mosquitoes on a fisherman.

Philbert knew they were after Buddy as sure as he knew that Buddy had gone amok and probably destroyed the RadioShack. He gunned Protector in reverse, and the huge rear slicks squealed as rubber burned on asphalt. Protector lurched forward at full throttle, and it was shut down my little deuce coupe in the streets of Sheridan, Wyoming! That valiant war charger became a snorting, fire-breathing dragon; a flaming, smoking locomotive bearing down on the terrified pedestrians, scattering like Cherokee into the hills when they saw their first thunderous choo-choo train. God, did they run! God, did Protector roar! God, did Philbert feel the power of Casey Jones comin' round the bend!

He was going forty by the time he approached the intersection and saw Buddy appear, on cue, in front of him, at a dead run. Rifle shots exploded from up the block behind him, men were running after him, a Star Wars police cruiser careened right past him and screeched on its brakes as it realized its mistake. The brakes locked and it flipped completely over a Salvation Army bell ringer on the sidewalk and flew upside down through the picture window of Zales Jewelers. A tremendous crash erupted of flying glass and raped siren shrieks and motors and metal and the jewelry store's burglar alarm. All hell had broken loose! Armageddon had been delivered by two horsemen in an apocalyptic Buick!

Philbert turned right up Star Wars Avenue and Buddy was packing cheeks right alongside. Phil threw open the passenger door and Bud leapt on it like a relay runner receiving the baton of life. A rifle bullet zinged through Protector's rear window and out his front, leaving two tiny holes as a remembrance. But boy, did that get Protector mad! He furiously leapt forward to fifty,

fifty-five—unheard-of velocities! Waylon Jennings broke through these sound barriers at breathtaking intervals.

"Holy goddamn shit! Fuckin' Jesus Christ, go! Go, go, Philbert, baby!" Buddy yelled, still clinging to the open door.

"Protector!" Philbert corrected, through the wind.

"Protector Baby Fucker! Protector, *go, go, go,* you mad mama!"

The cruiser in the jewelry store's window had not burst into flame, and its disappointed kamikaze pilot crawled out with diamond rings in his hair. A blood-lusty crowd cheered. Five more cruisers were hot on the trail of the mystery hot rod.

"What happened?" the kamikaze asked the Salvation Army bell ringer, who was still lying flat on the sidewalk. Urine was soaking through his blue uniform.

"You almost killed me, that's what, you goddamn maniac!"

The kamikaze looked around at his beautiful starfleet cruiser upside down in the store, stumbled twice, and fainted.

Meanwhile, back at the chase, Buddy "Buster Keaton" Red Bird was inching his way along the door to the interior of Trigger, when Philbert "Fatty Arbuckle" Bono turned the corner on two wheels and Buddy flipped out on the end of the door as it swung wide open again.

"Jesus, God!"

They went up one-way streets the wrong way, they went through red lights, they went up on sidewalks and down alleys and between hysterical Christmas shoppers, all the time Buddy clinging for dear life and yelling joyous obscenities. Philbert was driving like a virtuoso, not unlike a Cheyenne warrior hanging sideways from his pony as in the Old Days, shooting arrows from his bow at the soldiers gaping aghast.

The cavalry went up one street and down another, crisscrossing each other, wandering like angry hornets through their streets in search of trouble, but the crazy hot rod had no sense to its meanderings. It went nowhere fast, and Philbert's instinctive guerrilla maneuvers had the well-disciplined troops in a tizzy. Philbert also had on his CB.

"Adam-12 and Abel-21, go up Main," he heard one of them instruct two others, so he went *down* Main and they sped right past him.

"Cain-21, I spotted the fugitive on Twelfth and Fourth Avenue. We'll approach from both ends pronto."

"Was that Adam-4 to proceed to Twelfth and Twenty-First?" Philbert asked. He couldn't resist.

"What?"

"Twelfth?"

"No, Fourth."

"Ten-four."

"Twenty-one."

"This is Whirlwind, and out!" Philbert giggled. He jumped as Buddy fired a shot from some pistol at one of the tires of a cruiser as it came on a perpendicular collision course toward them. The cruiser spun sideways out of control and slammed into a brick wall. Another cruiser slammed into it and they were both out of it. Buddy had been quite a marksman in Vietnam.

"Starsky and Hutch!" Buddy whooped, leaping into the car finally, and closing the door, which had been scraping more than a few walls. He looked at Philbert and they went berserk.

"Whoo-whoo-whoo-whoo!"

"Hit it, Tonto!"

"Yah-ta-Hay, Kemosabe!"

"What the fuck, Hiawatha!"

"Whoo-whoo-whoo-whoo!"

In the folklore that arose ever thereafter, no two opinions were the same as to the description of that war party. Some said they were renegades, others that they were chiefs, some that they were whitemen dressed as Indians, others that they were demons disguised as human beings. One description listed the car as a '49 Chevy, as orange and black as Halloween. Another cop swore that it was a '71 Dodge Challenger with racing stripes. They all secretly confided to their wives and sweethearts that it was probably a professional inside job (whatever that meant). They all agreed on one thing—it was impossible that they could get away. But probably because they were the best fighters the crack city, county, and state soldiers had ever seen, they *did* get away. Therefore it was supernatural, and out of the range of radar.

They were just a couple of goddamn redskins. No one could ever figure *them* out.

Back at the chase, the purist beside the campfire would probably like to know how the two goofballs *did* get away. For indeed they did. Again it was Philbert's inherited instincts.

"I feel a great thirst upon my tongue," he said as they cloverleafed past a cruiser with three hornets hanging out the window, shooting in all directions but the right one. "Let's find a liquor store."

"Damn right," Buddy agreed, reloading his Colt .45 antique. He twirled it once like he'd seen Clint Eastwood do.

The Keystone Kops attempted a four-wheel-drive turn, jumped onto the sidewalk with three wheels off the ground, and got a trash can stuck in their rear axle. They were out of it.

"What the hell happened?" Philbert asked, in a moment of academic calm.

"Took an ax to RadioShack. Busted it to shit, broke the windows, you know."

"Kowabunga," Philbert breathed.

"Is that Indian talk?"

"No, Howdy Doody."

"I got the ax out of a hardware store next to RadioShack," Buddy explained, hanging out the window and taking a potshot at a sidewalk Santa Claus, who ducked. "Saw this fine pistol next to it. 'Never know when you're gonna need a weapon,' I said to myself. So I took it. You got the tape deck to work, huh?"

"Yeah," Philbert replied, careening over a curb and squealing out onto the "Strip" of Sheridan leading back to the Interstate. "You punch the dial."

"Oh."

Protector took a sudden leap across four lanes of traffic, and a Greyhound bus swerved into the fourth cruiser that was on their tail. It was out of it. The fifth cruiser was lost somewhere back in the labyrinth of ravaged downtown Sheridan. Protector went back a block, slowing down to the respectable, frenzied speed of the rest of the traffic. It lost itself in the anonymity of so many other ponies, like Gary Cooper escaping from the desperadoes by holding on to the belly of a horse stampeding out of a corral in the midst of a herd.

One more sharp right and they disappeared behind OWL LIQUORS—OWL LIQUORS—OWL LIQUORS of the blinking neon light. They pulled up to the drive-up window.

"Yes, sir?" the fine, respectable dispenser of drugs asked from inside his prefabricated box.

"A case of Bud and a quart of Jack Daniel's." Philbert was a man who knew his mind.

"Better have some chips and peanuts," Buddy added. "We'll have to drive all night."

"Some chips and peanuts too."

"Yes, sir."

"And a carton of Camels."

The respectable dispenser started passing them their provisions. Who knew when it would be before they would find another cache of supplies?

"That'll be $35.88, sir," the fellow said. "With tax."

They gave him two twenty-dollar bills. "Keep the change."

"Thank you, sir."

"Merry Christmas."

"Merry Christmas."

Filled with the holiday spirit, they pulled back out into the stampede. Reckless as their evening had been, it would have been unthinkable to have robbed a man of food and drink. Refreshments were sacred to a true warrior. Hospitality forbade the thought of nutrimental larceny. They both felt shame, for it had occurred to both of them to stick the gun in that jerk's face back there and demand a case of bourbon, a truckload of pretzels, a barrel of beer! Oh, the exhilaration of the moment! And the restraint they had exercised! It was another illustration, albeit minor, of the subtle developments in the growing character of each man.

They pulled behind the unsuspecting fifth starfleet cruiser. At a red light, Protector nudged its bumper, kissing its rear end like a dog smelling another dog. Oh, the perverse satisfaction! Buddy leapt out and stuck his long-barreled Colt in the front window. Baretta and Ironside sat exposed.

"Get out!" Buddy ordered, sticking the pistol up Baretta's nose.

They got out.

"Strip!"

"What?"

Buddy tore off Ironside's coat (sexual humiliation!). The light turned green and hooting cowgirls honked by, laughing and pointing, as the two representatives of law and order ran naked to some trees beside the road. Buddy took the keys out of the ignition and threw them on a passing hay truck. They were out of it.

Coup! Coup! Honor had been preserved!

No further incident was recorded that night. Protector obeyed the speed limit, yielded at the merge ramp onto I-90, and drove off into the night. No further messages or clues about the case ever came into the police dispatcher again, in what tomorrow's paper headlined as RENEGADE RAMPAGE REAPS $200,000 DAMAGE IN DOWNTOWN. No highway patrolman ever identified an obsequious Buick heading south as the notorious culprit of Sheridan.

And that, listener beside the campfire, is the end of the first improbable day of this mythical tale.

CHAPTER 4

How Jane and Sky Red Bird
Alerted Their Friends of Their Peril

THE JUVENILE DETENTION hall in Santa Fe is a two-story government building. It is bright, modern, and airy. It does not have bars over the windows, nor gloomy venetian blinds. The windows are large and clean, and they have curtains draped cheerfully over them. They let in the cheerful New Mexico sunshine.

Jane McNamara had her escape plan all prepared. She and her big brother, Sky, would crawl out the window on the main floor while the other kids were watching *Sesame Street*. She had been there two days and had cased out the joint. They were watched closely in the evenings, but during the day security was more lax. She had decided on a daring daylight break. The big window in the television room had two side panels, both of which could be opened by a child. Only a screen would then stand in the way of a four-foot leap to the ground and the nearby sidewalk, to freedom. No fence barred a good impression of the detention hall to passersby.

Jane had removed the window screen the day before, while the other kids laughed at *The New Mickey Mouse Club* cartoons.

She and Sky had their suitcases ready to go when Sky froze up.

"I can't do it," he whimpered.

Jane McNamara grabbed her brother by the shoulders and slyly moved him off into a side hallway. No one was looking.

"Whaddaya mean ya can't do it?" she demanded, shaking him roughly.

"I . . . I just can't," Sky sniffled. He was not as tough as his six-year-old sister. She had always been the one in the family with confidence. She had always been the one their daddy had loved to wrestle with, the one who had the looks, the brains, the moxie. Sky was always sitting off in a corner, coloring or reading *Peter Rabbit*. He was the shy, sensitive one.

Jane knew how to deal with him. Some people you could slap around to get results. But some people needed friendly persuasion, a gentler nudging. It got just as many results, maybe more, than the usual strong-arm tactics. Sky could be moved to great feats, but he had to be talked into them, not beaten into them. Jane put on her little-girl act.

"Mommy needs us, Sky," she said sweetly, and looking a little lost. "We have to get her out of jail. You know how we've always had to take care of her. She'll be helpless without us."

Sky nodded, wiping his nose on his shirt sleeve. It was true. They both knew their mother was a nymphomaniac, but she loved them and they loved her. They had gone over this many times.

Jane saw that he was with her again. She picked up their suitcases, dropping the little girl con. "So c'mon."

She led the way into the TV room—a confident little girl with somewhere to go. Sky followed. An attendant noticed their entrance. She was watching *Sesame Street* with a dozen of the other hard-core brats abandoned or beaten by their parents.

"Whatcha got in the bags?" she asked Jane.

"Tinkertoys," Jane replied sweetly. She sat on the floor and prepared to open them. The matron nodded and turned back to enjoy the Cookie Monster knocking the hell out of Big Bird.

Jane pulled out a can of Tinkertoys she had planted in her

suitcase, among her panties and little dresses, and closed the suit-case again quickly. She commenced dutifully to play with them, keeping one suspicious eye on the matron. Sky snickered.

"What's so funny?" Jane demanded.

"Your panties." He giggled.

"What's so funny about my panties? Your wiener is what's funny!"

"Just 'cause you don't have one."

"Daddy's wiener is a lot bigger."

"So?"

"You kids quit fighting," the matron said, standing up to go to the john.

"We're not fighting," Jane said. "Sky was being nasty."

"Damn Indian kids," the matron said, leaving the room quickly. She had kidney trouble. A few of the other kids turned to look at them, then turned back to the TV. They were mostly Spanish and had kept away from the damn Indians.

Sky and Jane stared at the empty doorway when the woman had gone. Jane quickly jumped up on the couch under the win-dow and rolled it open. A cool December breeze wafted into the overheated room.

"What did she mean, Jane?" Sky asked. He was still sitting on the carpeted floor.

"Oh, shut up!" she commanded. "Let's go." She jerked Sky to his feet, grabbed the suitcases, and threw them out the window. She pushed Sky through first. He put one leg out, then the other, and sat on the ledge, looking down at the dry grass outside.

"Hurry up!"

He jumped and landed on his feet. She swung her bare legs out and hung them over the edge. She had put on a dress for the occasion; it made her feel sexy. She turned to look back into the room, but the doorway was still free of her captors. The other kids were watching her attentively.

"Geronimo!" she said, and jumped. Her dress flew over her

head and she rolled onto the grass. But she was up in the blink of an eye and moving.

"Run!" she whispered to Sky, who stood there dumbly. They each grabbed a bag and started running away. Sky looked back at the other kids crowding around the open window, staring silently at the fugitives. None of them jumped after them or made a sound, no bells rang, no adults shouted, no dogs barked, and no gunshots went off.

They had gotten away, clean.

They had known that they had to. They would have been raised in the savage ways of the heathen. Perhaps an unconscious memory of other times had made them do it, and perhaps it hadn't. As they ran up one street and walked across another, looking for pursuers, listening for sirens, perhaps some instant replay of Indians shot down in the snow a hundred years ago bleeped across their subconscious visions. And perhaps they saw only the moments of their own lives bleep like colored lights before their eyes, in the marvelous way children have of freezing experience out of the slushy moments that adults pass over.

To their parents New York City had been a living, breathing memory. To Sky and Jane it was only the name of the place where they had been born. A hot dog in a park on a warm sunny day may have been New York City, or it may have been Oklahoma City. A horrible night when Daddy beat Mommy was only a bedroom, a warm blanket, a wet pillow. It could have been anywhere, but it was an experience that captured a moment forever. Sky remembered trying on his mother's tennis shoe in a musty living room while it was raining outside, but where it was or how old he had been, he didn't know. It was something he wanted to ask his mommy sometime, if only to see if she had the gift of special memory. He remembered only how pretty her foot was, and how brown it was against the white shoe. He remembered how patient she had been as he tied the laces into knots time after time.

Jane remembered fighting with her mom about a dress. Jane didn't want to wear it, but her mom had made her, and what a witch she was. Jane screamed at her how she hated her, and then crept up beside her in the kitchen where she was crying. Jane started crying, too, and they hugged each other, and she even let her mom put ribbons in her hair then, and didn't make faces about it. But where it was or how old she had been, she didn't know. But it was something she wanted to ask her.

They walked and they walked, and the sun cast long, loving afternoon shadows. They were getting cold, and it had been hours since lunch. But when were they going to see their mommy?

Sky had not handled the past two years as well as his sister. Once he had tried to stop his daddy from hitting his mommy, and he had been thrown over a couch. He remembered how his back had hurt, how his mommy had tried to stop the furious beast that was his father, and how he had run to his room and locked his door. He never again went near his father.

Jane went outside to play whenever a fight erupted. Even at night she would crawl out their bedroom window and play on her swing set. She ignored hassles. She would not let them get to her.

Her daddy treated her like a treasure. He always bragged to everyone about her, called her "toughie," and was stern but never hit her. She loved to take a bath with him and look at his wiener and ask questions about it. She loved to sleep with him and Mom, but Mom usually put her back in her own bed.

So she was glad when she went away with Daddy and Sky. She knew her mom didn't like her. Sky had sat in a corner of the car on the whole trip, and he had sat in a corner of the bedroom in Santa Fe too. He never talked to Shirley, Daddy's girlfriend, but Jane was glad to hear stories of California and bikinis and surfer boys. She asked Shirley questions about the boys' wieners, and Shirley told her about what wieners do, and about how they put them inside girls. Jane liked Shirley.

They had been walking for an hour when they noticed the

buildings were getting older, the streets narrower, and the sunlight a color of apricots on the brown adobe. They met more walkers, they saw more shops and restaurants. They heard Christmas music come out of a doorway. They came upon the cold Plaza del Monte Sol, bustling with shoppers and drivers. The trees on the square were almost barren of their leaves. The flagstoned ground was packed hard from thousands of visitors who came every year to see this lovely little city. The packed dirt was slowly strangling the roots of the trees.

Sky and Jane sat on one of the whitewashed metal benches that lined the walkways on the plaza. Few people were sitting there, for it was cold; the three-story buildings surrounding the little plot had cast it into premature shadow, as the apricot light still shone bravely up Old Santa Fe Trail and Don Gaspar Avenue. Sky and Jane sat on the bench wearily. Across the street, to the east where the winter sun shone from the south upon them, sat the main attractions of the fabulous tourist trade.

Perhaps the Pueblo and Navaho and Hopi were also the main source of income. They were the ones the tourists had come to gawk at. They were the ones Hilton and Sheraton and the Best Western motel chains had considered a good investment—for Hilton, Sheraton, and Best Western. And they were the ones Sky and Jane, like everyone else who came there, were staring at. Their foreign ways were a source of delicious anxiety to the visitors.

But curiosity is often a stronger urge in six- and seven-year-olds than fear. Sky and Jane crossed the street to where the Indians sat under a ramada of the museum. Some of them were packing up to leave for the day. They were joking among themselves as a few puzzled gawkers politely stared at the human sounds. The gawkers knelt gingerly beside the merchandise, silver and turquoise treasures spread out on blankets on the cement sidewalk. One old lady in a velvet green skirt, leggings, and a wildly colored blouse and fringed shawl put cans of Pepsi, potato chips, and her knitting into a vacuum-sealed Thermos jug that she was storing away in the cooler. Her hair was bound in a tight gray knot up on her head. These people were not as scary up close.

"Hi," Jane greeted the old lady. She turned to face her customer.

"Sorry, I'm closing up for—" She stopped, startled at the little girl who squatted beside her blanket of jewelry. The little girl had the brown hair and friendly, aggressive manner of her father. But it was the boy who stood several feet away that caught the old woman's curiosity. He was a handsome, dark-haired boy with the smooth auburn skin of his mother. He held a little suitcase in his hands in front of him and was looking shyly down at his feet.

"You are an Indian," she stated flatly.

"Yes," Jane answered, shrugging. "I guess so." Sky looked up quickly, then just as quickly looked back down.

"He is your brother?" she asked the girl, who was trying on rings. Jane nodded.

"How much is this one?" she asked, holding up a coral and turquoise ring. She met the old woman's gaze, and something about it stopped her impertinent manner. The wrinkled old face had two brown eyes that scared her. She didn't like them. She turned with studied interest to watch the couples and families stroll past the line of Indians under the porch. Then she turned back to the old woman, her childish maturity restored.

"Could I have some of your potato chips?" Jane asked, as nothing escaped her observation.

The old woman continued to think in Jane's manner. She did not stare, she merely stood there. Sky looked up again, puzzled that his sister's two questions had not been answered. The old woman obliquely drew his eyes to hers.

"What tribe are you?" she asked him. She was looking at him, only after he felt inclined to look at her. He quickly looked back down to his feet. Jane looked from Sky to the old woman, and back again to Sky. She suddenly felt excluded from something, and she put the ring back on the blanket.

"You do not even know," the old woman stated flatly. She sat wearily on the lawn chair that was against the adobe wall of the museum where the Indians were allowed to sell their products. She offered the bag of potato chips to Jane, who took a handful and passed it to Sky, who took a step closer but refused the chips.

"Come, boy," the old woman beckoned, smiling at him. The two kids drew closer to the woman, whose face was as brown and wrinkled as rawhide. She took out a jar of Noxzema skin cream and began rubbing it on her worn old hands.

"I am Acoma Pueblo," she said conversationally. "Keresan. We have lived on top of our mesa for a thousand years, and who knows how many more thousands we had lived in other places on this land? I don't know. But for a thousand years we have known. Sky City is one hundred twenty-five miles from here, and it will be dark before I and my family get there, but it will be much darker on this spot that the Pueblo built and the Spanish named Santa Fe. It will be much darker here."

"Why?" Jane asked.

The old woman looked up at the red clouds in the sky, then out across the blue plaza, where cars and trucks were circling the trees.

"My name is Sky," the boy said, grasping the old woman's meaning.

She jerked her head at his voice. Sky looked hard at her, and she nodded approval.

"Sky," she repeated.

"We need help," he said. The woman was not surprised, and was listening. "Our father is in a hospital and our mother is in jail. We have no money or friends. We are lost and hungry."

The old woman nodded. "I can do nothing for you." She stood up and began putting her jewelry into boxes. A middle-aged man was calling over to her from the next blanket, asking if she was ready. She said almost, and looked at the kids, as if she had just remembered them. "You are running away from someone. Go back to them."

"Could you give us twenty cents to make a phone call?" Jane asked. She was getting belligerent and had already dismissed this old woman as a phony. The old woman handed her two dimes.

"You may call from La Fonda," she said, pointing to a rambling lump of adobe across the plaza.

"Thank you," Jane said, and started off. Sky turned to follow her.

"Boy named Sky!" the old woman said, harshly commanding him to stop. He turned back to the old woman. Jane kept going. "You are not Pueblo. A whiteman is more welcome in a Pueblo lodge than an Indian who has gone away. A boy named Sky is especially not welcome. He is a dangerous boy."

"No," Sky said.

"There is a legend about Sky City," she said, "and about a boy named Sky who lived long ago. Have you heard it?"

"No."

"He was a shy boy who admired greatly the shyness of the deer he had seen running through the mountain forests. He dreamed of becoming a deer. He did not want to be a human being. So he decided he would no longer love his father the Sky, where he lived with his people. He would come to love his mother the Earth, where he would be pleased with all her beauties. So he went down from Sky City, and he ran away from his people, and he became friends with the deer. He ran all about the world with them. One morning he woke up and found that he had turned into a deer himself. He rubbed his antlers against the trees. He fought other stags for the honor of his mother and his sisters and his wives. He was very happy. But the years passed and he was growing old. He was growing frightened of the women around him. He began to long for a glimpse of the sky through the trees. He ran and he ran, looking for the sky through the trees. He ran and he ran, looking for a way out, looking for a clearing in which the tree branches would not block out one last view of the sky that he had known once as a human being. But he could not find a clearing, and he died."

She stopped and said nothing more. Sky was stunned and confused.

"I have to catch up with my sister," he said politely, and left.

The old woman's lumbago hurt. Her rheumatism ached. Her varicose veins were swollen. Her back was shot. She watched the handsome boy run off across the street and the plaza after his sister. She shook her head.

"I can't talk to kids anymore," she said quietly to herself. Her son of forty-five came over.

"Who were those kids?" he asked.

"Oh, some half-breeds looking for a handout," she said, and then added loudly, "I can't be taking in every stray cat that needs a bowl of milk!" Her son looked at her in surprise. The Indians were packing up their jewelry and blankets and Thermos jugs. Their pickups were waiting to take them home.

Noise, shouting, and the clanging of a cash register burst upon Sky as he entered the La Fonda Hotel. People were busy, lights were lit, displays of jewelry and "Enchantment Tours" to Taos Pueblo were displayed upon every spare inch of the walls. He was back inside a building, back in a more familiar world.

Jane was standing on her suitcase near the heavy swinging doors of the north entrance. She was reaching up to a phone, one of half a dozen lining the walls. A mob of another kind nudged past Sky—they were dressed fashionably. He went over to stand beside the suitcase upon which his sister was standing. She held the phone in her hand as her face contorted. She was staring up at the dial of the phone.

"I can't read!" she whined in absolute frustration. She knew she was just as capable as any of the chattering adults swarming around, but she lacked a few of their technical abilities.

"What do you want to read?" Sky asked. He could barely see the telephone from where he stood.

"I want to call one of Mama's friends in Oklahoma," Jane explained. "Rabbit always seemed like a nice person. She might help. But I don't know how—"

"You kids quit playing there," a voice of authority broke in. They turned to see a white-haired Spanish man standing beside them. He had on a blue bellman's coat. A smartly dressed couple stood behind him, waiting to use Jane's phone. All the other phones were busy.

"I'm not playing," Jane said. The bellman lifted her from the suitcase and put her on the floor. She kicked him and fought to get back on the suitcase. A few chatterers looked upon them disapprovingly. The smartly dressed man moved to use the phone.

"That's our phone," Sky said, stepping in front of him. The man stared at him sternly, attempting to instill some measure of respect, but the boy saw nothing in the man's eyes to instill anything. The smartly dressed woman stepped up beside her husband.

She said, "Oh, Derrell, they both look so lost." Jane was back up on the suitcase again, and grabbed the phone firmly.

"Do I call zero for information?" she asked the woman, in whom she recognized a sympathizer.

"They both need a spanking," the man said, unnerved, still trying to stare down the boy. A spanking would instill what authority could not.

"Yes, little girl, I'll help you," the woman said in a Texas drawl, taking a step closer to Jane and the phone. The bellman gave up and went back to his post. "Put your dimes in and dial zero."

"I'm not a child," Jane said.

The woman picked up the dimes to put them in, but Jane snatched them from her and did it. The woman let out a short laugh, to show she had not been embarrassed. The dimes clinked, and Jane listened for a tone. Her glowing face was proof enough that the magic transmitter was working.

"Now dial zero, right there," the woman said patronizingly. Jane dialed zero and listened.

"What?" she said into the receiver, which made her head look very small. Abruptly she handed it to the woman, who listened for a moment.

"She said, 'Where are you calling, honey?'"

"Oklahoma."

"Oh. Oklahoma," she said into the receiver and listened. "Where in Oklahoma?"

"Oklahoma City," Jane said, as if amazed at the woman's stupidity.

"Oklahoma City." A pause, then she repeated, "231-555-1212. Thank you, Operator," and she hung up. The dimes clinked down through the intestines of the oblong box and rattled into the change bowl. Jane's fingers made a dive for the bowl and retrieved them.

"Okay, honey," the woman explained, "put them in again, and then we dial 1-231-555-1212 and you ask for the person you want and they'll give you another number and we'll dial that and you'll have your party."

"Sure," Jane said surely.

"Are you calling collect?"

Jane shrugged ambiguously. She didn't want to show she didn't know what the woman was talking about.

"You better call collect," the woman decided. "You don't seem to have much change."

"Oh, fer cryin' out loud!" the man suddenly erupted furiously and stomped away. The woman ignored him. They had been married for twenty years.

Jane had put the dimes in, and the woman dialed eleven numbers while Jane held the phone to her head. She jumped as a voice came on.

"Oklahoma City," she said in response to some silent question the others couldn't hear. "Rabbit," she explained further.

An odd pause as Jane's face contorted again.

"Rabbit?" the woman repeated. "No, honey, give your friend's name."

"I did."

"Well, then, what's her first name?"

"I remember. Laloosh," Jane said, and waited.

"Laloosh Rabbit?" the woman repeated. Jane looked at her like she was an idiot. The woman looked at her like she was one more burden sent by Jesus to test her. Jane suddenly handed the phone to the woman.

"Could you repeat that, Operator?" the woman asked. "555-4242. Thank you." She hung up. The dimes clinked again, and Jane's hand dove gleefully for them again. "Now we're getting somewhere." Jane clinked in the same two dimes, and the woman dialed another eleven numbers.

"What?" Jane said into the receiver again.

"It's a recording," the woman said, then listened some more. She fumbled in her purse for a pencil and wrote some more numbers on the phone book. "Thank you," she said to the recording, and hung up.

The dimes clinked down again, and Jane's hands dove again.

"Your friend—is this your mama?" the woman asked, suddenly getting personal.

"No, my mama's in jail," Jane explained. "I'm calling a friend to get her out." It was the simplest thing in the world to Jane. Why or how this old bag couldn't already know it was beyond her.

"Oh," the woman said. It had suddenly gotten beyond her. She had never even gotten a parking ticket before. "What's she in jail for?"

"I don't know," Jane lied. She knew her mother was a witch, that was why.

"Where's your daddy?"

"The pigs beat him up," Jane said. It was how her daddy would have referred to it. "He skipped town."

"Oh."

"Where's Rabbit?" Jane asked

"What?" The woman was taking a pill.

"Rabbit," Jane patiently repeated. "You took another number and were about to—"

"Oh, yeah, Rabbit," the woman remembered. She hoped the Valium would stop her head from swirling. She was not well, and these little Mexican kids were throwing off the "reality equilibrium" Dr. Buzhardt had spent so much time and money developing in her. "She moved to Austin." The woman knew where it was. She was from Fort Worth.

Jane clinked in the dimes again. The woman dialed another eleven numbers and they waited.

Sky did not look directly at the other phone callers lining up on either side of Jane and the woman. The pretty young woman next to Jane did not see him looking at her. She was talking angrily about how her car needed a jump. The other conversations were about having a drink later, meeting Bob and Carol at the restaurant, calling for a room in Albuquerque, and a noisy guy with a mustache was yelling at the Public Service Company about his bill. Sky was fascinated by it all, and quickly bored. He took to watching the chic travelers file in and out the swinging doors. They were dressed like Indians, they were dressed however Fifth Avenue and the Champs-Elysée told them they should dress. It was all very fascinating, and quickly boring. Sky turned to watch salesmen in the turquoise gift shop take cases of gems from under the counters to enrapture the fascinated buyers. But the gems only made them more tolerantly bored. A newsstand across the lobby held no interest whatsoever.

"What's yer name, honey?" she finally asked Jane.

"I told you, Jane McNamara."

"Jane McNamara," the woman repeated in the phone, and listened. "She says she doesn't know any Jane—"

"Is that Rabbit?"

"Is this Rabbit? Yes, Operator, yes, I know this is a collect—" The woman listened. A twitch was developing on her cheek.

Doris was on the line on the other end in Austin. She could hear the Texas voice on the other end, and some tiny child's voice as well. But the operator was keeping the communication garbled. When she heard Rabbit's name mentioned, she called into the other room, while the operator was lecturing the smartly dressed woman about abusing long-distance privileges. "Rabbit?"

"Yeah?" Rabbit's twangy drawl grunted from the bathroom.

"You know any Jane McNamara?"

"Who?"

"Jane McNamara. Some old broad calling collect from Santa Fe?"

"Hell, no!"

"Operator I—" Doris said but was cut off by the operator, chastising her about talking to her. Would she accept the call or not? ITT insisted.

"Operator, I am not Jane Mc—" But the smartly dressed woman was also chastised. She was growing irate. Never had she been treated like this! Except maybe that time when—

"Wait a goddamn minute!" some fifth voice suddenly butted in. Rabbit was buttoning up her jeans as she grabbed the phone from Doris. "Is that Bonnie's Jane?"

"What?" the operator asked. She took a pill.

"Who?" Doris asked, lighting up a joint.

"Bonnie's! Bonnie's!" Rabbit demanded, exasperated with the system that couldn't answer a simple question. "Bonnie Red Indian Bird!"

"I don't know," the operator said, "but ma'am—"

"You Indian?" the smartly dressed woman asked Jane. Sky was suddenly alert.

"I guess so," Jane replied.

"Yes," the smartly dressed woman said into the receiver. "Yes," the operator said, relaying the message.

"Fuckin' A, we'll accept!" Rabbit decided in her succinct way. The operator, flustered, made the connection. The smartly dressed woman fainted. The bellman ran over to her as all hell broke loose. People crowded around to see some action, finally, and in the crush a man put his elbow through a glass window display of squash blossoms, cut an artery, and blood spurted four feet into the air. The burglar alarm went off as well, just as the smartly dressed woman's smartly dressed husband was returning with two gin and tonics. Somebody jostled him and spilled the drinks on the noisy man with the big mustache who was still on the phone yelling at the Public Service Company. The noisy man hit the smartly dressed man on the nose. Sky watched it all, fascinated, and not bored a bit.

"Jane, is that you?" Rabbit asked on the phone.

"Yes," Jane replied, unfazed by the chaos erupting in the lobby of the chic hotel.

"What's all that noise in the background?" Rabbit asked.

"I don't know."

"Well, how are you?"

"Fine."

"How's yer mama?"

"She's in jail."

"What?"

"Can you get her out?" Jane asked. She watched a kitchen dishwasher apply a tourniquet to the pale man whose arm was already a shrunken relic of its old self. Four men were fistfighting, including the noisy man with a mustache and the smartly dressed man. The bellman was on the floor, slapping the face of the unconscious smartly dressed woman. Her green skin was but a relic of its former altruistic exuberance.

"What jail?" Rabbit asked, then covered the phone. "Bonnie got busted," she said to Doris, who was lying on the couch.

"Shit," Doris said.

"I don't know," Jane replied.

"Well, it's cool, I'll find out," Rabbit said reassuringly. "Say, where the hell are *you*?"

"In La Fonda Hotel. We crawled out the window of that place where they put us and we got no place to stay."

"Oh, wow," Rabbit said, impressed.

"Can you send us some money?" Jane asked without shame. She was getting sleepy and hungry, and it was up to grown-ups to take care of these things.

"Sure, baby. Goddamn, ain't yer mama a good buddy of mine? Give me the desk clerk of that hotel. We'll put you on my American Express card."

"Okay," Jane said, putting the phone down, crawling off the suitcase, stepping over the smartly dressed woman who was now starting to revive, and threading her way through the firemen who were running into the building. Whistles blew somewhere and another window broke.

Sky reached up to the telephone receiver, where it lay in its stainless-steel booth. Police EMTs brought in a stretcher and started arguing with the firemen about who had jurisdiction over the man whose artery had been cut. An elderly woman tripped over the stretcher as she tried to get out of the way and fell down. Police were taking away the four men who had been fighting, and some order was returning to the hotel lobby. Except that the elderly woman who had fallen down was screaming at the top of her frail lungs.

"Rabbit?" Sky asked into the phone.

"Yeah, who's this?"

"Sky."

"Sky? Oh, yeah, Sky, how ya doin', boy?"

"Fine."

"Goddamn," Rabbit cursed. It was worse than she thought. Something in his voice told her so.

"Rabbit, can I ask you a question before Jane gets back?"

"Now don't you worry, Junior, we'll git ever'thing straightened up."

"That's not what—"

"Where's yer old man, anyways?" Rabbit asked. "The worthless fuck. So you kids escaped the pigs, eh, some juvenile hall, eh?"

"Yeah, I guess, but—"

"You lay low till we get there."

"Okay, but—" He stopped, for he could see Jane leading a disgruntled desk clerk past the hysterical elderly woman. They were almost to the phone.

"Rabbit, what tribe are we?" Sky asked.

"What?"

"An old woman said we don't know what tribe we are." Sky tried to explain. He was close to tears.

"You mean what Indian tribe are you? Your mama?"

"Yeah, what—"

"I don't know, she never—no, wait," Rabbit said, thinking, but got sidetracked. "Say, where's that desk clerk, we gotta git you kids under shelter."

"They're coming," Sky said. "But what—"

"Now wait a minute." Rabbit was thinking. "Cherokee? No. Caddo? I can't remember, Sky; she might have told me once but I'm not sure."

Jane grabbed the phone and gave it to the desk clerk, who took numbers from Rabbit. Jane scrupulously oversaw it all.

Sky wandered across the lobby to the newsstand. The firemen had the elderly woman and the man with the cut artery well on their way to St. Vincent's Hospital. Ceiling-high stacks of

Western history and books and magazines and newspapers were crammed into the tiny alcove of the newsstand. Sand paintings of Navaho rainbow gods were displayed and on sale. Sky looked up and around at the mysterious world of art and literature and journalism. His eyes landed on a picture book. He couldn't read very well yet, but he saw the cover painting was of a bald-headed Indian scalping a frontiersman. It was a beautiful and bloodless painting.

He opened the book. The woman behind the counter eyed him suspiciously, but she was more preoccupied with the screams of the running men in the lobby to bother him. He thumbed through the pages of history, thoroughly captivated. Then he turned a page to see an old brown photograph of his mother! But she was dressed funny. He stared aghast at the photograph. It was in a foreign place and time. He took the book up to the woman at the counter.

"Please," he said, holding the book up to her, "can you tell me what it says under this picture?"

"Are your parents with you?"

"Please."

The woman sighed heavily and looked at the caption under the photograph and read: "Skiowejea, a Cheyenne Woman at Fort Keogh, Montana, 1881."

She stumbled six times over the strange words, mispronouncing them all.

"Thank you," Sky said, and returned the book to its shelf and left. He saw Jane making a beeline for him.

"There you are," she said. "We have a room. Rabbit will be here tomorrow or so. C'mon, they're going to feed us too."

She walked briskly ahead of him, carrying their bags down a hallway, away from the noise of the lobby, her task fulfilled. There were more folk-art shops and paintings of conquistadores and Franciscan friars on the walls, but Sky was barely aware of them as he trailed behind Jane. One word was running through his head and his heart. It blocked out all the fine old viga beams in the room of the antique hotel. One word made all the rich paintings on the walls fade away into a blur. Sky was memorizing the letters of the word, so that he would never again forget it. He even dared to whisper it aloud. When no one was listening, he whispered, "Cheyenne," mispronouncing it.

 **CHAPTER 5**

How Philbert Came to Know Love

PROTECTOR WAS A cruisin' down I-90 at a cool forty-five miles per hour when a crossroads warning startled Philbert from his Sheridan reverie. He was running his hand over Protector's dashboard like it was the mane of a prize palomino. Buddy had lit the Coleman stove in the backseat, fashioned a vent of beer cans running from it and on out the rear window, and had fallen asleep in the front seat, wrapped in the warm glow of Jack Daniel's, Coleman butane, and one of the electric blankets. It was not plugged into anything, but Buddy dreamed of coup sticks and cavalry tactics and big-titted redheads nevertheless.

$$\boxed{\text{I-25 JUNCTION—2½ MILES AHEAD}}$$

Philbert knew that I-25 went south to Denver and Santa Fe, and that I-90 veered east into South Dakota. Philbert was a scout—he knew this country like the seams in his blue jeans.

South Dakota! The Black Hills, the Sioux, Wounded Knee, Mount Rushmore, Bear Butte. Bear Butte?

Bear Butte . . .

Inspiration wafted across his face with the swiftness of sexual realization. His eyes glowed and then they cooled into brown-hot intensity. His nostrils flared and then contracted in one smooth sign of thought. His mouth and cheeks and chin and all the other wrinkles and tensions of a smile leapt upward in sudden joy and descended into equally sudden relaxation. "Bear Butte," they said. The Sacred Mountain of the Cheyenne. The womb of Sweet Medicine.

I-25 NEXT RIGHT

I-90 NEXT LEFT

Protector effortlessly swung left, circled around ceremoniously on an overpass over I-25, and headed into the sunrise-to-be of the still-darkened east. Philbert rode his pony surely and drained another beer to stay awake. They would ride all night to be at Paha Sapa by dawn.

To stay awake, Philbert thought of the legends. He thought of the savior named Sweet Medicine, who came to the prairie people many centuries ago, beyond time. Before Sweet Medicine came, the Tsitsitsas were indeed savages, living without law and killing one another. It was said that a god named Sweet Roots came to a chaste young maiden in her sleep for four nights in a row, and in the end the dream had made her pregnant. Her parents were ashamed and sent her out of the village. No one helped her when she had a baby boy beside a creek. After it was finished, she made a shelter of driftwood and left the baby behind and went home.

An old woman found the baby, wrapped it up, and took it home with her. She went into her hut and said, "Old man, I found a baby boy that somebody throwed away." And the old man got up praising and was happy, and put his hands up kind of thankful and said, for some reason, "That's our grandson. And his name shall be Sweet Medicine."

Oh, those goddamn old blanket Skins, Philbert thought, smiling again pleasantly. They had a way with words.

That crazy, old Sweet Medicine performed all kinds of miracles too. He made a hoop out of an old calfskin hide once, when there was a famine on the prairie, and shot an arrow into the hoop, and it turned into a buffalo with an arrow in it, and it fell over and died and everybody had all they could eat. Philbert thought, *They probably ate it raw.* Another time Sweet Medicine shot an arrow at a beautiful red duck, but the duck flew away with the arrow. Sweet Medicine followed the arrow for four days over many miles and finally wangled it away from the duck, which had been captured by a medicine man (who was really an old woman), who killed the duck (but not really). On his way home, Sweet Medicine was tired of walking—this was way before horses, and they couldn't ride dogs around very well, so everybody walked—so he put the arrow to his bow and shot it far toward the north, the direction from which he had come. It disappeared from sight, but when it struck the ground, he was standing right beside it. Then he pulled it out again and shot it again, and again it carried him for many miles. He did this a third and a fourth time, and then he was just a short distance from his own village. And he returned to the village in this way and kept the arrow with him there among the people.

Jesus, I could really get into being the tribal soothsayer or something, Philbert was thinking. *I could really get into something like that. Weave the old stories into something pretty far-out. There's always a place for historians, and I have a way with words.* It was a goal he set for himself that night. It was the first time in his life that he had ever set any kind of goal for himself.

Outside, it was cold. Snow lay on the land in freezing monotony. The sky was clear and their good weather was holding, but it was cold as donkey throbbers. They crossed Crazy Woman Creek, which was named after some woman or other who probably went crazy from the cold weather. The whitemen probably had some legend about it. It was at Crazy Woman Creek, where it went back into the Big Horn Mountains, that a Lieutenant MacKenzie had ambushed Crazy Horse's camp a few months after Custer's comeuppance and taken care of a few hostile women and children.

Philbert didn't notice. He was fiddling with a Leon Russell tape. Philbert sang along with the music and popped open the last six-pack. Buddy was as dead to the world as a lump of last year's horseshit.

They crossed into the Powder River Country. Two enormous penis-snouts sprang up into the sky from beside that ancient and once-beautiful river, which had always been Sitting Bull's favorite. The city-sized gasification and power plant looked almost like Pittsburgh in sleepy repose at night. Lovely fuchsia lights blinked from atop the smokestacks; twinkle-twinkle little stars formed the Peabody Coal constellation on earth. From ten miles away it was the essence of orderly enterprise. It was the whiteman's contribution to intergalactic space travel—the mother ship to a scratching brood of space shuttles. Enormous strip-mining shovels crawled about their big mama, digging up natural resources. The two tremendous lamps of each shuttle rose and fell as they crept up and down the stubborn little hills, picking out scoopfuls of nasty little bituminous waste that hadn't done anybody any good for millions of years. Oh, it was a gleeful romp! Oh, the merriness of the times, that aliens could bring their knowledge and technology to this primitive planet! Why, but a few miles away, a few tidbits in the light-years of discoveries still to come, rested Devil's Tower National Monument—home of a movie! *Close Encounters of the Third Kind* had visited this dismal and isolated spot! The gasification plant had arisen from the dead and flown over the Devil! Strip tractors tumbled and twirled like gyroscopes romping into the twenty-first century! From afar, it was a quiet reassurance; from within, the primitive little ponies sneaking past in the dark, the mother mare slurping from the mother river was the hope of a better life.

Crash! Roar! From outside—only Protector's skin crawled to hear the crunch and grind of the machinery, to smell the stink, to see the black-and-white proof billowing twenty thousand feet above the propaganda. Protector galloped across the long bridge on the Interstate River, snaking over the slimy yellow Powder River far below. The mother beast upward had two digestive tracts—one farting into the air, the other shitting into the river. It grew great and fat and wise from its nutrition.

Inside the passing pony, peace and song occupied the warm and comfortable and drugged Indian, who didn't notice. Philbert didn't care. His mind was on myths.

Sweet Medicine had been exiled from the tribe for arguing with an old man. The soldiers who ruled the tribe at that time came after him, but his grandmother tipped her soup into the fire in their lodge and it made an explosion and ashes and steam and Sweet Medicine flew up through the hole at the top. When the soldiers came in to catch him, he was gone. In a moment someone saw him on a ridge beyond the village, so they all ran after him. His body was painted, and a stringless bow was in his hand and feathers were on his head. His dress later became that of the Fox Society. But when the soldiers reached the top of the valley, this time he was carrying an elk horn and a crook-ended spear wrapped with otter skin and hung with four eagle feathers, the insignia of the Elk Society.

He signaled them to come on, and they ran after him, but again he disappeared, and was seen again on the next ridge, wearing feathers in his hair and painted red, the insignia of the Red Shield Society. And they tried to reach him again, but he vanished a fourth time, appearing again with a rawhide rope on the side of a belt and a doughnut-shaped rattle decorated with feathers in his hand. He had become a Dog Soldier.

The fifth time he had a buffalo robe and a sacred pipe and one eagle feather stuck through the braided lock of his hair, and he had become the first Cheyenne chief. After that he was not seen again. It had been a busy day. The soldiers searched the entire country to find and punish him for showing off so much, but he was gone, and he did not come back for four years.

He had gone to Noahvose, the Bear Butte where the Goddess lived. Philbert and Protector were going there, too, but first they had to stop in Gillette, Wyoming, for gas and a pee.

The all-night U-TOTE-UM was just off the exit for quick access. Philbert took a three-minute leak (a minute per six-pack), pumped 19.1 gallons into his ravenous steed, bought four candy bars and a whip-it girlie magazine from the half-wit in the store, and he was back on his way with a delay of only nine and a half minutes. It was a thoroughly satisfying system, worthy of the Pony Express. Buddy only stirred once, muttering, "Where . . . what . . . huh?" looked blearily out the window into the neon interrogation, and turned back over to sleep.

They were back on the road, four lanes divided nonstop, Philbert back on his fancies, chompin' on a Three Musketeers and wishing it weren't so dark that he couldn't ogle at the glossy breasts and buttocks beckoning from the whip-it book in his back pocket.

Yep, ol' Sweet Medicine was a heavy bro. He had been called by some great power to the Black Hills Country, just as Philbert felt himself sucked toward that eerie place. Sweet Medicine found a place there like a big tipi, where old women were sitting along one side and old men along the other (but they were not *really* people, they were gods!). And Sweet Medicine saw four arrows there, which were to become the Four Sacred Arrows of the Cheyenne—

A sudden blackness overwhelmed . . .

. . . Philbert and Protector . . .

. . . at just the moment they thought . . .

. . . the sacred thought . . .

Philbert froze, terrified. Protector steered steadily ahead. The black omen passed. Perhaps it had been a cloud passing over the moon, or the last gasp of night, for now an azure blur was rising in the east, the first warning of light on the infinite horizon. Philbert had his own theory about that big tipi at Noahvose. He thought it was a cave. It was a big cave in the mountain where all the secrets of the earth were kept, and ol' Sweet Medicine had found him some sweet grass and stumbled in there and heard the mysteries of meat and grain and blood and sky explained; but explained not in definitions or descriptions, but in visions and rituals. He was a heavy bro, after all. Probably a sorcerer, like Jesus. A Poet-Chief.

Anyway, the Old Ones around that cave called him Grandson and began instructing him in many things he should take back to the people. They taught him first about the arrows, because they were to be the highest power in the tribe. Two were for hunting and two for war. Many ceremonies were connected with them, and they stood for many laws. He was taught the ceremony of renewing the arrows, which must take place if one Cheyenne ever killed another. The arrows had to be kept by a special warrior in a sacred tipi, covered at all times unless the Arrow Ceremony was under way.

He learned next that he was to give the people a good government, with forty-four chiefs to manage it, and a good system of police and military protection, organized in the four akicita societies he had already established. There was so much more to learn besides these things that he was there for most of the four years. Then he was sent forth to carry the laws to the people. One of the Old Ones came out before him, burning sweet grass as incense to purify the air for the arrow bundle. He had to be cool with that, for it was heavy shit, like the Ten Commandments. With it in his arms, he started for home and established the Cheyenne religion and culture and the whole trip. Medicine men made endless commentaries and interpretations of the Sweet Medicinaic Law over the centuries, and it was a real source of unity to his descendants. They wandered and split up into bands

97

and were forced out by various invaders and diasporized, but they were like skunk juice—they just kept coming back stronger and stronger every time.

Protector rattled and clattered over the Belle Fourche River; bypassed Sundance, Wyoming; and slipped over the invisible line that meant they were in South Dakota.

The horizon ahead beckoned ever more brightly—now a dirty amber with tints of indigo, shades of sapphire, promises of unspeakable wealth luring the gold seekers back to the East, of high-paying jobs in the wholesale and legal and political bonanzas where the real gold lay. "Yippee in the saddle!" Philbert nodded, a weary cowpoke, his plodding pony taking the reins down the trail. "Take me home again, Old Paint," Philbert said in his dreams, nodding intermittently in his own fanciful saddle. "Make with the hunt, my brown charger," he whispered, petting his stallion's neck.

Buddy tossed and turned over, mumbling aloud unto his own dreams. The Coleman stove blazed a suffocating drowsiness into Philbert's exhausted memories. Protector slowed to thirty miles per hour on its own as it trotted through deserted downtown Spearfish, South Dakota. The black smudge of the sacred Paha Sapa to Philbert's right did not awaken him from the somnolent stare at his pony's head and neck in front of him, slowly trudging out the miles. At Sturgis, they drifted off on a trail to the left. A mile, two miles . . .

. . . became a minute, five minutes, ten minutes . . .
. . . amber announced saffron, jasmine, and . . .
. . . finally . . .
. . . the great chrome sun burst out of the ground in an imperial rudeness right into Philbert's bleary eyeballs.

"Holy shit, what the—?" he asked metaphysically, stunned at the radical changes of Nature. "Oh, it's you." He squinted at the carmine-and-platinum fury that was his eternal father. "How ya doin'?" he asked agreeably, and got a suitable response. "Good. Oh, I'm okay. It's fine to have another beautiful day to—Holy of Holies!" he gasped, and slammed on the brakes. Protector didn't exactly slam shoes to linings to drums too well, but he did manage to stop eventually.

He sat in the southwestern shadow of Bear Butte, which was but a few miles away. It eclipsed the sunrise at an angle that cast divine sunbeams only on the car, only on that particular spot on the deserted side road and nowhere else.

"It is a sign from the Powers," Philbert murmured. He turned off the car. He got carefully and quietly out and stood on the road. "I will try to be worthy."

He watched as the sun rose, its red-and-white grace ascending into a yellow grandeur. He stared directly into it, or at least into the sliver that rose like a lover's caress up the slopes of the cone-shaped volcano. It reached a fold in the snowy garment that covered the modest lady and came like a silent orgasm into full, rounded view. Philbert had to close his eyes then. They were wet from the glands that protected them, and from love.

Humility had never known such bounds as it knew in Whirlwind Philbert that moment. He stood, in a trance. He stared at the sun, in rapture. He could have married that mountain, he loved her so much. There was nothing vulgar to the thoughts of this man standing in the deserted road. If they betrayed that his loins were a little horny, these same loins had nothing on his swelling heart. Love and sperm might burst from a man in his utter jubilance, but only love burst from Philbert in the road. He had respect and fear for the sun. If its sunbeams were sperm irradiating into the Holy Woman, then they were splattering all over Philbert too. It was an occasion for humility. It was a moment to exercise supreme submission.

Without taking his eyes off the nuptial ceremony taking place before him, he got back in the car and started it up. Buddy did not stir. Philbert drove closer to the Mountain. He reined Protector into the deserted parking lot, next to the Visitors' Center. It was even too early for the Rangers to be at work. Or maybe because it was Saturday they were at home in bed, still grasping for perfection in their wives and girlfriends and creating dreams of more luscious thighs somewhere else (granted, some had created the thighs of their wives and girlfriends as obtainable perfection, and were satisfied, but these were still myths).

Philbert reeled back in his seat, staring up and all around him. Up and out of sight and filling the entire windshield was the Holy Mountain—smothering the world! It's rocky, wooded slopes were right there!

He got out of the car. He zipped up his denim parka. He took a leak. He took his hat off. He closed the car door. He scratched his nose. He put his hat back on.

All the important movements of life became ordinary schlepp beside this massive thing. Nay, they became hogwash, puny and contemptible! No, they were elevated, edifying, significant. Oh, hell! Oh, Goddess! The Mountain made him feel everything good and bad and indifferent about life! He was a worm, a mortal nothing beside this incomprehensible thing. But this thing made him feel that a worm was also an eagle, an immortal something beside Her that he could experience and share. Oh, boy, but it was good to be a bug in a big world!

A trail led down from the parking lot to a gully, and then rose up a gentle slope a few hundred yards away. A long, flat clearing on the plateau of the slope stretched out of sight on the southeastern side of the Mountain. The sun was shining more indifferently now, rising into the sky perceptibly, accepting its responsibilities to the rest of its lovers around the world, waiting for a word or two of encouragement. It warmed the southeastern slope that Philbert could see from the parking lot. It invited him.

Exercise had always been loathsome to Philbert, but this little walk looked easy enough to him. It was mostly downhill and flat. It beckoned. Something in his legs cried out for movement.

Some antigravity tugged at him, and he took a step! He took another step! He was walking! He stepped over a curb and onto slush! His boots glurped in the old snow and fresh mud on the trail!

It was an odd, involuntary sensation, this phenomenon called movement. It was downright foreign to Philbert. After ten yards he was grunting, but it felt good! For some damn reason his body was leaping with joy! He slid on the packed snow of the trail, one foot hit the air, and Philbert slid thirty yards on his butt to the bottom of the gully! He was wet from snow, slurpy from mud, his hat had gotten crumpled, and he was laughing his ass off! He sat in the snow and fingered his hat back into shape and felt his skin throbbing from cold and wet and morning air, and he was overjoyed! It was silent and clean and fundamental in the bottom of that gully, and Philbert knew that it was a good moment. It was a very good moment indeed.

The Mountain watched him disapprovingly. It was a very serious thing to be a mountain. It had to maintain a standing in the surrounding countryside. The pastures and cornfields looked to the cold and shadowy queen that had hovered over them for eons to set an example. This solitary volcano the newcomers called Bear Butte and the older newcomers called Noahvose had sat alone in the surrounding plains. She rose iconoclastically from the prairie. She was the northernmost sentinel of the Black Hills, and even then she was separated by a significant number of miles from her community to maintain an individual identity. Only a supply line of pine trees and gullies connected her to the somber black line of the other hills. But she was growing old like her former neighbors, worn down by age, and like many old women, she was growing irritable. She had to put up with the sun pawing her most every day. Only occasionally could she gather clouds about her to keep out that old nuisance. Ah, then! then she could have a good cleaning, let loose a few good screams, have a knock-down, drag-out storm!

Ah, it felt good sometimes. She had to put up with deterioration with every cleansing, though. She had to hold her rumblings when the puny loudmouths ogled at her and called her beautiful. She had gotten worn down to nothing, damn them! They should have seen her when she was younger, when her trees were stately mountains themselves, when her children pranced all about her in a chain of graceful hills unto the horizon. There was Beauty! But now her children had worn down into nothing. They should have seen her fire and fury erupt in earth-shattering glory if they wanted to know what majesty and finery were really about! Beauty? Her passion had cooled now, into the embers of wisdom. What the hell had the loudmouths ever known about it? And now some idiot down there has to schlepp around on his ass. It would take another snowstorm to clean off the splotches.

Philbert was up again and moving, the smooth soles of his new cowboy boots not exactly suited to hiking, so he continued to slide and slip his way on up the gully to the plateau he had seen from the parking lot. He was vaguely aware of some huge something watching him, but when he turned around and saw only a few swifts and sparrows frolicking among the rocks and trees, he gave it up to exhaustion. He was tired, goddammit! This uphill stuff wasn't as fun as the downhill ride.

But he reached the crest of the plateau and sat on a rock, panting. It was a lovely place; huge boulders and small boulders decorated slopes. They had orange moss and green lichen clinging to them, to add contrast to the gray granite colors of the stones. Some black ponderosa pine testified that this was technically a member of the Black Hills too. Cedar, fir, and spruce increased the sense of contrast that is such a vital element to an artistic composition. The pines were long thin lines, the stones short round circles. The lines and circles of the land transcended any abstract or representational categorizing of Nature's chaotic art. And the slope of dirt and snow and tufts of stubborn weeds and bushes sticking out of the surface was the canvas. It was not a neat painting, but it had an element of honesty in it, and even though Philbert didn't know anything about art, he knew what he liked. The sun had Rembrandt's feel for lighting and cast skillful shadows and tones on the scene. Rabbits and marmots gave it some of Van Gogh's spontaneous fluidity. Birds zoomed by like time-exposed photographs of traffic in Paris at night—one long, white-and-red blur of life passing by. Philbert said, "Gee, it looks like one of them Hamm's Beer pictures I seen in bars."

He was getting his breath back, he was forgetting the pain of the climb that brought him here. He stood and walked across the slope. He felt real damn good, to be a part of Nature and all. It was silent and clean and fundamental.

A frame of wood braces was built in the shape of a small hut behind a large rock. Philbert came upon it suddenly and stared at it. He was astonished. A red handkerchief hung from the little willow beam across the doorway. There were no walls.

"It's a Cheyenne sweat lodge," Philbert whispered. His voice and body heat startled a mouse that lay inside the hut, preoccupied with its own worries, sunning itself. The mouse scurried away under the big rock. "Sorry, my brother," Philbert apologized to the mouse. The Mountain seemed to heave an exasperated sigh as Philbert crawled into the hut and sat down in the middle of it, facing the sun. It felt good.

Noahvose is occasionally a place of worship for Cheyenne. Some come here to make with a fasting and to make a plea for visions; some to pray for the end of whatever war happens to be in progress at the time; and some to dig eagle pits to capture eagles for their feathers. Philbert's Uncle Fred Whistling Bull had liked to point out ancestral eagle pits to Philbert when he was a boy. They would drive around the reservation or go to Devil's Tower and Uncle Fred would stop his old Packard and point to a hole in the ground and say, "There's an eagle pit." Philbert was grown before he discovered that most of those eagle pits were outhouse holes, full of old shit and Monkey Ward buttwipe. It was a great joke to Uncle Fred.

Philbert sat cross-legged, Indian style, and closed his eyes, wishing he had brought a joint with him. It would be good to make a smoke of peace.

This is not to say the medicine men who often came here to hold some private ceremonies were smoking dope. They weren't. Often they were told in dreams to come to Bear Butte to hold ceremonies. So they came. Paying attention to dreams was just about the main requirement to being a medicine man. God knows what would happen if a guy ignored a summons or a request in a dream. It was too scary even to imagine what would happen.

So here they set up shop. These were the old camping grounds on the south of the butte. These were the happy hunting grounds that so impressed the good citizens of nearby Sturgis that they wanted to make the Mountain into a shrine. Privately owned by a rancher, they wanted the U.S. government to buy it and set it aside in a warehouse or a museum. But instead the Indians were given special camping privileges and it was left where it was.

Kiowa and Arapaho and Apache all got important religious power there too. The Kiowa got the kidneys of a bear, and the Arapaho got medicine from a sweet smoke from hot coals, and the Apache got horse medicine. The Sioux claimed they got a pipe from the mountain, but everybody knew the Sioux came from Minnesota and already had the pipe. Or else they had stolen it from the Cheyenne.

Philbert had the place to himself that day. But something was wrong. He was trembling. He was gritting his teeth. His eyes were clenched shut. An insane vision was making him sweat. He was remembering the sacrifices made on this spot. He was seeing a small but difficult task set for him by the Powers, a punishment for the presumptuous goal he had set for himself earlier that morning. He was being commanded to prove his worth as an aspiring historian of the tribe. He had to accept it. He had to accept it. He had to accept it! His doubts reached their climax, then they slowly settled into a calm resolve. He would do it. He had accepted it. He didn't like it, and he wished to hell he had stayed in the car, but the task had drawn him into it and there was no way out, especially since he had just sworn to the Powers that he would do it. So, he would do it.

He opened his eyes. He stood up inside the skeletal little hut and was taller than the roof. He turned to look at the smooth slopes of the volcanic cone that rose above him disdainfully.

"Well, hell," he said, taking a deep breath. "It ain't that big. It won't take no time at all." Panic seized him, but he dared not show it. If he had to climb it, then he had to climb it. It could be worth it, he rationalized; there could be some great reward on top that the Powers wanted him to have—if he didn't have a heart attack first.

So he found the trail again and started up. He tried not to think of each tortuous step as the unrelenting incline grew steeper. The trail wound around the east, and to the snowy north face, where the slopes had a much gentler grade. It was the easiest way to go. On the north was where Sweet Medicine's cave was.

But Philbert was still back down on the south face. He was resting after the first hundred yards. In fact, he was sprawled out on a rock, gasping for dear life. His mind was flashing through scenes of senseless crucifixion, his eyes were red and hot, his lungs were outraged at this unspeakable affront. But he caught his breath, his brain told him it was really just a little hill, the most intense pain was forgotten, and some nameless will drew him to his feet and pulled him forward. He continued. He was moving. He was doing it!

What makes a man attempt the impossible? What force drives mankind to achieve extraordinary feats of strength and valor? Is it adrenaline? Is it desperation? Is it fear? Is it God? Or is it his own cockeyed notions of pride and peace? Peace of mind, the effort to keep all them yapping ideas and hopes in the brain quiet for a minute. Does a man work his ass off all day to keep his wife off his back about the bills? No. Does he do it to keep all those starving, widemouthed chicks in his nest in a full refrigerator? No. He does it to give his mind some breathing room. He does what he hates to get a little peace and quiet.

So Philbert trudged. He slipped. He fell down. He panted and collapsed. He gasped and got back up. He cursed mud and rock and sky. He went into the cold shadows and came back out again into the warm glare and hated them equally. He knew only his own gut cramps, his own deoxygenated throat, his own anguish and sense of victimized frailty. He stopped every two minutes and rested ten. But vipers and devils and foul, nameless Defeat kept him from turning back. Shame forced him forward. Self-pity drove him to new heights. The proud pines watched him pass, contemptuous. The squirrels played in the snow and scurried for nuts, indifferent to his difficulties. And most of all, the Mountain—it sneered at him, it fought his every attempt at self-respect, it mocked his very mortality. It would kill him and not even notice. He could lie on the muscle of her slopes for eternity and it wouldn't matter a bit.

"You bitch!" he croaked at her, immediately regretting the waste of breath. He stopped, putting his hands on his knees, gasping for life. He had learned already that it was too hard to stand back up if he sat down. As he recovered, his ire returned. "You . . . you"—he struggled for a thought, but spent oxygen could not supply him with one—"bitch."

Despite it all, the sense of peace increased. He *knew* the view was magnificent, for one thing. He *knew* he was great also, just as he knew that his own greatness was but a puny reproduction of the pines he was struggling by. He was not worthy to wear the sap off their barks. They were hundreds of years old, they stood erect against blizzards without down parkas, they withstood cold and wind like no man ever could. They were the goddamn power!

These rocks and these birds and these insects on this mountain made the power of Hitler and Einstein and Buddha look like dingleberries on a cow's ass!

"Jesus goddamn shit fuck, I'm on the top!" Philbert gasped, and collapsed.

The circle of the world surrounded him. His face lay openmouthed in a snowbank, staring in bewilderment upon the hazy vastness of but one small part of the earth. The triumph of the moment was spoiled by the incomprehension of the moment. He had conquered one summit to emerge into another. The circle of the world was so vast that Bear Butte itself was more puny than Philbert had been when he was at the bottom.

He lay facedown in the snowbank on top of the world and closed his eyes. He dreamed. He saw his own memories of himself unwind in glimpses of self-understanding. His debilitated brain remembered his life as it had been, as a part of the lives of others who had camped on the now irrigated prairie surrounding the Mountain.

The plains cossacks had often gathered in the lap of this guardian, in the old days. The many bands of the Cheyenne would gather here for feasting and visiting their relatives in the summer. Philbert saw all this again, in his revelations.

The Arrow Renewal Ceremony was often held there, too, although never on top—that was too presumptuous. Philbert was a part of it. Horse races and gambling and laughter and fights were there, too, and Philbert was a part of it. Love and courting and secret sex in the dark were there also. But Philbert could not see himself here.

He opened his eyes suddenly. He stood and brushed the snow off his new clothes. They already looked a year old. He walked around the small peak, which showed no indication of a volcanic cone. Maybe it hadn't been a volcano. He tried unsuccessfully to grasp the awesome panorama circling his aerie perch. He was a lonely eagle, looking out on the glorious world and wondering if there was some small spot out there where happiness was waiting for him. His eagle binoculars could see to the ends of the world with unerring perception, but they could not keep him from his own nervous pacing.

He turned inward to explore the pines that had also scaled the summit. There were perhaps a dozen of them clothing the peak. Did they know the position they had attained? Had it made them happy? Philbert continued to pace, exploring every rock and tree, every view north and south and east and west and all the fractions thereof.

He found a scarf tied to the limb of a tree—some token left by another hawk. He found a strand of yellow beads draped carefully over a rock—the sacred graffiti of another woodpecker. Indians had been here before! Other restless man-birds had come to light on this perch for a moment of revelation, and to catch their breath. Many had asked—what was it that made a bird fly? But Philbert wanted to know—what made them not fly? What had made them stop, and perch, and stare?

He found a comfortable rock to lean against and sat down, facing the sunny south. It was midday. The morning haze was being burned off by the sun reaching its full erection. Philbert watched some buzzards circling to his right, meadowlarks licking their wings to his left, and the holy black hills of Paha Sapa stretching from the horizon to within a few miles of him—nay, to within a few finger lengths. He was sad, motionless, and unbearably excited.

His body wanted him to dance, but the Mountain would consider that profane. It was already sacrilegious to be on top. His brain warned him of the arrogance of it. His heart told him he had too much love for his own good. His dick chastised him for loving without fucking.

The Mountain had once been a sacred sepulchral isle, like Avalon, a place of orgiastic ritual for the priestesses of the Goddess.

A corner of his weakness had not forgotten the whip-it book in his back pocket, you see. He pulled it out in a quick parry to strength. Pleasure sighed unto the eagle's Reason for Being like the clean kill of a doomed rabbit.

Women! Women! Women made the eagle perch, just as men made women fly. Women were a fact that a man could grasp unerringly! In the midst of infinity a hot breast explained a lot of things. A wet pussy overcame sorrow or joy with an unerring sense of equality and objectivity. Philbert opened the pages of the tasteful magazine with unmistakable relief. A tiny 8½ × 11 page with even tinier photographs of something familiar made the limitless horizon more lucid, more significant, more endurable. The first glimpse of naked tits and smiling human teeth and luscious pink ass cleared up a lot of Philbert's confusion about Nature. The first inviting thighs and velvety labia brought the truth of the Mountain within grasp. She was a woman! These buxom ideals in print were the elusive soil and slopes of the world!

These axiomatic idiocies satisfied Philbert. He didn't know much about women, you see, except what he knew from contemporary literature. He had been fat and stupid all his life was why. He knew the basics of being a man—he knew how to fall on top of women and thereby trap them into amorous surrender (although it was only infrequently successful); he knew how to talk big and pretend misunderstanding and boast of hatred and sigh at the fascinating mystery of the things, but he had never known much reciprocity. He was fat and stupid, and girls kept clear of him. He had never been loved by anyone.

So he beat his meat a lot. He was a normal, healthy guy, after all. He idolized the beautiful women in *Playboy* and *Penthouse* and *Argosy*. He went to the porno flicks in Billings whenever he could. He was an idealist; he believed in Beauty.

But his hog needed reality. "For every pure impulse there is an equally impure repulse"—Philbert's law.

He had his jeans unzipped, his bare ass on the cold rock, his hot Throbber in his protective fist. His eyes and his fantasies alternated between the voluptuous nudies on the pages and the voluptuous scenery spread out on all sides of the pages. His libido shifted from nipples to frosty tree branches to luscious lips to pubic twists of cottonwoods down by the old millstream. A timid lady stepping modestly, and nakedly, into a swimming pool became a yellow meadow of rippling wheat (and Throbber rejoiced!); a suntan became a brown pasture; a belly button an eagle pit; a calf a calf; a beaver a beaver; a crevice a crevasse; a mammary a mountain (Chomp! Smolder! Avalanche! Moo-moo!).

A spread eagle wed a golden eagle!

Philbert undulated on and on, his endurance truly phenomenal. He had too much love to endure the absence of sex. He squirmed and groaned. His cherubic face had too much compassion to endure neglect. He turned the pages with one hand and turned his life away from ugliness with the other. A brunette smiled at him. A blonde thrust her large, happy breasts at him, a brown-head held her vagina open to him, a blue-eyed goddess invited him into her body, a black woman welcomed him into her heart, an Indian princess gathered him into the moist folds of her soul.

Oh, god, he was lonely! He was happy! He was hot, hard, and rising into the sky! He was ablaze with the heat of his fathers! He turned to the soil beside his rock and erupted into the Lady, returning her youth to her with his own fertility. He buried his penis into the dirt and became the sun . . .

. . . Drained . . .
. . . of every human fallibility . . .
. . . he slept . . .

In his dreams he saw that he—like the other lovers who had been here over the ages—would remain here forever.

CHAPTER 6

How Life in Lame Deer Went On, and
How Billy Little Old Man Oversaw It All

SATURDAY AFTERNOON IN Lame Deer is a magic time, especially on a warm December day. The pale yellow light of winter reminds the inhabitants of their mortality, and they move more cautiously. They are satisfied just to sit on their porches and glow with the philosophic idleness that comes with the afternoon. Even the boys shooting baskets over at the gym dribble slowly. The ball itself loops lazily into the basket, whooshing through the net with a reluctant sigh.

Billy Little Old Man crossed the street back to his office, scornful of a truck that had to slow down for him. He had been to the veterinarian's, the bank, and a couple of houses. They had all glowed with the gloomy listlessness of the afternoon. His wrinkled old face sagged more than normal. His closely cropped head of pure white hair wouldn't stay combed. His golf shirt, sport coat, slacks, and Hush Puppies had lost their crispness.

He had been to the vet's to see Mary Jane and Roscoe. Mary Jane was a nervous wreck. She had always been a shy little cat and had never understood the madness that came over her when she was in heat. It had therefore been a shock when she had kittens. She panicked. She ran away; nobody had known where. After the kittens had all died without her, she reappeared under Billy's couch. She was trembling, and had an insane look of guilt in her eyes. Billy gently called her to him, petted her for hours, and took her to the vet's for fallopian rehabilitation.

Roscoe had fallen off a rafter in John Young Bull's barn, stumbled dazedly out into the road, and a pickup ran over his tail. Billy found the old tom by the side of the road, staring at the bloody lump that had been his tail. He had about a two-inch stump left. Billy took him to the vet's also.

"He looks like he has distemper," Doc Sits in Timber said.

"No, he's looked like that for years," Billy explained.

Billy had stopped at the bank next. He was given the canceled check for $2,000 that had just come in from Birney. He had talked to Sven Sundersen on the phone the previous night, so he knew something was up.

"I'll take care of it," Billy had said to Sven.

Billy went to Buddy's trailer next, but nobody was there (or at least he couldn't see anybody there). His parents in the trailer next door didn't know where he was. Billy politely watched the basketball game on TV with them for a few minutes and then left. He always marveled at how clean they kept their trailer.

"How they raised a maniac like Buddy, I'll never know," Billy said to himself, walking two blocks back to his office. "How I ever trusted him, I'll never know. I ought to have my head examined."

The tribal headquarters was in a prefab building next to the prefab recreation center. It was a long, narrow building and looked very small. It was very small. A number of secretaries were never in, but IBM Selectric typewriters testified that this was a busy place of business. Billy came in the front door and saw that all the desks were empty. The secretaries were off on Saturday. He went back through the cheerful front rooms to his office. It said on the door:

TRIBAL PRESIDENT
BILLY LITTLE OLD MAN

He went into the office and closed the door behind him. He sat behind his modest desk. It was clean. He was known as a "clean-desk man." He always kept his paperwork current. A photograph of his deceased wife and their three daughters who had disappeared years ago sat in a five-by-seven frame on the corner of his desk. He lived alone in the Casa Loma Apartments up the hill. A feathered shield was hung on one wall. It was the insignia of the Medicine Arrow Chief. Billy stared out the window, trying to decide what to do about the wild young man who held so much hope and promise for the tribe.

He knew he should call the police. Not the tribal police but the State cops, or even the FBI if he had gone into North Dakota or Wyoming. He knew he should pick up the phone right now and give that maniac a dose of his own medicine.

Medicine . . .

Billy continued to stare out the window. It was a lazy afternoon. A few dogs trotted importantly up the street. Billy thought about getting a dog. Cats could be nothing but trouble sometimes.

He knew he had responsibilities to his people. He was serving his second four-year term as president of the ten-member council. He hadn't become the spokesman in Washington and Helena of tribal sovereignty by being soft. He hadn't opposed the coal and gas and uranium companies by being naïve about human nature. He knew what it would take to preserve his culture and to take that culture out of its present oblivion. Compromise. It would take compromise to survive.

It was the traditional role of a chief to do the unpopular, ignoble thing. Compromise had earned Dull Knife the hatred of the idealistic young warriors a hundred years ago. But his compromises had saved a lot of Indian lives. Compromise had turned Sitting Bull into an embittered old man, hated by just about everybody for his political scheming. But he gave the white-men a legacy to remember, and he gave the Sioux half a dozen reservations on their favorite lands.

So Billy stared out the window. He, too, was called an Apple Indian—red on the outside, white on the inside. The militants in the American Indian Movement hated his compromises, but he tolerated their vanities. It had always been that way—the old man chiefs against the young warriors. It had always been that way.

Billy thought of Buddy. He had been a boy chosen by power. He became a man who foolishly resisted it. He wanted to be a whiteman, or at least *not* an Indian. He wanted an even break out of life, but no person chosen by power was permitted his privacy. Billy knew Buddy well, for Billy had also been oppressed by power. He knew he would have to compromise on this matter.

"I will wait until he comes back," Billy decided, and put his feet up on his desk.

CHAPTER 7

How Big Lester and Rabbit Felt
the Stirrings of Social Consciousness

IT IS SAID that for every good thing there is an evil thing. That very evening near Austin, Texas, three people were wavering between good and evil. Each one of them sat in the living room and struggled with their own personal moral crisis.

To Rabbit LeLouche, there was no dilemma that she was conscious of. She knew that Texas was a myth. The Alamo, the oil wells, John Wayne—they were attempts by Texans to create Texas. Actually they were hallucinating. John Wayne's genius was to live with the hallucination of cattle drives and colossal adventures. He could not create the actual reality of the stupid miserable lives of cowboys. He never lived in Texas himself. After filming for a few months on the prairie, he went back to his swimming pool in Hollywood, just as any cowboy would. He hated the prairie.

Big Lester Mardewcki believed in the myth. He was from Delaware. He loved to sit out in the middle of the prairie and feel lonesome. It was better than the ocean, where you could only sit on the beach.

Doris Keselring liked the prairie, but she didn't love it. She liked to be able to walk naked out in the front yard because there wasn't a neighbor within fifteen miles, but she missed the stimulation of neighbors. She wanted more people to be naked with, to drink with, to talk with. She was from Baltimore.

Lester was on his third martini. It had been a busy day of drug dealing. He had flown back from Lubbock about an hour after the girls had talked to Sky and Jane in Santa Fe. He had made a couple of grand selling marijuana and cocaine to the students of Texas Tech University.

"This place never gets old," he was saying. "The people are for shit, but there's no end to the land, especially from the sky. It's great." He had leased a Cessna and had covered four hundred miles from Lubbock to Austin in two hours. He loved to fly.

"Texas is the asshole of the universe," Rabbit stated flatly. She was from Oklahoma, after all. There is no greater animosity on earth than that between neighbors. They pretend solidarity, but let one of them cross a fence and he gets his head blown off.

"The people are *not* for shit," Doris protested. "This place is swarming with good heads, especially in Austin."

The prairie sat outside the ranch houses and the chuck wagons all over the state, and the prairie waited. As tensions mounted, it waited. The people inside the ranch houses and the chuck wagons knew that it was waiting, and it made them tense. Its terrible wealth would turn them into good things one day, and evil things another day. The people knew that the deserts and bayous of Texas were a waiting devil and that the money and power were a waiting god, and that both devil and god were waiting for them.

"So what about Bonnie?" Rabbit asked. They had been discussing it for an hour. "I know you have expenses, Les, but we can't abandon her."

"You said her arraignment is Tuesday?" Big Lester asked.

"Yes, in three days," Rabbit replied. She had made several phone calls to Santa Fe.

"The day before Christmas," Doris said dreamily.

"It's not enough time," Big Lester said. "We can't raise twenty grand in three days. Maybe in two weeks, but not—"

"I know, I know," Rabbit said. "But there must be some way to get it."

"We can't let her stay in jail over Christmas," Doris added. "Maybe even months."

"She was working for Parelli," Les said. "Why not let them—"

"Goddammit!" Rabbit exploded. They had already been over that too. "That was a fling. She was gonna come back in with us. We've gotta get that dough."

Good tugged them one way, evil another. The prairie waited outside their windows, exerting its pressure. They sat and had another drink, and did not look at each other.

Lester said tentatively, "Maybe I can call Vito."

Rabbit and Doris looked at him, wondering which direction he had been pulled in.

"He could probably loan it to us."

They looked at him, and the prairie waited.

"A loan."

Doris felt her nipples go hard. Rabbit felt flushed. Les was scared.

"I'll call him."

He got up and went into the next room, and the women soon heard his solo voice. They heard him laugh a few times, then listen silently for a long time, then talk again. They heard the phone return to its cradle, and Les reappeared.

"They want to see Rabbit and me in Dallas in three hours. I'll gas the plane."

The three men in the restaurant in Dallas did not waver between good and evil. The prairie did not lurk outside their window. The men gulped their Bloody Marys and looked at the pretty girls passing by outside. They were morally confident of their lives.

The prairie was many miles away from the concrete and asphalt of the morally confident city.

Vito Scarlatti hated the movie *The Godfather*. He knew the Mafia was a myth. It was a hallucination to say that it was vicious and sentimental. It was neither of those things. It was a damned good business enterprise, that was all. Efficient and patriotic. Vito hated violence and family sentiment.

FBI Special Agent Tom Washington was cool and collected. He had gone over the dossier Agent Lewis had telexed from Kansas City. He knew the case well, and he was a specialist in the Indian field. He was prepared, and a little excited. This could mean a real breakthrough.

Sandy Youngblood loosened his tie. The vodka tasted good after a frustrating day of meetings. The phone call from Tom had come as a welcome surprise.

"I think that summarizes it, gentlemen," Tom was saying. "This girl, Bonnie McNamara, may be the spark we've needed. Vito, I'd recommend you front the money to your man. We'll see that you get it back, of course."

"When the girl is caught escaping to the reservation?" Vito inquired. He was a perfectionist. He liked to have all the details understood. He was the regional consigliere of West Texas and all of New Mexico.

"Sandy?" Tom turned to the man with the high cheekbones, who was dressed in an impeccable glen plaid suit.

"It's hard to tell where she'll go," Sandy said. "She hasn't been to her own reservation for twelve years—"

"But the phone call to her brother?" Vito reminded him.

"Yes." Sandy suddenly tensed. "Buddy Red Bird. I hope to hell he does come, because I want his ass."

"So do we, Sandy," Tom gently added.

"Gentlemen, you're forgetting business," Vito said. "We want the entire network, not one or two radicals."

"Vito," Tom said sternly, showing a side that caused new respect from the other men, "that 'radical,' as you put it, has assaulted at least one FBI agent. That is—"

"I know, but we need those coal rights on the reservations if—"

"*Attacked* an FBI man!" Tom said, raising his voice uncharacteristically. A couple at another table looked curiously at them. Tom shrank down in his seat, ashamed of his indiscretion.

Sandy said, in a cold-blooded tone, "Tom, we'll get him. The reservations will be gone soon, it's only a matter of time, then the scum hiding out won't have any more refuge. They won't be able to infect the decent people there anymore—"

"Now let me get this straight," Vito said, interrupting. "There are decent Indians on the reservations who don't want the militants?"

"Indians hate AIM more than white people do," Sandy explained.

"Is that right?" Vito questioned skeptically.

"Don't you have young hotheads disrupting your organization all the time?"

Vito sighed. "I see what you mean."

Sandy continued making his point. "The Oklahoma reservations were dissolved years ago, and things are better for Indians than ever. They got six hundred and forty acres each—"

"And what's left over is parceled out to the open market," Vito said shrewdly. "That's a lot of undeveloped land for sale. Not to mention mineral leases."

"Whatever," Sandy said, warming to his own pet hopes. "But the time of the reservations is over. Even the Indians know that. They'll secretly be relieved. They can all get their own ranches or farms and live free of tribal politics. I, for one, look forward to it." Sandy Youngblood was the president of one national Indian organization committed to the preservation of the reservations, and a member of numerous other responsible groups. He was a Southern Ute, from Colorado. He already had his eye on a mountainside resort development for his ex-reservation.

"It'll be for the best," Tom said. "The crime and drugs have become epidemic. We can't have inviolable jurisdiction in the midst of our country, fomenting revolution. We know there are stockpiles of weapons."

"Just be fair, Tom," Sandy said. "Not everybody's a revolutionary."

Tom and Sandy laughed. Vito grinned at them. Little did they know what fools they were, he thought. He saw Lester and the girl come in, and he winced, because they were in jeans and serapes. He stood and motioned them over. They all stood, introductions were made, they sat, drinks and dinner were ordered.

The Trojan Restaurant is part of the Greenwood Plaza in northern Dallas. It is in the entertainment district of town. Elegant restaurants with excellent food dot the cobblestoned streets. Gas lamps light the way for merry pedestrians toward the exotic discos, the chic nightclubs, the ice-cream shops, the movie theaters, and all the clothing and jewelry and antique and gimmick stores without which any American mall is not complete. The Scarlatti Trucking Company owned preferred and common stock amounting to fifty-five percent of the total capital investment.

"How was your flight, Mr. Mardewcki?" Tom asked. Tom had been introduced as one of Vito's lawyers. Sandy was introduced for who he was. Rabbit had given him a dirty look, but no one noticed.

"Good," Les replied. "Flying is the only way to go." He was nervous. He didn't like being forced into this. It was none of his business, what happened to Bonnie What's-her-name. But Rabbit had made herself an indispensable part of his operation and she had been adamant about this thing. For a moment he wished he were back on the road, a happy-go-lucky hitchhiker. But one drug led to another dollar, and here he was with these creeps. Oh, Vito was okay, he didn't ever interfere, as long as he got his cut and an audit every month, but he wasn't exactly the kind of guy you made friends with.

Rabbit sipped her soup as the others chitchatted about airplanes and cars and the Trojan decor of the restaurant. She was the only woman at the table. It gave her a feeling of arrogance. She knew she had good tits, but her face prevented any danger of having to fight off these hotshots. To them a beautiful woman was a beautiful face. A body was needed, too, but they could overlook skinniness or plumpness in lieu of long lashes and helpless lips. Rabbit wasn't plain, and she wasn't without shapeliness, but she knew as sure as road apples she wasn't *their* type.

So she relaxed with her salad and puzzled over the flight. They had not spoken two words after Doris dropped them off at the tiny municipal airfield at Jollyville. Lester had seemed to drift into thoughts opposite from Rabbit's. He looked straight ahead, as if avoiding the black presence of the earth below. She had stared down at it for some sense of relief. Every house light or car light below lit up the blank expanse for an instant, and she grasped desperately for each glimpse.

"Well, Rabbit," Vito said with a deprecating smirk, "tell us about your friend."

They all looked at her, eating their dinners hungrily, as it was almost eleven o'clock. The dinners made them all feel more cordial toward each other.

"She got busted," Rabbit said simply. "She needs twenty thousand bail. We'll pay you back when she shows up for her indictment and trial."

"Why should we trust her to do that?" Tom, the lawyer, interrogated. "She was working for the Parellis."

"That's what I said," Lester added.

"Don't jive me!" Rabbit said loudly, and stood up to leave. "I don't need you guys! You talk about trust?" She spat the word, looking directly at Sandy, and started to leave.

"Sit down, young lady," Vito calmly commanded from his seat. The quiet authority in his voice did more to stop her than the clumsy attempts of the others: Les had grabbed her, Tom had scooted his chair back noisily, and Sandy had stared angrily.

"Why should I?"

"Because you'll get your money. I apologize for the devious ways of the legal profession." Vito continued eating his artichoke veal without looking at her. She returned and sat. The others took up their forks, and the rest of the restaurant calmed down as well.

"But I have a request," Vito began. Rabbit was way ahead of him.

"Crack the drug traffic from Colombia?"

Vito looked at her, impressed. "Yes."

"No problem."

"I see why Lester wishes to keep you happy," Vito said, finishing his veal. "It is the sign of good management." He patted Lester once on the back. "Tom will have a cashier's check for twenty thousand at the Austin bank on Monday morning, made out to the city of Santa Fe." He stood up. "Gentlemen, and lady, will you excuse Mr. Washington and me? Order anything else you would like, but I must see that my well-rounded personality"—and he jovially patted his slightly paunchy stomach—"doesn't get out of control with dessert. The chocolate mousse is particularly excellent. It has been a long day for a Saturday."

The others all stood and said how pleased they were to meet each other. Sandy left as well, for his wife and kids in the suburb of Garland. Rabbit and Lester had two desserts each, wrote a fat tip for the waiter on Vito's tab, and went next door to a disco to celebrate.

"That girl is too smart for her own good," Vito said to Agent Washington as his black limo pulled out into the street. "I want her busted when this thing is over."

"Sure, Mr. Scarlatti. We have to show a quota."

"And another thing," Vito said, reclining luxuriously in the velour backseat of the Caddy. The chauffeur and bodyguard in the front seat could not hear them. "I want Saturdays off from now on. This conspiracy racket is tiring."

"Sure, Mr. Scarlatti," said Tom pleasantly, and they both laughed. The black Cadillac limousine whinnied sweetly down the endless asphalt track away into the night.

The prairie waited.

 **CHAPTER 8**

How a Powwow in South Dakota
Brought New Warriors into the Quest

MEANWHILE, BACK IN South Dakota, Buddy couldn't figure out where in the hell he was. He looked out at the strange parking lot and assumed they were at least in Colorado. The mountains around there didn't look right, they were too small, but where else could it be? It was where they were supposed to be, so he assumed they were somewhere north of Fort Collins, Colorado, and that Philbert had stopped for a leak or a candy bar and they would be moving again shortly. So he turned over and went back to sleep. It was the best way to pass the endless hours on the endless prairie.

He awoke again several hours later and looked out the window to see where they were not. He vaguely remembered having stopped somewhere else before and wondered why they kept stopping. It took his brain a few more minutes to remember where he was going and who he was with and all the events of the past twenty-four hours. He grinned contentedly at the recollection of pleasant embarrassments and opened his door to take a leak. He was halfway through his pee, watching the urine splash on the black asphalt, when his sun-dazed eyes became aware of another car tire next to his puddle.

"Hey"—another voice arose out of the aroused awareness of his returning consciousness—"You born in a barn?"

Buddy looked up from his puddle, squinting in the midday light. He kept peeing. It was an endless whiz, built up after many hours. "What?" he said to the voice.

"You're peeing on my tire," the voice said, amused.

Indeed, Buddy's puddle had grown into a lake and overflowed onto the big snow tire. Buddy saw it was attached to a pickup. The pickup was attached to three grinning Indians looking at him. As he kept peeing, he looked around to see where he was. Half a dozen cars and pickups were hitched in the corral, but no people seemed to be peering out of them.

"Must be in Denver, huh?" Buddy said. "Anyway . . ."

"Denver?" the Indian voice repeated.

"Yeah," Buddy replied. "Jesus, it's kinda cold," he said, shaking his wang of its last drops and returning it to its nest. "Looks like a purty nice day, though."

"You actually drive that thing?" another Indian said inside the pickup cab, pointing to Protector. They all laughed. They were in a pretty nice Ford Ranger XLT, only about six or seven years old.

"No, he just shakes it." A female voice laughed, indicating Buddy's retreated wang.

"Shake it, baby." Buddy laughed, alert to the female presence. He leaned in the window of the pickup cab. Two pock-faced fellas of about twenty with straw cowboy hats grinned at him, and a rowdy woman of about forty-five sat between them with her arms around them. She was Indian, too, looking more than just a little frowsy.

"Excuse me, ma'am," Buddy said, "I hope I didn't embarrass you."

"Embarrass me?" And she laughed boisterously. Her voice had a whiskey raspiness full of a life of hard luck. "You might've embarrassed these shorthorns, but not me, for chrissake!" and she reached over and cuffed Buddy on the chin.

"What tribe y'all?" Buddy asked.

"Blackfeet," the driver replied softly. It was obvious he was intimidated by this floozy his pal was pawing. The floozy stuck her hand in the pal's jeans and laughed in his ear. They had obviously been on a three-day toot and had gotten a little tired of propriety. The driver ignored them and put on his sunglasses.

"You?" the fella asked.

"Cheyenne."

"Yeah? Well . . . we're goin' over to Pine Ridge. There's a Christmas powwow. You goin'?"

"Pine Ridge?" Buddy repeated, incredulous. "That a helluva long way from here."

"Not so far."

"I bet there's a powwow at the whatchamacallit," Buddy said, trying to think. "The White Buffalo Council. I been to powwows there before."

"That's in Denver," the fella said, his voice taking on a little of the puzzlement that was in Buddy's voice. "You'd never get there in time tonight."

"I don't know," Buddy said, "just where the hell are we? These mountains don't look much like . . . Did I sleep through Denver? Hell, I bet we're close to Pueblo. What is this, a rest area?"

The fella looked at him closely. "I think you slept through the last month. I always heard Cheyenne was—"

"Down around Pueblo, the mountains get far off like this," Buddy said, squinting at the hills. "The road goes straight south, but the Rockies back off southwest. It makes 'em look smaller far away. I been on this road before."

"I think you been on acid, pardner," the Blackfoot said. "Them're the Black Hills."

"What? That's crazy. We're in Colorado."

"You're in Disneyland, chief," the woman said, and laughed. They all grinned broadly at him. "I've done lots of goofy things before," she said, "but I usually knew at least what state I was in."

"Yeah," the other fella said, "a drunken state." They erupted in laughter and fell all over each other.

"I ain't crazy," Buddy said.

"Go look at them license plates," the driver said as he stuck a wad of Copenhagen chewing tobacco under his lip.

"I will," Buddy said, and stumbled out into the middle of the parking lot. He surveyed the license plates of the six vehicles. One of the pickups said Montana, three Ranger pickups said South Dakota, and a station wagon said Wyoming. Protector didn't have any plates. Buddy turned to read the letters on the wall of the small building in one corner of the parking lot:

VISITORS' CENTER
BEAR BUTTE STATE PARK
SOUTH DAKOTA

"South fucking Dakota?" Buddy muttered, incredulous. He turned around in a circle, looking from the cars to the building to the little hill in front of him and back to the cars.

"South fucking Dakota?"

"Hey, Cheyenne," the woman's voice yelled, "you doin' a dance?"

"What?"

"C'mere," she yelled, "we got something to put you back together."

Buddy walked back over to the pickup. "I think I need a new mother to put me back together," he said.

"Smoke this," she said, handing him a lit joint through the window.

"*Yaaa-ha-ha-ha-hoooooooo!*" suddenly echoed out of the Mountain, and the four Indians froze. Buddy flipped the joint out of his hand unconsciously, and it disappeared.

"What's that?" the woman dared to whisper.

"I don't know," Buddy dared back.

"What happened to the joint?" the other fella asked.

"I don't know," Buddy whispered, thoroughly spooked.

"It's somebody up there," the fella with the sunglasses and the Copenhagen teeth said.

"I don't know what it is," Buddy said.

They looked up the steep southeastern face of Bear Butte, off to their left. A ranger in a green suit came out of the building and looked up the slope. A tourist family of four appeared off to the right, from the gentle ridge where they had been hiking on the trail. They looked up the slope.

A small rockslide began to roll down the slope. Boulders on the steep face were jarred loose by some frenzied animal that was bounding down the slope. It looked a little like a rabbit from far away. Perhaps it was a marmot or a small dog. No, it was getting bigger as it came leaping down the slope, out of control. Perhaps it was a deer, a cow, or a horse.

"*Ya-ha-ha-ha-hoooooooooooo!*" it yelled.

"Hey, you!" the Ranger yelled. The rocks rolled. Bushes were crushed. Dust rose in great clouds. Stones leapt through the air as if trying to take flight. The whole front of the hill seemed about to come loose and roll like lava over the Visitors' Center and the parking lot. And still the figures ran, and leapt, and jolted the slope loose.

"Ohmigod, it's Philbert," Buddy whispered. "No, it couldn't be . . . but it is . . . no . . . Jesus, yes . . . no . . ."

Philbert eased back on his reins when he hit the more level slope at the bottom of the Lady and slid maniacally into a sitting position as gravel and boulders cascaded all about him. He was gasping with utter exhaustion and happiness. He skinned his elbow as he sat from his dead run into gravity's lap. The Mountain threatened to break off in one murderous chunk, and the people in the parking lot below cowered expectantly, but Philbert just sat and gasped and was ready to accept whatever decision the Mountain made.

The stones and gravel shifted, one rock rested precariously on another, thousands of rocks waited to establish balance on thousands of other rocks, and they eased into uneasy inertia. The Mountain stopped moving. But it made it clear that it would annihilate the next trespasser. So much as one more ounce of foreign mass, one more decibel of intrusive sound, and it would devastate all life within five miles.

Everyone knew this. No one moved or made a sound. The Mountain slowly settled. The dust gradually came to rest in fine powder on the rocks. Like a city united in all its many million parts, nothing moved in a crisis unless everything was to die. Every plane and angle found a corresponding plane and angle to rest up against. With everything back in uneasy order, Philbert stood up and brushed himself off.

"Hey, you!" the Ranger yelled, coming up toward him. The Ranger was an ecologist. He knew when danger was imminent, and when the danger had passed.

"Yeah?" Philbert said, loping down toward the Ranger. He felt as if he were moving like an antelope.

"What's the idea of charging down that slope like a rhinoceros?" the Ranger angrily demanded. They came up to within a few feet of each other and stopped. Philbert smirked sheepishly. The Ranger could have killed him.

"I guess I did knock loose a few rocks."

"You guess you—" The Ranger was livid. He was rabid. How dare anyone abuse his mountain! She was his! "How dare you— What were you doing up there, anyway—" He kept interrupting himself, he was so incoherently jealous. "You can't just—what if—there are certain rules to—if I had known—" It was hopeless. His private romance had long ago been spoiled by tourists and imperfect women.

"Get out of this park!" the Ranger ordered.

"I—"

"Out!"

Philbert left him to his misery. He walked on down to the

parking lot, where Buddy stood with some people. He smiled as he came up to them.

"Hi," he said. "I decided to come down the shortcut."

They stared at him. He didn't know that he looked like a bear that had rolled in the mud and snow and then covered himself with a fine brown icing of dust. His lips and eyebrows were muddy smears on a dusty face. The white of his eyes shone spookily through the muck. His hat was crushed beyond hope of ever regaining any shape.

"What the hell are you doin'?" Buddy asked.

"Nothin'," Philbert replied truthfully.

"You know this thing?" the floozy asked.

"No," said Buddy.

"Hi," Philbert said to the others, "where you guys from?"

Buddy suddenly grabbed Philbert by his filthy denim parka. "Where the hell are we, Philbert? What in the goddamn hell are—"

But Philbert grabbed Buddy by his arms and lifted him off the ground. Buddy was a tough, lanky guy, but he was no match for giant Philbert when his ire was incited. Unfortunately for Buddy, nobody had ever seen Philbert's ire incited. He had never even known he had ire before, was why.

"Nobody grabs me no more," Philbert said simply. He kept Buddy up in the air, where he was dangling helplessly. "Nobody grabs me no more."

"Sure," said Buddy.

Philbert let him down. "We're in South Dakota, Buddy, and that is Noahvose," he added, pointing to the Mountain.

"Sure," said Buddy, uncertain what Noahvose was. Buddy was not as versed as Philbert in the tribal legends or language, nor could he figure out why the hell they were in South Dakota when they were going to New Mexico.

Philbert read his face. "We are gathering power, Buddy, as you said."

"Oh, okay." Buddy couldn't remember ever saying that.

Philbert turned to the three Blackfeet partiers in their pickup. A cloud passed over the sun and immediately dropped the temperature ten degrees, making it about twenty.

Philbert explained himself. "We are making with a raiding party to New Mexico to rescue a maiden from the savages. Wanna come?"

"Naw," the driver replied, "we gotta get to the powwow in Pine Ridge." He started up his engine.

"A powwow in Pine Ridge?"

"Yeah."

"When?"

"Tonight," the driver explained.

"Yeah?"

"Yeah."

"Maybe we'll go too," Philbert said.

"See ya there," the driver said.

"If that old nag makes it," the other fella in the truck said.

"Don't let yer shorts ride up," the woman hollered after him, and they backed up and drove off.

"Bye," Philbert said, and turned back to Buddy. "Nice folks."

"Blackfeet."

"I thought so," Philbert said. "Or Flathead, anyway. Well, I guess we better get goin', huh?"

"Yeah, sure."

It was not intimidation that made Buddy suddenly so docile. Nobody had ever intimidated Buddy and nobody ever would. He was groggy from sleeping all morning in the car, that was all, he told himself. It was all too weird to deal with, that was all.

They got back in the car and drove off. Philbert went slowly, looking back at the Mountain frequently. Even when they stopped in Sturgis at a drive-in for a sack of grease, he kept his eyes on the hill. He savored it. When he reached in his pocket to pay for the burgers and fries, he found a small rock. It had rolled into his pocket in the landslide. It was a sign from the Powers. That little hidden rock would be the first medicine sign for his own warrior's bundle. Three more sacred objects and he would be a warrior, protected from all mortal harm. He hid his excitement and looked at Buddy to see if he noticed anything. Buddy had a slightly sick look on his face, but otherwise he didn't seem to have noticed Philbert's newfound aura of power.

They pulled back out onto Interstate 90, heading southeast toward Rapid City and Pine Ridge. The road followed the front range of the Black Hills, on their right, on the west. To their left was the prairie. They chomped on their grease and slurped from their large root beers.

"You climbed that hill, eh?" Buddy said casually. Only a slight quaver in his voice betrayed his inexplicable trepidation.

"Yep," Philbert said, smacking his lips.

"And, uh . . . we're goin' to a powwow at Pine Ridge?"

Philbert nodded.

"Philbert," Buddy said apologetically, "we gotta get to Santa Fe."

"I know," Philbert said. "I had a vision. This is the best way."

Buddy put on the radio to an FM rock station in Rapid City and looked out the window. *Jesus Christ,* he was thinking, and his thoughts assumed the sophistication of this objective narrative: *That sucker lifted me off the ground!* Philbert the Weird was not all blubber with jelly beans for brains like everybody had always thought. Well, the jelly beans were probably right, and he *was* mostly blubber, but to them the jelly beans and blubber had some other more substantial ingredient. Maybe there was some muscle there. Nobody had ever gotten the jump on Buddy before, but nobody! And this guy, this laughingstock of the tribe, this lowest of the low, this most certifiable loser of Lame Deer, had flat cold-cocked the psyche of number-one Macho Warrior and spooked him out of his shorts! How? Why? What?

Crackers had always been Philbert's nickname. He always got the worst grades at the Mission School. He couldn't grasp math, the catechism, literature, civics, or gym. He always got straight Fs. Once he got a D in English because he loved poetry, but technically he never even passed the first grade. They would have sent him to the School for Mentally Handicapped except that his mother wouldn't let them. She knew he wasn't a retard, and so did everybody else, really. It wasn't that he was retarded, he wasn't a spastic or a CP or an MD or even a special-ed case. He was stupid, that was all. He had crackers and cheese for a cerebrum. He could count and read and talk, he just couldn't get out of the bottom of life.

Crackers sat off alone all the time too. Before his mother died, she would sit off with him. Buddy never paid much attention to them; he didn't remember much except that she choked on a piece of lettuce at a church supper and croaked on the table in everybody's salad and spaghetti. It had been a great, amusing joke among the kids then. He must've been ten or twelve. He didn't know who Philbert's old man was. He thought he had been passed around to uncles and aunts, but he wasn't sure. The kids used to chase Crackers around and ask if he had slept in barns and badger holes. They couldn't help it. It was impossible not to tease the moronic slob. He was a total pig. That was a fact.

But . . .

Buddy gazed out the window. They were coming into Rapid City, the biggest town in western South Dakota, and it had about as many people as a city block in New York.

"Wanna stop at Kitty's for a beer?" Buddy asked.

"Sure," Philbert replied.

Buddy took a double take when he looked at Philbert. His face had a cherubic bliss upon it. Crackers was out on an adventure with the star of the tribe, and he was already the Terror of Sheridan, the Ya-ha-ha-hooo of Bear Butte. God, how could it be?

And, rapt listener beside the campfire, how could such branding iron–hot insights come from these two very different schmucks? Crackers grasping the prescient truths of Sweet

Medicine at a single bound up a volcano? And the Red Bird improvisationally going along with it? It must be a trick of sorcery, a storyteller making it up. It must be. It couldn't be accurate. Nobody could *think* such thoughts of beatitudinous perception and *do* such idiotic things.

Protector skidded harmlessly into the curb in downtown Rapid and stopped up on the sidewalk against a parking meter. Philbert and Buddy got out and went over to Harry's Place, which Kitty Wells owned. No one knew who Harry was, or why Kitty's place was called Harry's Place. Except maybe Kitty. It was just another sleazy Indian bar. Nobody cared what it was called.

"Howdy, Bud," an Indian called from the street corner. "What's happenin'?"

"Hiya, W. T.," Buddy said, and waved. He and Philbert went in Kitty's Harry's. It was full of Indians of every complexion and consciousness, and some white people. There are only a million Indians in the United States, so of course they all know each other. They've all been down the powwow highway at one time or another. They all have a friendly word for each other, and Philbert and Buddy are no exception.

"Look what the cat dragged in."

"Did a horseshit truck just drive by?"

"Howdy, Marilou."

"Hiya, Buddy."

"Well, goddamn if it ain't Geronimo himself."

"How ya doin'?"

"What's happenin'?"

"Get a brew, bro."

"Been here a long time, ain't nobody bought us a drink."

"Get the hose, we gotta wash down some Skins."

"Whoo-whoo-whoo-whoo!"

"Kitty, you 'member Philbert?"

"Sure I do."

"We'll have two short ones."

"I'll say!"

"Now, Selma, mind yer manners."

"You heard the one about the robin that flew south too late?"

"No, but I'll bet I'm about to."

"It seems he was crossin' South Dakota and hit a snowstorm. He got ice on his wings and crashed into a barn, landing square into a pile of fresh cow shit. It broke his fall and saved his life. It was also very warm and kept him from freezin'. So he figured he'd stay there fer the winter. He was so goddamn happy, in fact, that he started to sing. Well, a cat in the barn heard the song and come to investigate. He couldn't figure out how a pile of cowshit could be singin', so he stuck his paw into the pile, pulled out the robin, and ate him. Now, there's three morals to this story."

"Hey, horseface, how's it goin'?"

"What's happenin', snag killer?"

"Eeee, my main snag is here."

"*Hau, kola.*"

"The first moral is that it ain't always bad to be up to yer eyeballs in shit."

"Hey, Big Tom, long time no see."

"The second moral is that not ever'body who pulls ya out of the shit is always yer friend."

"How 'bout a dance, Lucille?"

"Shove off, pimple face."

"The third moral is to keep your mouth shut when ya got a good thing goin'."

"*Ha-ha-ha-ha!*"

"Goddamn!"

"Shit!"

"*Ha-ha-ha-ha!*"

"Well, see ya later."

"Take it easy, bros."

"Or any other way ya can get it."

"*Wasteyelo.*"

"Yep.

They gassed up at the Conoco station, bought a case of Schlitz, and headed straight south on State Road 79. It was getting to be late afternoon as they drove along the front edge of Paha Sapa, the sleepy hills of the Sioux. Somewhere back in there, the immigrants gawked at Mount Rushmore, another of the whiteman's ever-amazing conquests of Nature. Somewhere back in there was Custer State Park, and Custer National Forest, and the town of Custer. Somewhere back in there, lots of people were making lots of money selling the myth of the land. It made Buddy and Philbert too sick even to think about. They drank their beer and drove on to the Pine Ridge Reservation of the Oglala Lakota.

They didn't have to think of the sacred history of the Black Hills, or of the buffalo herds, or of the countless fastings and feastings their people had enjoyed over the millennia. It was not something they had to think about to know about.

Dusk hit the village of Pine Ridge at about the same time it hit Lame Deer and Mission and Fort Yates and New Town and Timber Lake and all the other reservation villages in the west. Perhaps it had been a hundred years ago that the Ephemeral Dusk had come here, and perhaps it was only this one evening as Protector clattered into the cluttered sprawl of Pine Ridge. And perhaps it didn't matter.

Depression hung upon every rusty animal that lay gutted beside the road that led into the village. A muddy sunset lay its gray pallor over the gray and miserable town. Dogs didn't care where they were going—they just loped slowly along in aimless indifference. Misery had achieved its ultimate consummation here. Sorrow and tragedy were open wounds on the very hillsides of Pine Ridge. Utter despair was a festering shriek in the slimy trickle of White Clay Creek, which could hardly be said to "run" through the garbage that was Pine Ridge. To call the agency headquarters of the descendants of Crazy Horse and Red Cloud a spiritual pigsty would be a kindness.

But it didn't matter, either. The "bros" of the Sioux Nation fought off defeat and despair with the best weapon any nation had ever had for fighting off Defeat and Despair—they laughed in its face. Failure was a fucking joke! Fuck depression, they weren't gonna let stupidity and foolishness get them down!

Ah, bitter Comedy, raise thy ugly head! Buck at thy black rider, humorous bronco! Despair, thou art a tenderfoot on the back of the Burlesque Devil!

Tote that barge, shatter them myths, it's the only way out of slavery, brother!

It's the only way left.

Protector rolled into town, looking for the party.

Philbert kept putting his hand in his pocket, holding his rock.

Buddy felt terrible that he had fallen so low as to be in such company.

Oh, brother, lead me to the laughs, I can't last much longer.

I'm fadin' . . .

I'm fadin' . . .

I'm fadin' . . .

away

Practical considerations had to be made first.

"We're low on dope, Philbert," Buddy said. A furtive glance from the cherub bespoke more than a thousand photographs. "Let's go by Luther's."

They turned right, down a tree-lined residential boulevard—three diseased cottonwoods and a two-block row of identical cracker boxes, that is. They went past a very nice house. It had hedges and a paved driveway and two goons guarding the front door. It was the home of Bull Miller, the tribal president.

Protector clattered slowly by, its one walleyed headlight winking at the goons. They glared, alert to a possible commando raid. Inside their parkas, they put their hands on the .41 Magnums the government had issued them.

But Protector went on. He went on past this, the most fashionable part of town. He crossed a bumpy dirt road that goat-tracked out across alfalfa fields and gullies full of trash. Tar-paper cottages spewed haphazardly from the fields and gullies. It was flat countryside, pimpled by Indian estates. On the banks of these gray ridges and pastures had the human beings of the fiercest band of the Teton Dakota come to rest and to lick their Wounded Knees. Dusk had become the oppressive twilight of a race.

The boys knew where they were going. Buddy had to give only a few directions. Like all the refugees of the Powwow Highway, they had friends on just about every reservation in the country. They had been to parties and fights and romantic rendezvous on just about every reservation in the country. It was a network of such haphazard and chaotic symmetry that the FBI spent millions of dollars a year worrying about it. It had a tremendous potential as the next pattern for revolutionary fomentation. The FBI was pulling out its bureaucratic hairs. It bugged wine parties; it surveilled beer softball games; it wrote expensive reports on drug transactions behind chicken coops.

And Pine Ridge was the nexus of this aboriginal network. The siege of Wounded Knee had taken place only a few miles away. FBI men had almost been *killed* here. Two of them *had* been killed at Oglala, also a few miles away. Political hoodlumism was rampant. Storehouses of bazookas were found. Letters from Marxist sympathizers were uncovered. Overtures from Arab potentates to their tribal brothers were a part of the daily communications in this hellhole of anarchy!

Protector pulled up in front of a house. Well, it should more accurately be described as a wad of weeds and muddy heaps of dirt surrounding a roof and walls. A tipi had more room than the tiny shack they sat in front of. It was dreary. It was dismal. It was foreign. It scared the hell out of the FBI; they imagined it was how the Russians would have wanted everyone to live if those atheistic Mongols conquered North America tomorrow.

Philbert and Buddy got out and stretched. The gray twilight lingered and lingered. Buddy idly wondered if it was ever going to get dark.

"Who's there?" a voice challenged from inside the house. The two musketeers turned. A rifle stuck out of the window. A cold fear huddled inside the shack.

"Buddy Red Bird from Lame Deer. And Philbert." He was cool under fire, Buddy was.

"Well, I'll be horsewhipped!" the voice declared.

A very short man with very long black hair came out onto the "porch." He held the 30.06 at his side. "I almost blew yer brains away," the man said. "But they wouldn't have made much of a splatter."

Buddy walked up to the man and gave him a great, gentle bear hug. For some idiotic reason his eyes were moist and his voice tender. "Hiya, Luther." And they hugged each other fiercely and tenderly for a very long moment. "Things kind of nervous around here still?"

"Yeah," Luther said. He broke the hug and took a step back. He tried to examine the Cheyenne critically, but he couldn't, and he dropped his head. "Come on in the house." And he quickly went back in.

Buddy waved at Philbert, who stood by Protector, taking in the scene. "Bring the beer, willya, Philbert?" It was not a command and Philbert felt somehow honored to do that one simple little service. Buddy went in the house. Philbert easily hoisted the remaining two six-packs of Schlitz in their case and followed Buddy into the house.

"Wolf Tooth's here too," he heard Luther explaining to Buddy. "No shit?"

The room was dark, uncluttered of unnecessary furniture, bursting to the seams with people, sitting and standing.

"Everyone," Buddy said, "this is Philbert, my good buddy."

Philbert felt a thrill of friendship at Buddy's genuine tone. "That beautiful woman over there is Linda, Luther's lady."

"Hi." A short, petite woman of about thirty waved from a chair.

"Well, hell, I ain't even met Philbert, have I?" Luther asked.

"No," Philbert said.

They shook hands, thumbs up, revolutionary style.

"You weren't at Wounded Knee, were you? Or Oglala?"

"No," Philbert said, "but I remember hearing about it. I've always admired Leonard Peltier."

Buddy added, "He's a great warrior."

Everyone shuffled.

"That's Curly and Alvin and John, Luther and Linda's kids," Buddy continued. On the floor, three boys in underwear and dirty corduroy shirts ignored the adults.

"Sit down," Linda said. Buddy grabbed a six-pack and handed it to her. Philbert sat on a coffee table.

Another person came running into the shadowy room. "Buddy!"

"Imogene!"

They clasped clumsily and he swung her off her feet. "Oh, Buddy, Buddy, Buddy! Oliver will be so glad to see you!"

"Where is he?"

"Went down to the bus station. Be back in a minute. God, you look terrible."

"I feel okay."

"Shit," the woman named Imogene said. "When you gonna get married?"

"When there's a woman invented who doesn't feel she has to give me shit."

"If men could get pregnant," Linda said cheerfully from her chair, "abortion would be a sacrament."

"What outhouse wall d'you read that on?" Buddy asked. He knelt beside her and put his arm around her. Imogene knelt, too, and put her arm around Buddy. Linda popped open the beers and gave them each one.

"Tribal president's office."

They roared with laughter. Philbert roared, too, even though he didn't get the joke.

"Miller still got the Gestapo running loose?" Buddy asked of no one in particular.

"Yep," Luther replied. He sat on the floor across from them, rolling joints.

"Faggots, that's all they are," Linda said, and spat on the floor. The others laughed. "Caught one of Miller's goons over at Porcupine wearing panty hose."

"Oh, bullshit," Buddy said.

"It's the truth," Linda retorted. "*Oglala sari oglala!*" she cursed in Lakota. They all laughed again. The good cheer was a beautiful thing.

"Goodness gracious," Imogene said, gasping. "Who's King Kong?"

"Philbert, ma'am," Philbert said.

"Oh, I'm sorry, I forgot," Buddy remembered, taking a joint from Luther. "This is Philbert, Imogene. Imogene is Wolf Tooth's old lady."

"Hello," Imogene said politely. "That's Marie in the doorway."

A tall, thin girl of nine stood in the kitchen door, silhouetted by the gray twilight coming in through the small windows behind her.

"Mom," she said, "I can't find my green dress."

"Look in the second drawer, honey."

"I did."

"Look again," Imogene gently reproached. The girl turned away and left the doorway.

"What're you guys doin', staying here?" Buddy asked Imogene. She passed the joint to Philbert without smoking it.

"We're moving to Denver, Buddy," Imogene explained.

"What?"

"They've been here a couple of days, Buddy," Luther said, taking the joint from Philbert. "The pigs broke into Wolf Tooth's machine shop a couple of days ago. Wrecked everything. Wolf's been raisin' hell at the council meetings, you know, never knows when to keep his mouth shut."

"Good for him," Buddy said angrily.

"Good for you, maybe," Imogene said. "I can't take it anymore. We're getting out of here. There's a shooting a week."

"Tommy Yellow Nose got killed three days ago," Luther said, passing the joint to Linda.

"We're getting out of here," Imogene repeated.

"I don't blame you a bit," Linda added. "I wish to hell we would too."

"No way," Luther said. The three boys on the floor looked from one parent to another.

"Tommy Yellow Nose? Goddammit! Goddammit!" Buddy exploded, and threw his empty beer can against the wall. "The pigs?"

"Miller's goons."

Silence and bad cheer wedged its way back into the retreating interlude of friendship. Another joint was lit and circulated. Beer cans popped open. Even the boys on the floor colored silently in a Flintstones coloring book. One lamp was turned on.

"We're going to Denver," a soft voice interrupted through the gloom. "You can come with us, if you want."

They all looked at Philbert. He took the joint from Linda, fashioned a roach clip from the flip-top of her beer can, and began snorting in great wafts of smoke from the weed. The boys on the floor watched him raptly. He snorted louder and they giggled. He swallowed the burning roach. He said in a deep bass voice, "Great buffalo bull, *snort, snort!*"

Smiles from the adults.

Philbert got down on his hands and knees on the floor and

reared his head up and down. "Grandfather buffalo has an itchy back. A candy bar is in his pocket for the calf who scratches his back."

The three boys piled on top of Philbert, scratching his back furiously. They were as gnats on a dinosaur.

"You're tickling, you're tickling." He started to laugh, rolling over. The boys tickled him and they all four shrieked with laughter. He grabbed them and tickled them. Marie came into the room, in exquisite torment to keep from joining the melee on the floor.

"Ah, young cow must scratch too," Philbert bellowed from the floor. He crawled over to her, with the three boys clinging to his arms and legs like cockleburs. He grabbed her and tickled her and she shrieked with laughter trying to get away. They all five tumbled into the kitchen.

The adults hooted with delight.

"What the hell!" Linda declared, and went and jumped into the pile. One of the boys got the candy bar out of Philbert's dirty coat pocket. Another boy grabbed it. Marie grabbed it from him. Philbert grabbed it from her. They all fought over the Milky Way and it got torn, smeared, and demolished in the fight.

"What in the hell is going on?" a new figure declared from the front door.

"Only a couple of Cheyenne come to give the Lakota a hard time." Buddy laughed, standing up. The candy-bar wrestlers on the floor lay in a sprawl, exhausted and giggling.

"Buddy."

"Wolfie."

They hugged. Oliver Wolf Tooth had very short hair and conservative clothes. Imogene was a conservative woman. But he and Buddy had an unshakable bond that neither fashions nor economics nor the vagaries of social upheaval could ever rend asunder.

They didn't know what to say to each other. There was so much to say that none of it could be said. So they stood an arm's length apart, their hands on each other's shoulders, and grimaced meaningfully. Their careworn faces spoke of everything between them.

"So," Wolf Tooth said, "what're you doin' here?"

"Just passin' through," Buddy explained. "Me and Philbert are goin' to Santa Fe, by way of Denver. You might as well come with us. That's Philbert."

Wolf Tooth waved at him. "What's happenin'?"

"We also need to score some dope," Buddy continued. "Luther, you got any for sale?"

"Couple of bags, sure," Luther responded.

"Full price, too, man."

Luther got up and went out the front door.

"We've already got bus tickets, Buddy," Imogene said, then she looked at Philbert, around whom the kids clustered as if for warmth. "Thanks, anyway."

"Shit, Imogene," Wolf Tooth said, interceding. His voice betrayed some excitement. "That bus trip is a pisser. We have to go to Rapid City and then Casper, where there's a three-hour layover. It's an eighteen-hour trip."

"Yes, honey, but—"

"You guys goin' straight through to Denver?" Wolf Tooth asked.

"Straight," said Buddy.

"After that powwow," Philbert added from the floor.

"Sure, that'd be perfect," Wolf Tooth said.

"But you already got the tickets," Imogene argued. It was clear she was reticent about the whole thing.

"I'll cash 'em in," Wolf Tooth said. "Is that your car out there?" he asked Buddy.

"Mine," Philbert said.

Luther came back in. The screen door clanged shut. He closed the other door. He gave Buddy two plastic bags full of brown grass. "Ditch weed," he explained. "Fifty dollars each for you."

"Yeah, we came into some money," Buddy said, handing him five twenty-dollar bills from his thick billfold. He knew that the money would be spent for food, and that Linda was silently attentive to the transaction. The three boys had the wide eyes and bloated stomachs of hungry children. "Now let's all go to the Burger Baron, treat's on me and Philbert. We'll catch up on news on the way. Then Philbert and me need to take a shower at the gym."

The powwow had been going on all afternoon. When Protector and Luther's pickup pulled up in the dark outside the high school gym, it was just about to get its second wind. The cars and trucks were lined up around the block. The A&G parking lot was full. A new moon, with a massive yellow ring around it, lit up the sky.

"It's going to snow," Luther said, looking up. The others were awkwardly getting out of their wagons. Linda had put a beaded barrette in her long black hair. A red satin shawl with fringe was folded neatly over her arm. Luther still had on his jeans, flannel shirt, cotton jacket, cowboy boots, and hat. The boys ran full blast into the gym. Their parents ignored them.

They waited in the road for the others. Buddy and Philbert were immaculate. They still had on jeans and boots and hats, but they were clean. Philbert's hair was still a little wet but he looked like a million bucks. They had taken a quick shower at the gym, ripped off towels and shampoo from a locker, and returned to the Buckhorn Estate to pick up Wolf Tooth and his family. Wolf Tooth had put on slacks, brogans, and a Choctaw squash-dance shirt. It was a bright yellow corduroy pullover with red silk stripes on the cuffs and across the heart. A Choctaw had given it to him at a powwow in Mississippi once. Imogene wore an elk-bone rosette around her neck. She carried a paisley shawl over her arm. Marie was in a red felt dress with leggings. Conch shells and porcupine quills decorated the dress. She ran into the gym to join her friends.

"Well, Saturday night in the big city," Buddy said. "Oh, hell," he suddenly remembered, "I forgot something." (Why is it when somebody remembers something they say they forgot it?)

The others waited in the road for him as he ran back to Protector. They could see him rummaging in the backseat for something. They chattered about the imminent storm.

Buddy came back. He had something around his neck.

"Whatchoo got there?" Linda asked.

It was an elk-bone necklace, but the rosette was made of three bronze medals welded together on a leather circle. Green Hudson's Bay Beads decorated the simple piece of jewelry. It hung halfway down his chest.

"I thought I'd put this goddamn tin to *some* use," Buddy explained rather sheepishly. He slapped Wolf Tooth on the back.

"It's beautiful, man," Philbert said.

"Let's get inside," Buddy responded unsentimentally. They walked slowly toward the gym doors, enjoying the night air and the prospect of a relaxed evening.

Kids from three to eighteen loitered around the doors. Light and noise increased as they approached the building. A goon watched them sullenly by the brick wall. He was smoking a cigarette.

"Hiya, Leroy," Wolf Tooth said. Leroy shot him the finger and Wolf laughed, enjoying the joke immensely.

They went inside.

BOOM-BOOM-BOOM-BOOM

The drums were booming out their steady cadence from the gym within. No one in the lobby seemed to be paying them any attention. People of all ages and dress chattered, or hurried to the bathroom, or stood in line at the concession stand for fry bread and Coke and coffee. A handmade sign by the booth said:

BUFFALO STEW $.75—WOJAPE $.30

Philbert loaded up on two bowls of stew and three helpings of pudding. Three short, fat women in white aprons dispensed the delectables from the booth. Several long tables were set up, and jewelry and leather goods sat on them for sale. A few stoic old women sat behind them, apparently indifferent to whether anybody bought any or not. Fluorescent light, cracked government paint, and a dirty tile floor completed the anything but extraordinary scene.

The Buckhorns—the Wolf Teeth, Red Bird, and Bono—went on through and into the main arena.

BOOM-BOOM-BOOM-BOOM

HIYE-YA-YA-YA-HI-HEY-HEYYA-HEYYA-HEY-YI!

Three large drums sat out in the middle of the basketball court. Two of them, in the middle and at the nearest end to our new arrivals, were encircled by folding metal chairs. No one sat on the chairs. No one beat the drums. Only at the drum on the far end did six men sit on the chairs and beat the drum with tomtoms. They were of all ages—well, from about twenty to fifty. Several wore cowboy hats. Several wore Caterpillar caps. The younger ones had long hair. The older ones had crew cuts. They had on their work clothes—jeans and cotton shirts from Penney's. Not a bead or a feather or a streak of war paint was in sight on the six men.

But they were singing, all of them, together. Some were wailing in a falsetto that sent chills down every spine. And they beat the drum in unison, fiercely, fast, and steadily. No syncopated rhythms here. The steady bass detonation counterpointed the monotonous songs of war and glory and buffalo hunts.

HIIIIIIIIIIIIIIII-HI-YA! HI-HIIIIIIIIIIIIIIII-YA-HI-HI!

The bleachers were packed. Most people sat and let the ancient sound zap them. Kids seemed oblivious to it, running importantly back and forth. Most folks were in their Western wear, but there were a few notable exceptions. A hawk-nosed man in full buckskins, feathers, and fearsome paint walked casually past them to get a cup of coffee. Half a dozen preteen boys jangled brilliantly from across the room—they were in full fancy dress regalia, with bells on their bare ankles, eagle rattles in their hands, and explosions of beads, paint, and coup sticks. Several wore glasses over it all. They all chomped on gum.

The drumming stopped abruptly. No dancers had joined in the last song.

From a dais in the middle of the far bleachers a genial man leaned up to a microphone on a table. Several other middle-aged men in crew cuts sat at the table. A beautiful middle-aged woman sat there, too, joking with them. She had on a light tawny doeskin dress, beaded blue leggings, and copper bracelets, and an enormous beaded rosette hung down between her breasts. One fluffy blue feather anchored her glistening ebony hair.

"That's the Coyote Singers from the Lower Brule Reservation, ladies and—wreeeeeeeeeeeeee!" The microphone shrieked, and everybody cringed. The genial old boy tapped it a few times and looked genially helpless until it stopped. "Let's give them a big hand, ladies and gentlemen," he said, and about half the people clapped semi-vigorously.

"GRrRAAAAAAAAAAAAAAAAAAaAaAaAaAaaaaaaaaaaaaakkK!" went the microphone again. "I guess I stepped on the wire, hee hee."

Everyone shook their heads genially. The Coyote Singers were wandering back to the bleachers. Another group of men was assembling around the drum in the middle. A gimpy teenager sat outside their inner circle, holding a large portable tape recorder.

"The Sunshine Yodelers will now do a social dance for us,"

the genial old boy announced, "so everybody get up there and dance."

BOOM-BOOM-BOOM-BOOM
YO-HOOOOOO-HO-HO-HEY-HI-YA-HI-YEEE-YAT-HO-HO-HO!

They were not just sounds, though, they were Lakota ballads. A few people got up to dance.

"Merry Christmas," an unpleasant voice said behind the Buckhorns—the Wolf Teeth, Red Bird, and Bono—who were still standing by the entrance, looking for a place to sit.

Buddy turned, and the others took their cue from him. A short, fat, pock-faced man stood behind them. He had the penetrating flair of worldly-wise intelligence and the fat cheeks of corruption. His hair was short. He had on too many turquoise rings, a too-loose ribbon shirt of the traditional Sioux, and carried too much trouble in his baggy middle-aged bearing. Four monstrous thugs stood alertly around him. They were crew-cut brutes, pure Indian. The short man in the middle had addressed Wolf Tooth.

"Big Chief," Wolf said in greeting.

"I hear you're leaving," the short man declared, rather than asked.

"Come on, Oliver," Imogene said, touching his arm, "I see some seats for us."

"That's right, Bull," Wolf muttered, clenching his teeth. "I want to thank you for destroying my shop."

"I didn't hear about that," Bull said. "What happened?"

"Your baboons stumbled over all my equipment. My tools were stolen, windows broken—"

"I don't like what you're saying," Bull said, bullying in. "I don't like what you're saying at all."

"Oliver, come on!" and Imogene forcibly pulled him away. Luther and Linda and Philbert started walking away too.

"Good to see you again, Mr. Miller," Buddy said. The others

turned back. The music continued, and a few dancers did the two-step, but most ears were on the conversation at the door. The ears couldn't hear the words, but they were attuned to the subtle shifts of weight from the lead actors, the slight changes of expression in their faces, the signals of communication.

"Do I know you?" Bull asked.

"Wounded Knee, March 1, 1973, behind the bunker, I kicked you in the balls," Buddy said, "but you didn't have any, so of course you wouldn't remember."

Two goons grabbed him faster than it took to think about it.

"Let's go have a talk, Red Bird," Bull hissed. "I heard you were coming."

"From where?"

"A little Rapid City voodoo, let's say. Move it!"

The goons were hustling Buddy to the door.

DANG-FHWOPP! *fhwop-fhwop-fhwop-fhwoppppp!*

Something struck the basketball backboard over their head. The music stopped. A hush settled over the gym. Bull looked up.

A huge Buck Knife was throbbing from the board where someone had thrown it. It was embedded two inches in the wood. Bull turned furiously to the crowd. All the faces were blank. Not one betrayed the identity of the assailant.

"Who threw that!" Bull roared. "That's a felony, and I'll find out who did it if I have to—"

"The next one might be lower," Buddy said, strangling in the grasp of the goons. "It might be just a little chickenshit of a scalp lock lower."

"Don't you threaten me, buster!"

"I'm not," Buddy said, gesturing to the crowd, "they are."

Bull turned back to the crowd.

AI-AIIIIIIIIIII-YI-YI-YI-YI-HOOOOOOOOOOOOOOOOOO!

The Sunshine Yodelers chanted. The drum beat again. Bull looked at them hatefully.

"Ain't it nice to be loved," Buddy said.

"Let him go," Bull ordered, a look of frustrated fear in his eyes. The goons shoved him away roughly.

"And you, you primordial fucks!" Buddy sneered at the goons. "Your days are numbered!"

"Get out of our town, Red Bird." Bull sneered right back. "You AIM sons of bitches have had it. You hear me, you're going to find yourself raped in prison, and pretty goddamn soon. You and that fuckin' Leonard Peltier."

"AIM," one of the more articulate goons growled. "Assholes in Moccasins. Har-har-har!"

"You and your kind get out of here, creep," Bull Miller growled, "and we'll have us a better place to live."

"Fuck you," Buddy said, and walked off.

"No! Fuck you!" Bull yelled, and stormed out. The goons followed him.

Philbert had crept up the closest to the confrontation. His eyes were the first eyes Buddy saw when he left the tribal president and his bodyguard. Philbert's eyes betrayed the wonder of Buddy's lesson. They shone fiercely of wonderment.

"It's okay, Philbert, we'll stay for a while, then go out the side door. They probably don't know your car. Who threw the knife? That was great."

"Jimmy," Wolf Tooth said. He had come up beside Philbert.

"Jimmy Campbell?" Buddy asked.

"Yep."

"Where is he?"

"Up there." Wolf pointed to the top of the bleachers. A pale, thin young man sat at the top, very still and very alone. Buddy started up the bleachers toward him.

"We'll watch the door," Wolf said after him, "in case Bull has someone watching." No one made a move to remove the knife from the backboard. It would stay there for months.

Jimmy Campbell had been in 'Nam too. Everyone at Pine Ridge loved him and was terrified of him. He always carried a knife and a gun. He stuttered incoherently, drank peppermint schnapps twenty-four hours a day, and, as far as anyone knew, he never ate anything. He only had three of his ten fingers, but he was faster with a knife than the Vietcong, who kept him in a tiger's cage for thirty-one months. He slit four of their throats and escaped into the Cambodian jungle. He got the silver medal with clusters, four Purple Hearts, a bronze, the DSC, and damn near the Medal of Honor for overrunning almost a whole battalion of Khmer Rouge. He had been in Buddy's and Wolf's intertribal unit. They were the only three of fifteen who enlisted together to come back.

"Hi, Jim," Buddy said, sitting down beside him, putting his hand lightly on Jim's mangled right hand and rubbing it. Jimmy always appreciated having his stump rubbed. It itched all the time.

"Ol' B-B-B-B-B-B-Bull," Jimmy said, chortling. "He-he-he-he-he full of shit."

"He's full of it now. You musta made him crap all over himself."

"Ha-ha-ha-ha-ha-ha-ha!" Jimmy laughed with pure, malicious delight. "It-it-it-it-it-it—" But he couldn't finish his thought. He struggled fiercely, his face contorted and growing furiously scarlet. "It-it-it-it-it-it-it-it-IT—oh, oh, oh," and he started weeping pathetically. Buddy clasped him in his arms roughly.

"Shut up, goddammit, you don't gotta say nothin'!" Buddy choked, his own tears bursting out from the nightmare they had shared together and would never escape. "Don't say nothin', Jimmy boy, don't say nothin'."

"I-I-I-I-I-I-I—"

"Think of them squirrels in the trees back home. Think of the squirrels, and the nuts, and just lyin' down on the grass, and doin' nothin', and lookin' at the sky." He rocked the soldier in his arms. Several kids nearby stared in wonder at the two men. The adults were all moved to thoughts of their own shame and ate buffalo stew.

Two thin men came over and sat down with them. They were in jeans and had very long hair, tied back in a single tail with rubber bands. One had a beaded insignia on the back of his denim jacket. It was a red fist with a feather in it.

"Hey, Jim," Buddy said, and Jimmy looked up, composing himself a little. "Mad Dog Malloy and John Big Hand are here."

"Hiya, Buddy, Jimmy, where ya been?"

"What's happenin'?"

They all stared at the dancers down on the floor, satisfied just to be in each other's company. There was too much to say to say anything. Wolf and Imogene and Marie and Luther and Linda joined them. They all sat, listening to the drum and the singing. Four more frightening-looking men joined them, and a tough woman. They were all in their early thirties, militants bred in the turmoil of the 1960s. They all sat solemnly around Jimmy. He was their center. They wore a few more beads, their hair was a little longer, and their faces were a little more grim than everybody else.

Philbert watched them all from down below. He was not a member of that desolate fraternity. He finished up his stew and pudding and found some Cheyenne. They were going to sing in a minute. He asked to join them, and they didn't say no. A pow-wow was a hotbed of insouciance. No one seemed to care very much *what* happened. They all just sat and waited, it seemed.

"There's the Gray Thunders," Buddy said to Jimmy, "and Haskell Collins, Gallatin Taylor and his three girlfriends—"

"Hard Woman McPhyre is over there," said John Big Hand.

"And Fat Lulu and Amy Tucker," Wolf added, continuing the litany, much to Jimmy's delight. "The Harris family is in from Kyle, and Long Jaw, Movie Jean, Mutilation Hat, Hiram Pritchard and his family, Walker Rising Sun, Rocky Roads, Notch, and there's Starving Elk."

"Look," Linda said, "Travois Schofield dares to show his face here."

"And Hazel's with him," Luther added. They shook their heads.

"T-T-T-T-T-Turkey Leg too," Jimmy said, pointing to another long-haired young man joining them.

"It sure is, Jimmy," Imogene said. He made her uncomfortable.

"Wallowing Bruce is over there," Wolf Tooth added. "And Whistling Hog, George Lee, Lindbloom Banks, Marshall Moons, Harrison Jones, Lydia Young Mule, and Winnebago Smith."

"Yep."

The music stopped.

"That's our own Sunshine Yodelers who blaaaaaaaaaaaaattttttttttttt-shaakkkkkkkk-zeeeeeheeeeeeeeeee-wjiiiiiiiiiineeeeeee. Thank you, boys. Now we have some Cheyenne come down from Monton-zoooooooooonnnnnnnkkk-aa. They call themselves the Happy Times Boys. Come on, then—"

"They'll do a few war dances," the beautiful middle-aged woman in the doeskin dress said, leaning into the microphone.

"I'd like to do a hose dance with Colleen," Mad Dog Malloy said. The others grinned.

The Happy Times Boys took their time setting up. Everyone waited, but it didn't seem to matter if it took an hour or a minute. They were on Indian time.

"We'll have some fancy dress contests this time," the genial old boy at the mike said. "Plus, Cliff Maroon will lead the circle. So everybody—waaaaaaaaaa-waaaaaaaaaaawaaaaaaaaaaa-leeeeee-heeeeeehikes!—get up and dance."

The hawk-nosed man in full paint and feathers sat in front of the dais, tying the leather laces on one of his soft, beaded moccasins. He talked to the others as they got up from behind the dais and went down to the floor. The beautiful woman carried a shawl. The genial old boy stayed at the mike.

The drummers started beating. Philbert carried a folding chair over and wedged his way into the circle. The others made room for him, and he had a tom-tom he got somewhere and beat in time with them. It was a moderate beat. They were warming up.

The hawk-nosed man started dancing slowly around them. He lifted each foot just a few inches, just twice, shifting his weight only slightly. He stood very erect and dignified. Only his knees were bent a little. He held an eagle feather in one hand, a fan of feathers in the other.

A few more men in ribbon shirts and slacks and moccasins joined him, slowly circling the singers. They were very close, at the near end of the gym.

Clang-clang-clang-clang, came the fancy-dress preteenagers. They immediately went wild (no warm-up needed!), jumping and leaping, gyrating and twisting in the air, all the while keeping strict adherence to the discipline of the two-step. Step-step and step-step. They could elaborate from the basic move with their shoulders and rump, etc., but they could never deviate one beat from it. The judges were watching them.

The women draped their shawls over their shoulders and formed the outer circle. They were somber and painfully dignified, barely lifting their heels off the floor, moving like concentric snails around the flip-flopping males. Circles moved at various paces, however, disunited.

The drumming stopped and immediately started again, much faster. A sudden piercing wail arose from the singers. Everyone jerked, moved to the quick by the falsetto shrill that bespoke more of prehistoric longings and urgings than it seemed human vocal cords were capable of. It climbed up the wall to the rafters and out through the roof into the universe beyond. It pierced one old man's eardrums. It sent dogs howling for cover. The dancers exploded into an involuntary unity.

Philbert had brought the cave truths of Bear Butte into the high school gymnasium. He had never sung before, nor played before, so his thirty-three years of solitude had a lot of steam to get out of their system. The great boiler-furnace of his body sent thousands of BTUs through the soft whistle of his larynx.

The other singers could only accompany. He was singing an old song, of wild maverick horses. He closed his eyes and gave every ounce he had to it.

"Wi-hi-yi-wi-hi-yi-yi-yi-yi-yi-yi-yi-hi-hi-hi-hi-yi-yi-yi-yi-wi-wi-wi-wi-wi-wiiiiiiiiiiiiiiiiiiiiiii!"

"D-d-d-d-d-d-dance," Jimmy said from the bleachers.

"Naw, hell, I don't dance." Buddy snorted. "That's fer old farts and kids." But it was hard to resist the pull of Philbert's sonic boom.

Half the gym was out on the floor, circling the center. The boys were clanging wildly, the men were twisting and stomping deliberate patterns, the women and girls were parading in their shawls in twos and threes on the outside.

"D-d-d-d-d-ance. P-p-p-p-please?"

Wolf Tooth bolted up and lurched down the bleachers, not looking behind him. Linda followed, draping her shawl over her, as did Imogene. They all got on the polished floor and circled.

The others took their cue from Buddy, who sat. So they sat. He was in turmoil. He hated stupid-ass powwows. They were idiotic family affairs. Kids and old ladies crawled all over their previous Indian heritage like it was some goddamn Indian blanket. They acted like a few lousy beads and some smelly feathers were a big deal, a culture. It was pitiful, that's what it was, pitiful. Look at 'em, traipsing around on a basketball court in a dying town like it was something alive, like *they* were something alive. They didn't know they were already dead. They died at Wounded Knee, and at Verdun, and Corregidor, and Khe Sahn.

BOOM-BOOM-BOOM-BOOM.

"I gotta get outa here," Buddy said, standing up. The others stood up. "C'mon, Jimmy, we'll go smoke a number."

"N-n-n-n-n-no!" Jimmy said, and sat angrily. "You-you-you gotten m-m-m-m-m-m-mean!"

Claymore land mines exploded all around him. Mortar fire,

napalm fire, M16 bursts, blood, guts, gore, and cavalry charges, frozen Indians in the snow. "Wi-hi-yi-yi-hi-yi-yi-wiiiiiiiiiiii-hiiiiiiiiiii-yiiiiiiiiiiii!"

He was dancing, Jimmy and his brothers all around him. He must have flown there, it was so far. His bronze-medal rosette slapped up against his chest. His feet picked up and picked down, up and down, step-step and step-step.

"Wooooooooooohooooooooooooooooohooooooooooooooowooooo ooooooooo!" was a wind blown out of him, a memory, a loss, a love, and raw, unbearable pain lifting his legs, bending his back, shoving him in a circle, running around and around and around.

Dance!

Dance out thy turmoil.

Dance!

Dance pony unto the wind!

Dance!

Dance! sang the furnace of the Whirlwind!

Dance!

Sing! my brothers, sing!

Dance, my sisters, dance!

Around and around and around they moved, the circle closing tighter, the flames of the sun leaping like slashes of amber paint, then rolling back into the gaseous, molten ball at the center, the infinite heat drawing in closer, the dancers pressing in tighter to the singers, the central song, the sun, the wail—

Wi-hi-yi-yi . . . wi-hi-yi-yi . . .
They all sang, the dancers sang . . .
The singers sang.
Dance!
  Dance!
    Dance.
Wi-hi-yi-yi!
  Wi-hi-yi-yi!
    Wi-hi-yi-yi!

They crushed into the center, all turned inward to the song of ponies and buffalo hunts, all moving up and down, step-step and step-step, a huddle, a pep rally, a go-go-go charged with atomic fusion at the center of the solar system, the Young Mules, Buckhorns, Starving Elks, the Wolf Teeth, Magpies, the Red Bird dancing, the Bono singing, Mercury and Venus and Pluto slurping from the fountain of fire and music and perpetual motion—Wi-hi-yi-yi!

> Wi-hi-yi-yi!
> Wi-hi-yi-yi!
> Wi-hi-yi-yi!
> Wi-hi-yi-yi!
> Wi-hi-yi-yi!
> Wi-hi-yi-yi!
> Wi-hi-yi-yi!
> Wi-hi-yi-yi!
> Wi-hi-yi-yi!

Old ladies sang beside young children, men of politics and men of apathy danced shoulder to shoulder, Brule and Yanktonais and Oglala and Arapaho and Hunkpapa and Cheyenne and Blackfeet all knew the words, hurt and joy and heresy and honor all said to hell with their prejudices . . .

> . . . and danced . . .
> . . . and sang . . .
> And forgot everything else.

There are two parts to every story: the part that is believable and the part that is not. It is impossible to determine which of the two is the truth and which of the two is a lie, for a lie is an extension of the truth and nobody knows what the hell the truth is. Perhaps it is a lie that is so exciting and preposterous that it has to be true. But nobody really knows.

It is the same with dancing and singing. Dancers and singers were the most articulate of the storytellers around the campfires, and they never knew what the hell they were talking about. They acted out the day's hunt, but did they understand the hopes and the fears of the hunters? They sang dear and silly significance into every eclipse and breech birth that terrified the cave dwellers, but did they understand the stars and their effect on the female uterus? They calmed down the first *Homo erectus* with soothing and exciting lies of gods and ghosts, never dreaming that they might be true. It was only with the sophisticated advent of the Age of Reason that the first part of storytelling reached new heights of obscurity. Reasonable Man was the first to deny that mankind had been full of jerks since creation. Hence our contemporary confusion.

So, of course, half of the wild Indians spilled out of the powwow when it was over and went to the Jimbo's where the real action was. They had fulfilled the dull obligations of cultural preservation in the first part of the evening, and now it was time to have fun. It was time to forty-nine.

Remember? Buddy and Philbert and the boys and girls had said they would be on their way after the powwow. And they would be. But Jimbo's was the second part of the powwow, as natural an extension of a powwow as a lie is to the truth. (Oh, whiteman, get yer cryptic shit together and cut out this reason hogwash! It gums up a story!) It did not even occur to them not to go, or that they were violating decorum. That was the way it had always been done, and it was a way that tradition had legitimized into habit.

Jimbo's was a dive. It was a prefab saloon with one neon Coors light in one window. It had a wooden porch, a hitching post, swinging doors, and a honky-tonk country-western band throbbing out the beat. Thirsty toe-tapping redskins poured out of the gym and stampeded to the Haven.

It was packed with dancin' and drinkin' and laughin' folk with funny cheekbones and clay-raw skin. A few normal palefaces added some chalky contrast to the crush, but not much.

GOOOOOOOOOOOOOOOOOOOOOOOOOOOOOOOOOOOOOOO OOOODDAMN!

They were twirlin' on the dance floor, bouncin' up and down, stompin', chompin', hoppin', jiggin', flingin', and shufflin'.

SHHHHHHHHHHHHHHHHHHHHHHHHHHHHH— ITTTTTTTTTTTTTT!

There were a hundred stories unfolding in that square little room, and a hundred more ending. Olin and Vicki Gray Thunder had reconciled and were getting back together. Haskell Collins had just gotten his divorce papers that afternoon from Xerepha and was annoying Cindy Kennedy, one of Gallatin Taylor's three girlfriends. Hiram Pritchard was getting drunk and embarrassing his wife and kids again, who sat primly at their beer-soaked table. Rocky Roads came over and tried to soak up the beer with Walker Rising Sun's pack of Chesterfield cigarettes, and Walker shoved Rocky up against the pool table and spoiled Kyle Long Jaw's bank shot. With the pool cue, Kyle hit Walker, who shoved Rocky, who landed on Turkey Leg Krutsinger, who had bent over to clean the instep of his boot. Fate hung in the balance—violent destruction or peaceful forgiveness were the alternatives. The second choice prevailed, unfortunately, and the four boys fell on the floor laughing. Peace had nipped action in the bud again. Kyle got wet when Walker spilled Starving Elk's beer on him, but Starving Elk was dancing with Kathy Jiminez and didn't notice. Notch had gotten his penis caught in his zipper in the bathroom and was screaming bloody murder, but Whistling Hog, at the next urinal, thought he was screaming happily to the music. The screams were very much alike, after all.

WHOOOOOOOOOOOOOOOOOOOOOOOOOOOOOOOO-Woooo-Woooo-WOOOOOOOOOOO-WOO!

YIIIIIIIIIIIIIIII-HI-YI-HI-YIIIIIIIIIIIIIIIIIIIIIPPEE!

Buddy and Philbert were lost. Perhaps it was Philbert lounging contentedly at the bar with a quart-sized paper cup of tap beer, and perhaps it was three other guys. Cecilia Torres wasn't sure if she had danced with Buddy, or if it was Marshall Moons who had put his hand under her blouse to retrieve a hot joint. Juvida Petter remembered being swung wildly around the floor by Buddy, and so did Noisy Lillie and Loretta Looks Behind and Edna Silver and Cleo LeFevre, but Amy Tucker had seen Buddy go outside with Big Tits, and Loretta threw her ashtray against the wall. She was sweet on Buddy, you see.

Jimmy Campbell had gone home, where he lived with his mother.

Luther and Linda Buckhorn had left their kids with Imogene and Marie at the house. Imogene didn't want to come. They had to pack, she had said, and she suggested to Wolf Tooth that he should help, but he ignored her and went with Buddy. Linda had tried to console her red-eyed friend, but Luther had honked the horn to get going. She felt bad about it, but Wolf Tooth sat sullenly drinking at their table and wouldn't talk about it. They were smoking a joint. Mad Dog Malloy and John Big Hand sat at the table with them. They were in a drug daze and stared dull-faced at the dancers. Luther was getting pretty blasted himself, and he kept trying to get Linda to go out to the truck for a "little fooling around."

"Luther, you stink," she said.

"Thank you," he said amiably.

Buddy plopped down next to them. Big Tits sat on his lap.

"It's anoooooooooother tequiiiiiiiiiiiila sunrise!" he sang. They all joined in with him, singing at the top of their lungs, making absolutely no impression on the cacophonous roar created by the Muddy Water Boys, who blasted away at the small room from their massive amplifiers. They were white hippie rednecks from Lincoln, Nebraska, brought in by the tribe especially for the Christmas powwow. They wore straw cowboy hats and long beards and hair and cowboy clothes and weren't as sure it was going to be quite so groovy to rock and roll with their red brothers as they had been at the beginning of the evening. One cretin kept passing out on their expensive sound mixer, for example, and spilling his beer. They would chase him off, he would go get another beer, come back, and pass out again on the sound mixer. They couldn't believe it. They didn't know that the cretin was called Chief Donald and that he usually passed out in the fresh vegetables at the A&G on Saturday night, but this was a special occasion. Monday through Friday he passed out several times in the intersection at the elementary school, and on Sundays he passed out several times in Lydia Young Mule's Chevy. It had a cozy backseat.

"Back agaaaaaaaaaaaiiiiiiiiiiiin in Margaritaville!" the Muddy Water Boys sang, and Buddy and his boys and girls accompanied. The Fosters sang at the next table, the Blackfeet trio from the Bear Butte parking lot and the Stewarts and the Swallows and the Tall Bulls never stopped dancing, and Amy Tucker left with Whistling Hog. Olin and Vicki Gray Thunder had another fight and vowed they'd never see each other again. Gallatin Taylor cold-cocked Haskell Collins, and Cindy Kennedy kneed Gallatin in the nuts and took Haskell home with her. Gallatin's other two girlfriends produced a bottle of white rum and left with Loretta Looks Behind and Cleo LeFevre to go drink it and vow hatred for all men for all time. Linda Buckhorn took Wolf Tooth home to his wife and would bring them back to the Haven to leave from there for Denver with Buddy Red Bird and Philbert Bono. Cecilia Torres had her eye on Hiram Pritchard, but Mrs. Pritchard started crying and the Pritchard children took their mother out of that filthy place. Kyle Long Jaw kicked Hiram's butt, Hiram ran off after his wife, and Kyle put the moves on Cecilia. Rocky Roads and Walker Rising Run both asked Big Tits to dance, and she jitterbugged with both of them. Buddy was glad to be rid of her, so he could talk about AIM strategy with Luther Buckhorn and Turkey Leg Krutsinger. Starving Elk told Kathy Jiminez he was a homosexual and he left with Notch.

The band played its last song, "Macho Man," and then got out of there as fast as they could, vowing never to come back. The lights came up (and half a dozen drunks fell down), the beer stopped running (except on the floor), everyone lingered too long outside (looking for lost companions), and the war dance was over as suddenly as it had begun.

CHAPTER 9

Of Bonnie's Boredom in the Tower,
and of Her Five Conclusions

A PRINCESS TRAPPED in a tower by an evil lord gets awful bored. While heroic knights battle the forces of the evil lord and have a helluva good time, she sits and looks pretty and twiddles her thumbs. Although many legendary adventures are swirling all about the land in her name, she doesn't get to partake of these spoils of victory. She gets to brush her hair and do her nails and gaze out the window. She is the Ideal. She cannot wriggle out of her dignity like it was a girdle. She must maintain.

Bonnie was therefore about to do something foolish. Her first onset of panic was Friday night, *because* it was Friday night. She loved to go drinking and dancing on Friday night. She could really cut loose on Friday night. Friday night was a symbol, and it was a symbol she felt slipping through her fingers, hour by hour. It was agonizing. She had to sit in her solitary cell and stare at the sink. She even let her leg go to sleep once so she could wake it up. She asked the matron if she could have a few magazines to read, and the old crow grudgingly brought her an issue of *Sports Afield*, which was eight years old. She thumbed through the crinkled pages, staring at photographs of men holding up trophy

Mackinaw salmon in Alaska. She threw the magazine at the sink and it knocked over her shampoo, which spilled into her fashionable leather boots, but they were already permanently stained with a big purple grease spot. She lay back down on her cot, cried herself silly, and the lights went out. She stared at the darkness, and listened to the automated noises of a jail, and mercifully fell asleep.

Saturday was a miserable day for a lot of reasons, but the main one was that it was Saturday. She loved to get up early on Saturday and drink coffee and watch cartoons with the kids. They would have breakfast and then they would go shopping. They would buy some T-shirts or a pair of shoes and have cheese dogs at the Orange Julius. Then they would go for a drive or she would drop the kids off at a matinee and go ball with some boyfriend or other. It was exquisite to lie naked on some man's dirty sheets and smoke a cigarette and think about the kids throwing popcorn and Coke on the other kids at the movie.

So what was she doing instead? Staring at the sink.

Saturday night? Foolishness was overwhelming her. She let panic possess her again as she thought of Life and Freedom Out There. Panic led to foolishness, and vice versa. Instead of locking out all the dangerous progeny of imagination that kept lifers behind bars sane, she opened the doors to all her hopes and fears "If She Ever Got Out of There." She got a message from Rabbit that they would be there in a day or two. Rabbit also said she had her kids secured. It depressed the hell out of Bonnie. Everybody was doing, going, doing, going! She was staring, thinking, staring, thinking.

She forced herself to consider some startling conclusions, as much to keep from being bored as well as to figure herself out.

First conclusion: She couldn't go another weekend behind bars. She would die. It was as simple as that (already she felt panic constricting her libido, and her libido was her lifeblood). So she had to get out of there and *stay* out of there.

Second conclusion: How? A question was not normally a conclusion, but to Bonnie it was (it was a major step, in fact, in her agonizing assessment).

Third conclusion: It had something to do with men. Not just whitemen, brownmen, but *all* Men. Maybe, just maybe, if she could find a man her children could love, who she wouldn't be afraid of . . .

Fourth conclusion: The man who got her out of there would be *the* Man.

The princess twiddled her thumbs and thought of home for some strange reason. Something of Lame Deer seemed to beckon, and to answer her questions, and to squeeze the fifth conclusion out of her: It didn't matter anymore if he was one of the ruling elite or not. She was sick of looking for Mr. Perfect. She would take anything now.

Thus did foolishness beget wisdom. The princess masturbated, fantasizing about working men, smelly men, basic decent down-to-earth slobs, and then fell asleep peacefully.

CHAPTER 10

How a Holy Blizzard Sweeps in upon the
Journeyers, and How the Spirits of Their Ancestors
Cheer Them On, and How a Dragon Is Involved

THE PEOPLE OF the prairie do not swear. They do not take the
Lord's name in vain. This is of course understood to include the
rural people, not the city people of the prairie. The city people of
the prairie *do* swear, and take the Lord's name in vain, and per-
form a multitude of other perversions. But the country folk, the
ranchers and the farmers, whether Indian or German or Pekingese, *do not* swear. This point must be made very clear, otherwise
the significance of the forthcoming episodes will be lost.

A few snowflakes in December on the prairie are cause for
rejoicing only among the heartiest of the hearty, by which are
meant the people of the American prairie. A few snowflakes are
a welcome source of moisture to the wheat farmers and the cattle
ranchers. They love a few snowflakes. They bless God for the
water that sustains their rich soil. Alfalfa and buffalo grass are
the fruit of their lives.

But let more than a few snowflakes fall and they grow silent.
Let the wind come up and blow their seeds into snowdrifts and
they mutter about the cruelty of Fate. Let two feet of snow pile up
and they curse the land (unprofanely, of course). Let three feet

come and they airlift hay to their stranded cattle. They grumble impotently, they work ferociously, they call out the National Guard. They stare bitterly at the prairie blizzard that is as bad as any storm that haunts any man-infested area of earth. They hate the blizzard, but they will not swear; this must be understood.

For the prairie blizzard, as evil and cruel as anything on earth, is also one of the most truly beautiful phenomena. It is Violence and Beauty incarnate. It is so awesome that it prevents any profanity from escaping the lips of the prairie people. They are afraid to curse the storm. It would kill them; or worse, ignore them, and not include them in its glorious fury. They would have to stop believing in God if they had to start cursing Him. The prairie people are simple folk this way.

The first few snowflakes on the windshield of Protector took a startling form in this theological confrontation. Philbert thought they were pretty. Their little lacy patterns stuck lovingly to the glass. Philbert thought of jingle bells and one-horse open sleighs.

"Holy Jesus, it's starting to snow." Buddy gasped. Buddy was not a simple-minded bumpkin who'd been born yesterday. He knew a raw deal when he saw one. "I knew our ass was grass when we got off the Interstate. Holy Jesus *shit!*"

"Buddy, shhhhh!" Imogene whispered, horrified at his blasphemy. She knew the impending storm would have to kill them now that its name had been taken in vain.

Silence descended inside the car, taking many forms as the storm slammed full fury into the sleigh. Silence was upon Oliver Wolf Tooth, who was passed out in the front seat between Philbert and Buddy. Philbert was trying to remember the words of the song "Silent Night." He drove innocently and fearlessly. Buddy sat in shock, scared to death. He knew what this could mean if it turned into a blizzard, as it looked it might. Imogene, in the backseat, was also scared to death, as much because she hadn't insisted they take the Greyhound bus, which would have been much safer, as she was because of the weather. She was wedged up against the makeshift Coleman stove. Marie slept fitfully in her arms. The backseat was a wad of their luggage and Buddy's sleeping bags and some old wet blue jeans from somewhere and a heap of empty beer cans and whiskey bottles. It smelled of grease and marijuana smoke and butane. She had almost gagged when they'd first piled in at the Sioux Haven, Jimbo's.

They were in Nebraska, cutting across the northeast corner. It wouldn't be long before they picked up the southwest corner of Wyoming and then on into Colorado, and Denver, which wasn't so far, Imogene told herself. They might be there by morning, if this darn storm petered out.

It was always the way of mankind to deal with Fate by hoping it would go away. All a body had to do was think positive.

"It's getting worse," Buddy said with a moan. He had long ago resigned himself to defying Fate. He wasn't going to let superstition keep him from getting an even break. He'd already had enough shit come down on him in 'Nam and for being an Indian to let Nature push him around too. "Here's our turn up here, Phil. Turn right."

Protector spun a little on the white road and managed to get rolling around in a right turn, to the west. "It'll probably get better this way," Buddy said. "It looks to be moving back off to the east."

The wind slammed into them with double the force it had had before. They were heading directly into it now. One valiant window wiper scratched the windshield glass back and forth, leaving long half ellipses on the glass, and Philbert had to lean over Wolf Tooth to see out, but a tiny path was kept cleared and they kept going.

"It's gonna let up pretty quick," Buddy decided.

Inches piled up faster than minutes. In five minutes, six inches of snow threw up barricades on the road. The wind blew much of it into the borrow pits on the side of the road, but the same wind blew ten inches of snow back out of the borrow pit onto the road.

"It's not slippery, anyway," Buddy said. "I think we'll do all right."

Protector came to a slight curve and did a wheelie, turning around three hundred and sixty degrees and stopping up against a road sign that said CURVE.

Wolf Tooth was awake in an instant. The instant a car stops, most car sleepers are instantly awake. Being an intuitive child of the prairie, Wolf Tooth instantly assessed the situation.

"It's snowing," he said.

"We gotta keep moving or we'll die," Imogene wailed from the backseat. Marie was awake and staring out the window. "We gotta keep moving or we'll die."

Indians had borne countless prairie blizzards through the millennia. They knew every trick of survival. They were the toughest, boniest people of a tough and bony breed. An Indian always had had twice the stamina of a pioneer, and an Indian pony always had had quadruple the staying power of a big pioneer horse. If anyone could get out of a natural mess by sheer shrewdness and toughness, it was an American Indian.

Philbert gunned Protector and his big rear slicks spun madly on the slick road. He gunned it more and smoke clouds of burning rubber arose from behind. Protector, like ponies out of yore, was digging himself a hole in which to hole up until the storm blew over. Indian ponies had always gotten real pissed off when their heroic masters tried to forge ahead over hill and dale to find a party. They didn't like the wind and the snow blowing up their assholes any more than Protector did.

"We better turn back to Pine Ridge," Wolf Tooth said.

"And get murdered in our sleep by Bull Miller? No thank you," Buddy said. "We get out and push. It ain't so bad."

He opened the door and the hobgoblins came screaming gleefully in.

Roooaarrr!
Whoooooooooooosh!
"Holy shit!"
"Close the door!"
"Come on, Wolf, we'll push!"

The door closed and peace reigned again inside the coach. Snowdrifts were heaped up against the people inside and in every corner and every direction. Philbert and Imogene and Marie were covered with it. The stove hissed and steamed from the water that had infiltrated its sacrosanct chambers. And the roar still buzzed in their ears.

Outside, Wolf Tooth and Buddy were yelling at each other and couldn't even hear themselves. The icy cataclysm threw them brutally up against the car, then threw them back away from it. It swirled like insects into their ears and down their collars and up their noses. Blindly, frantically, they both leaned on the trunk of the car and started rocking it. The tires weren't dug in too deeply, and there was good solid pavement only ten inches down. So Buddy and Wolf Tooth pushed. They grunted. They strained. They nearly popped their hernias. It took them several excruciating minutes to realize the wheels were not spinning. The car was sitting idly.

They screamed, "Philllllllll—hilllllll—bert you *@=_** ##@*!"

They pounded the trunk. They jumped up and down. And still the Furies roared and carried their frail shouts off to never-never land.

Philbert was getting the snow off the stove; he was wiping the inside of the windshield with a rag where it had gotten frosted up; he was consoling Imogene and Marie.

"You know the words to 'Silent Night'?" he asked them. They glared back at him like he was the Creature from the Black Lagoon.

Some monstrous banging hit the passenger door. Some beast

was trying to get in, but the rickety old rump-sprung door wouldn't open. The harder the beasts outside tried to open it, the more adamant the metal got. They kicked it. They cursed it. It remained noncommittal.

Philbert leaned over and rolled down the window a crack. "You guys ready to push?"

Gloveless hands reached murderously through the crack to pull Philbert's face off. But the crack was too small. Fingers got jammed and wedged in the crack like octopus tentacles severed from their carcass.

Philbert leaned back over in the saddle and gave Protector a little gas. The tentacles in the window retreated into the deep. Protector started to rock. Philbert gave it the gas on the forward push and let up when it rolled backward. The rockings got longer and faster. Then, in one mighty heave, he lurched out of the rut and back on the trail! He was rolling! He was running!

The snow beasts outside were hoofing it too. With extraordinary grace and agility Philbert kept one hand on the reins and reached over to the passenger door, gave it a knowing shove-push, and it flew open.

The snow was swirling in a whiteout, the road was rolling by with an occasional glimpse of graveled blacktop underneath. It was a new storm; ice had not had an opportunity to freeze its way into the prairie's heart yet.

Philbert stuck his hand out (for he was a giant and had great capacity of breadth), and another hand, out of the ocean's black deep, grasped it. He pulled the hoofing car pusher back onto the pony's back, and Wolf Tooth caromed beastily into the front seat. He was gasping. He was dripping. But he was safe.

In his safety did he think of vengeance? No. In his security did he think of himself? No. With nary a thought to his nauseating hangover or the shrieking outrage of his soaking body, he reached out for Buddy.

"We can't stop!" Philbert yelled, for the roar was deafening. "We'll get stuck again!"

"I know!" Wolf Tooth said. He leaned way out the door. Buddy was back a dozen feet, packing full cheeks. Protector was throwing shovelfuls of snow at him. The storm itself was trying to throw him under Protector's galloping hooves. But Buddy was fearlessly hauling ass right next to the car. Wolf Tooth could see his mouth working. Expletives were fueling his do-or-die chase. He was cussing with every heroic stride. His face was contorting to keep his eyes and mouth clear of the snowy assault upon them.

"Slow down a little, Philbert!" Wolf Tooth yelled. "Imogene, you and Marie get over on the other side of the seat. I'll roll down your window and pull him in!"

"But the stove's in the way and—"

"Then crawl underneath it on the floor, goddammit!"

The females sidled on their bellies under the platform of camping gear and over to the left side of the backseat. Wolf Tooth crawled over the seat and rolled down the window on the right rear. He hung halfway out the window. His hand was a foot away from Buddy's outstretched arm.

"Slow down some more, Philbert!" he yelled.

"I can't, or we'll lose momentum!" (Momentum? From Philbert?)

The hands inched closer. Buddy packed his cheeks as fast as he could. His slick cowboy boots threatened to fly out from underneath him at any moment on the wet snow. Wolf Tooth was hanging out the window up to his knees. The joints of his body flip-flopped in the wind precariously. Any moment he could lose his balance and fly out the window. In addition to that, his hangover gut threatened to spill the beans.

Their fingers touched. Their hands grasped wrists! Contact was made! Man afoot and man abreast were one!

So now what? Buddy was still running, only his equilibrium was thrown off because one arm couldn't pump in rhythm with his legs. It was nailed out in front of him. He lost control and went down.

Wolf Tooth would have been pulled out and down into sure death with his friend if he had not grabbed the window frame with his other arm. He was splayed out against the side of the car, hanging by his ankles and one hand.

Imogene screamed and grabbed at his waist. She held him by his belt, but she wasn't strong enough to pull him back in. Plus, she'd burned her arm on the stove, reaching over to save her husband.

And Buddy? He was a fish at the end of his line. He flip-flopped on the snowy road, thrashing to grab hold of some solid reality. That was probably why he wouldn't let go of Wolf Tooth's wrist. His head was just behind the right rear wheel. The soft snow was keeping him from being fatally bruised by the blacktop, but sooner or later something was going to have to give.

"I'm stopping!" Philbert yelled.

"No!" Wolf Tooth yelled back.

"No!" Imogene relayed the message.

"He'll be sucked in underneath!" Wolf Tooth added.

"He'll be sucked in underneath!"

Buddy knew how to keep his cool. He refused to panic. He grabbed the bumper with his free hand. He pulled himself up to the bumper. Wolf Tooth kept him tethered with one arm. Buddy put one foot on the bumper, and then the other. Squatting there, he decided his only hope was to crawl on the trunk, up on the roof, and in through the passenger door. Wolf Tooth would keep him from being blown away.

He lay flat up against the trunk. Wolf Tooth eased himself back to his waist in the window. Unfortunately his feet kicked over the stove in the backseat and spilled hot fuel on a down sleeping bag, and it exploded into flames.

Imogene screamed. Philbert flailed at it. Marie smothered it with a Marine blanket, and it was out in eighteen seconds. But the reek of burned goose feathers almost made Imogene puke. And the stove lay on its side on the floor, its neck broken.

Buddy was crawling up the rear window, wondering why he smelled smoke. He slithered up on the roof and the wind whipped him sideways, and then back into position. Wolf Tooth clung to him for dear life, twisting upward to follow Buddy's progress. He wasn't sure exactly what the hell crazy Bud was doing, but communication was impossible, so he went along with whatever he did.

A face appeared in Philbert's windshield, upside down. A foot dangled in the open doorway, kicking sideways, searching for solid horse. Wolf Tooth was twisted in two, holding onto the creature spread-eagled above him. He grabbed the other leg with his other arm and it stepped in his face. Solid footing at last! An arm reached for the car door, still open and swinging noncommittally. It was a very helpful door, that passenger door. Already, in just a little over twenty-four hours, it had saved Buddy Red Bird's life not once, but twice. He clung to it. Wolf Tooth turned his face sideways so Buddy's boot could have a more solid surface on the side of his face. The two men got their legs and faces tangled in the steel bar that divided the front from the rear of the stagecoach. Buddy grasped inward and flopped in, onto the floor. Wolf Tooth had his own arms tangled in the window.

It was then that Philbert started to laugh. It was not just a giggle or a chuckle. It was a genuine chortle, an uncontrollable guffaw. It was an ape noise of pure, contagious delight. Buddy's tangled, sopping excuse for a body on the front-seat floor was a hilarious picture. Wolf Tooth looked like an ivy vine wrapped around the pilaster of a small liberal arts college administration building in Vermont.

Philbert howled.

"Close the door!" Buddy barked, unable to extricate himself from himself.

Imogene tittered.

"I can't," Wolf Tooth groaned.

Marie giggled.

"Oh, ooh, unh, ugh," Buddy grunted, trying to get his leg out of his armpit.

Wolf Tooth ha-haed.

The passenger door suddenly swung closed by itself, narrowly missing Wolf Tooth, and Philbert died.

Buddy gave up and snickered.

Wolf Tooth collapsed out of the window and rolled over the front seat and landed on Buddy.

They screamed.

Imogene crawled over the stove and rolled up the rear window.

They were in stitches.

The stove slid into the pile of beer cans as Protector eased on down the road.

It snorted in time to the merriment.

Oh, did they know how to have fun!

"Siiiiiii—hiiiiii—lent night . . ."

"Hooooooooo—hooooooooly night," Imogene started to sing. Philbert and Marie joined her.

"Allllllllllll is caaaaaaaaaaaalm,
Alllllllllllll is briiiiiiiiiiiiiight."

Buddy and Wolf Tooth were assuming some more normal positions on the front seat. "Let me kill him," Wolf Tooth pleaded happily to Buddy. "Let me kill him, please, please, please."

"Round yon vir-hir-gin
Mother and Chiiiiiild . . ."

"Oh, okay." Buddy grinned. "But slowly. Save me some."

"Sleeeeeeeeeeeeeep in heavenly peeeee-eeeeece,
Sleeeee-eeee-eeeeeep in heavenly peace."

"I hate Christmas songs," Buddy hollered. "Stop that racket!"
And he put his hands to his ears. Wolf Tooth joined the singers,
who, if anything, sang louder, and he leaned closer to Buddy,
deliberately torturing him.

"Jingle Bells, jingle bells, jingle all the way,
Oh, what fun it is to ride in a one-horse open
sleigh—hey!"

"Yikes!"

"Oooooooooooo—dashing through the snow,
In a one-horse open sleigh,
O'er the hills we go,
Laughing all the way!"

Good King Wenceslaus took them through the storm as Buddy
rigged up the stove again. It was soon pumping out its good
smelly heat. They screamed "Hark! the Herald Angels Sing"
through Hay Springs, Nebraska. Buddy screamed through "The
First Noel," and lit a joint in the midst of "Adestes Fideles," but
by the time they got to Chadron and "The Twelve Days of Christmas," he was bellowing with them.

Protector rode the storm. He ran faster the worse it got. Philbert drove more carefully when the snow and the wind eased up
for a moment. More danger lay in deceptive complacency than in
howling turmoil. The prairie blizzard drew him and Protector's
charges onward, onward, "Onward Christian Soldiers," onward
to one of the most holy places on earth.

They were destined to pass through Fort Robinson, Nebraska.
There was no way they could avoid it. Highway 20 was the only

road to Wyoming, and Denver, and Santa Fe. Is it destiny that decides on the routes of the ancient Indian trails? Or is it just cheaper to build highways where Indians followed the buffalo herds and found the best way to go over buttes and to straddle the Niobrara sand hills?

Did the first man (or animal) who passed by here choose this route for convenience, or did it happen that some magical rock or tree pulled him that way?

Be that as it may, destiny or geography put Fort Robinson where it was, and dealt its blows to the people who had died there, and now drew our adventurers to it. Sentiment did not dictate the tragic events at Fort Robinson in 1877, and again in 1879, and sentiment does not compel the warriors of the Quest to lapse into silence from their merriment. Power demanded silence. Respect for this spot was permitted only to the red people of the prairie, who sorrowed for the power that had been destroyed at Fort Robinson but would never be lost.

Protector drove closer. Philbert breathed deeper. The others vaguely got drowsy and tried to forget. Philbert's genius, however, was that he was determined to remember. He was too stupid to know what was futile. His sentiment was a rarity in a breed saturated with melodrama—his was a practical sentiment. He derived religious strength from history. The whiteman did not. That was the curse of the history-loving redman. The whiteman hated his history (as he should have, given its vicious record). He thought it was past.

The blizzard-covered sand dunes and buttes and grasslands of that part of the Great Prairie that had now come to be known as northwestern Nebraska, United States of America, howled with history. The great buffalo herds were still there. Their ghosts and their bones and their manure supported the grass and cottonwood trees still thriving there. Their ancient spirits, along with Pleistocene camels and mastiffs and dinosaurs, were the stuff of the soil and stones. Volcanic upheaval, endless swamps, and arid, mountainous turmoil survived in the awesome limitlessness of the place.

Philbert shivered. The others were silent. They passed through the village of Crawford, only a few miles from the Spot. The wind and the snow howled, but Protector was invincible.

Young-Man-Afraid-of-His-Horses rode over a bluff. His was a peaceful family. His father, Old-Man-Afraid-of-His-Horses, had forged an aristocratic heritage. Like his father before him, Young-Man-Afraid-of-His-Horses educated his sons well. They were trained in the social graces. They were handsome, intellectual, awesome bastions of personality. Young-Man-Afraid-of-His-Horses was the superhuman culmination of his line. He intimidated the bejesus out of every cavalry general and peace commissioner that came to negotiate with the Sioux. Any woman on earth would have wilted in his presence. He was Robert Redford and Clark Gable rolled into one, with long black hair wrapped in otter fur.

Spotted Tail and Fast Bear rode over the bluff to have a look at their heirs. Old Bull, Little Wound, American Horse, and Little Big Man rode up, too, and sat on their ponies on the bluff and watched the pony wagon crawl down the trail they called the Thieves' Road.

They argued among themselves. Some said they should let the jerks go merrily on their way. Some said they should kill any whiteman in sight. Some said they could get a big price for the minerals on their land.

Spotted Tail said, "The Great Father has a big safe, and so have we. This hill is our safe. We want seven hundred million dollars for the black gold in this hill."

Old Bull said, "Stick it up yer ass, Spotted Tail. You cannot buy and sell the earth."

They wrangled. They accused. They threatened. They drew their weapons.

Young-Man-Afraid-of-His-Horses sat on his spotted pony

benignly. He had but to raise his arm and the hotheads and the kiss-asses alike looked to him. "Look," he said, pointing to Protector on the highway below. "That is what we are to become."

"What?" Little Big Man asked. He was kind of a dummy.

Young-Man-Afraid-of-His-Horses gave him a withering look. "That which you, Little Big Man, took part in."

The pony wagon down below approached Fort Robinson. Little Big Man held his head high and rode off. He would maintain his individual warrior identity.

"Little Big Man!" Young-Man-Afraid-of-His-Horses shouted after him.

Little Big Man stopped and turned defiantly to his chief. "It is not my fault that the Light-Haired One became a legend. He was a pain in the ass. All he ever wanted to do was raise hell and get freaked out."

The others on the bluff top lowered their heads at Little Big Man's shame. He rode off and they let him go. They, too, had often felt irritable about the Light-Haired One's intransigence. He *was* a nut; they all agreed on that. But it was hard to cross a nut who knew *why* he was a nut and was proud of it. He could also kick anybody's ass who got in the way of his impossible dreams. He was the toughest son of a bitch who had *ever* lived. (The whitemen called him Crazy Horse.)

Touch the Clouds rode up to them. He was nearly seven feet tall. He made his pony look very small and very tired. He had to change ponies often. He had four extra ponies with him, leashed to a long rope. He Dog rode up with him. Black Shawl followed on a bay mare.

They were the Light-Haired One's closest friends. Black Shawl was his wife. Perhaps Little Big Man had known they were coming, and that was why he had galloped off so hastily. The others on the bluff dared not criticize the Light-Haired One now, not even in their hearts. For his father and mother also rode up to the bluff.

His mother was panting. "What's up?" she asked.

"I don't know," Young-Man-Afraid-of-His-Horses replied. "Some warriors have come in a storm to see how it is with us."

"Warriors?" He Dog questioned. He had been with the Strange One on his first kill, when they were still boys. He had ridden with him in every fight, except the last one.

"They *are* warriors," Black Shawl said quietly. The others turned to her. "Any who have come like these to pay homage to our dead are true."

They all sat on their ponies and watched.

Philbert stopped Protector by the side of the main road. The snow was too deep to take the side path. They were in Fort Robinson, which once had been Red Cloud's Agency. Neat and trim barracks huddled about a compound on the right. A tall flagpole—without a flag—sat in the middle of the compound. A wagon gun was beside the flagpole, aimed at the bluff towering over the fort from the north. The skeletal limbs of large cottonwood and box elder grandfather trees were draped with the fresh snow. A few streetlights lit up the deserted fort. The highway ran through the middle of it. It was still snowing and blowing like the frozen breath of hell.

But it was a place of supreme peace now, because it had once been a place of utter anguish. No more evil could even penetrate into this hallowed ground, for evil had purged itself from here with its own foul breath. Like a suicidal cannibal, it had eaten itself whole.

Philbert turned off his engine and got out quickly and closed the door. The others were surprised but did nothing. They knew where they were, and they waited. When Buddy made no fuss about Philbert's nutty behavior, they made no fuss. Buddy was learning that nothing could stop Philbert from his weird excursions.

The storm blasted into Philbert through every pore of his being. He crossed the highway and walked into the dark, away from the barracks compound. He had never been there before, so he trusted to his instincts to find what he was looking for. He trudged through the snow. He slipped and fell down. He followed a dirt road (that was now a snow road, of course) that wound around by a streambed that had no stream in it. It seemed like he walked for hours. He found himself coming up and around on the road in the same direction that he had left the car. He had walked in a large semicircle. He saw the car back up a few hundred yards west of where he had started, but he must have walked a mile in all. And still no—

Wait. . . . He turned around and looked behind him. Two large shapes huddled back in the dark. He tromped toward them. His heart was beating with more than blood now! More than snow was falling into his boots and soaking his socks! More than thought and awareness and consciousness filled his mind.

The first shape was a log building. It was small and square and simple. Whirlwind peered in the window but couldn't see anything. Only a little light from a streetlamp back on the road shed any photoelectric illumination on his search. The snow gave off a white reflection from the swirling clouds, somehow, but it wasn't much. The point is, Whirlwind was pretty much stumbling around in the dark in a blizzard looking for even God didn't know what.

The second shape was a log building also. A sign over the door said QUARTERMASTER.

Whirlwind stumbled on . . .

. . . something . . .

. . . was ahead . . .

Yes, here. . . .

Incomprehensible power pulverized him. He fell to his knees; unable to withstand the explosive pressure in his head, tears burst from his heart. He fell on his face and spread his arms and legs in the snow. He felt that he had to give some of his warmth to this Spot. He felt the Spot returning his gift. And his heart stopped for an eternal instant.

A small, lithe man struggled in the arms of half a dozen cavalry troopers, screaming to the heavens for Justice. The guardhouse was only a few steps away. The man thrashed insanely at the sight of the bars on the windows. His great golden heart thundered for Honor to rescue him. A mob of blanketed nomads milled about the troopers, muttering cliquishly at the irrational reaction of the small, lithe man. Others muttered outrage. No one did anything. The man kicked and screamed and fought like a hundred wildcats for Truth to rear its courageous head and end this nightmare. He broke free of the terrified soldiers with raw, brute force and arose above them all like a tornado growing thousands of feet in the air. Cyclonic madness swept the Spot, and all mankind cowered at the murderous ascension of the small man.

"I will be free!" reverberated to the ends of the earth.

The soldiers drew their Remingtons and fixed their bayonets. The excitable nomads roiled and broiled restlessly. The small man drew a knife hidden in his buckskin tunic. He flipped his waist-length brown hair around and fastened the ends to the transcendent silver beams of a sorcerer's wand. They had all seen him prepare for battle this way many times. But he had not his war paint now, nor his medicine bundle (for they had ridden into the fort in peace), and this gave Little Big Man his opportunity. The fierce wildcat had not his magical tools with him, the wildcat could not go into the Other World where he was invincible, and Little Big Man seized his destiny. Jealousy hurled him at the small man. He grabbed his arm. The wildcat slashed at him, but the troopers moved in. A bayonet sank to the hilt in the wildcat's back. The trooper drew it out and thrust again.

All the eagles of the earth screeched, as one of their sacred fraternity fell to his knees and collapsed in a bloody heap.

"I nursed him that evening," Touch the Clouds said.

"And I," his father said. "While Black Shawl huddled in a corner of the quartermaster's little log building."

He Dog was delirious with emotion. "I . . . was . . . not . . . there!"

His anguish spoke of his love for the man whose name could never be spoken. Love? Hatred of evil and hatred of the whiteman's utter contempt for truth and hatred of the redman's treachery and weakness were He Dog's love for his great friend, as they had been the Strange One's love also. Their feelings ran higher than injustice or dishonor or lies could ever erase. Legends could grow of the wild man's raping of pioneer women and sneaky cutthroating in the night, but the truth ran higher than that lie. Legends could also grow of his religious magnificence and uncompromising heroism, but the truth ran higher than that too.

When the last drop of his blood ran out of his heart that night in Nebraska in 1877, more than a man died, and more than hope was conceived. Millions of years of mystical understanding came to an end, but a new era of Power began. Power turned the Strange One's last drop of blood into his people's first drop of hope. With every year another drop of renewal beat into the desperate bloodstream of Indian America. With every year they grew stronger, while the lust and greed of the Strange One's murderers and traitors lost their bone and muscle.

Philbert felt it coursing through him—the Power of the Unnamed One.

He lay there, growing into a transcendental monster, gulping the spiritual nourishment.

And the liars? The cowards? The winners of the West? They could never convert this boy. He had a Power Spot. He had lots of them all over the country. And it is a law of physics that for every action there is a reaction. For every injustice done to the North American natives there is at least one spiritual goofball gulping up the inevitable Power of avenging justice. It's unavoidable! Good will triumph! We *will* overcome!

Philbert felt pretty good about that. He felt good about something, and it wasn't physical because he was cold and wet and hungry and sleepy all of a sudden. He stood up, brushed himself off, and froze—

A small white stone was stuck to his coat.

It was his second medicine sign.

The Strange One had trickled another drop into the human race.

Philbert pressed it against him.

It was of no small significance that it was exactly over his heart (the largest organ in his body, besides his stomach).

Comedy's profanity weaseled its way back into the picture. Philbert stood here, on one of the holiest spots on earth, clasping a gift from the gods, and his stomach growled. His salivary glands sudsed over. He thought of a package of peanuts in the car and hurried off.

But first he put the stone in his pocket with the stone from Bear Butte and said "thank you" to nothing and everything in particular.

"Could have been worse." Young-Man-Afraid-of-His-Horses shrugged from atop the bluff. "Not exactly the Second Coming, but who's counting?"

They all rode off and out of sight, perhaps even to the unknown place where the parents of the Strange One had buried their tempestuous son.

Make no mistake; only the highest reverence is intended with the telling of this tale. If comedy intrudes upon tragedy in its willy-nilly way, that is not the fault of the tale-teller. It is the fault of Truth. Following the physical equation already postulated that there is a ludicrous element for every serious element, an action for every reaction, then the forthcoming events can be excused under the title of Farcical Tragedy.

Philbert couldn't believe his eyes as he approached the

highway. A blue-eyed dragon was burying Protector in the snow! It couldn't be! But it was! The dragon completed its grisly task and continued heedlessly up the road, shoveling snow into the ditch. It had no time to bother with cars blocking *its* way from *its* appointed rounds.

And Protector sat up to its eyeballs in snow. The people inside were trapped.

Saint George was bilious! He was provoked! He was cross! He ran—yes, *ran!*—headlong at the dragon approaching him. A head-on collision was imminent! The joust was about to begin.

Dull Knife walked up to the top of the bluff and watched. His wife and family were with him. So were seventy-eight other Cheyenne, mostly women and children. They were the only survivors out of 142 who had escaped from the Fort Robinson barracks on a night very much like this one on January 9, 1879, sixteen months after the Strange One had been murdered. They were in rags. Some had no shoes, and their feet were already green with death. But they were the survivors. Sixty others were dead in the snow. Five warriors had stayed behind at the barracks, keeping the soldiers busy while the others escaped from captivity in the foul pens where they had been corralled. Fifty more dead were shot down as they escaped and were piled into wagons and brought in. Some of the wounded would not be taken by the savages from across the sea. Big Antelope stabbed his wife and then killed himself. Thirty-two women hid in a hole, until the soldiers had killed all but three of them. One of the warrior-women stabbed her child and then herself. The remaining women stood on the bluff and stared blankly with the others at Whirlwind attacking the beast. They were the remains of Dull Knife's band, which had marched a thousand miles from Oklahoma Territory, had outfought five American armies on sheer desperation, only to be captured and finally slaughtered in the snow.

History?

Whirlwind saw it all again in the yellow Caterpillar that

scraped and raped the holy earth from coast to coast. *Its* hideous steel and unconscious march westward were again out to bury the purple riders of the sage. Again? The rape had never stopped.

Whirlwind was up on the dragon's lip in one leap, up on its face in another spring, and up into its brain with another vault of adrenaline. He opened the door into the very marrow of every bullet and railroad tie and barbed-wire fence that had killed, displaced, and discouraged every single Indian in America.

"Hey, what's the big idea!" the voice of the Enemy said. But Whirlwind glommed onto the greasy barbarian like the sneaky savage that he was. Good god-fearing sodbusters a hundred years ago had known the fury of similar Abominable Snowmen. He was the sneaky savage of old, terrorizing wagon trains and farm families out of their Christian sleep. He had only to vault full-blubber onto the snowplow driver to crush him half to death. The driver was out like a light, and the dragon skidded stupidly to a stop, deprived of its brain.

The Cheyenne on the hill cheered.

The tractor idled in the middle of the highway. Spurts of black diesel smoke came out of the smokestack, like the smoke of a dragon's extinguished flame.

Whirlwind got clumsily to his feet, a little surprised at his heroic feat. Untangling himself from the gearshift levers and hand brake and the mechanical marvels that propelled such uniform destruction, he sat in the driver's seat. He looked at the flattened driver, scrunched in a corner of the cab.

Whirlwind thought, *I've stopped progress.*

The road wouldn't get plowed that night. People wouldn't get to church the next day. Trucks wouldn't get to Chicago. America would stop.

What is the only thing worse than a nation without its ponies? A nation without its pony trails. No trails, no ponies.

Whirlwind grinned. It was an unspeakable thought. He would have to bring it up with the boys sometime when—

189

The boys!

He remembered the moment, and that his fellow travelers were probably suffocating in the car. Or at least shitting in their pants.

Suddenly, very tired, he crawled awkwardly out of the dragon. It must have been ten feet down to the ground. It took him forever to get down, because there didn't seem to be any ladder or steps on the damn thing. He caught his toe in a wedge of metal frames and tumbled head over heels into the fluffy white powder. Well, no one said a hero can keep up his heroism twenty-four hours a day. And Philbert especially could not keep it up. He *floofed* like a beached walrus into the snow.

It was the first good laugh the Cheyenne on the hill had had in days.

Philbert got to one knee and slipped disjointedly around on his butt.

The Cheyenne hooted. They jumped up and down. They made quite a scene of themselves.

Philbert finally got to his feet and stood very still.

The snags snickered.

Philbert waited, expected, to fall down again, just out of the orneriness of his own fleshy momentum. The papooses clapped their hands.

Floomp! Down he went again, like a ton of bricks!

They rolled around until they got sick, up on the hill. They held their stomachs. They let go of their stomachs. It was unbearable. Tears rolled down their cheeks. They choked. They gagged. They hugged each other. It was excruciating. It was torture. It was merciless.

It was a massacre.

The big, fat dumb shit crawled humbly to his hands and feet. He lifted up one hand and crawled. He withdrew the other hand and kept upright. Well, sort of. If he'd had longer gorilla arms, he thought, he might do better. But he slipped and shodded his way back to his buried horse.

He almost cried to see it so helpless and abused. But the pale-face interlopers had never been against cruelty to animals, and it was obvious they were never going to amend their ignorant ways.

Philbert brushed three feet of snow away from the left rear window. Half mad, Imogene glowered at him from the window. Philbert grew a little frightened of her. She looked like a crazed animal in a zoo.

She rolled the window down and screamed, "Get us out of here! I'm never going to—oh, God—I—if I ever again reach civilization, I'll never—I promise I'll—" And so on.

Wolf Tooth quickly wriggled out the window. Buddy wriggled out right behind him. Buddy said, calmly going for Philbert's throat, "I'm gonna kill you now, Philbert. I'm gonna kill ya."

"Why?"

But Wolf Tooth interrupted. "Look."

Buddy looked.

"Holy goddamn Jesus, Mary, and Joseph," Buddy gasped. He could gasp and talk at the same time. "The tractor stopped. It's coming back for the kill!"

"No," Philbert said, "I think it—"

"Whaddaya know?" Buddy hissed at him. "You stop for some goofy—"

"It's not moving, Buddy," Wolf Tooth said.

"What?"

They ran to have a look. Philbert patiently waited for them. They crawled all over the dragon, shouted, and ran back.

Oh, when were they going to stop underestimating Philbert?

"What happened?" Wolf Tooth asked. Buddy had his mouth open but couldn't talk.

"Nothin'," Philbert said.

"Uh-huh."

"Okay."

"Well, uh . . ."

"You can drive a Cat, can't ya, Wolfie?" Buddy asked.

"Yep," Wolf replied. "We can back her up, hook up a chain, and pull that baby out. I may even plow on ahead for a few miles while you follow."

And that's just what they did.

The Cheyenne in their graves rested more peacefully that night, and the people of the prairie—whether Indian, German, or Pekingese—*did not* swear, because the blizzard blew itself out. The clouds went on by and Great-Grandmother Moon came out to supervise the whole operation.

 CHAPTER **11**

Of Sunday Morning Worship
at St. Andrew's in Lame Deer

MR. AND MRS. Chester Red Bird went to six o'clock Mass every Sunday morning at St. Andrew's Catholic Church in Lame Deer. They got up at five o'clock every morning, anyway, and it was a nice change not to make breakfast and turn on the big color TV and watch the *Today* show out of the NBC station in Billings. *The Pentecostal Hour* and *Meet the Press* were the only things on, anyway.

Unida Red Bird was the only full-blooded Cheyenne in the Red Bird family. She was a short, fat, silent woman. She kept an immaculate trailer. She kept an eighteen-hour vigil in front of the color TV. She made Chester put up a fifty-foot rotating antenna so they could get reception from four states and Canada.

Chester was half Cheyenne and a quarter Assiniboin. His father was Assiniboin and French. He had been the janitor at the Mission School for twenty-five years and was living on a nice pension now. He had pictures of his son Buddy all over the trailer. He had pictures of him in his Marine fatigues, he had pictures of him at a party holding a drink and hugging Chester. One small snapshot of their long-lost daughter, Bonnie, was in a corner of the pantry, next to a fifteen-by-eleven blowup of Buddy scoring a touchdown against the Lodge Grass Devils.

Unida and Chester Red Bird got in their 1975 Toyota pickup and drove four blocks to St. Andrew's. It was still dark. A foot of new snow from the previous night's storm was only a dark nuisance in the predawn murkiness. Unida had on a black cotton dress she'd gotten at the grocery store for $19.95, and a long gray cotton coat. She had on her inevitable matching white hat and gloves. Chester wore a blue serge suit he'd gotten in 1945, when he got out of the Marines.

The little prefab church was packed when they got there. Indians always got up early, and they always would. They'd always worshiped the sunrise and they always will. So the six o'clock Mass was a very popular one.

Unida and Chester wedged their way into the back pew, next to Myron and Farnett Stump Horn. They nodded hello silently, for Father Murphy had entered and the show was beginning.

The savages chanted Kyrie Eleisons along with the altar boys. They gazed raptly at linen chasubles and remembered buckskin antelope capes. They prayed for themselves, and their sons and their daughters, and cast furtive glances at the one stained-glass window above the altar. Blue-and-yellow glass formed the cubistic picture of John the Baptist doing his thing at the River Jordan with Christ the Savior. The aborigines watched the light trickle through the glass. By some haphazard stroke of construction, the window faced east. The redskins converted to Catholicism in droves, primarily to watch the sunrise trickle through the stained glass. The poor Lutherans and Mormons didn't have a chance. As Father Murphy raised the host in the Consecration, turning the Aramaic rabbi's body and blood into bread and wine, the heathens held their breath. The window was glowing.

The infidels filed up to the altar railing for Communion with Joshua-bar-Joseph. They held their mouths open, took the host from the priest on their quivering tongues, and kept an eye on

194

the window. It was luminescent from the light arising outside. Phosphorescent chunks of blue glass and amber Jesus radiated! Throbbed! Oh, God, God, God, Thou art our Savior!

The Untamed Ones shuffled out of church. Father Murphy greeted them at the door. He thanked them for coming. They congratulated him on the sermon. (What sermon?) They shook hands. They stood out on the porch and took big breaths of the good, fresh air. The sun shone happily on their faces. They all went home for big breakfasts and to catch the NBA game of the week.

They all agreed it had been a good service.

CHAPTER 12

Of Protector's Glory, of Wihio the Trickster, and of the Fate of Another Whirlwind and Red Bird

PROTECTOR WAS IN his glory. He had five lives dependent on the smooth functioning of his ball bearings and piston rings, and he was functioning smoothly. He whinnied and pranced and fairly leapt down the highway. His old joints and hardened arteries barely complained at all, and then not in any sort of irritable manner. They creaked and crunched and squeaked, but they were the happy groans of a contented old gentleman with his grandchildren on his lap. He was, in short, a prosperous machine.

He had followed the dragon for thirty miles until they crossed the Wyoming border. Then Wolf Tooth drove the thing into a ditch, where he was sure it would take at least five wreckers to pull it back out. The road was snow-packed, and only occasionally did they see any other travelers.

The brain and marrow of the dragon crawled up the steep slope where his hideous charger lay up to its eyeballs in snow. He stood in the road, shaking his fist at the sneaky savages who had come in the night, wreaked havoc on his cozy little world, and now drove away into the mist from which they had come. ("Remember, Pa? Remember, Ma? The night them red devils swooped in on the Morgan place and killed ever'body in their sleep? Half the valley moved back to Missouri after that.")

Philbert gave Protector the reins and dozed as they trotted westward. All the passengers were asleep and counting their blessings after the harrowing night. Philbert awoke briefly in Lusk, to feed and water his faithful horse, and then they were back on their way. The sun came up behind them on a clear and white land.

Another forty miles and an hour later, they stopped at the Western Cafe at the junction of Interstate 25 (Interstate at last! Interstate at last! Thank God, the Interstate at last!) for breakfast. Everyone went to the bathroom, washed up, woke up, then chowed down. The flapjacks flew, the overeasies were sopped up, coffee was slurped, and Buddy paid the bill. They piled out to the car, sucking on their toothpicks, patting their satisfied bellies, feeling real damn good and glad to be alive. They rolled onto I-25 and headed just as south as they could go. The Interstate was snow-packed, too, but it was sanded and scraped and that's all an adventurer could ask for.

It is at just such times that it is real damn fine to be alive. Intellectual discussions arise with the sun. Pensive musings flow upon a body like sweet, warm milk.

"Look at this lousy place," Buddy said sweetly. The others turned to him, then turned to look out their windows. Eighteen-wheelers blasted past them like they were standing still, and at forty-five miles per hour on an Interstate, they might as well have been. A refinery was on their right. A dam on the North Platte River was on their left.

"You'd think at least way the hell out here," Buddy said from the backseat, "there'd be a little bit of countryside left."

"We're getting close to civilization," Wolf Tooth said from the front seat, "Denver's only two hundred miles from here."

"Denver!" Buddy cursed. It was a foul curse. It was a blasphemous oath.

"There's lots of pretty country here," Imogene said from the other corner of the backseat. "And Denver is a good place. Keith and Donna are very excited to see us, Oliver has a good job with the Sunbeam Corporation all lined up, and we have lots of friends there." She reached up to pat Marie on the head, who sat between Philbert and her daddy. "Donna said the school where Marie will be going is very nice. It's in a nice neighborhood, she said."

Buddy ignored her. "Wyoming is a piece of shit. They've sold out. Strip mines everywhere. Gasification plants. Why, hell, Rock Springs is so full of whorehouses and cheap trailer parks from the oil and coal boom that it'd make ya sick."

"That's what I heard," Wolf Tooth said. "I been reading the *Denver Post*, ya know? I read about in there where you can't replace the soil when it's been stripped."

"The aquifers," Buddy added, "the underground water. It gets cut off. You can't put a river back. Look at West Virginia. It's one big pit. The Powhatans are gone, man. There's only about fifty of 'em left. Fifty. Fifty!"

"Jesus," Wolf Tooth said.

"Yeah. It makes me sick."

Philbert said to Marie, "What is your Lakota name?"

The girl looked anxiously to her father.

"Little Sweet Grass," he said.

"Oh, yeah," Marie said, "Little Sweet Grass."

"Do you know what the Arapaho is for 'come and get it'?" Philbert asked her. "You know how when you're hungry, you say 'Come and get it!'?"

"Yeah. What?"

"*He-est-tan-i-winna*. The Cheyenne is *He-est-tan-its*. You see how they're alike?" Philbert asked.

Marie nodded. "*He-est-tan-its*."

"*He-est-tan-its*. The first four allies of the Cheyenne were the Suhtai and Arapaho and Apache and Sioux. They are all very much alike. The old name we Cheyenne had for ourselves was

Ni-oh-ma-ate-a-nin-ya, which means 'desert people.' But the Sioux started calling us *Shi-hel-la*, which was a misunderstanding. When we told your ancestors in sign language that we were the desert people . . ."

And here Philbert made some quick hand signs, holding the steering wheel steady with his belly. Imogene leaned upon the seat to watch.

". . . they misunderstood the sign and thought we were saying that we always used red earth paint on our faces and bodies, so they gave us the Sioux word for that."

He made another series of hand signs.

"It changed into *Shi-hen-na*, and the name was picked up by early white travelers, and it is Cheyenne today."

"That's very interesting, Philbert," Imogene said. "Isn't it, Marie?"

"It's neat," the girl said. "But why did they get the signs all mixed up?"

"Our people did not write anything down, Little Sweet Grass," Philbert explained. "They wandered around a lot, always looking for game and fuel, and got separated into different groups after many years, and so languages changed. They had to invent sign languages so that they could talk to each other. Today there are the Northern Cheyenne in Montana and the Southern Cheyenne in Oklahoma, and we have forgotten many of the old words. But we all came from the same stock of long, long ago. You, Little Sweet Grass, are also my relative."

"Really?" the girl said, her eyes lighting up. "Wow." Imogene and Wolf Tooth were also listening raptly. Buddy was scowling.

"Where'd you learn all that stuff, man?" Wolf Tooth asked.

"From my uncle Fred," Philbert said. "He used to tell stories all the time."

"Too bad those stories don't tell us how to keep our reservations," Buddy said, "and keep up with progress, and—"

"But they do," Philbert said, interrupting.

"Oh, is that right?" Buddy asked. "I don't mean to tromp on your show, Phil, I really don't, but what are we gonna do about two hundred and twenty million taxpayers out there who are getting sick of one million of us not trying to be Americans? They're sick of us, man, and they ain't gonna feel guilty about what they done to us much longer. They need our coal, our oil, our uranium. They're hungry, man. We got fifty million acres of land that's got one fucking trillion dollars worth of energy on it that they want! And they're gonna get it, just like they got that sewer put up over there!"

They drove past the largest power plant in the country, near Wheatland, Wyoming. It belched. It farted. It pissed. It shit.

"No, they aren't," Philbert said. The others turned to him. He drove silently for a minute, for effect. "Wihio the Trickster won't let them, for Wihio is also the creator of the universe. He will play a little trick on the whiteman, you wait and see."

"Oh, fer cryin' out loud," Buddy muttered, and stared out the window. He said in a tone of utter mockery and sarcasm, "Wihio the Trickster won't let them. God, no less."

Buddy smirked, and Marie snuggled closer to Philbert, and Wolf Tooth rolled a joint in delicious anticipation, and Imogene put her chin on her hands in the back of the seat, and Philbert told this story: "In a way Wihio was an animal, and in another way he was a Cheyenne, but his name was the same word we use for whiteman. So he was many things, but mostly he loved to pull antics and tell dirty jokes. He had many adventures, but I will only tell you one."

"Thank God," Buddy muttered, accepting the joint from Wolf Tooth.

"One day Wihio was out looking for some fun, the way he always did, and to get away from his tipi, where his wife was always putting him to work. He came to a little creek and sat down under a plum tree to rest his dogs. Pretty soon he saw some beautiful purple plums floating in the creek. Now, Wihio is always hungry. He will eat anytime he can. He especially loved Indian food, like turnips and squash and plums. Indians are responsible for most of the food of the earth, you know. 'You never know when you'll eat again,' he used to say. So he reached out over the creek to get those plums, but they disappeared and he fell in the water.

"Well, he crawled back out of the creek, soaking wet. After a minute he saw the plums shimmering on the water again. He dived at them this time, just to make sure that he would not miss them, but all that happened was that he found himself on the bottom of the creek again. So he crawled back out and lay on the bank under the tree. He lay very still, and when he was sure the plums had forgotten about him, he grabbed for them again. He spent the whole day, and the whole next day, trying to come up on those plums from every angle, but it was no use. They were very tricky plums and Wihio could not hold on to them. He kept falling in the water.

"Pretty soon his wife came looking for him. She found him splashing around in the creek, under the plum tree.

"'Woman,' he cried, 'I am glad to see thee, for a very wonderful thing has taken place on this magical spot. During the day some very juicy plums are floating in this creek. But at night they go away. I have been thinking upon this miracle, for I wanted to bring the plums home to thee.'

"'You stupid dog of a dog,' she screamed at him. 'Those plums are hanging over your head. Those are shadows you see in the water, worthless fool of a husband.'

"His wife hit him over the head with a pan and took him home. He never did get any plums."

Protector ambled happily down the highway.

"That's it?" Buddy asked.

"Yes," Philbert replied. The others were smiling gently. They glowed with sweet, pensive musing.

"That's gonna do it?" Buddy asked. "Fairy tales?"

"Yes," said Philbert, "and there are many other stories too."

"I don't know about you, Philbert," Buddy said, shaking his head. "Navaho uranium miners are getting cancer, Indians are getting fifteen cents' royalty on a ton of coal while white landowners get a dollar and a half. The per capita income on reservations is a thousand dollars per year—one seventh of the national average, and you gotta tell fairy stories?"

"There are also stories of our ancestors," Philbert said. "Stories that tell of problems and of how the Old Ones handled the problems. Often problems do not change, nor do people."

"Oh, so now you've got soap operas," Buddy said sarcastically. "Congress is trying to pass what they call the Native American Equal Opportunity Act and you're passing out *The Guiding Light* on Channel Two? Hey, man, those racists want to chop up our land into small farmsteads. The Mafia and the FBI are out to eat us up. They don't want us yelling racism because they say that only *causes* racism! They pack the BIA with apples and the prisons with AIM! Yeah, AIM is mostly full of crazies, but at least we wouldn't let another 'Allotment Act' knock our land down from 398 million acres in 1887 to 48 million fuckin' shittin' kiss-ass acres now!"

"There was a policeman named Red Bird who was cursed by a witch in 1897," Philbert said calmly. "Was he your great-grandfather?"

"Oh, Christ," Buddy said, "I don't know. It doesn't matter, anyway, whether some old—"

"A very wise and cautious old man had an answer for our problems once," Philbert said. "It had to do with another warrior named Whirlwind. Which, Little Sweet Grass, is my Indian name."

Little Sweet Grass smiled at him and snuggled closer.

Philbert was in control again. "The trouble started when Sam Crow; Blue Shirt or Whirlwind, another Whirlwind; Ben Shoulderblade; Tangled Yellow Hair; and Spotted Hawk were out one day looking for some fun. These six came to the camp of John Hoover, a sheepherder who worked for a man named Barringer.

"He gave them a meal, and then either Blue Shirt or Sam Crow started to steal something and the sheepherder shot at him. So Blue Shirt rode around the wagon and shot the sheepherder from the other side, killing his dog too. Then they left.

"They found the body a few days later, and the whiteman threatened to go to war against the Indians. Blue Shirt lost his nerve and took his wife and camped out in the hills. The rest of the Cheyenne moved to Tie Creek and made breastworks on a hill.

"But the soldiers did not attack. Later Blue Shirt came in. He was related to the policeman, Red Bird, who gave Blue Shirt a big feast in his tent and then handed him over to the Indian superintendent, who put him in a log jail at Lame Deer. The next day the sheriff came out and took him to Miles City.

"They got the other five a few days later, and held a trial down there. Blue Shirt lied in court and blamed Spotted Hawk, but Spotted Hawk had a good lawyer and they hung Blue Shirt. The other Indians dug a hole in the jail and escaped, except that Tangled Yellow Hair got stuck in the hole because he was too fat. The police searched for the others, but it was a long time before they could catch them, because they were hiding out in the hills. But they finally caught them and took them back to jail. They had to serve extra time.

"The sheepherder killing was the last war scare for the Cheyenne. There was trouble after that, but troops were not called out. The soldiers left the reservation not long afterward, and the scouts were disbanded."

"What about the witch?" Marie asked.

"She was a religious person," Philbert explained. "She was down getting water from the river when she saw Red Bird patrolling along the edge of the brush. She didn't like him because he was too strict. He would arrest anybody. And so she did a thing that religious people are not supposed to do. She pointed at him and said, 'Let my finger pass through that man.' And in just a few days he was dead."

Protector rode through the city of Cheyenne. The Cheyenne did not say a word for half an hour.

"It happened on ration day," Philbert continued, as if there had not been a pause. "They were branding some cattle, and Red Bird was sitting on a plank across one of those high gates, helping push the cattle into a chute below with a long pole. He lost his balance, fell off backward, and broke his neck."

They crossed into Colorado. The sun was as mellow in its afternoon glow as were the riders down below.

"But," Philbert said after a while, "the curse came back upon the old woman, as it always does. A bale of hay fell on one of her relatives and broke his neck too."

They drove through Fort Collins. The Rockies loomed menacingly on their right, growing ever closer and meaner.

"Who was the old man?" Marie asked.

"What?" Philbert asked.

"The old man you're talking about."

"Oh, that was my uncle Fred. He told me a lot of the old stories. He told me that one. He said he was a boy when it happened—I mean, when they hung Blue Shirt. He said all the kids got out of school when the tribe went up to Tie Creek to hold off the soldiers. But when it was over, they had to go back to school. They did not want to. He said he remembered that day Blue Shirt was caught, and that he wished somebody would kill a sheepherder every day."

Protector rumbled into the murky outskirts of Denver. His old bones ached now. He was tired. He was being outrun by sleeker and prouder animals. Herds of them jostled him and laughed at his old swayback. He was a little sad to see the sun disappear behind the great cloud of smog enveloping them.

 CHAPTER **13**

How Success and Happiness
Became Possible for a
Southern Ute Living in Texas

EVEN THOUGH IT was Sunday afternoon in Dallas, Texas, and Sandy Youngblood would rather have been at home with Elaine and the kids playing Ping-Pong in the den or frying steaks on the hibachi, he didn't mind going to the meeting he was now going to. The Olds Cutlass Supreme was on cruise control, the roads were clear of the previous night's blizzard, and the heater blew its sweet heat uniformly throughout the luxurious velour interior. Sandy's crisp white shirt smelled of Downy fabric softener, his woolen blazer fit him as only his tailor in London could make it fit him, and his Bass Weejun loafers hugged his feet just right. He felt clean, smelled manly, and knew that he looked just as he was supposed to look. The best part was that it was how he wanted to feel, smell, and look. He was a happy man, he truly was.

His wife and he had worked out their differences over eight years of a topsy-turvy marriage. He had wanted more freedom, she had wanted more love, they had fought about it, compromised, and come to accept each other for who they were. It had been a struggle to make sacrifices for their three children, but

Sandy came to earn their demanding love through an uncompro-misingly relentless display of integrity. He knew that children could see through hypocrisy and unhappiness quicker and clearer than legions of psychologists and wise men ever could, and he wanted his children's respect. So he was honest with them. He did not lie, he did not hide his feelings, nor did he tell truths that would unnecessarily damage their fragile egos. He was stern and yet fair with them; he was fun-loving and yet very adult.

He was capable of such wisdom because he had a challenging job—he had goals. He believed in something. And he did not kid himself by expecting too much out of life. He was thirty-five, half Indian, and he knew that human nature was an imperfect thing; he knew that only the best people accepted great responsibilities by remaining humble about their own mortality. He knew that power was a passing illusion but that illusions were the only things in life that were fun, and that having fun was essential to every human endeavor. Therefore he was a mature man who had fun with power.

He played at controlling the lives of other people, because he played at controlling his own life. He was a man who had a hell of a lot of fun. Consequently he had a hell of a lot of friends. Con-sequently he had a hell of a lot of power.

He had mastered the politics of fun. He was a successful busi-nessman. He was president of the Rotary Club. He was a mem-ber of the prestigious Dallas Athletic Club, as well as the Golden Grove Country Club. He was the assistant chairman of the Texas Democratic Party. His name was being mentioned for a post with the BIA in Washington. After that, who knew? Maybe he would be the first Indian candidate for the United States Senate. He had powerful friends, drinking friends, fun-loving friends.

He pulled into the parking lot of the federal building complex in downtown Dallas. The lot was practically deserted on this

Sunday afternoon. Only a handful of other cars were parked there. Sandy Youngblood parked his car. He got out of his car, locked the doors carefully, and strode briskly toward the modern, thirty-story building made of Vermont marble and Texas know-how. A security guard inside the swinging glass doors checked his ledger for Sandy's name, scowled a little at Sandy's suspicious bone structure, checked his IDs and credit cards, and finally let him pass. Sandy thought how he had enjoyed the going-over as he rode the silent elevator to the seventeenth floor. His minority status had opened many doors for him, and it would open many more.

He thought of that day's meeting. It was a rather important meeting. It was a rather secret meeting, but only because the undersecretary of the U.S. Department of Interior was going to be there. It was a meeting of the Council of Energy Resources Tribes.

CERT had been described to the president as "the Native American OPEC." It was an organization of American Indian tribes that was determined to get its fair share out of the minerals on their land, just as the Islamic Arabian tribes in Asia and Africa were determined to get their fair share out of the oil-thirsty tribes of Europe and North America. The red devils had a lot of leverage, too—four percent of all the land in the country, one-third of the strippable coal, half of the uranium, and enough oil to bedazzle Saudi Arabia. It was time to circle the wagon trains again. They were, in short, going to put the screws to the industrial nations. The undersecretary of the Interior "was thus encouraged by the Indians' understanding" of the economic facts of life. He had come to Dallas to negotiate the terms. Dozens of Indian spokesmen and tribal presidents and lawyers and consultants would be at this, the first of a week of "private talks" about the course of sovereignty and self-improvement in Indian country.

Sandy Youngblood was the spokesman of four such Indian

self-help organizations. He was one of the most glib of the Indian spokesmen. He was a rising red star on the horizon, and he looked forward to the horizon.

He took his place at the huge walnut table in the Department of Interior offices (after greeting a host of friends), and a Department of Interior clerk banged a gavel at the head of the table.

"Gentlemen, can we begin?"

 **CHAPTER 14**

How the Knights Came to the Wicked City, and How They Were Tempted, and How They Resisted Temptation

THIS STORY WILL now grow more unbelievable than ever, if that is possible. Our noble voyagers have now come upon the most unbelievable episode they are to encounter on their voyage. Therefore it is the most authentic episode of the voyage.

Denver, Colorado, was the fourth fastest-growing city in America. The Denver Broncos were a championship football team. The region's oil, coal, gas, and uranium made Denver, with only 1.8 million people, second only to Houston, Texas, as an energy giant. And that meant second in the world. It had the best dry-powder skiing in the world. Numerous corporate mergers commanded bullish opinions of Denver's Rocky Mountains' *high* profits. It was the marketing and distribution center of the mountain states. Six railroads, 160 interstate trucking lines, and hundreds of thousands of square feet of warehouse space helped fill the needs of a region as large as Western Europe. Thirty-five thousand federal jobs, 150,000 university students, 300,000 airline flights a year, and 1,000,000 automobiles were all just a small part of its greatness.

Its people made Denver, the Mile-High City, great, not its

official elevation of 5,280 feet above sea level. It had one of the highest percentages of out-of-state residents of any city in America, second only to Los Angeles. And that meant second in the world. Its healthy climate gave Germans from Ohio a new breath of life. Its vigorous pace gave Jews from Long Island a feeling of home. Its easygoing manner gave Gambians from North Carolina a touch of the old country. Its cross-country skiing satisfied Swedes from Wisconsin, its alpine skiing satisfied Italians from Texas, its sense of bon vivant and esprit de corps and antelope-meat hors d'oeuvres at Renee's were adequate for the Frenchmen from New Orleans. It was a city where many, many people wore T-shirts that said: I LOVE YOU, DENVER!

Imogene Wolf Tooth gave Philbert directions through all of this magnificence. Protector was in terror to be only one of a million, but he merged left and picked up Interstate 70 east. They were bound for the suburb of Aurora, and the condominium of Donna and Keith Harris, who lived in the condominium that they owned (with only eleven years left on their second mortgage) there. Donna and Keith Harris, as Imogene Wolf Tooth explained, were members of minority races who had successfully integrated into the mainstream.

"Keith is Oglala, of course," Imogene explained. She was very excited.

"Donna is Mexican, and they have two girls."

"Well," said Buddy, looking out the window at the great downtown skyline of the great city, "this is where the action is." He was only a little excited.

Philbert wondered idly if an Arapaho camp had once nestled beside the Piggly Wiggly on Colorado Boulevard. He had an idea that Cheyenne had followed bison along the draw where Broadway crossed Colfax Avenue, but it was hard to tell. He was pretty sure a party of Sioux had gone fishing in Cherry Creek, where the Golden Slipper Inn now was, but he couldn't be positive. He did take courage from the many, many remnants of his culture still visible: there was the Comanche Lounge, the Navaho Trucking Company, Kiowa and Seminole and Bannock and Huron streets. He took hope from the Jeep Cherokees passing him (whooping madly!), the Ford Pintos (whinnying furiously!), the Chevrolet Cheyenne pickups ("Run down them slowpokes!").

The miles and miles of concrete and machinery and well-made plans of urban men went on and on. They crossed Vasquez Boulevard, they went past the refineries of Commerce City, they circled the planned community of Montebello, they went under a 747 on the north runway of Stapleton International Airport. They stared and gawked and yakked, getting into the contagious excitement of an American city—the most exhilarating center of human endeavor on earth.

They turned right on Peoria Street, which was just about the easternmost edge of the metropolitan area. But Interstate 270 was being built a few more miles to the east, to make room for the growth that was to come, and soon Peoria Street would be only another important trail in the metropolitan area that formed a fifty-mile radius in all directions from downtown.

"Take the next right," Imogene said, navigating. She had done a splendid job of it. Wolf Tooth hadn't hollered at her more than a dozen times.

Protector gingerly swung right at the next street. Ten-foot walls of imitation redwood encircled the planned community like the walls of a flimsy fort. The two-story condos huddled inside like fashionable barracks. The streets had bumps in the middle so that no one could run down the children. Signs warned of speeding. Dogs warned of canine infringements. Lawns warned of territory. Sidewalks. Streetlights. A swimming pool. A police station.

"Over there, over there," Imogene instructed, beside herself with anticipation. "Over there." She was gathering her Kleenex in her purse, she was putting Marie's coat on Marie, she was fiddling, fidgeting, and fussing.

They parked between a Mustang and a Cougar. The sun was

threatening to set, just to see if anybody noticed. And they did notice, what they could see of it through the brown haze, for these were outdoor people, these Denverites. All across the city the black-headed travelers had seen golf courses crowded with golfers, tennis courts crowded with tennis players, jogging lanes and bicycle lanes and soccer fields crowded with joggers and bicyclers and soccerers. It was a warm yellow day. It was sixty degrees. People were *out*.

Philbert turned off Protector, but Protector continued to gurgle, to stomp his hooves, to bounce and kick and shrug off the weariness of a long day's run. But he wheezed and shuddered and finally breathed loudly through his mouth and let his mind wander to the barn. He thought of hay and a good long drink of water. And sleep.

The five weary voyagers got out and stretched, looking about them in varying stages of curiosity. Buddy was the least curious. He saw through all the plastic bullshit. Wolf Tooth was the next least curious. He wondered why it was so warm there. Marie was next on the scale—she was moderately alert to a gang of kids playing on the yard in front of them. She looked anxiously to see if there might be a place for her in the games, and if there were any boys her age. Imogene loved everything already. She loved the way the fort was clean, the way all the barracks had tiny lawns, the way plants were hung in the windows, even the way jets from Stapleton and C-47s from nearby Lowry Air Force Base roared overhead on their way to somewhere exotic. She loved the whole modern, new, fashionable, *progressive* smell of the place. It was civilized.

Philbert, though, outdid even Imogene for pure astonishment and rapture. He had been speechless on their drive across the city. If he had not been a little worried about the safety of his pony in the endless stampedes, he would have felt perfectly magnificent. As it was, he still felt rather exalted. Now that his pony was bedded down for a while he could let his tremendous powers of observation and description take a particularly lucid turn in their very astonishing development. The ponies hitched in their stables, the ponies congregated in the parking lots, the car washes, the shiny car lots that stretched for blocks and beckoned from out of the ages, even the graveyards—these and many other glimpses of equine behavior in their drive across the city left Philbert speechless and stunned and full of happy wonder. What a truly extraordinary civilization this civilization-on-wheels was! Philbert felt no cynicism about it. He was truly impressed. It was an awesome accomplishment and he was genuinely impressed, for he was an awesomely genuine type of guy. He was down-to-earth. He knew magnificence when he saw it.

"Marie! Wolf Tooth! Aunt Imogene!" several voices shrieked above the other little shrieks of the children playing normally on the lawn in front of them. Two girls emerged from the nameless normalcy and ran full speed at the entire Wolf Tooth family. Jenny hit Wolf Tooth himself and would have flown into sure death if he had not caught her with his neck; that is, she looped her little arms around his neck like a doughnut thrown at a peg and which spins madly about the peg, as if anchored to some uncertain buoy. She showered him with kisses. Kathleen tackled him about the knees. She crawled all over him. Marie stood by in exquisite torment, aching to join in the melee. Philbert giggled. Buddy pretended to observe something down the street.

Imogene walked up to the front door of the condominium, where a man had come out onto the porch.

"So," the man said, "I was about to send the highway patrol out after you guys."

"Hello, Keith," Imogene said, and gave him a big, slow hug. A woman came out on the porch behind him.

"He doesn't even bother to sneak off in the night for his affairs," the woman said, "he just brings them up on the porch now."

"Donna." Imogene grinned, and the women hugged. Keith

stood over them and noted the contrast between them. Even though Donna had always been more attractive than Imogene, she now looked more alive, more . . . alert than their friend from the reservation. Donna was a dark beauty, with the long straight hair and olive skin of a Sonoran peasant. She was short and thin and rather elegant in an undernourished way. But Imogene had gotten a little stout, her skin a little gray, and even though she had on a nice pantsuit and her black hair was combed and cut in a stylish neck-length swirl, she didn't look at ease. She didn't have Donna's knack for casual elegance. Although they were both of peasant stock, Donna had simply grown up in a city and Imogene had not. Imogene didn't have the . . . confidence of a city girl. She was uncomfortable.

"You look wonderful," Donna said.

"Oh, nonsense," Imogene said (and Keith winced), "I look like hell. You wouldn't believe our trip."

"In that thing?" Keith said, pointing a long finger at Protector, lounging in the parking lot. Even his finger seemed to sneer at the vehicle.

"I'll tell ya about it," Imogene said, "in a year or two, when I recover."

Wolf Tooth came up the walk, the two girls in his arms. "Howdy, folks. Looks like I'll have my hands full for a while."

"C'mon in, Wolf," Keith said. "If the girls bother you, just tell them to get off."

"I will."

"Uncle Wolf," Jenny, the younger one, said. She looked like her father. "Tell us the story about—"

"No, no," Kath interrupted. She looked like her mother. "You gotta give us a piggyback ride."

Marie trailed behind her daddy. The other kids on the lawn watched the show jealously. They knew Jenny and Kath were showing off, showing how many neat friends they had that came and visited them. They began to wander off. Philbert watched the drama attentively.

"Oh, Keith," Wolf said. Keith turned back from the door. Donna and Imogene were already inside but turned in the dimness also. "This is Buddy and Philbert, who brought us here. That's their car."

"Well, come on in," Donna greeted from inside.

Buddy came up to the porch and shook hands with Keith. "Hi."

They appraised each other. Keith had Buddy typed immediately; here was a dangerous person. Buddy saw immediately that Keith was a faggot. Even though he was married and had kids, any army veteran knew a latent homo when he saw one. And this Keith was a dilly. He had on a shiny purple polyester shirt unbuttoned to the middle of his hairy chest. He had on tight faded blue jeans where his throbber was deliberately conspicuous. Blue-and-white Adidas tennis shoes. No socks. Stylish short hair with bangs. Bushy mustache. Yep, a real nellie.

"Keith is a capitalist Republican warmonger," Wolf Tooth said amiably.

Keith laughed out loud and put his arm around Wolf Tooth (which Buddy duly noted). "You old hippie pinko faggot Fascist subversive imperialist dog."

"And Philbert there," Wolf interceded, "you should hear that guy sing at powwows."

Philbert waved shyly. He liked Keith a lot. He was easygoing, no phony bullshit, just friendly and clean and mellow.

"You kids beat it," Keith said. "Oh, Kath, bring us four beers." He patted Kath on the rear and she ran inside. The other girls went inside too. Keith suddenly jumped off the small porch and sat on the grass. "Let's stay out here for a minute. The goddamn women'll have to chatter and look at the new curtains, anyway."

"Yeah," Wolf Tooth said, sprawling on the grass. "They'll have to talk about us too. Might as well give them a chance to get it all out. They get resentful if we hang around too much so's they can't talk about us."

"Gotta compare sex notes," Keith added.

"Figure out what's wrong with us," Wolf said.

"Yeah."

"I never seen a woman yet who wasn't worried about another woman ruining her life before she had the chance to let a man ruin it first." This was Buddy's contribution to the masculine repartee.

"That's about it."

Kath came out carrying four beers in her arms. It was clear she was mighty proud to do these masculine chores for her daddy. She gave each man a beer, then ran back inside. Philbert sat on the porch stoop and popped open his can greedily. They all sat, staring vaguely to the west, and to the far-distant mountains, and at the hazy red sun about to set.

"Yep," Buddy continued, "they love to think we ruin their lives. We're out to get 'em. And they get so paranoid about it that I for one get awful sick of it. They drive me to the point where I feel like I *am* out to get 'em. And it's only because that's what they think."

A respectful pause from all.

"You guys ain't Sioux, are ya?" Keith asked.

"Cheyenne." Philbert gulped.

"Me 'n' Buddy were part of the radical horde at Wounded Knee, Keith," Wolf said.

"Oh, Jesus," Keith said, and the men rose to the topics of war and politics and men things with delicious trepidations. "AIM?"

"That's right," Buddy said tensely.

"Keith," Wolf Tooth interceded, for already the ideological camps were sharply defined. "Bull Miller's gone and destroyed my machine shop. I had to escape, man, fucking escape my own home because of my political beliefs! Now that's the way it is on the reservations now, man, right fucking now!"

"Hey," Keith said, "you gotta live like a human being. You're welcome to stay here as long as you want, until you're on your feet. You know that—I said it a year ago and I'm saying it now. But don't expect me to like what's happening at Pine Ridge. It's my reservation too."

"I was just trying to make a living, man," Wolf Tooth said. "A good small-businessman capitalist pig. The whole hog, man, *and it didn't matter.*"

"Politics are life," Buddy said.

"And," Wolf Tooth said, "city ideas ain't country ideas. You can go to your fancy office, Keith, and write grant proposals and form committees and read books and really get an idea of what's going on at Pine Ridge, but that ain't nothing like living there."

"I'm outnumbered." Keith shrugged. "You guys outnumber me."

"Buddy and Philbert are on a trip to Santa Fe," Wolf Tooth said. "Buddy's sister is in jail for being an Indian. They're gonna get her out."

"Great," Keith commented. "Is she in jail because she's an Indian or *because* she's an Indian?"

"We don't know," Philbert said. "But I heard your wife say something about dinner."

They all stood up. Keith made a speech. "If you two must go to Santa Fe, at least stay the night. We have plenty of beds and plenty of hot water, for even anarchists get hungry and dirty and need to relax from the pursuit of their high ideals of a revolutionary utopia."

"Oh, you're a smart man," Buddy said with a grudging smile. "You city liberals have a helluva deal going for yourselves. Fat jobs, fat houses—"

"We read a lot." Keith laughed, and they all went inside.

It was a fat house, indeed. A strong lodge, Philbert thought. It was a two-story condominium in a duplex. It had 2,500 square feet, four bedrooms, three bathrooms, two fireplaces, and one helluva modern kitchen. It had deep orange wall-to-wall carpeting, even in the bathrooms and the closets. It had color-coordinated drapes and paintings; soft, comfortable orange and oak furniture; and, most of all, a cozy, lived-in feel. It was secure, luxurious without being ostentatious, middle-class without being monotonous, upper-class without being preposterous. It was realistic. Every adjective was honest. Every description was absolutely ordinary without being customary. Philbert loved it. He sank down in a soft easy chair. Someone produced another beer for him. A large bowl of peanuts sat obligingly on the table next to his left hand. A large lazy Susan (to be redubbed a lazy Philbert), full of olives and pickled beets and cheese dip and barbecued Doritos, sat within easy reach of his right hand. Both hands worked in an unconscious rhythm up and down to his mouth, a steady stream of nuts and dip and beer, up and down, down and up.

A stereo played a Roberta Flack album. Everyone gathered about the large oak coffee table—which obligingly sat in front of Philbert—where Donna had put a hot pot of green chile fondue and homemade bread. They all sat on the couches flanking the table. Keith brought out a two-gallon pitcher of sangria. Bouquets of pineapple sticks and sliced apples and wedged oranges and fat red grapes floated succulently in the cauldron. Everyone enjoyed Philbert's immense delight in attacking these ambrosial goodies, and Philbert in turn amplified their delight at his delight with an even greater delight. They laughed at nothing. They ate every-thing. They toasted the Christmas tree that presided regally from a corner by the big front window. The sun went down outside and Donna brought them steaming trays of her homemade enchila-das. Keith brought them cocktail glasses of Cuervo Gold margar-itas, with the rims lined with salt. Imogene helped. Buddy told jokes. Kath refilled the grown-ups' glasses and brought grena-dine Roy Rogerses to the kids. Donna brought out her stuffed sopapillas. Imogene passed the bowls of natural honey to everyone.

With the feast in its last fulfilled stages, the conversation turned from the weather, personal anecdotes, and endless com-pliments to the cook and bartender, to more personal and endear-ing topics. It was time to be unselfish, to warm the hearts of thy fellow human beings, and to celebrate the well-fed joy of a Dickens Christmas.

But it takes time to research the depths of the human heart. It takes diplomacy and tact, and an even circumvention for a civilized human being to arrive at his true purpose. And so the probings for truth began with an allegory of plum pudding.

Philbert had the children utterly fascinated with his story of Wihio and the elusive plums. Marie had told Jenny and Kath about it and they had forced it out of him. When he was through, Donna led the applause.

"I tell ya," Wolf Tooth was telling them, "this Philbert is a marvel. He's full of surprises."

"That's not all," Philbert added, patting his immense stomach, growing even more immense by the evening's feast. They all laughed uproariously. "I tell ya," Philbert said, "I get so fat sometimes that even I can't figure out how fat I am. Why I'm so fat—"

"Tell us how fat ya are, Philbert." Wolf Tooth hooted.

Philbert grinned broadly. "I'm so fat that I don't even know I'm ugly."

They roared, Philbert leading the roar. They knew that that was funny only in their uniquely jubilant situation, and that it was not really funny, and that that was what made it particularly funny. They knew that "you had to be there," and the fact that they *were* there made them unique, and privy to the secret zest of life, and that that made life exceedingly unique and zesty. And so they laughed. Philbert's inflections had been just right, his timing was perfect, and his face was priceless.

"Let's play 'Make Fun of Yourself'!" Wolf Tooth shouted. He was really into the spirit of things. "Whoever humiliates himself in the best way wins."

"Who would want to win that?" Buddy asked. It was a reasonable question.

"No, I like this," Donna said. "Whoever loses gets to do the dishes." They all screamed. The dishes and glasses were piled up in every direction. Oh, there was a dishwasher, but the dishes were still a psychological nightmare, and everybody knew it.

"Great!" Wolf Tooth hollered. "Only the humblest wins this game, while the proudest, the biggest ego—"

"The horse's ass," Imogene added slyly.

"—loses. And does the nigger work."

"I don't like that word," Donna said.

"I don't, either," Wolf Tooth said humbly. "'Work' is the curse of the drinking class."

"I didn't mean 'work,'" Donna insisted.

"Neither did I."

"Oh, I give up."

"So," Wolf Tooth decided, "we all take turns making fun of ourselves, and then we all decide, unanimously, who *didn't*, who really flattered themselves or whatever."

"Can we play?" Jenny asked, meaning the kids.

"That'd be perfect."

How does a party game begin? How, in fact, does the party itself begin? One person goes to the bathroom, and another one lights up a cigarette, people cross their legs, other people remember something they wanted to ask each other, another person adds a comment, two more join in the conversation, and they all magically discover they have similar interests, they enjoy listening, they have something witty to say, the others laugh, the others listen, and everyone feels like somebody good and important. They all wonder why life couldn't be as spontaneous and meaningful as this all the time.

"Who goes first?" Wolf Tooth said.

"Ah ha!" Keith commented. "The first shall be last, et cetera."

"What?"

"Whoever goes first," Keith elucidated, "is the proudest, the biggest ego—"

"The horse's ass," Imogene added slyly. She was on her fourth margarita. She was loosening up. She stood up. "Wanna see me throw up? I could do a pretty good imitation of Oliver wrapped around a toilet. Wanna see?"

"I guess Imogene goes first," Wolf Tooth said.

"Go for it, Imo baby!" Keith applauded.

Imogene looked at them. "Oh, I didn't mean—"

"That's why it's perfect." Keith applauded again. "Go for it."

"But humiliate yourself," Wolf Tooth cautioned tentatively. "Yourself."

"Oh, not you, lovey-dovey?" Imogene said sweetly to her husband. "Snookums, big brave chief, *I do, I will* have and hold thee in the rut of my life, for worser and worse, till politics do us part. It's a woman's duty to obey her husband, an Indian woman's tutti-frutti. It's a woman's duty to"—and here she sang "Stand By Your Man"—"for richer or poorer, while an Indian woman's for poorer and poorer and poorer." She sat down calmly. The others gaped at her in amazement. She knew she had their full attention. "But seriously, folks, let's talk about humiliation. You know how humiliating it is to live with a jackass who smells of grease and bear oil twenty-four hours a day? Oh, I know it's his job, I *know* it's a sign of manhood to be filthy and smell of diesel farts, but what I don't *know* is why he feels he has to stick those slimy hands up me without at least washing them first!"

Donna howled with laughter. The men and children stared at each other.

"I see I'm losing you," Imogene concluded. "Mine is a repertoire for a limited audience. Perhaps that is why I should win. My problems are so stupid and so universal that nobody even knows about them. They bore even me. I make so much fun of myself by being married to this big dumb schmuck that I can't even stand myself. And the clincher is—now get this, this is the limit of debasement—"

"Is debasement like deattic?" Keith asked.

"Shut up," Imogene warned. "The clincher is—I like him. Can you believe that corn? Anybody who can stand this bozo, let alone actually love him, *has* to get the booby prize of the year. I rest my case."

The others applauded. They cheered. They shouted for encores.

"No, wait a minute," Wolf Tooth interposed. "I'm not so sure I like this all that—"

"Shut up, schmuck," Imogene said, and gave him a big hug.

"That's a tough act to follow," Keith announced. "So maybe we should hear from the peanut gallery. Jenny, you're a big show-off, do some of the dumb things you do about a million times a day."

"Like what?" Jenny asked sarcastically with her hands on her hips. "How about the time I put a frog in Mommy's purse?" Jenny was only six and hadn't grasped the ingratiating flavor of the game yet.

"No"—her daddy smiled—"that's something that's not nice. We want you to do something stupid so we can laugh at you."

"But you always tell us not to do stupid things?" Kath inquired.

"I know, honey," Donna said, "but this is part of growing up. The more stupid things you do, the more grown-up you are."

"Only kids do smart things," Keith said.

The kids looked at him like he was crazy. They knew he was putting them on and wondered why he was being so stupid.

"I know what," Marie said. She had been with the gang for a whole day now and had a better grasp of the absurdity expected of her. She picked up Jenny's plate of enchiladas and tostadas, which were only half eaten. Very carefully she lined up the plate on the floor in front of where she was sitting, stuck her tongue out like she was fainting, rolled her eyeballs, and fell full-face into the plate of food.

"Marie!" Imogene squealed, and moved to rescue her only daughter from the enchiladas. Oliver held her arm and the others applauded. Kath was appalled and pointed a finger at her berserk peer, then scooted away. She was also giggling uncontrollably.

Jenny jumped up. "C'mon, Kath," she commanded, and the two girls ran upstairs.

"A mysterious mission," Keith commented.

"God knows what they'll come back with," his wife added.

"I thought I raised you better," Wolf Tooth said to Marie.

"You raised her worse," his wife added.

"Um, good." Marie grinned from behind dripping red tortillas.

"Go wipe it off now," her mother instructed.

"No," the girl said. "I gotta keep it on if I'm gonna win."

"Let's hear from somebody else," Wolf Tooth said.

"I'm too humble," Wolf said. "How about you, Keith?"

"I'm a very sophisticated guy," Keith droned in a pseudo-sophisticated English accent. He sat back luxuriously on the couch. He crossed his legs daintily. He brought his cocktail glass delicately to his lips and took a sophisticated sip. Then he smacked his lips loudly and boorishly and belched grotesquely. The others roared but he kept a straight face. He looked at them in amazement. He looked down his nose at them with patronizing haughtiness. "Peons," he said. "Slime of the earth. Slimy fingernails, slimy morals. You're all a pack of antedeluvian ignorami." He scratched his ass. "You know nothing of Beethoven." He picked his nose. "You know nothing of Voltaire." He slurped his drink noisily. "You know nothing of dignity, rococo architecture, table etiquette." He took his shoe off and began clipping his toenails. "You think you have a place in this world? You think you have a say in how you live your life? Freedom? Opportunity? You have nothing but what I give you. If I give you scraps from my garbage can, you should count yourself lucky." A toenail flew into Philbert's drink. "You will never, never be worth two warts on a cow's ass. Because I—I!—say so. I alone understand civilization. I control the money and the power of the world. I have risen by my bootstraps to boot you in the ass. I am the urban dweller. I am the educated. I am the privileged. I am the quintessential achievement of the Age of

Reason, of human nature gone mad with sophisticated good sense. I am the City Slicker." Keith farted and put his bare foot on Donna's lap. "Would you mind picking out the toe jam from my toes? I almost have a whole jar now, and I want to trade it in at the Gourmet Shoppe for some chocolate-covered ants."

"Oooooooh!"

"Ugh!" His wife scowled. "You're disgusting."

"Thank you." Keith beamed. "Do I win?"

"You lose, which is the same thing," Imogene said.

"What, no applause? No cheers?" Keith asked, hurt.

"That was good shit, man," Buddy conceded.

"Hey, thanks, man," Keith said. "Say, man, what's it *really* like to be an Indian?"

Buddy grinned.

"Ohmigod," Imogene gasped. The others looked at her. She was looking up the stairs. The others looked up the stairs.

Jenny and Kath were walking down the stairs precariously. Jenny was sitting on Kath's shoulders. Kath had on bright red high heels. Her head stuck out of an unevenly buttoned skirt wrapped around Jenny's waist. It was one of their mother's skirts. Jenny was bare-chested except for a black lacy bra that practically covered her whole chest. She had on gobs of garish makeup, her father's cowboy hat covering up most of her face, and in one hand she had her mother's six-inch battery-powered vibrator.

"Let's go dancin'!" Jenny cooed in a sultry voice. Kath was a giggling silly skirt. They reached the floor and pranced with mock sexiness toward the adults—who were howling, by the way, at the outrageous costume. The disjointed disco queen paraded up the room, and paraded down the room, and the adults fell off their couch, and fell back on the couch, and the two Innocents chanted a barrage of sexy comments.

"Hey, big boy!"

"Come and get it!"

"Oooh, ooh!"

"Not in front of the children, Keith!"

"Oooo-la-la!"

"Aw, c'mon, honey, just a quickie!"

Jenny accidentally turned on the vibrator, it leapt out of her hands and landed in Philbert's lap, he leapt to his feet, but the insidious thing stayed with him. He brushed it off and it fell to the floor, squirming around and around like a milk bottle in the old game, spin the bottle. It finally stopped and pointed at Buddy. Everyone else pointed at Buddy.

"C'mon, Bud, go for it!"

"Show the disco queen what it's all about!"

Buddy got up and went over to Jenny and Kath. Jenny had her hand on her hip in an imitation of a sultry saloon girl she had seen on a TV Western.

"Hiya, baby," Buddy said to her.

"Hey, big boy, buy me a drink," Jenny replied. Kath began laughing, the totem started to topple, and Buddy caught them as they fell apart. Kath wriggled her shoulders seductively. "Come on up and see me sometime." Then she ran out of sight.

The room was in chaos. The party was at the summit that all good parties reach. Nothing is planned, and yet everybody knows what makes them feel good and they are all doing it. Philbert lounged in his chair with nuts and a drink resting on his belly, staring at the opposite wall, taking in all the good cheer around him by not taking in any one portion of it. He absorbed the totality, the meaning of the experience, in his dull blank ability for sensory absorption. Kath and Marie winked meaningfully at each other and giggled. Buddy put the vibrator in his pocket and poked Imogene with it. Imogene made cracks about "half-pint men" and laughed herself silly at her own joke. Wolf Tooth smirked mildly at his wife and thought profoundly about her idiotic personality. Keith put his legs in Donna's lap and sang "Yesterday" by the Beatles at the top of his voice. Donna turned off a lamp and rubbed her husband's feet and felt glad that people could feel so comfortable in her house.

Organization collapsed. Wolf Tooth pressed for the continuation of the game, but Jenny came back downstairs with two decks of cards and asked if anyone wanted to play Polish rummy, and Kath, Marie, and Philbert sat on the floor with her.

"Hey, Philbert," Wolf Tooth pleaded, "you gotta make fun of yourself first."

"Oh," Philbert said, looking anxiously at the cards being dealt to him. "Well, I'm fat, ugly, stupid, shy, and have no common sense."

The adults gaped at him. The kids argued about the rules of the game.

"How's that?" Philbert inquired.

"Not bad."

"Donna," Imogene said, "how about you?"

"Didn't I already go through enough with that spectacle my children put on?" Donna said. She had a good point. "You talk about husbands? It takes a mother to know real mortification. Pregnancy? Labor? Diapers? If they aren't peeing all over themselves, they're peeing all over me. The little darlings, they'd sell me to the Nazis for a bag of candy. I love them dearly. Just take away their TV privileges and they'll make life a living hell for me. They know every trick in the book, and, I swear to God, they're *born* knowing every trick in the book. They only begin to lose their edge when they get older. They get so much responsibility and maturity pounded into their heads that their heads get blunted with the pounding and they become adults. And they find it so boring that they deliberately, maliciously go out and get pregnant and perpetuate the whole silly process. Talk to a parent. I got more ways to demean myself than any, *any* fool on earth in any profession."

"Donna teaches first grade, too, you know," Keith annotated.

"We won't even talk about that."

"Hey!" Keith expostulated. "Who wants to play Perquackey?"

"Hey!" Buddy asked. It was a remarkable question.

"Perquackey. It's a dice game with letters on the dice and you spell out words."

"We haven't finished this game," Donna said.

"Well . . ."

"Buddy," Wolf Tooth said, "we haven't heard from you."

"And you're not going to," Buddy said definitely. "Oh, come on, man."

"No, you come on, man."

"Why not? Jesus."

"C'mon, Buddy," Imogene said. "It's good to get off the high horse sometimes. Everybody—"

"No, it isn't," Buddy insisted. "I'll wash the dishes. I don't mind that, but there's too much absurdity in the world already for me to add to it." He stood up and picked up some dishes.

"You mean you ain't even gonna try?" Wolf Tooth asked. Philbert was watching Buddy closely.

Buddy sneered sarcastically. "No, I ain't even gonna try."

"No humility at all?" Donna inquired.

"Humiliation is not humility." He carried a stack of plates to the kitchen. It was past the stairs, which were in the middle of the main floor, so they could see him from where they sat.

"Heap big warrior too good to be laughed at?" Keith chided.

Buddy blew up. "Don't push me into a corner, man!" He came back over to them. Even Jenny stopped shuffling the cards to watch him. "Okay, I don't like being laughed at, is that so bad? I've had enough of that garbage all my life. Sure, I can be a jerk just like anyone else, I've had people shooting at me, I knew I could die just like that, and I knew that made me as much of a jerk as anybody else. I could drop dead in twenty seconds, and that's *exactly* why I can't take myself lightly. I guess that's my way of making fun of myself, eh, Wolf?" And he went back to the kitchen.

Wolf Tooth went over to him. "I know, man." They looked at each other and weren't as sure of the unspoken things between them as they had been before.

Buddy turned to him, and a rare, new look of confusion was in his eyes. "Why did you move to this city, man?"

Wolf Tooth did not answer. He picked up some dirty plates and began scraping the leftovers into the stainless-steel garbage disposal. Buddy stared at him. Wolf Tooth turned on the disposal and it ground and growled up the wasted food with a smooth, functional whir.

Philbert and the kids resumed their card game. Marie asked, "Did Daddy and Uncle lose the game?"

"Yes," said Philbert.

"How 'bout some Perquackey?" Keith said cheerfully.

"Sure," said Imogene. Donna nodded assent.

The party regained momentum. Keith and Donna and Imogene had a rousing game of Perquackey. Wolf brought them coffee, and Donna got a bottle of Irish Mist liqueur out of the sideboard. Buddy and Wolf joined them after the dishes were done—the dishwasher humming contentedly—and they sipped liqueur and played Facts in Five. Philbert went upstairs with the kids to play Monopoly, and Donna was the only one who watched them go.

After a while she wondered why it was so quiet and went upstairs to investigate. Philbert sat on the floor telling a story about a coyote that turned into a boy. Marie and Kath lay on their stomachs on the deep carpet, their heads propped up in their palms, listening to him. Jenny lay asleep in his arms, her head nestled up against his chin.

Donna Silva-Harris, whose grandfather, Emiliano Silva, had come to Denver from Cuauhtemoc in Mexico fifty-five years before, came into the bedroom and squatted beside her children. Philbert looked at her and wound up the story.

"Okay, you dirty little girls, get in the bathtub," she said.

"Aw . . ."

"Go. Kath, you can show Marie where the towels are." The two girls got up and left.

She and Philbert undressed Jenny, who squirmed and cursed in her sleep, and put a flannel nightie on her and put her in the bottom bunk bed.

"I'll give her a bath in the morning," Donna explained.

"Sure," said Philbert. "I could use a bath too."

"C'mon," Donna said, "I'll show you your room."

She led Philbert out into the hall and down into another room. It had two twin beds in it. There were blue down quilts on the beds, flowered wallpaper on the walls, and tidy little chests of drawers that were a little too small for the room. With Philbert standing mightily in the room, it looked like a dollhouse.

"This is your room. Yours and Buddy's."

"This is where *I* sleep?" Philbert asked, amazed. He had never even *been* in a room like this, let alone contemplated sleeping in one. Donna laughed softly. They were both talking softly. Sleeping children made adults who loved children talk softly.

"I guess it is a little cutesy," Donna said.

"No, no," Philbert replied. He looked skeptically at the little bed. "Are you sure I won't break this?"

Donna laughed. "Your bathroom is right there. There should be plenty of towels and shampoo."

"Thanks."

Donna nodded and left.

Philbert sat on the bed and sighed. It was very soft. He took off his boots. He began to realize that he was very tired. He had been driving for three days and two nights, with only a short catnap on Bear Butte. He seriously questioned whether to take a shower or not. After all, he had taken one just last night at the gym at Pine Ridge. Was that last night? Well, maybe he'd better take one. He didn't want to get her clean sheets too dirty. She was a nice lady. Awful pretty. And he had said he wanted to take a bath. Why did he say that? Maybe because she had looked so pretty and he felt kind of dirty.

"I'm tired," he said aloud. "I'm talking to myself."

He got up and went into the bathroom. It was a spick-and-span, white, porcelain model found in a hundred million middle-class homes. The steel faucets all gleamed miraculously. The towels were monstrously soft. The toilet paper matched the towels. It was the apogee of sanitation. Deodorant cans conquered the subtleties of perspiration. Plastic shampoo canisters were full of the most existential juices and formulae yet discovered by science. Body creams and skin lotions and bath emollients burst out of their jars and bottles and tubes with all the knowledge that herbalists and pharmacists and the witch doctors of beauty over the ages could beg, borrow, or contrive. It was a paradise of hygiene. Philbert loved it. He wanted to try everything. He took off his grimy clothes and ran the bathwater, he shook green substances into the water, he lined up a dozen shampoos, cream rinses, and conditioners along the edge of the tub. When it was full and he was sure it was boiling hot, he stuck a toe in. He got in and sat down. Water flooded over on the bathroom rug but he didn't notice. He sat in a foot of water in a dinky little tub about four and a half feet long. He splashed about in the chemically treated reservoir water, softened by water softeners, and kicked, and squeezed tubes of beauty goo all over him, and scrubbed his hair, and washed his ass with the back scrubber, and had more fun than a barrel of monkeys on a Saturday night. He got out soaking wet and wiped off, using four extra-large towels. He soaked them all clear through. He brushed his teeth with spare toothbrushes in the medicine cabinet, savoring the minty taste of the toothpaste, squirted deodorant in his pits, surveyed all the bottles and gewgaws in the room to make sure he hadn't forgotten to test any, and strode naked into the bedroom.

He turned out the light and got between soft, fragrant sheets smelling slightly of peaches. He sighed. He felt human again.

The door opened suddenly and the hallway lights dazed his eyes. Two little bodies ran into the room. They came over to his bed and kissed him.

"Good night, Uncle Philbert," they said.

"Good night," he said, and kissed them back.

They both ran out of the room and closed the door. Just as he was dozing off, visions of sugar plums already dancing in his head, he heard the shouts of adults downstairs. They were playing charades.

CHAPTER 15

Of a Commercial Derailment, of Flight, and of a Surprise Meeting among Conflicting Forces

THE FIRST NATIONAL Bank of Austin, Texas, opened promptly at nine o'clock on Monday morning, December 23. Jody Tilbert was the head teller and she was already growing great in her newfound position. Already, at twenty-seven years old, she was responsible for eighteen tellers and the $1,000 in cash each teller was responsible for in their cash drawers. Jody Tilbert had one girl make coffee each morning, another girl apportion everyone's cash and deposit receipts, and one of the boys see to the proper functioning of the coin changers. When Jody Tilbert saw that her charges were in their stalls, that their glass walls and Formica counters were spotless, that the calendars and the skirts and the suits and the coiffures were all in place, she nodded to Joe Garcia, the security guard, who only then opened the doors on another business day.

FBI Agent Tom Washington, alias Counselor Tom Washington, was the first through the door. He winked at Jody Tilbert, who smiled correctly. He halted at the first window, where a sweet young Mexican girl attended to his business.

Within minutes the customers were humming about busily,

the tabulators were ringing, the network of model railroad trains choo-chooed from a large, flat table in the middle of the festive lobby. A white plastic Christmas tree ten feet tall rose cheerfully from the midst of the train table to the ceiling. Miniature trees and bridges and snowy farmhouses reproduced an idyllic New England village for the trains to chug-chug around and about and throughout. Jody Tilbert patrolled the stalls and approved or disapproved checks, and enjoyed the swish of her new outfit on her new stockings as she hurried back and forth.

Rabbit barged her way into the commercial merriment wearing jeans and boots and her full-length rabbit coat and with her hair wrapped hastily in a few bobby pins and stuck in her cowboy hat. She chewed on a toothpick and surveyed (to her) the astounding scene. She had Jennifer by one hand. Jennifer's beautiful, long blond hair had been brushed a hundred times. She had on a nice dress. She had on a nice cotton coat. She was a pretty little girl of eight, slightly spoiled, not too bright, a great whistler, but (as it has been said) very pretty. Big Lester Mardewcki came in behind them. Doris Keselring came in behind him. He was in his work clothes, jeans and boots and hat. Doris had on a long wool dress of Mexican cut and a striped Navaho serape.

"Look at that stupid-ass train, will ya?" Rabbit exclaimed. She and Jennifer went over to explore its stupid-ass details. They looked at the tiny cow standing beside a barn. They oohed and aahed at the Datsun pickups on a flatbed, on one of the trains on its way to Pittsburgh. Jennifer pushed a switch and a red sign went up, and a train changed tracks and went over a bridge instead of around a water tower. They giggled. Half a dozen other kids, including a pensive white-haired grandfather, giggled.

Tom Washington came up to Lester and Doris, who were watching Rabbit and Jennifer watch the trains.

"Good morning, Lester," Tom said.

"Oh, hi," Les replied. "You're already here, huh?"

"Yes."

Rabbit joined them in the middle of the lobby. Jennifer remained at the train table. "Hi," Rabbit said crisply to Tom Washington. She was all business now.

"Good morning, Miss LeLouche," he replied. "A fascinating display, don't you think?" he added, meaning the trains.

"Yes."

"They do it every year, I understand, and add something new. The head teller was just explaining it to me."

"Oh?"

"I guess that little tunnel is new this year. See? Where the deer are grazing on the snowy hillside over the train? That's a new tunnel."

"Where never is heard a discouraging word."

"Pardon me?"

"Nothing," Rabbit explained. "Is that the check?" she asked, pointing to a plastic leather bank pouch Tom had in his hand. It was green and had stamped on it a white ink sketch of the bank and its name and address.

"Yes," he said. "A cashier's check for twenty thousand dollars made out to the city of Santa Fe." He handed it to Lester.

"Great" was all that Lester could think to say.

A man across the room took a photograph of the two men exchanging the pouch. Only Rabbit thought it odd that they would conduct this transaction in the middle of the lobby of a busy bank. Only Tom Washington didn't know that the man worked for Vito Scarlatti and not the FBI.

"Thanks," Rabbit said.

"You're leaving this morning, then?" Tom asked.

"Yes," Rabbit replied. "Les and I and my little girl will be flying out from Jollyville."

"You know, I was thinking," Tom interjected. "You said her arraignment is tomorrow?"

"Yeah."

"Well, that's the day before Christmas," Tom observed. "I

would think all the state offices would be closed for the holiday."

"I guess not in New Mexico," Les said.

"They're probably making Bonnie an exception," Rabbit said quietly. A stern set was forming to her mouth.

"Well," Tom concluded, "if you need some legal advice, give me a call at this number," and he handed her his card. The man across the room took another picture. "I have some friends in Santa Fe."

"We probably will, Mr. Washington," Les replied gratefully. "That's very nice."

"Your friend's in a jam. She's gonna need all the help she can get. Well, I have to catch the ten o'clock flight back to Dallas. Have to be in court this afternoon. Merry Christmas."

"Merry Christmas," Les responded. Tom Washington walked across the lobby. Joe Garcia held the door open for him; Jody Tilbert found time to wave good-bye to him. He waved to her and was gone.

"That was nice of him," Les said. "I guess we haven't given much thought to Bonnie's defense. It could be a real showcase for legal harassment, surveillance, everything. But she's gonna need a lawyer."

"Bullshit," Rabbit concluded. "I wouldn't trust that jive-ass lawyer as far as I could chew him up and spit him. Those fuckers are double-timing us, I would bet on it. Something stinks in Denmark."

"Rabbit," Doris pleaded, "Bonnie *is* gonna need a lawyer."

Rabbit looked fitfully around the room. She caught the eye of Jody Tilbert, behind one of the teller stalls. She gave her a dirty look. "Bonnie's gonna need a miracle, if what I smell is fish." She shot Jody Tilbert the finger. Something about the cute little brunette's cute little hairdo and cute little dress made her sick. "And I have a pretty good nose for a double cross. Let's get out of here, I feel like I'm in a bad science-fiction movie."

"Rabbit—"

"We'll figure out somethin'. C'mon."

She grabbed Jennifer and they left, but not before she would not let Joe Garcia hold the door open for her, and not before Jody Tilbert stared indignantly after her. One of the toy trains jumped the track and sparked clumsily over on its side, crushing a plastic maple tree.

Doris drove the Mercedes-Benz 300SL to the Jollyville Municipal Airport. Lester's leased Cessna 310 was already gassed and checked out, weather charts and log and navigation charts were already prepared, and Doris walked them out to the plane. It was a fine clear day, a crisp portentous day, or so they all felt. Doris hugged Lester for a long time and squeezed his nuts playfully. She hugged Jennifer. She hugged Rabbit, even though she had been sleeping with her old man. In fact, Doris and Lester were on rocky ground and this trip probably wasn't going to help matters. Nobody said much. It was still too early for feelings to overcome their friendships, and they didn't want words to jeopardize what was very good in many ways. So they didn't say too much, except good-bye.

Les and Rabbit and Jennifer crowded into the cockpit, Les put on his headset and hit the switches, and Doris backed away as the turbo engines roared to life. Jennifer waved madly out the window. The plane pulled out to the taxi ramp, Les got clearance, and they gunned down the concrete and off into the wild blue yonder.

Flight. Fifteen thousand feet, two hundred miles an hour, over the clouds, into the jet stream, under the clouds, out of the jet stream—the people within the bird took it for granted. Machinery did its job. They snoozed (the passengers that is, not the pilot), looked at their watches, and wondered when they would get where they were going.

They said very little on the four-hour jaunt. Over Abilene, Rabbit said, "Want some coffee?"

"Sure."

Over the vast oil fields between Lubbock and Hobbs, Jennifer said, "I have to go to the bathroom."

"It's in the back, honey."

A hundred miles later, over the Pecos River, Rabbit said, "Wanna smoke a number?"

"Naw," Les muttered. "We have to talk to cops or whoever this afternoon."

"So?"

"So?"

There it was—fear and defiance in one word. Lester was basically a good guy. Rabbit was not. Lester would go through life afraid—and successful. Nothing scared Rabbit—she was doomed to quiet failure. It was not the law of nature, it was the law of man.

"Since when does getting high stop anything?"

"Cut it out, Rabbit."

"All right. Jesus!"

The machine swooped over the Sangre de Cristo Mountains. It flew of its own will. A red-bearded man sat at its controls, but the plane was the one flying. The wind and air slapped up against its fuselage, not the hard-ass woman and her pretty little girl inside. The people inside luxuriated in the sensations of the wind and the air and the machine, but only a song could explain this thing that the air and an aerodynamic wing could accomplish.

> Alone am I the windhover,
> Alone am I the windhover,
> Desperate am I for love and company,
> Content I am without them,
> Alone am I the windhover,
> Alone am I the windhover.

The pilot would have argued unto death that he was the

windhover, not the machine. It was an eternal debate, without a verdict.

They came over the last mountain and Santa Fe lay below them. For an instant of hope and memory, they were above its problems, they were apart from its problems. And it made them anxious to land. They got clearance from the tiny municipal airport that was the only perch for the humble birds that came out of the wind. Jumbo transcontinental jetliners had to land in Albuquerque sixty miles south. Santa Fe did not even permit the Santa Fe Railroad to stop any closer than seventeen miles away. Santa Fe would probably not allow buses or cars onto its ancient pathways if the people had not insisted at least on that one concession to the outside world. Windhover swept over the trucks and motorcycles scurrying by the thousands down below in the abundance of the Santa Fean concession. They scurried in and out of the piñon hills. They disappeared in and reappeared out of the chamisa gullies. And Windhover let its awkward talons down as it, too, floated past mesquite ridges and drifted clumsily over hard pueblo sand and touched—squeaked!—rubber to concrete, bounced, lurched, held matter to energy for several precarious moments, and then rolled resentfully down the little runway and stopped in front of the little hangar.

It took an hour to get a taxi to take them into town. They, like their bird, resented this inefficiency of land travel. They stewed and fumed, but the land was relentless. By the time they got downtown, it might as well have been mañana. It was four p.m. They had gained an hour on the flight when crossing from the central time zone to the mountain time zone and had lost that same hour again while waiting for wheels. By four p.m. both the banks and the city treasurer were closed for the holiday.

"America has shut down," Rabbit muttered through clenched teeth. They went over to the municipal building. A pert young Mexican woman in shellacked black hair sat anxiously at a desk waiting for five o'clock.

"Can we give you the bond money to bail a person out of jail?" Rabbit asked the pert señorita hopelessly. She knew there were channels to go through for this sort of thing and that they hadn't gone through any of the channels yet.

"Sure," the señorita said. Rabbit stared, a little disappointed at her inaccurate assessment. Lester hoped beyond hope that it would be that easy. He had a vision of taking off that afternoon for home. Jennifer stared longingly at a pop machine up the hall. It was an impersonal hall, with an echo.

"What name?" the señorita asked.

"Bonnie McNamara."

The woman looked in her book. "Do you have twenty thousand dollars?"

"Yes. Here's a cashier's check."

The woman looked at it and stood up. "I'll make sure this is okay."

"You don't think there'll be any problem?" Lester dared to ask.

The woman gave him a deprecating glance. "No." She went up a side corridor and disappeared in a side office. Rabbit clenched the edge of the tall counter that stood as a bureaucratic barricade in front of the señorita's spotless desk. She thought of the many things that hung in the balance in this tiny moment. Les was hot. He was sweating. The room was stuffy. He wanted to run. Why had he, a well-known pusher, *walked* into a police station? It was crazy. Jennifer sat on a plastic leather chair next to the pop machine and fanned herself with a magazine. She took off her coat.

The señorita returned after a long time with a señor. He was a bulky man in a wrinkled suit. He was nearly bald, but his chubby face had a hint of humanity in its sorrowful weariness. Rabbit thought he looked like a kind man. She thought he caught her eye curiously and gave her a kind look. He held the cashier's check in his hand.

"We're closed until Wednesday," he said abruptly. "We'll keep the check and Miss McNamara will be released first thing

Wednesday morning." He turned away wearily and went back up the side corridor to his side office, where FBI Agent Doug Lewis waited on the telephone.

Rabbit could have cried. Then she could have yelled after the bastard for justice, for mercy, for Christmas. But all she could do was feel sorry for herself and ask the señorita, "Can we at least see Bonnie?"

It was clear that any heavier tone would have inspired resistance in the woman (who had her orders), but instead, Rabbit's sense of pity, her quiet plea, invoked a humanitarian impulse in the woman.

"Come with me," she said, and the three adventurers followed her up another obscure corridor. They went past offices that sprang out of the wall like monks' cubicles. The stylish sequestered workers inside the cubicles were having coffee, they were joking, they were ready to go home for the holiday. Their desks and their papers would be abandoned for a day or two. They had a less jaundiced view of humanity now, with the prospect of escape so close at hand.

Not so the criminals within the more inner recesses. Corridors opened onto more narrow corridors; cubicles were revealed—like boxes inside boxes shrinking into infinite diminutiveness—within cubicles. They approached another guard, another Mexican señorita with shellacked black hair and a lumpy blue uniform.

"Hi, Vengey," the first señorita said to the second guard. Vengey nodded disagreeably. "Is it okay if these people see Bonnie McNamara for a minute?"

"I can't—"

"They came to pay her bail, but we're closed until Wednesday."

"Maybe you're closed," Vengey growled. "I gotta pull swing swift tonight and tomorrow night, Christmas Eve." She was obviously a horrible person. She took a long, horrible pause, staring at the three adventurers like they had a horrible disease. It was no wonder—they were in a dark, dank, dismal phantasmagoria of a corridor. The walls were a cheerful government green. The floor was tiled a pleasant pattern of red and white. Soft lights, cool ventilated air, soft chairs—it was a nightmare.

"Only a minute," Vengey decided. "Go in there," she instructed horribly, pointing to a side door.

"Thanks, Vengey." The first señorita smiled. But Vengey had opened a grate in a big heavy door next to her desk and yelled, "Hey, Judy, bring Bonnie McNamara to the interview room." And she slammed the grate horribly. She turned and looked surprised to see Rabbit, Lester, and Jennifer, all still staring at her. The first señorita had already retreated back up the corridor to the safety of her own desk.

"Well?" Vengey asked. "You," she growled at Jennifer. "You can't go in. That door!" she concluded to the adults, pointing to the door again. Jennifer sat on a plastic leather chair next to Vengey, who pretended not to notice her. Rabbit and Lester went in the side door.

They sat on two folding chairs in front of a short table. Several more chairs were situated on the other side of the table. Another door was at the other end of the room. The room was lit brightly by fluorescent lights. The walls were Sheetrock. A mirror was on a side wall. It was a small, clean, white room. Rabbit thought of a soul and how it must be a little like this room buried deep inside other rooms buried deep inside the municipal building. She felt at once afraid and secure, both exposed and invincible.

The other door opened. Another uniformed woman came into the room. Bonnie came in after her, wearing a plain blue prison dress.

Rabbit didn't have to think. She didn't have to consider all the dramatic possibilities possible in this moment. She jumped up from her chair and screamed. "Bonnie!"

They were in each other's arms before Judy the guard could stop them. Then it was impossible to stop them.

Who said only men understand camaraderie and bravado? Not these two women, who had shared many exploits. They had quarreled, grown jealous of each other, and had even hated each other at times. It was a greater bond than camaraderie and bravado.

"Oh, Rabbit, Rabbit!" Bonnie wept. She didn't know how much her friend's presence could mean. "And Lester." Les smiled bravely.

"Okay, that's enough," Judy said, acting the referee. The two women respected the other woman's strong hand on their shoulders. They broke. "You have five minutes. Chow's on pretty soon."

Rabbit retreated to her chair more demurely than she had ever retreated anywhere. Bonnie sat numbly. They sat at opposite ends of the table. Les sat beside Rabbit. Judy stood behind Bonnie.

"Rabbit, I don't know what—" Bonnie started to say, but Rabbit interrupted.

"We got twenty thousand."

"Oh, thank God," Bonnie prayed.

"But they can't process it, or some damn thing, until Wednesday."

"Wednesday?" Bonnie repeated. It was an unfathomable word. It was light-years away.

"We'll get a lawyer to represent you at the arraignment tomorrow. "

"Oh . . . good," Bonnie managed to say.

"But I don't know how we're going to pay him."

"Pay him?" Bonnie repeated.

"We haven't seen your kids yet, but we'll go over there as soon as we leave here."

"Fine," Bonnie managed to say.

"I guess we should just take them back to Austin with us."

"No," Les said, "Bonnie won't be able to go out of state while she's out on bail."

"Oh, yeah," Rabbit realized, "it could be months before a trial. Maybe you could—"

"Months?" Bonnie repeated. Her hopes and fears were being bounced up and down like a yo-yo. The presence of her friends was—

Noise intruded into her thoughts again, from outside. Her sterile meditations were being jostled again, from without. Was it Rabbit speaking? And about what? No, Rabbit and Lester were looking at the door. Shouts of men were coming from the outside. Someone burst chaotically into the room.

"No one's going to tell me I can't see my sister!" Buddy insisted as he and Philbert wedged their way into the room, with Vengey the guard breathing down their necks.

CHAPTER 16

How Philbert Was Growing in Virtue

PHILBERT WOKE UP suddenly before dawn in his Goldilocks bed in Denver. He was frightened. He did not know where he was. The room was dark. The curtains were drawn, and he could not see the sky outside. Hastily he pulled off the strange blankets and stumbled nakedly to the window. He pulled open the strange curtains. He breathed a sigh of relief. The first light of dawn made the sky a dark blue. Stars were still sparkling dimly. Streetlights glared on the street on the other side of the fence that enveloped the condominium compound. A few cars zoomed by, their headlights another contrast of white-on-blue darkness. Protector sat there, waiting loyally for him.

He heard snores elsewhere in his suffocating little room. His brown elk eyes focused for dimness and saw Buddy asleep in the other bed in the room. He stumbled nakedly to the bed and gave Buddy a gentle nudge.

"Huh? What?" the man muttered.

"Buddy, get up."

"What? Huh?"

"We have to get going," Philbert whispered.

Buddy sat up suddenly. "Philbert? Jesus, put on some clothes."

Confident that his compeer was conscious, Philbert stumbled into the bathroom. He took a long satisfying leak in the dark, made doubly satisfying by the knowledge that he could hit the pot almost by instinct. Only after he shook off the last few drops, took a few pleasurable pulls on his hog, out of habit, scratched his nuts vigorously, out of itching, did he turn on the light and blink wildly at the sudden intrusion. He brushed his teeth, brushed his hair, and fastened it in one long braid with his two green-and-white beaded barrettes. then he surveyed himself in the mirror. It had two side panels that could be adjusted for any angle of narcissistic contemplation. He contemplated himself at length. He admired his flat, round, massive nose. He thought it very admirable that he had no double chin. His chin was a massive round ridge, but it was noble, not double. He stood back from the mirrors and admired his massive body of smooth brown skin. It was very pure skin. Not a hair on it, except, of course, at the crotch. It was a pretty impressive body.

"Philbert? Will you get dressed?" Buddy stood in his shorts in the doorway. "Jesus."

"Oh . . . yeah."

Action replaced contemplation. They were soon dressed and sneaking down the stairs in the dark, so as not to disturb the sleeping household. But it was no use. Pancakes and coffee and eggs hurled their irresistible odors at them. Donna was up, in her pajamas and robe, humming contemplatively in the kitchen over breakfast.

"Good morning," she whispered cheerfully as the two men floated like unconscious odors themselves into the kitchen.

Buddy began, "You didn't have to—"

"I'm always up this early," Donna explained. "I have to get the kids to the school bus by seven-thirty, and then I go to work from there. And we always have breakfast together, when I can drag Keith out of bed. He doesn't have to be downtown until nine."

248

She poured them coffee during this (to them) incomprehensible speech. She turned on KHOW-FM for some easy listening morning music, and for the news and weather.

Oh, they talked (whispered) and ate (gobbled), but Philbert was oblivious with wonder. He had never known such a perfect woman. Out of courtesy he had ten pancakes and six eggs, and she gasped gratefully, as any good cook and perfect woman would, but his heart was on the wonder of it all. They got up to leave, but he didn't even want to. The dawn was beckoning, however, and Donna made them swear to come back every time they were in Denver. Then she gave them a map on how to get back to the Interstate, wished them luck on their mission, and waved farewell from the front door.

Philbert was glad to be outside again, though, the minute he was. The air was cool but not cold. It was gray and blue with the approaching sunrise, and Protector was damp and sullen with the dew of the receding night. Buddy wiped off Protector's damp windows with his sleeve while Philbert got inside to crank up the old buggy. It didn't want to start, but Philbert floored it mercilessly (immediately wondering why he was compelled to such a cruel tactic) and it grumbled cantankerously to life. It had waited all night for hay and a drink of water but in vain, and now its neglected digestive system wasn't about to function in an orderly manner for several minutes. It sputtered and missed heartbeats and gasped in its alimentary canal, so Philbert and Buddy patiently waited inside, shivering. Finally piston coordinated with rod, rod adjusted to valve, and valve got in gear. The miracle of the machine was performed once again. The old buggy was once again raring to go out into the magic of an American Monday morning.

And magical it was, to Philbert. They crept up one street and down another. One street lined with shops and buildings and lights of all shapes became another avenue of shining new cars hurrying on their way to infinite other streets and avenues bursting to their seams with an infinite array of other shops and buildings and colored lights. It was a gleaming, glistening thunder of disproportionate dimensions. The traffic was still thin at this pre-commercial hour of sunrise, but to Philbert and Protector it was already a crush of modern new possibilities. They drove agape.

To Buddy, it was witchcraft. Dracula lurked behind every shop and building and neon light that promised good service and a fair deal. Frankenstein's monster had reproduced a hundred million-fold. The Trojan Horse concealed the bacteria of internal decay hidden within. It was Huck Finn's river, Dorothy's yellow brick road, the Ho Chi Minh and Santa Fe Trails, the end of the Powwow Highway. Buddy felt defeated. He could oppose the immoral bloodsucking phantom that lurked within the very definition of this city. The city was only a small creation of the mad doctor, only one corpuscle of the monster. This society was riveted solidly together by the rubber bolts of its virulent belief in its own manifest inevitability. Buddy knew it the first time he left Lame Deer. He saw the inexorable intellectual wealth at Yale University that filled up any subjective holes with the scientific objectivity of great minds. They could think through any problem and solve it. He saw it in the Marine Corps. Any nation that is to succeed needs a core of warriors to defend it from enemies. The Marines were fanatics, and greatness is predicated on fanaticism. He saw it at Wounded Knee in the awesome eye of the media. It had perfected the ugh-how communications of the cave with global satellites, dictionaries, and computers. Buddy was defeated. His ways had only one hope—to become their ways.

They picked up Interstate 25 and beat the morning rush hour by a matter of minutes. They had the southbound lane to themselves, comparatively, as they left the greater metropolitan area, and the greater metropolitan cloud of brown smog. The northbound lanes were already bumper to bumper with machines, and men and women on their way into the heart of their society.

Buddy and Philbert envied them. They had a job to do. They were going to work to solve their problems.

It was an overcast day for Buddy, but Philbert was on the sunny side of the street. He had his CB on and was talking to the truckers. He stopped at Vicker's in Castle Rock for gas and coffee to go, and took a dump. He gave no thought to oil or water for his car; his thoughts were on his future. He flew past Colorado Springs to the tunes of KHOW-FM, still coming in from Denver. He rolled through Pueblo as the sun got high behind thick, gray clouds that threatened snow, but Philbert only saw the dry pavement stretching into the horizon in front of him. He stopped in Walsenburg for hamburgers and fries and more gas, but no car complaints for oil would he hear of. He picked up an Oklahoma City rock station as they breezed across the Colorado prairie, tapping his toes to the revolutionary beat of guitars. He talked to Buddy about Comanches who had roamed these southern plains and listened to Buddy about artificial foods that caused cancer as Protector vainly warned of aches and pains like a neurotic cynic. The prairie stretched ahead and behind forever. They rolled through Trinidad, crawled up Raton Pass, said farewell to the Spanish Peaks and the Colorado Rockies, and inched to the top of the pass and into New Mexico.

"New Mexico," Buddy said with a foreboding finality.

Extinct volcanoes of another great era lay before them on the lovely plain like a heartache. The border turned their thoughts to their impending task. The closer they got to their impossible goal, the closer Buddy felt to a sense of irretrievable failure that he had been fighting all his life. Perhaps he was self-destructive, he thought, summoning a psychological phrase he had learned in college. After all, success in a world that one despises is the highest form of failure.

No, analysis was foolish. Buddy was a jerk, that was all.

Philbert? He dreamed on. The fact that he *knew* he was a jerk as well gave him hope. He knew their only chance for success was in foolishness. So the best he could do was to continue to do nothing, trust in accidents, as he had done with such success all his life.

He drove. Protector drove. The sun crossed the sky. The highway crossed the villages of Springer, Wagon Mound, Las Vegas. The prairie watched them ascend into the Sangre de Cristo Mountains; marijuana helped them ascend into great understanding of the Sangre de Cristo Mountains (for Buddy had kept the joints moving all day). It was only sixty miles, now, to Santa Fe.

Time had passed in a more normal way on Monday, even for Indians. Adventures may have occurred, and indeed very definitely *have* occurred, on other Mondays in other lands, but very rarely do they occur in this land in this time. This is a business day. This is a day to get things done. This is a day to see to the business of survival.

The sage and mesquite and piñon watched them pass. Trucks and buses and even an old 1942 pickup passed them, but they were unfazed. They were in no hurry. Destiny would wait. They crawled to the top of Glorieta Pass. Philbert gave no thought to Protector's screaming agony up the long steep climb. He had faith in the thing (even though, as an Indian, he had no idea what faith was). He had his favorite Waylon Jennings tape on his cherished R3 Road-Rated Receiver and tape deck with CB. They cleared the top at ten miles per hour. Buddy was slightly alarmed but not much. He was staring out the window. He was preparing his battle-ready mind. He wondered how in the hell he was going to find Bonnie. She could be anywhere. He didn't know Santa Fe very well. Hell, he'd never even been there before. He wondered vaguely what he was going to do about the bail money that had already been spent. He checked his pistol for ammunition, found it loaded, and put it back in the glove compartment. He looked at Philbert. Philbert was smiling. He had one hand on the wheel, the other hanging out the open window by his side. It was warm outside now, and he had rolled down the glass halfway—as far as it would go. He looked like he didn't have a care in the world. Buddy shook his head. *He* wouldn't be any help.

Protector barreled down the mountain on the incline. He was a lot happier going downhill. He went past adobe churches, adobe shacks, adobe graveyards. They were in a different world suddenly, it seemed. The Jemez Mountains across the Rio Grande Valley loomed in eerie clarity from out of a past of Pueblo uprisings and Cibola cities of gold. The land, the air, time itself grew radically different. And over a rise they arose over the squat, brown city of Santa Fe. Its adobe blended indecipherably into the earth down below; far, far below.

"There it is," Buddy said.

And down they coasted into the valley of death.

CHAPTER 17

How the Warriors Found Their Princess, and of Their Surprises, and How the Talisman Was Left Behind

OF COURSE, WHENEVER two or more volatile spirits crowd into a tiny room—as indeed two or more volatile spirits had crowded into the tiny interview room within the municipal building—a volatile situation is bound to ensue. And ensue it did.

"No one's going to tell me I can't see my sister!" Buddy reiterated. "Bonnie!"

"Who in the hell?" Rabbit wondered.

"Buddy?" Bonnie wondered.

"Buddy?" Rabbit repeated.

"You people—*out!*" Vengey the guard commanded.

"I'm her brother!" Buddy explained, at the apogee of his frustration. He moved to his sister, the dark-haired woman who in her confused and trammeled manner was an unmistakable relative of the misguided warrior. He put his hand carefully on her shoulder. He looked in her eyes. She lowered them. She was ashamed.

"I told you I would come," he said.

She could not say anything. He put his arms carefully around her and held her. She could not respond. She kept her arms at her sides and put her face into his chest and could not show anyone anything of herself. It was a change in her personality, for sure. Something, something in this room in this moment compelled her to regress into a shy background. New York City and conscious motives and escape faded into this unconscious reaction of hers.

She caught Philbert's eye, who was trying desperately to avoid hers.

This is not to say the action in the interview room ceased. It did not even desist for a moment for Bonnie's moment of Cheyenne truth. Judy and Vengey the guards were insistent upon the proper discharge of their duties, and they discharged vociferously.

"All of you—*out!*"

"But—"

"Judy, call the guards!" And Judy rushed out.

Rabbit was annoyed as well. "So what the hell's the problem? This is family, I guess. Nobody else has been here to bother Bonnie yet, have they?" This was all directed at Vengey.

Vengey redirected to Rabbit. She thrust her breasts against Rabbit's. "Get out."

"Why?"

"Because I said so!"

"Now look—"

"No, you look, girlie. You've got ten seconds to clear out or you'll go back to the cell with your friend, *comprende?*"

"Who's the tough guy?" Buddy asked Bonnie, meaning Rabbit. Bonnie looked up.

"That's Lester." Lester was sort of standing against the wall, inching his way around to the door, but he had confronted a formidable obstacle in Philbert, who was leaning dizzily against the same wall. Philbert managed to smile at him.

"Hi," Philbert said. Les nodded.

"Hi," Buddy said. Les responded to their double-barreled

greeting, coming from both ends of the room almost simultane-
ously, with less than commensurate simultaneity. He jerked his
head fatuously from one hi to the other, smiled stupidly, and
stopped inching along the wall. Vengey glared at him.

"I meant the chick boobing it up to Godzilla," Buddy said to
his sister, meaning Rabbit.

"You mean Rabbit?" Bonnie asked.

"Chick?" Rabbit pronounced distastefully. She turned her at-
tentions to Buddy.

"Rabbit?" Buddy pronounced sardonically. He turned his at-
tentions to her.

"That's right, Rabbit. So you're her goddamn brother she's
never talked about. And don't call me 'chick.' Jesus, I hate that
shit."

"You just hate it all you want, baby," Buddy replied. "Because I
don't give a good goddamn what you think, but I think I can
guess what you're doin' here: screwin' up everything with all yer
stupid-ass feminist bullshit."

"Stupid-ass! *Baby?*"

"We ain't got time fer it now, we gotta get my sister outa this—"

"You're telling me about what we gotta *do?*" Rabbit asked in
semi-outrage. "We got the bail money, peckerhead, twenty thousand strong, and I'm here to tell ya it wasn't easy!"

"Twenty thousand?"

"Jerk off!" Rabbit concluded. "You expect to just charge in here
like a pack of wild Indians and—"

"Please, please." Bonnie pleaded for order, but to no avail, of
course.

"I'm telling ya all what's happenin' now!" Vengey barked horribly, and she had the last word, of course. Jackboots thundered
up the hallway, and within no time at all the room was surrounded by six officers of the law. What was more, six 20-gauge
shotguns were cocked, readied, and aimed at the five troublemakers.

It tended to take the edge off the situation. Silence took the fort with more sureness of foot than a savage skulking over the fence in the dark looking for scalps. Everyone froze, as if they had heard the sounds in the night of a murderer but were not sure where he was or who he was after. Death stopped everything. It took the potential out of breath or movement. Utter stillness cut through the air like a tomahawk.

"No one . . . move," one of the officers of the law uttered firmly. He knew it was awful not to move, that it was a deathly inconvenience, and that motionlessness was a test of obedience. No one moved, not even the guards.

Well . . . Jennifer moved behind them. They had forgotten about her. "Mommy," she said, "can I go get a drink?"

Eyeballs flickered wildly to the impertinent sound. Shotguns swiveled ominously to the attack. Six barrels crowned her face instantly. She started crying at the horrendous sight and shrank to her knees.

"You bastards," her mommy said quietly, and scooted courageously to her little girl. She knelt beside the child and cradled her in her arms and defied the 20-gauge presence.

"Oh, hell," one of the officers cursed. He lowered his cannon. The others followed suit. The fun had gone out of the moment. They glared at the madonna and child on the floor. The madonna gloried in her righteous moment and seized the opportunity.

"Let's go, honey," she said, and they stood up. They started off down the hall.

"Now wait a minute," Vengey began, unforgiving.

"Go ahead, blast us," Rabbit said, and kept walking. Lester eased out the door and eased after her. Buddy gave Bonnie a reassuring pat and eased his way between the shotguns. Judy grabbed Bonnie and yanked her to her own doorway.

"Uh . . ." someone said.

It was Philbert. He wanted to say something. Bonnie looked at him, and Judy stopped yanking her. Bonnie had noticed him before (it was impossible not to notice him) and had wondered who he was. The guards looked at him. The officers and the shotguns looked at him. He stood his ground in the middle of the room.

"We'll get ya outa here, Bonnie," he said. He marveled at his words. They were colloquial. He didn't feel very poetic in this room at this moment.

It was all he said, but it was all that Bonnie needed to hear. Judy yanked her out of the room, and Philbert eased out between the guards in the opposite direction.

"Don't you people expect to come back," Vengey warned. "You don't know how lucky you are."

Philbert continued off down the corridor. The guards and the officers returned to their posts. They were the ones who felt a little lost, however, not the imprisoned and defeated ones.

Philbert wandered down the corridors, and he wandered up the corridors. He finally had to stop at a cubicle and ask directions. Two men with shoulder holsters and .357 Magnums in the holsters sat in a room playing cribbage. Philbert came upon them like a phantom.

"Uh . . ." was all he got out.

They stood wildly at the sound and drew their pistols. Philbert stood in the doorway, astounded. He sure had had a lot of guns pointed at him today. And these two guys *really* had them pointed at him—they were crouched, both hands on their cannons, eyes wildly controlled.

"Freeze, mister," one of them barked. He was in a brown suit without a jacket. He was obviously a plainclothesman, a detective or something. The other man was in a black uniform.

"I just wanted to know how to get to the front door," Philbert explained. Strangely he felt no fear, as he had felt no fear back in the interview room. The cops glared at him, relaxing their crouches a little. They had seen plenty of crooks, but this big dummy probably was telling the truth. He probably *couldn't* find his way out of a paper bag.

"Whad're ya doin' here?" the plainclothesman asked.

"I was visitin' a friend of mine who's in jail. I'm sorry if I scared you."

The cops had to grin at that. This guy scare them? They hastily put away their guns as they put away their caution. Philbert took a step into the little room and they grinned wider. Philbert concealed a gust of shock that swept through him—along one whole wall there were two large safes. One of them was as tall as the ceiling. The other was open. Long rectangular drawers were inside. Wads of green money were inside the drawers, within easy reach of where Philbert stood. He looked twice at the door through which he had just stepped. It was four feet of iron, with long metal bars and handles and shining dials winding around and behind it like miniature plumbing. He was in the city's vault!

"Follow that hall, take the second right, the first left, and the third right," the plainclothesman explained. "That'll take you right out."

"Second right, first left, third right," Philbert repeated.

"Sounds like a combination," the cop in black joked. The plainclothesman smiled appreciatively.

"Thanks," Philbert said, and turned to go.

"*De nada.*"

He walked slowly up the hall, his heart beating furiously, his bowels squirming oddly. The third door down from the vault, before he took the second right, said gentlemen on it. Philbert ducked inside and barely got his pants off in time as he plopped in the second stall. He closed the door and released his anxiety into the spotless porcelain bowl. He did not think his lack of control was the result of fear and guns and a long drive. He was sure it was—

Somebody else came into the toilet, whistling. He plopped onto the bowl in the first stall and closed his door. Philbert heard his grunt, his splashes, a few farts echoing up from the bowl, and then the pages of a magazine crinkled.

"Oh, baby, suck my hose!" Philbert heard the other person declare, in response to the nubile declarations of his magazine. Philbert froze. The voice was the voice of the plainclothesman from the vault! Philbert leaned over between his own naked legs and looked under the wall between them at the other squatter's feet—brown slacks laying in a pile over brown shoes!

Philbert stood up, pulled his pants up, yanked them back down, wiped, pulled them back up again, and flushed. He tiptoed out of his stall, tiptoed to the door, and was almost out when—

"Hey, have a Merry Christmas," the plainclothesman said from his stall.

"Yeah," Philbert muttered, "don't let the hogs get ya."

"I won't."

And Philbert was back out in the hall. In his confusion he turned left instead of right, and was hurrying back up the corridor in the direction from whence he had already come when the cop in black stepped out in the hall in front of him to have a cigarette. But all he got was Philbert, who ran him down like a Mack truck squashing a grasshopper. The black cop bounced off him at zero leverage and conked his head on the wall and was down and out before Philbert knew what hit him. And then there was just a coldcocked cop lying on the floor at his feet.

It took Philbert no time at all to assess the open door of the vault beside him, and even less than that to decide to do what he had to do, and even less time of all to weigh the moral complications. He opened a door beside the conked-out body on the floor, and, of course, as fate had decreed this development, the door led to the janitor's closet. Philbert easily stuffed the cop into the closet and closed the door. He checked out the hallway and nobody was in sight.

He stepped into the vault. Capitalism was at his feet. Excitement—excitement? nay, his heart was fibrillating, his penis was bursting out of his jeans—did not prevent action. He stuck his hand in the open safe. It came back with a wad of five-dollar bills in it. He stuffed them in his pocket. He peered into the safe. A drawer of twenty-dollar bills found itself short by several fistfuls. He grabbed fifties. And then, in a tidy stack on the shelf, bundles of hundred-dollar bills extracted from traffic fines and parking meters and the nickel-and-dime larceny of the City and County of Santa Fe found their way into Philbert Bono's pocket. But it was no time to gloat. His treasure would have to be analyzed later. Now the stuffy little room taunted him. It tempted him to clean it out. It wriggled its seductive hips at him. "Take more!" It squirmed. It opened its legs to him. "Take more!" its juices dripped enticingly. But he knew that old line, and he got the hell out.

No sign yet of anybody in the hall. He made no sentimental pause as he strode casually past the door to the janitor's closet, he hesitated upon no reflective irony as he shuffled, a little more bulky than usual, past the door to the men's room, he veered off and away like the masked man in the correct direction of the sunset, taking the second right and the first left and the third right.

He smiled at the señorita at the front desk, stopped at the water fountain for a quart of revitalization, and emerged out into the receding dusk with exactly $22,455 more in his pockets than he had when he went in.

He found the others by listening for Buddy's and Rabbit's voices, which were rising in decibels upon decibels as each out-did the other for sheer crudity and outrage. They were standing beside Protector out on the street, arguing at the top of their lungs. Philbert strolled up to them like nothing had happened.

"So whaddaya suggest, then?" Rabbit queried of Buddy.

"Well, I sure as hell don't see what good it'll do to get some flunky shyster to represent my sister! Jesus Christ! We don't want some shit-eating—"

"What the hell d'ya think *I'm* saying, fer goddamn's sake?" Rabbit returned. "I'm the last one to say, 'Oh, fuck, talkin' to you is like fartin' in the wind.'"

"Don't give me that garbage," Buddy retorted.

"Bonnie didn't tell me she had a jackass for a brother."

"If I'd known she was runnin' around with bubbleheads I would've—"

"You would've what?" Rabbit asked sharply, moving in for the kill. "Come help her like ya never did all them years? She told me how nobody ever gave a shit about her when she was a kid."

"Oh!" Buddy cursed, thoroughly offended now. "That is such a goddamn lie, I don't—she *said* that?"

"Goddamn right."

"Here's Philbert," Les interjected.

"Okay," Rabbit said, "we can go now, seein's how you're the only one who can drive this thing."

"Hi," Philbert said to her, feeling rather flimsy about it. "Bonnie always was a pretty shy kid."

"See," Rabbit added triumphantly, in Buddy's face.

"Oh, Christ."

"You gotta admit, Buddy," Philbert continued as they all crawled into the car, "you were pretty famous and she was nobody."

"The hell!"

"I can believe it," Rabbit added. "Good Jesus, fuck, what's all this garbage in there? And Christ, it smells like skunk!" She had crawled into the backseat with Lester and Jennifer.

"Welcome to Indian country," Buddy muttered.

"Yer ass, ya mean," Rabbit said.

"Let's get a drink." Les sighed. "Phil, take the first right up there, around the jail. We'll go to La Posada."

"I'm hungry," Jennifer dared to say.

"They got good sandwiches there. And chile con queso dip."

Protector picked up speed but not before Philbert observed the municipal building fading off behind them and the bars on all the windows at the back of the building.

"Bonnie was my kid sister," Buddy felt compelled to say.

"So?" Rabbit inquired. "I mean, God, didn't ya ever wonder why she took off?"

"And never came back?" Philbert added, turning another corner.

"I was in Vietnam, dammit," Buddy said, growing more defensive. "I didn't have time to worry about some little girl's insecurities. I was gettin' my ass shot at."

They pulled into the parking lot of La Posada Inn. It was getting dark. The brilliant oranges and reds of a typical sunset were already fading, and Philbert regretted not having said good-bye to his father. It was bad luck.

They crawled out of the car like primeval coelenterates and meandered across the parking lot and single-filed into the luxurious wood-and-adobe building. They went past a crackling fire in the lobby where several Spanish businessmen recounted the day's business and schemed for tomorrow's, and went on into the luxurious bar with chandeliers and green velvet wallpaper and photographs of historical businessmen crammed from ceiling to floor on the green velvet wallpaper. More businessmen recounted more of the day's business. The five troublemakers found a corner and established themselves on antique divans. It was a warm, rich room. Vivaldi tinkled soothingly from stereo speakers situated throughout the network of small, warm, rich rooms. They ordered drinks and asked for menus.

"So you were in Vietnam?" Rabbit asked, resuming conversation.

"Yeah," Buddy replied resentfully. "I woulda thought Bonnie woulda told ya, she told ya everything else lousy about me."

"Oh, kiss my ass," Rabbit responded. "She didn't tell me hardly anything about ya, and I guess that's the best she could say."

"Whatever else," Les interjected, "we still gotta get her a lawyer. Her butt's in a sling."

"I hate lawyers," Buddy said.

"I picked that up right away," Les replied, "but God, she's got

264

eight counts of felony lined up against her. She could go to prison for ten years."

"Ten years?" Philbert repeated.

"At least," Les confirmed. "Now, I hate the system as much as you guys, but let's be real. They got her. We don't."

"We will, you said so," Buddy argued. "Wednesday, right? Then, hell, we're bustin' ass back to Lame Deer. They can't touch her there."

"Are you kiddin', man?" Les exploded. "They'll have you before you get a hundred miles. You don't think they'll be watchin' her? I *know* the FBI is interested in this case. Not to mention Mr. Scarlatti, who I'll bet money has got some wop eyes keepin' eyes on his twenty grand. God. You'd be crazy to pull some shit like that. They'll kill you. They'll kill *me*, if I lose that bread."

"We'll make it," Buddy said confidently.

"And they'll kill Bonnie," Rabbit added. "There was that guy in Dallas, Les, that Indian, what was his name?"

"Sandy Youngblood," Les said.

"Yeah," Rabbit confirmed. "There was somethin' about him that made me—"

"Sandy Youngblood?" Buddy repeated incredulously. "Jesus, that guy is the enemy. You're right. If he's in on it, the FBI ain't far behind, and that means murder."

"You know him?" Rabbit asked.

"Yeah," Buddy replied quietly, "yeah, I know him."

The waitress brought them green chile burgers, more drinks, and more dip. They ate for a while in silence.

Buddy started talking between mouthfuls. "In Nicaragua, you know, down in Central America, the U.S. government has been supporting the Somoza dictators for forty years. A few businessmen got rich starving and slaughtering the peasants. And America sends 'em millions of dollars of aid every year, because they're anti-Communist. Those millions of good American tax dollars go to the Somoza family and a few elite families in Managua to build up the army to protect their fortunes from the Sandinista guerrillas, who are the champions of the peasants."

"Shit," Rabbit commented.

"Yeah," Buddy continued. "I know some Indians from down there. They said Sandy Youngblood has gotten rich with the deals he's made with the Somozas and the other families who support them. He sells beans to them for exorbitant prices—rotten, mildewed beans—and the Somozas in turn see they are the only beans available to the peasants. At even more exorbitant prices, of course."

"He's an Indian?" Philbert asked.

"No," Buddy said.

They were all silent for a minute, leaning back on their divans, warm and fed and troubled.

"I met him in Washington at a seminar when we took over the BIA Building," Buddy continued. "He was with Bull Miller, and the fucking secretary of the Interior, and a dozen other pigs. We had a debate on 'law and order.' I was with Luther and Jimmy Campbell and everybody, and we had just destroyed a government building to the tune of a million dollars. And we still knew more about law and order than they did. You know how you've met someone you know is absolutely evil? Like Hitler must have been? They just scare you, they're so cold and empty and proud of it? That was how I felt about Sandy Youngblood. I spit in his face."

"What?" Les asked.

"I spit in his face. In the middle of the debate, after he made a speech about justice and responsibility, I went over to him, knowing what I knew about Nicaragua, and I spit his evil lies about patriotism and fighting fer yer country and liberty for all right into his filthy, lying Indian face."

"Good for you!" Rabbit declared, slapping the table firmly.

"The motherfuckers."

"Literally," Buddy added. He grimaced at Rabbit, and she returned the salute. "And college professors at the University of

Colorado are really FBI provocateurs too, working against the people, pretending to be AIM."

"Let's kill the fuckers," she said.

Buddy nodded to Philbert. "A sheepherder a day."

"What happened then?" Les asked.

"We left. And we're never going back until Washington, D.C., is a pile of junk."

"Well, that's what I'm going to be if you skip out on the Mafia's money," Les cautioned. "Oh, Jesus," he breathed. He had glanced over at the bar. He recognized Tony Parelli, drinking and talking business with another well-dressed young man in his late twenties. He didn't know the other man was Doug Lewis, whom Tom Washington had phoned earlier from Austin. Tony didn't know that Doug was FBI. He thought he worked for the Scarlattis.

"What?" Rabbit asked.

"That's Tony Parelli," Les whispered. "Now I know what Vito suspects—"

"Tony Parelli?" Buddy repeated loudly. "Ain't he the one Bonnie was hooked up with?"

"Yeah," Rabbit confirmed grimly. "He's the one who dumped her in jail. At least that's what I think."

"Me too," Buddy said, and stood up. Les and Rabbit tried to stop him but it was too late. He was already at the bar and leaning casually next to the Sicilian scion.

"Hi," he said. The two men turned distastefully to the long-haired, sweaty foreigner. "Is it true that if the Mafia ran the country we wouldn't have any crime?"

"What?" they both asked together.

"Just wipe out any nonunion crooks. Nobody'd mess with the Mafia. Is that the plan?"

The two men of power and wealth stared at the one insignificant renegade. The renegade continued pleasantly. "I'm Buddy Red Bird, Bonnie's mad-dog brother. I believe you're Tony Parelli of the Mafia. And who's this? CIA? Or just a senator?"

He offered his hand, but neither of them returned the peace offering. Buddy had made sure his volume had been sufficient for everyone in the bar to hear him. He got louder. "You raped my sister." And with that he brought his knee up into the immigrant's crotch with the force of nine Gs.

"OWWWWWWWWWWWWWWRRRRRRRRRRRRRRR-RRR!"

Before the screaming mass of ruptured flesh could collapse to the floor, however, Buddy elbowed him in the face and broke his jaw, nose, and sent eight teeth flying across the bar. Blood splattered on the chandeliers. Everyone in the room screamed and fought to get out of there.

Doug Lewis drew his gun and aimed it at Buddy's forehead. But Buddy was not surprised. He fell in front of what was left of Tony Parelli and threw the writhing body at Lewis. The gun went off straight in the air, and the .38 slug went through the face of one of the businessmen's photographs on the wall.

Lewis collapsed when Parelli's head hit him in the jaw and he bit off the tip of his tongue. He went down screaming—as much as he could scream without his tongue, that is. Buddy took his cue from his friends, who were packing cheeks to get out of there. Les grabbed him on the run, but not before Buddy yelled into the acrid, gunsmoked room, "Next time I'll kill ya!"

They fled out across the parking lot and fell to their knees on the brown grass under a tree in a lovely compound amid the adobe cottages of the inn.

"Oh," Rabbit gasped, "you were fucking A!" and she gave Buddy a big hug.

"Hey, tits as well as a mouth," Buddy said. Rabbit rolled over on top of him. "Hey, baby, if one leg is Christmas and the other is New Year's, why don't I drop in between holidays."

"You prick," and she kissed him.

"Well, I gotta split," Buddy said, coming up for air, but not before he grabbed her groin. They laughed.

Lester sat on the grass and looked at the new quarter moon that played hide-and-seek with the big clouds above. He felt relieved, yet saddened, at his loss. But as with so many losses, it made life simpler.

Jennifer was there, too, and she said, "Mommy, we didn't pay the bill."

Everyone laughed, except Jennifer. They sat on the grass and watched police cars swarm all around the parking lot. A dozen armed deputies ran inside the building.

Rabbit sat up suddenly. "Ohmigod, Jane and Sky!" She stood up quickly.

"What?" Buddy asked.

"No, Rabbit," Les admonished, "there's cops everywhere. We gotta cool it for a little while."

"But God knows how those kids are," Rabbit said, moaning. "Oh, God, how could I forget them?"

"Who?" Buddy asked.

"Bonnie's kids, of course."

"What? You mean—"

"Bonnie has children?" Philbert asked quietly out of the dark.

"Yes," Rabbit said. She felt, like so many others had felt these past four days, humbled to have forgotten Philbert. She waited for his thought in their silence. "You guys didn't know that?"

"No," Philbert said sadly. He stood up. "I'll go get them. Where are they?"

"No, you—"

"I'm the only one the cops won't bother," Philbert declared, and they all knew it was true. He was so passive that he was almost invisible.

"They were at La Fonda Hotel the last time I talked to them. Room 220. It's just two blocks and turn left."

"I will find it," Philbert said. His voice betrayed a returning poetic purpose.

"Can I go, Mom?" Jennifer asked suddenly. She was suddenly

afraid to be there without the gigantic man she had met that evening.

"Absolutely not. It could be dangerous."

"Let her come," Philbert pleaded. "We'll just be a minute." Some persuasive vulnerability in his voice penetrated her motherly firmness.

"Well . . ." Rabbit hesitated, and it was all that Philbert and Jennifer needed to disappear into the dark. The others watched them go. A sense of foreboding and hurtful loss swept in upon their grassy hiding spot, and they waited anxiously. Rabbit sat between Lester and Buddy, making sure to touch their shoulders with hers, and they silently lit a joint. The stars and the moon and the warm air held mute vigilance with them. Perhaps it could be said that they prayed for their next move, which was by no means clear, or that they prayed for their own clear visions in the sky, or perhaps they prayed for Philbert's safe return. They didn't know; none of it was certain. But uncertainty was the path they had all chosen for themselves.

Philbert and Jennifer walked hand in hand past the police cruisers in the parking lot. Blue and red lights flashed on their faces, static radio messages infiltrated their eardrums, cars and onlookers jammed the place. Finally there was some action. There was some turmoil . . . vigor . . . entertainment. The two sycophants crawled obsequiously into their car and flashed their one taillight, a cruiser obligingly moving out of their way, and they took the back entrance out of the compound.

They went two blocks and took a left. They found a parking place on the street in front of La Fonda. They went inside, still hand in hand. Tape was on a broken window where squash blossoms had been displayed in a display case, and a few brown steaks of old blood were still smeared in one corner of the broken glass (from some recent cataclysm), but Philbert and Jennifer thought nothing of the scar. They thought nothing of the stylish throngs in the lobby bustling off to throng about with other stylish throngs. They thought a little more about the location of room 220, but as soon as they obtained the necessary specifications from an overworked desk clerk, they didn't give the machinations of the hotel's ecosystem another thought. They dodged through the throngs hand in hand, they double-checked their directions from an overworked room-service waiter, wandered up a quiet hall, turned down an even quieter hall (as they left the lobby behind), and paused in front of the doors until they found Room 220. Then, and only then, as they stood before room 220, did they look at each other, smile, and knock three times together. They stood, tremulous, and waited, apprehensive, for it was not every day that either of them dared trespass these foreign halls and unfamiliar haunts of older, more chic folk.

The door opened. A TV blared a Clorox commercial. "Jennifer!" the little door opener declared. The two little girls shifted, uneasy about feeling glad to see a future rival again, but nevertheless glad.

"Hi, Jane."

"So you're here," Jane declared. "Is Rabbit here too?"

"Yeah. And Lester."

"Wow. Great. Who're you?" Jane asked of the bulky black-and-red mountain looming over Jennifer, holding her hand.

"This is Uncle Philbert," Jennifer explained.

"Hi," Philbert said.

"Where's Rabbit and Lester, then?" Jane pressed.

"Over . . ." Jennifer struggled to describe where the others were, but couldn't figure out what kind of place it was. She gave up, and Jane had lost interest. "I'll help you pack. You got stuff?"

"Yeah."

Jennifer led her hand holder into the room, as Jane had already turned into the room. It was small, with two twin beds of carved Mexican wood, Mexican tile on the writing table and bed tables, and a twenty-four-inch color TV. Sky sat on the floor in front of the TV watching a deodorant commercial. He gave Philbert a quick glance.

"Mom said to come get ya," Jennifer said for no reason.

The two girls moved to throw Jane's stuff in her bag, chattering about what a neat place this was and about Jennifer's neat plane trip. Sky moved to pack up his stuff, but he kept his eyes no higher than at a fifteen-degree angle off the floor. Philbert closed the door and stood awkwardly watching the activity. After a minute or two the girls took a pause in their chatter.

Philbert said, "You're Bonnie's children?"

The girls looked at him like he was a typical goofy grown-up. Jane replied, her good manners straining to the limit of their endurance, "Yeah, I'm Jane. That's my brother, Sky."

"Hi," Philbert said, smiling wanly. Sky gave him another quick glance. "Where's your father?"

No one answered, until finally Sky said, "We don't know. Mommy and him are divorced."

"Oh," Philbert responded. "I don't know, either. I mean, I don't know who my father was, either."

"We know who he was," Jane said belligerently.

"He's gone, though," Sky argued, not quite as shy with his sister.

"So? We know who he is."

"So?"

"So?" Jane said mockingly. "What about Mom? Is she still in jail?"

"Yeah, we saw her," Jennifer explained, remembering the exciting melee in the jail. "You shoulda seen all the guns and cops and everything. It was neat." Jane listened wide-eyed, and a little downhearted, to the tale of her mother's constraints of that afternoon. Jennifer could see a little movie oozing out of her rival's eyes, and she felt a little more insolent to see it. "And maybe Buddy will be Mommy's new boyfriend," Jennifer concluded. "He's an Indian."

They all looked oddly at Philbert, who felt compelled to explain. "We came down from the reservation to get her out."

"You're a Chee-annie?" Sky asked wonderingly.

"A what?"

"The . . . Indian that Mommy is."

"Cheyenne. Shi-hella. Maxkeometanio Ni-oh-ma-ate-anin-ya. Kipanna Kiwani of the Makatozanzan: the little awakening of the clear blue earth. I am Nagi Napeyapi, the Whirlwind Dreamer."

"Wow," Sky declared.

"Can you get my mom out of that place?" Jane inquired, not trying to show that she was also a little impressed by this weird fat guy. He only stared at her reproachfully.

"I don't know," he said. "Do you have any ideas?"

Jane was flattered to see that he was not humoring her. "No," she said, "but we can't leave her there."

"You're right," Philbert said. "The other grown-ups talk of lawyers and politics, but these are as the cotton of the cottonwood tree in a spring wind. They float about like snow, but they go nowhere and are nothing, and clog up the ditches. You, *micunski hunka*, do you have any ideas?"

Sky looked at him unashamed, as if he understood the words for "chosen son." "I saw a Hopalong Cassidy movie today, on the cable station from California. The cattle baron put him in jail, so he whistled for his horse. The horse came up to his window, Hopalong grabbed the rope on his saddle, tied it to the bars on his window, and the horse pulled the bars out of the wall. Hopalong escaped and he killed the bad man."

They all stared at Sky. Jane especially had never heard him make such a long speech before.

"*Hoka key*, we will do it." Philbert said. The children stared at the adult with new respect.

"Do what?" Jane asked. She was a practical little girl. She liked to clear up any minor details.

"*Micunski hunka*," Philbert said. "Adopted daughter, we will buy a rope, and tie it to my car, and pull the bars out of your mother's jail cell."

Nobody moved. The air grew thick and ominous with *Taku skanskan tawaiciyapi,* to use the Lakota phrase, an untranslatable aura of unreal freedom, an Indian reality at implausible odds with the rational world of whitemen. *Taku skanskan* was pure spiritual vitality that radioactivated the bejesus out of any foreign impurities. And Philbert would have driven a logical Geiger counter berserk with his illogical radioactivity, not to mention linguists with the way he mixed up Cheyenne and Lakotax.

He turned off the TV and grabbed their bags. "Let's go."

They went. They marched like a guerrilla phalanx through the elite hierarchy of America that thronged the fashionable hotel. They marched past the front desk and did not pay their tribute to the god. They marched up to their pony, which cowered a little to still have some of the blood and grease of America in its system.

Philbert mercilessly gunned his engine into action. The phalanx crowded soberly into the front seat, four strong. They drove like a Sherman tank across town to the Kmart, bypassing lesser men and lesser means of transportation like a starship bypassing a biplane. They marched into the Kmart, scornful of the Christmas shoppers, sneerful of the ropes and chains in the hardware department, contemptuous of the forty-five dollars Philbert paid for the fifty-yard heavy-duty rope out of the wad of money in his pocket.

They drove back downtown. They drove slower. They clenched their fists and wiped their sweaty palms on their jeans. Adrenaline and *skanskan* and regular gasoline pumped through children and beast alike. They slowed as they passed the front of the municipal building. They drove around the block, casing out the joint from all angles. On the south, the front of the building where the flagpole rose nakedly above the two-storied fortress, the lights were all out. No life stirred. On the east, nothing. On the north, an empty parking lot and bars on all the windows. This was the side the jail was on. On the west, lights, the fire trucks gleaming inside the fire station, and cop cars parked everywhere. It was the headquarters of the city police. They drove with particular insouciance past the west side.

They all had their own thoughts as they went around the block one more time. Yes, they all thought of happier times, of loved ones, of universal hopes and fears, but each commando was an individual, and each individual had unique hopes and fears that distinguished them from all the other individuals on earth.

Jennifer missed her daddy, whom she rarely saw. He used to visit in the summers from his dirt ranch outside Coalgate, Oklahoma, but he never came anymore. He'd gotten married again. She wondered if the violent man that Mommy had kissed tonight would be her new daddy.

Sky pronounced "Cheyenne" over and over in his brain. It was a monotonous repetition, a nightmare that would not leave his dreams. Cheyenne, Cheyenne, Cheyenne . . .

Jane said, "We're not really gonna do this, are we?" As no one answered, she shrugged. She was not really worried. She was just a kid. They wouldn't put *her* in jail.

Whirlwind had absolutely nothing in his brain. He had nothing in his heart. Only the pit of his stomach, where the spirit of Sweet Medicine dwelt, contracted ever so slightly. His internal dialogue had stopped. His pony and he were One, impeccably prepared for battle.

They drove around to the north end of the municipal building. Whirlwind doused his one headlight. They rolled slowly into the parking lot next to the jail. One streetlight glared from across the street. The quarter moon gave the signal for action as it ducked behind a cloud and plunged the night into full darkness. No other cars or pedestrians were in sight. Another municipal building—probably a courthouse—framed the remainder of the parking lot. It, as well as the municipal building and jail and the back of the police station, was dark. It was, after all, the night before the night before Christmas.

The marauders coasted to a stop in the parking lot and cut the engine. All five warriors—for Protector was now more than a machine—held their breath. No one looked out a window of the building to see what was going on. No one opened a door. No one gave a shit that they were there.

So far so good. The two car doors opened and the four warriors got out noiselessly. Whirlwind grabbed the huge rope from the backseat. They all crouched on his side of the car. He gave instructions in a whisper. "There's the jail. Jane, Jennifer, crawl up to the windows. Find which one is Bonnie's. Tell her to get ready, and quietly. Whisper. Sky, stay here with me."

The two girls tiptoed off across the narrow dirt trench that separated the pavement of the parking lot from the two-story adobe building. It was only about twenty feet across. The men watched them approach the closest window. No light shone from it. A few lights checkered the building at incongruous intervals, but these were far apart and, as it has been said, were only a few. Mostly it was dark and foreboding. Whirlwind and Sky could barely see Jane and Jennifer already. They could just barely make out the girls glancing surreptitiously about them, and they heard some whispering.

"Psssss," Jane whispered into the first window. She was too short to reach even the bottom of it, so she helped herself to Jennifer's back, which she motioned for the other girl to present to her, posthaste, which the other girl hastily did, seeing as how she didn't really have much of a choice. "Psss."

"What the hell?" a loud male voice boomed out of the window. Jane fell off Jennifer and rolled into the trench. Jennifer rolled after her. They could see a face and hands peer out of the window, but he didn't peer in their direction. They didn't move, and the face and hands eventually disappeared.

The girls crawled frantically back to the car, where the men were waiting.

"There's a man in there!" Jane whispered frantically.

"Okay, okay," Whirlwind whispered. "This must be the wrong end of the building. We'll try down at the other end. I'll drive Protector."

They all got in the car and drove two hundred yards to the inner crotch of the building. It was darker away from the street-light, and therefore they couldn't see very well themselves, either. But Whirlwind backed into the corner and cut the engine. They held their breath again. No one seemed to notice them any more than they had before. They might as well have been on another planet, as quiet and dark and dangerous as it was.

"Okay," Whirlwind whispered when they got out and crouched again on his side of the car, "you girls go try them windows."

"What're you guys gonna do?" Jane asked. She was getting a little perturbed at having to do everything.

"We're gonna tie the rope to the car," Whirlwind explained, "good and hard, under there." He waved his hand underneath the car.

Jane perused that possibility, and its commensurate difficulty with her task. "Okay. C'mon, Jennifer." Jennifer obediently came on after her bossy friend. They crawled off over the ditch, and after a minute the boys heard more *pssssssing*.

Whirlwind tried to crawl under the car from the rear with the rope, but he got stuck. Sky watched seriously. Whirlwind wriggled back out and said, unabashedly, "That's what I thought. Sky, you can do it. Tie the rope around the biggest piece of metal you can see. Wrap it around about five times and make about six knots. We got plenty of rope."

"Okay," Sky said. He took the heavy rope from his mentor and crawled underneath, where he felt it was doubly darker than usual. He felt around in the grease and mud and felt slightly nauseous to be feeling around in this gunk—like it was the guts of some animal—but he persevered. He flipped the rope up and over a big long round thing that ran between the rear tires. He pulled on it and threw it over again and again and again and again, each time multiplying his own filthy situation with flying mud and gunk and greasy rope. Then he made big clumsy knots in the thing—one, three, five, six. Grunt, squeeze, slurp, slide.

He scooted back out and grinned at Whirlwind. He looked like a tar baby, and it didn't look like that tar would ever come off. It was a joyous feeling to be so dirty.

"Get it?" Whirlwind asked.

"Yep," the tar baby replied, and grinned from ear to ear.

Meanwhile the girls weren't doing so well. They had *pssssed* at four windows and gotten chilly receptions from all four. One woman screamed, another thought it was mice in the walls and threw her shoe, another was sure it was the toilet flushing next door, and the latest one just kept snoring. But they were getting somewhere, they realized. They were at the women's wing. And Bonnie didn't snore—at least Jane didn't think so—so the last cell hadn't been her. They were eliminating, though. They crawled from one little window to another, right on down the line.

Oh, the odds that were against them! Bonnie could have been in a cell on the second floor. A matron might have heard them. An inmate could have reported prowlers. The possibilities were infinite. Luck was finite. Fate was bound to run out. It was the law of probability.

At the fifth window, on Jennifer's aching back, Jane saw a gray-haired old woman sitting on the pot with her head in her hands. At the sixth window a bald-headed girl stared directly at her from her cot and thought nothing of it. She made no sound or motion. Just laid on her cot. Jane stared for a minute. She had never seen a bald-headed woman.

At the seventh window—craps! Bonnie lay on the cot, cuddled up under her blanket, in the last stages of sanity. Imprisonment was draining the energy out of her as surely as Dracula drained his victims. She was awake, but her teeth were chattering with terror. Her soul was about to panic. The cruel temptations of that afternoon had given her the last tantalizing glimpse of freedom, and she had to be sedated after her friends left. Her nerves could no longer even bear the thought of a guiltless world.

"*Pssssss!*" her little girl whispered. Bonnie didn't hear it. Her brain was swirling with conscious demons. Snakes slithered all about the floor—

"Mommy! Is that you?" something whispered, outside her despair.

"Mommy! Wake up! Wake up!" She was weak. She could not bear the loss of freedom as well as most of the other prisoners. But she opened her eyes at the sounds of the whispering dream and stared at the concrete wall in front of her.

"Goddammit, get up!"

She turned over. She focused on the window, and the little head peering in through it.

"Jane?"

"Mom."

"Jane," Bonnie said, and stood up, but not before she checked the dark floor for snakes. "What—?" She put her fingers through the crisscrossed bars and touched the little face outside the open air. The little face was wet with tears.

"My bonnie little Jane, oh, how did you—?" But she choked on her own tears. Reality, luck, guilt, delusion flooded out of her, and she shook herself free of her terrible isolation for a moment. "I'm sorry, honey, if I—for all this. I know it—"

"Mom," the little girl interrupted, quickly recovering her composure, and a little annoyed with herself for jeopardizing the business at hand. "Get dressed and be quiet about it. We'll have plenty of time to talk later."

"What? Now, Jane—"

"Shhhhhhh! We'll be right back. Be ready to—" And she was

gone. Well, she was down in the trench again because Jennifer's back had had enough, and they both had sprawled into the gunk. Bonnie stood on her tiptoes and watched them run a few dozen yards to some heap of junk squatting in the shadows.

"We found her, we found her!" Jennifer blurted out.

"I get to tell!" Jane said viciously. "She's at the window." And she pointed at Bonnie. Bonnie could see her pointing at her. She hadn't the slightest idea what was going on. The Thorazine tranquilizer they had given her made her think she saw creatures from Uncle Remus and Lewis Carroll scurrying around in the parking lot. She shook her head to clear it, but the gobbledygook remained.

"*Ai good, washtay,*" Whirlwind whispered. "*Akita mani yo, Anpagliwin.*"

"What?" Jane asked.

"Observe everything now. Be careful. She is the returns-at-dawn woman," Whirlwind explained. "In your tongue. Jane and Jennifer, go twenty yards and keep the lookout. Let us know if you see anybody, my little *wiyanna*. Sky and I will back Wotawe to her window. Sky, sit on the trunk, here, and hold the rope. Make sure it does not get tangled. Go, *wiyanna, wanyaka tuwena icunsi*, keep the lookout. You will be the scouts, *tonweya*; alert us if the *tokahca* approach."

"Okay," the girls replied, and moved to the edges of the parking lot to take up their positions. Whirlwind got in the car, maneuvered it forward a little and around to the right, then backed it up a dozen yards so that it was as close to the window as possible. Sky kept a worried eye on the rope, which almost buried him in its great coils on the trunk. But luckily it did not get tangled in the axle. Whirlwind cut the engine. Then he and the boy unwound the rope carefully, down the trench and back up, and were almost to the window, when—

"*PHLLLLWWWWWWWTTTTTT!*"

One of the girls whistled shrilly. Whirlwind and Sky turned

and saw Jennifer waving frantically at them. They all hit the dirt.

A police cruiser patrolled by. Its spotlight was peering omnipotently up and down the alleys and the shadows across the street. It did not turn its gaze in their direction and, after an eternity, passed up the street and out of their range.

The *tonweya* and *wiyanna* and Wotawe still dared not exhale. Danger seemed to rear its ugly head at all of them for the first time now. This was stupid. They could get into trouble!

But none dared admit cowardice. Peer pressure again, like all the important events of history, prevented the marauders from running away. How many romantic adventures would be lost to the imaginative annals of mankind if so many would-be romantic adventurers had not been laughed at and jeered at and probed by their peers to go off and do some half-baked crime, out of shame? Many, many adventures.

When the cruiser was gone, they stood up slowly. They did not run. Whirlwind had the rope around his shoulder. He eased up to the window.

"*Winu!*" he whispered. "Captive woman?"

"What?" the woman breathed. "It's you?"

"Ai, Whirlwind Dreamer, Nagi Napeyapi and Wotawe. But you can call me Philbert."

"Philbert," Bonnie pronounced gingerly. His soft voice and great shadow in her window were a thick quilt of protection over her.

"We'll tie this rope around these bars and pull them out of this fucking wall," he explained.

"You're kidding," she said (but not disrespectfully).

"No."

He commenced tying the rope through the crisscrosses. The rope was almost as thick as the holes, and he grunted as he worked.

"Are you ready to go?" he asked between grunts.

"What?"

"Ready."

"Ready?"

"To go," he said, grunting again. "Get yer things together, put yer shoes on, wash yer face."

"Oh." And she hopped to it. First, however, she looked out into the hall to see if anybody else was hallucinating, too, or at least checking out the grunts and whispers emanating from her cage. They weren't. It was dead.

She put on her boots with the shampoo stain and washed her face and brushed her hair. She put a few odds and ends into her pockets, patted her dress to smooth it out a little, and waited patiently for the jailbreak.

The rope was wound insanely (she thought) through the bars like a crochet pattern from Mars, but it was knotted a dozen times and looked like it would never be separated from the thing again. And perhaps it wouldn't.

"There," Whirlwind breathed heavily. "Let's do it."

"Okay," Bonnie said. "So what do I do, just crawl out, or wait for the wall to cave in—or out, I guess—or what?"

"Find a hole and go." Whirlwind shrugged. "But wait until everything's all clear. We don't want you getting hurt. Okay?"

"Okay."

Whirlwind slid down the trench. "Okay, Sky, stand clear. Be ready to cut the rope from under the car as soon as we pull that place apart. Be sure it's all untangled from underneath."

"I don't have anything to cut with."

"Oh. Oh, Buddy has a knife in the backseat."

Sky hurried to get the knife. Whirlwind gave the high sign to the lookouts. They high-signed back. Sky got a big hunting knife and stood clear. Whirlwind got in the car, started it up, and put it in low.

When all was ready, he gripped the steering wheel and said a little prayer in Shi-hella, which may have sounded in English like:

Drums! Pain of the air in the Powers
    of laughter
Drums! To us, moccasined moonlight
    of laughter
Drums! With our all we battle ourselves
    laughing
At the drums! The drums! Drums!
    of happy death.

He floored the accelerator. Wotawe leapt into the air. The rope grew taut instantly. The token of war tugged mightily at the iron house, but the bars did not budge. Wotawe strangled itself on its axle, its wheels spun furiously, but the walls of Jericho did not come tumbling down. Nagi Napeyapi took his foot off the accelerator and the screaming rubber ceased screaming. Nagi Napeyapi did not panic, even when lights came on all over the municipal building. He rocked his war charger back and forth, reverse and low, low and reverse, jerk-pull, pull-jerk, the rope slacked, the rope leapt erectly, back and forth. The armed rider and his horse were One—madly leaping forward, madly squealing backward, and the commandos breathed hoarsely through their mouths as they watched the indefatigable madness.

Back and forth.
    Wi-hi-yi-yi!
        Low and reverse
Jerk-pull, pull-jerk
    Nagi Napeyapi sang
        to the Powers
    Wi-hi-yi-yi!
Wi-hi-yi-yi!

One of the bars budged. Plaster fell on the floor inside. Bonnie cowered in a corner. She heard faraway voices, in the hall.

Crack! the iron groaned
    Crack!
      Scraaaaaaape!
    Crack! the reinforcements complained!
      Wi-hi-yi-yi!

The madness was a smell of burned rubber, the squeal of agonized machinery, crack, groan, crunch. Rupture! Eruption! The bars moved. The adobe and concrete cinder block beneath the surface crumbled resentfully. Jericho's walls fought valiantly, but crumble they did, for Protector Wotawe was more valiant, and Whirlwind's song even greater still.

One jerk and a bar came out of its grave, two jerks, three—resurrection, ascension!

And the entire crisscrossed window frame flew in one piece out into the sky! Protector Wotawe skidded wildly clear across the parking lot as it was suddenly freed of its intransigent anchor and nearly plowed into the courthouse. The rope and its trophy flopped angrily out behind.

Out of the dust and impending collapse of the entire wall of the prison emerged Bonnie, coughing and stumbling blindly. She slid on her butt down into the trench and ruined her light blue prison dress, but she was up again in a second and running after her liberator, which was doing wheelies in a circle to get pointed in the right direction. And the commandos were yelling, and the back door of the police station looked like a wasp's nest about to explode with enraged policemen, and there was no way to describe the calamitous scene.

"Run, Mommy!"

"Oh, Sky, you're here too—"

"Holy Jesus Maria, look at that hole—"

"Who in the hell—"

"What in the hell—"

"Where's Jennifer?"

"Who—"

"What—"

"Here I am!"

"Get the rope off!"

"Oooooh, my foot—"

"There they are—"

"What . . . in . . . the . . . hell . . ."

"Run!"

"Get 'em!"

"It's kids!"

"What's that?"

"Where's—"

"What's—"

"Who's—"

"How—"

"Why?!"

There was no way anyone involved in any phase of the havoc in the parking lot that infamous night before the night before Christmas could ever reconstruct their own movements. All anyone could ever remember, no matter how astutely they were interrogated later, was being shot at, or doing the shooting at themselves, or running, or chasing, or falling down, or getting up again. The gunsmoke and rubber stink and cinder-block destruction obliterated ordinary experience. Memory and reality were reserved for more normal occasions.

The first thing that Philbert and Sky and Jane and Jennifer—and Bonnie—could remember was that they were all in the car and screaming idiotically up a street and away from the scene of the crime. They laughed and hugged each other as idiotically as their screaming escape, and Bonnie was laughing and hugging everybody more idiotically than they were, but not much. It was, in short, a screaming and idiotic scene, and was therefore equally impossible to describe.

"Mommy!"

"Honey!"

"We're not out of the woods—"

"Oh, Janey, Janey!"

"Not by a long shot."

"Jennifer, you're here too?!"

"I mean, there'll be APBs—"

"Oh, Philbert, Philbert, Philbert!!!" Kiss. Kiss. Kiss.

"Gee."

"Look at this—"

"What's that—"

"Where—"

"Turn here—"

"I . . . don't . . . believe . . . it . . ."

"Oh, honey, I'm so glad—"

". . . not . . . for . . . a . . . minute . . ."

"Did you see the way—"

"It was neat how—"

"I bumped my knee—"

"The car smells funny—"

"Out of nowhere—"

"Honey!"

"Bonnie?"

It wasn't far back to La Posada. By the time they pulled back into the parking lot, all the cruisers had sped off to investigate some hysterical reports coming in from the municipal building. Les and Rabbit and Buddy were on their fourth joint, still under the tree, but weren't so stoned that they weren't a little surprised to see Bonnie pile out of the junk heap on wheels and give them all slobbery greetings. Unfortunately it was another idiotic scene, beyond any narrative, lyrical, or operative powers of description.

"Bonnie?!"

"Hey, hey, hey!"

"Bonnie?"

"How—"

"We have to get going—"
"Where'd all the fuzz go in such a—"
"Bonnie?"
"Les!"
"Philbert? What the hell—"
"Oh, you wouldn't believe—"
"Want a toke of . . . uh . . ."
"You've been gone two hours—"
"Hey, man . . ."
"You go off on a simple—"
"What's happenin'?"
"Get in the car, we'll explain it—"
"What is *happening*?"
"Just get in the car!!!"
"Bonnie?"

They got in the car, eight strong, and took the back entrance out of the compound. They swung right on Paseo de Peralta and circled around the downtown plaza, which, as was obvious to any fool, had erupted into some kind of nameless anarchy. The eight strong were all talking and hugging at once amidst the chaos, and Philbert always remembered those few moments of jubilance as among the happiest of his life, no matter how long he lived. Bonnie sat firmly at his side, her children on her lap, and it was pure exhilaration to him. Lester and Rabbit and Buddy and Jennifer crowded around the confused Coleman stove in the backseat and frequently, taking turns, leaned forward and gave Bonnie various hugs and tweaks on the nose and other signals of endearment. They took almost as many turns patting Philbert on the back, and thumping him on the head, and passing them both joints, and generally wearing themselves out with gratitude and relief. Gradually, out of the exuberance and Wahupa, some practical good sense was bound to emerge. First Jane, and then Rabbit, and then Lester recovered their natural anxiety and remembered that their asses were probably grass.

"We better fly the hell out of here," Lester said nervously.

"And the Mafia?" Buddy added. "They'll find you even if you go to Bora Bora."

"Oh, God, the money, I forgot," Les moaned.

"I got the money," Philbert said simply. "Bonnie, reach inside my pockets. There might be enough for Wambli *gleska*. He has done so much for us."

"What?" Rabbit dared to ask.

"The spotted eagle," Philbert explained.

"No, I meant—"

"Look . . . at . . . *this*!" Bonnie declared, a little beside herself at the paper goodies overflowing from Philbert's pockets. "Twenties," she gasped.

"Fifties?" Buddy gurgled.

"Bundles of hundreds?" Rabbit croaked.

"Where—"

"What—"

"Is there enough for Wambli *gleska* to take back to the Tokahca?" Philbert asked. Jane grabbed the dough. They drove silently as she counted.

"$22,410," she concluded.

"Holy shit!"

"I spent some on the rope," Philbert apologized. But his heart was pounding. It was more than he thought. "Hooooooo-leeeeee shit!"

"Where . . . where . . ."

"Hooooooooo-ho-ho-hoooooo-leeeeeee Shhittttttttt!!"

"Where . . . where . . .

"Where?"

Philbert was not toying with their demands. He just needed a minute to get his voice out of his balls. It was more than he thought. "Vault. Corridors. Jail. Toilet. Janitor's closet."

"What?" someone asked, understandably.

"Safe."

"You mean you robbed the safe at the jail?" Rabbit explained. She was particularly astute in the matter of garbled communications.

"Yeah."

"You . . . just . . . robbed"—Buddy gulped, trying to get it straight—"twenty-two *thousand* dollars?"

"This afternoon," Philbert corrected.

"And four hundred ten," Jane accounted, "in all denominations." She smiled proudly, as if she had done it.

And Sky? Bonnie saw his pride.

"Should we give twenty to Wambli *gleska*?" Philbert asked.

"It's yer bread, man," Buddy said.

Philbert gave him a quick look. "Give him twenty thousand, Jane. And we'll keep two for Billy Little Old Man."

"Oh, wow" was all that the spotted eagle could say. Jane handed him all the bundles of hundreds. Everyone looked at him looking at the bread. Out of this he could fake his way to freedom.

"You have to go back, don't ya?" Rabbit declared questioningly.

Lester looked at her fondly. "I don't want to. But it's going to be tough enough explaining all this as it is, even with the money."

Rabbit gave him a long, hard look. "To the airport, James. Take a left up here."

They drove silently. Les asked, "Where are you guys going?"

They all looked at the driver. "Home," he said.

Les nodded.

"Here, Les," Buddy said, scribbling on a piece of paper, "Here's our address and my phone number in Lame Deer—"

"Where?"

"Montana. You're welcome anytime. Maybe we can get some deals going too."

"Buddy," Rabbit said, "the Mafia's been out to crack the reservations, as they put it, for traffic for a long time. They're perfect hideouts and a legal no-man's-land for drug traffic. We could really make a fortune, what with Les's connections and—"

"No heroin," Philbert said.

"No heroin," Les repeated.

Rabbit nodded. "Oh, wow, the shuckin' and jivin' we could do with that kind of bread. We could put lots of people to work. Industry, capitalism, it's what the BIA's been screamin' about fer years. Well now, we'll *join* the rat race and nobody'll fuck with us. What, one million Injuns pushin' and shuckin'—!"

"Ten million," Buddy corrected. "I know Indians in Colombia, Brazil, Guatemala, everywhere. They'd sell their crops to us— and I mean *cocaine!*—before they'd take any more shit from the big-crime and big-business assholes!"

"Right *on!* I just dare the Cosa Nostra to take them—*us!*— on!!"

"You're out of yer skull." Buddy grinned.

"Damn right. Here's the airport."

They pulled up to the plane. Rabbit said, "You got enough gas to get out of here?"

"Yep," Les replied, piling out of the car. "Well, maybe enough to get to Albuquerque to refuel—"

"Oh, Lester! Thank you for everything!" Bonnie exclaimed, and hugged him tightly.

He blushed. "I'd do it again."

"Come see us, man," Buddy said.

"I just might," Les replied. He turned to go. "Now you guys get movin'. Every cop in the state is probably lookin' fer that car."

The kids shouted good-bye, and Philbert said, "*Doksa.*"

Les hurried off. He felt like a damn fool leaving them. They were bound for trails that he craved, but he was going back to . . . Anger and pity swept over him as he got in the plane. He glanced around quickly to wave, but they were gone. He sat alone at the dark, deserted airport and stared at his instrument panel for a long time. Then he revved up the engines and taxied back into his own world.

The marauders left Santa Fe by some back roads that Rabbit knew. They drove silently, and a little sadly, on Highway 285 north.

Buddy kept rolling the joints, and Philbert had the radio on. They heard a bulletin on the hourly news about the breakout, and the robbery, and the brawl, and listened proudly. Then the news continued about wars in Africa and Asia, economic doom, corruption, elections, and earthquakes. They stopped at the fancy El Paragua Restaurant in Espanola and pigged out on burritos and beer.

Back on the road again, two cases of Dos Equis beer in the backseat, Philbert picked up the police band and they got the dispositions of roadblocks up ahead on Routes 285 and 68 to Taos, so they took Route 76 into the mountains.

"Indian land," Buddy said, consulting his map. "Hey, I know some Picuris Pueblo up here. Cat and Tommy Cuartelejo. They'd hide us for a while."

"We might need to," Rabbit said.

They drove. The road got hilly, and very dark, and very alone.

Protector Wotawe knew that his job was done. He was not even sure that the Shi-hella appreciated all he had done for them. He sobbed once as they went up a steep hill, and began to hemorrhage internally.

It all happened at once. The neglected rear end slurped its last drop of oil. The bearings dried up and shattered like crystal. The transmission flywheel broke. The generator, the battery, the starter, radiator, steering pi, carburetor, and distributor sparked fatally, ground to pieces, gurgled in their own deoxygenated blood, and rattled.

The racket and gasps scared the hell out of the passengers.

"Jump for it!" Buddy yelled. "It's going to blow up!"

"No, no," Philbert pleaded.

But the death rattle was unmistakable. Something large and vital fell out onto the road and punctured the rear tires as they ran over it. The machine swerved hysterically. A steep drop-off beckoned from the side of the deserted back road.

Buddy had the passenger door open and was throwing all the camping gear out. "Now you kids jump! We're not going fast!"

Jane jumped. Then Jennifer.

"Go, Bonnie!"

"Philbert!" she screamed.

Buddy threw her out, but Sky clung for dear life to his father.

"C'mon, Philbert!" Buddy yelled.

"No."

Rabbit and Buddy tugged at them but it was no use. The car was completely out of control by now, swerving back and forth across the road insanely.

Rabbit jumped.

"Goddammit, Philbert, Sky, c'mon!" Buddy screamed.

"It is my pony," Philbert muttered stubbornly.

"Please! Please!" Buddy was frantically weeping in the cool wind that blew inside the sedan. It felt fresh and cleansing and very close. He snatched Sky, who fought to get back to the great, silent whirlwind in the driver's seat. But Buddy held him tightly.

"Wotawe Wuni!" the boy screamed. Whirlwind looked at him suddenly, just as they went over into the chasm.

Buddy leapt clear at the last possible instant with Sky in his arms, and they rolled a dozen yards down the sandy slope, clasping desperately to each other's heads for protection. They slid into a cactus patch and were lacerated cruelly, but it hurt more than it did any harm. And they stopped tumbling. They were safe.

Not so Wotawe Wuni. It left the earth and disappeared into the darkness of another world. Buddy and Sky felt it sail over their heads, and heard it roar down the mountain, and saw it explode against a telephone pole at the bottom. They felt the blast of heat sear their faces and choked mournfully, wrathfully, at such senseless destruction.

And the breeze blew fresh and cleansing and very close.

Bonnie ran over the hill, screaming and sobbing. She ran blindly toward the fire. The others saw her disappear as well, into the flickering shadows.

"Mommy!" Sky yelled. But Buddy would not let him go near the conflagration below. He pulled him up to the road. Rabbit and the two girls were helplessly watching the fire and hugged the two men as they came up. They all sat in shock by the side of the road until only black clouds billowed up from the gully. They could not bear what they were feeling, and so tried not to feel anything.

Death, they thought, vicious death, vicious truth—

"Hey," Rabbit whispered, "what's that?"

They looked. Something was struggling up the hill. Phantoms could not have been more dreadful than the shapes they saw silhouetted by the chaos below. The shapes struggled toward them, and they wondered if it was death itself about to discover them too. They froze, hoping that motionlessness would make them invisible.

"Oooof, unghh," the shape grunted. And the survivors opened their eyes.

Philbert was carrying Bonnie in his arms. He looked up at the others. "Hey . . . how 'bout a hand. Jesus Christ!"

They ran down to them, leaping and screaming for joy.

"She's a little charred from the smoke," Philbert grunted, "but okay, I think."

The others looked inquiringly at him. Bonnie looked at him, too, a little dazed but full of wonder.

"She came to find me, I guess, and ran right past where I jumped out. I had to go down and get her. You big dummy," he said to her, and kissed her dirty face.

Then he looked at Sky. "Thanks," he said to the boy.

"Why?" Sky asked.

"Wotawe Wuni—the token of war that is captured by weakness . . . Well," he added, as the others shoved and pulled the two lovers up the hill, "let's get out of here. We've probably knocked down the electricity for a hundred miles."

They all limped across the road and up a hill on the other side. Indian land was nearby. He clasped and unclasped his hand on something both cool, like metal, and hot, from hell. It was the cigarette lighter from his pony. Now he had three tokens for his medicine bundle.

Bonnie hugged him.

"Say," he said to her, "will you make me a pouch for my medicine bundle? Make it out of the cloth of your prison dress, maybe?"

"Sure," she said.

Philbert smiled. It would be the fourth token for his medicine power. He would be complete now. He turned without remorse to the smoking ruin below, the dead American thing his people no longer wanted.

"Farewell, my brother," he said, and he and Bonnie hurried after the others.